FLAWED

By

Michael Fowlkes

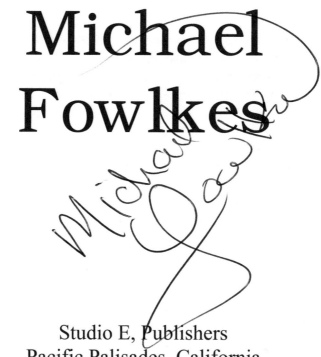

Studio E, Publishers
Pacific Palisades, California

Flawed

Michael Fowlkes

First Edition 2010   First Printing 2010

Studio E, Publishers
Studio E Bookshelf
Carol Givner LLC
www.studioebookshelf.com

STUDIO E

Cover Design by Jennifer Givner

ISBN: 978-1-58755-050-8
EAN: 9 781587 550508

Fiction

Published in the United States of America

10 9 8 7 6 5 4 3 2 1

Dedication

To courageous women, loyal dogs and wooden boats everywhere.

Acknowledgements

Running out to the grounds, during the night in a storm is never fun. But when a passenger breaks into the wheelhouse screaming someone has fallen overboard, the sheer terror that shoots through you is mind numbing. I could hardly breathe as I raced from stateroom to stateroom searching every inch of the boat for the missing passenger. The moment I realized he was no longer on board, a part of me shriveled up and died.

This all-too-real life experience, how it happened, and what happened next was the inspirational seed from which this novel was created. From there, you'll each decide for yourselves, what is real and what is fiction.

To the individuals who recognize themselves within these pages, I've done my best to represent you with the highest respect, and to the depth you've each influenced my life. Throughout our lives, it's the people we love, those that love us, and those that don't, that make us who we are. This book is dedicated to each and every one of you.

To my mother and father, to my grandmother and grandfather, who in their own unique way, taught me to love the outdoors, to love being on the water, and most importantly, to cherish and respect all living things, small and great, both above and below the waterline.

To my crew at the time, now Captains Zachary Story and Brian Fey, thank you, for your locality, friendship and bravery. To Larry Edwards and Lloyd Wolf for taking me under your wings and making sure we did it right. To Captains Buzz Brizendine owner/operator of the *Prowler,* Alan Fay owner/operator of the *Pronto,* and Frank LoPreste owner/operator of the *Royal Polaris,* for your willingness to work with a rookie operator, on a 6-pac no less, so green it wasn't even funny. You never knew it at the time, but the few words of encouragement you sent my direction over the radio meant the world to me.

To my dear friends, Tom and Gracie Rogers, Dave and Hallie Pfeiffer, and Joani Dickenson, for your invaluable insights into the storylines and characters. For your honesty, critiques and suggestions, without which this book wouldn't be what it is. Thank you for your support, encouragement and love.

To Carol Givner, what can I say. Without you, this book simply wouldn't have ever been published. Throughout the entire process you have been there. Your few, well-chosen words always arriving at just the right moment. From the bottom of my heart, thank you for believing in me and never losing faith. To Jennifer Givner for your creative vision and design.

And to my incredible wife, Kimberly, I owe you everything. You were there in the beginning, throughout the storms, and will be until the day I die. Your patience and unconditional passion are living testament to what love is all about. I love you.

Prelude

La Jolla, California

The infinite black heart of the wave began to swell under her. She could feel it gaining force from the offshore trench as it approached. She spun around, timing her move perfectly. Water was now being sucked off the shallows by the fury building behind her. Having had nothing in its way since it began its journey a thousand miles south, far off the coast of Baja, its unbridled dominance now being challenged by the coast and a little outcropping of submerged rocks that slashed outwards from the sheer cliffs along the southern most section of Blacks Beach. Its fury unleashing into madness at its destiny. The blackness giving way to a beautiful midnight blue.

She paddled. Deep, strong strokes. Effortlessly into the sweet spot...into the very heart of the wave. From the beach it looked as if the monster were going to swallow her whole, and spit her out in little pieces. Several tourists stopped in their tracks, staring wide-eyed. The locals were watching as well. Hell, how could anyone take their eyes off such a perfect pair.

Surrendering, her mind simply letting go, allowing pure instinct to take control, as the wave continued to build to her right. In an instant, she went from lying on her board to her feet. The blues changing colors behind her, turning white as the top of the huge wave began cresting overhead, forming into a perfect left. During a south swell, there was no place on earth she'd rather be. Shooting down the face, her left arm and hand gracefully reached out toward the wave. Her fingers, outstretched, not so much for balance, but because she loved caressing the face of the wave as she dropped in. The pure, silky blue melting between her fingers. It was her own special way of saying thank you. In her mind she felt as if she were touching the face of God.

Spray exploded overhead, surrounding her in holy mist. Completely obscuring her from anyone watching along the beach.

The wave continued to crash forward, unleashing tons of furious white-water. Its deafening roar filling the air for a thousand yards in all directions. The tourists, unable to move, stared in disbelief. One of the ladies forming a cross over her chest. Believing she'd just witnessed someone being killed by the giant wave.

But inside the wave, Jennifer couldn't have been more alive. Every fibre of her body charged with electricity. Words can't describe what it was like being inside a wave, especially a wave like this. After what seemed like an eternity, she shot out from beneath the crashing avalanche of white-water into the afternoon sunlight. Effortlessly flying down the face, then turning back towards the foam, hesitating for a split second, before jetting up its face again and dropping back down. Her body blending into the wave. A dance of pure harmony as their destinies carried them toward the beach.

"Unbelievable," one of the locals murmured.

"No shit. What a ride," another said, without taking his eyes off Jennifer, as she kicked out over the top of the wave.

Now outside the break, Jennifer's pounding heart began to slow. It had been an incredible ride. *Perhaps one of the best of my life*, she thought to herself. Closing her eyes and thanking the Gods once again for their gifts, for her sanctuary.

And for those few precious moments, the loneliness inside her wasn't all consuming.

Go placidly amid the noise and haste, and remember what peace there may be in silence.

Chapter 1

Seattle, Washington

The storm slammed into the coast just before dawn, exactly as the late night news predicted. It whipped down the inside passages east of Vancouver Island, providing a taste of what life was going to be like for the next six months—cold, wet and miserable.

Every year around the autumnal equinox, the weather in the Northwest turns. It's a part of life. Locals know it's coming, and there's no reason to complain about it, but they always do…as they have since the beginning of time.

Preparing for another Seattle winter, Karyn and I were winterizing the boat when old man Wilson shuffled by, the splintering wooden docks creaking under his weight. He stopped and eyeballed what we were doing. Being neighbourly, Karyn asked if he needed any help with his boat.

"Don't need no help. Can take care of her myself," he snapped back defiantly, nodding toward his floating pile of crap a couple of slips down from ours. "Been taking care of her my whole life," he said. "Certainly don't need no help from the likes of you."

"Just offering was all," Karyn answered him softly.

He grunted in return. I'd ducked behind the opposite side of the wheelhouse as I saw him approaching, and was watching them through the salon windows. There was a glimmer of a smile in her eye as she assured him she didn't mean any offence. How she had the patience to deal with him the way she did was beyond me. I couldn't stand the crotchety old prick.

"Yeah, well, you'd better be sure and do that right," Wilson said, looking at the braided mooring line she was holding. "It's going to be a bitch of a winter, and I don't want to deal with your boat breaking loose, banging up against my lady there," he added, jerking his stiff neck and cap-covered head toward his boat. "A real bitch of a winter," he mumbled to himself, turning and continuing down the dock. "I can feel it in my bones."

No doubt he could, I thought to myself as Karyn turned, flashing that incredible smile of hers. She knew full well how the old man would respond before she even asked if he needed help. He was as cantankerous as they come. Older than dirt and mean as hell. Couldn't blame him for being so pissed off, though. He'd been living on the water since the day he was born. One of a dying breed being forced out by the nouveau riche, who had recently discovered houseboat living along Seattle's ancient waterfront. Didn't matter to Wilson that I'd been born right here, onboard this very boat. As far as he was concerned, anyone under a hundred was scum.

What used to be a shantytown of makeshift craft, most of which, like Wilson's, were seemingly kept afloat by only their dock lines, were being run off by multilevel, built-to-the-hilt, wall-to-wall floating condos. Tasteless pieces of architecture that wouldn't last an hour outside the protected waters of the harbor. With deck-to-ceiling glass, tile roofs, recessed lighting and spiral staircases, master suites and fake fireplaces, the condos boasted heads with built-in Jacuzzis, heated floors and tanning beds. Seattle's new houseboats were anything but boats; the new generation of occupants, anything but boat people. But together they were the new floating armada of Seattle's waterfront. Karyn and I resented them as much as the old man did.

Like old man Wilson, my Dad was born and raised on the waterfront. Married to the eldest daughter of one of the most successful seafood processors on the coast, he'd spent his life fishing a deep-water trawler, working the Bering Sea until an Arctic storm took his life.

After he died, Mom and I moved off the boat and went to live with Grandpa and Grandma in the big house up on the hill overlooking the harbor. Mom never set foot on the boat again. The following day, Grandpa picked me up after school in the old truck and drove me down to the plant. He put me to work cleaning up the guts behind the cutters at the cannery.

"You earn your keep, boy," Grandpa said. "There ain't no free lunches in this world. The sooner you learn that, the better off you'll be. Understand?"

"Yes, sir." *I didn't have a clue what he was talking about.*

The cutters went through the fish like butter. Knives flying faster than the eye could keep up. But after a few days, I began to hate the smell of dead fish and dreaded when school let out. All the other kids took off to play, while I had to go slop fish guts into the barf barge. "I'm only thirteen," I'd mumble to myself, shovelling another pile of guts onto the barge. "This sucks. It isn't fair."

But every day after school and all day Saturday, I'd slop wheelbarrow after wheelbarrow full of fish guts and carcasses from under the cutters table to the barge.

The only good part about the whole ordeal was riding out to dump the barf barge when it got full with Angie Santos. Angie had been driving the barge for my Grandpa since the beginning of time. An ancient Portuguese fisherman, Angie been working fishing boats his whole life. Knew more about fish than any man I ever met. Taught me just about everything I know about fishing. Everyday when the barge got loaded up, and we'd head off. He'd drop back a hand line. At first, I thought he was nuts.

"You aren't going catch anything in here," I pronounced, nodding towards the busy harbor.

He glanced up at me, but didn't say a word.

No sooner than that did he get bit. I couldn't believe it. "What da' got!" I yelled excitedly.

Holding firmly onto the line with one hand, he reached down and pulled the old Union diesel out of gear. Looking back up at me, his words were soft. "Why don't come on back here," he said, offering me the line. "Pull him in and see for yourself."

I about tripped over myself, scrambling along the edge of the barge. "Really? Can I?"

"If you can keep from falling overboard or into the guts," he said, a gentle laugh accompanying his thoughts. "Here you go," he said, handing me the line as I reached the stern. "Hold tight, or it'll rip you up."

The fish almost pulled the line out of my hand. Burning my palms as the line seared over my skin. His hands were like leather. Mine turned white where the line burned through before starting to bleed, but I didn't let go.

"Jesus!" I screamed.

He nodded. Knowing how much it hurt, but liking the fact I didn't drop the line.

"If he runs again, let him go. Don't try and stop him. Keep just enough tension on the line so you have some control, but there's no way to stop him when he's this hot."

It was the biggest fish I'd ever caught, or at least fought. My dad had taken me fishing a few times off the docks, but the only things we'd ever caught were some scrawny bottom grabbers.

But this fish was something else. "What do you think it is?" I asked Angie.

"Not sure. What do you think?"

Visions of giant halibut raced through my brain. Or maybe even a King salmon. "I don't know, maybe a King."

"Maybe," he said, "but who knows."

It felt like the fish was beginning to tire. But then he made another long run after I'd gotten most of the line back, again burning my hands.

"Even pressure this time," Angie coached me. "Steady even pressure. You got him coming your way, no need to piss him off any more than he already is."

The fish circled under the boat a few times. Each time he came out from under the boat, I was able to gain a full arms length of line.

"That's it," Angie said as I gained on the fish. "Slow and easy. Keep his head up and just guide him toward the surface."

"Holly shit!" I screamed as the big flattie broke the surface. Shaking his head violently. Rocking me to my bones. Holding on with both hands as tightly as I could, he wasn't able to pull out any line, but he about jerked my arms out of their sockets.

"He's a beauty," Angie said. Reaching over the rail, grabbing the line. My body immediately quit shaking. My arms were numb and my hands were on fire, but none of that mattered. This was the biggest fish I'd ever caught.

Angie started talking out loud, not taking his eyes off the fish. "Now take it easy big guy, everything's going to be alright."

He was talking to fish as if it was a person and the weirdest thing was, I swear to God that damn fish was listening. It immediately quit thrashing around and let Angie pull him right up next to the boat.

"That a boy," he said softly. Reaching down and pulling the barbless hook out of his mouth in one easy motion. The fish hesitated for a split second, before diving for the bottom. Leaving a huge boil in his wake.

I was speechless.

"Nice job," Angie said, leaning back up and extending his hand.

Taking it, I shook my head in shock, "Why did you let him go?"

Angie pushed the shift level forward, putting the barge back in gear, before asking, "How your hands?"

"Fine!" I snapped back, slowly turning my palms up and looking down at them. I was pissed. My hands were bleeding and starting to really hurt. "That was my fish. Why did you let him go?"

"Look around you," Angie instructed calmly.

"At what?" *You crazy old coot.*

"What do you see?"

"Nothing. We in the middle of the bay surrounded by water."

"Not exactly. Look closer."

I had no idea what he was talking about. He waited, watching me. When he saw me look down at the load of fish carcasses and guts we were hulling his eyes flashed.

"What are you talking about? You want me look at the guts?"

He nodded.

"I don't get it."

Then he asked me, "Are you hungry?"

"What?"

"Hungry? Are you hungry?"

"No. I'm pissed off you let my fish go."

"Your fish?" he asked.

"Yea. I caught him."

"You certainly did. And you did a damn fine job," he added. "I thought he was about going tear your hands off on that first run."

Looking down at my throbbing hands again, I nodded, shrugging my shoulders. "He just about did."

"I know." Angie said. "You showed a lot of heart hanging on the way you did."

Lowering my head, my anger draining with the fading adrenalin rush. "Thanks."

He didn't say anything else for a while. Until I asked him, "Why'd you what to know if I was hungry?"

"Because that's the only reason to ever kill anything. If you're going to eat it, take it. If not, let him go." His eyes bore into my young soul. Holding me there until he saw that I understood what he was saying. I nodded. The corners of his eyes creased into the beginnings of a smile as he slowly nodded back. We understood one another. "Chances are," he added, "we might even fool him into doing battle with us again one of these fine days."

That was it. That was all he said. But from that moment on I was hooked. After that, I couldn't wait to fill the barge so we could ride out together. Angie continued teaching me everything he knew about fishing. I soaked it up like a dry sponge.

Born in San Diego, he'd fished tuna and albacore his entire life. At first from a small converted WWII jig boat, where he spent hours standing in a little area of the stern, hand lining fish. Tossing them in over his shoulder, before grabbing another line off the spreaders. Jig boat fishing was one tough way to make a living. But he loved it. From there he'd moved on to working the clippers. Running as far south as the Galapagos. Being away for months at a time. Making bait, and having to get their fresh water from waterfalls cascading over lush islands and into the sea. He explained to me how they'd row the bait skiff in under the waterfall, filling it with fresh water. Then row it back to the clipper, "...full to the gunnels...," he'd say, before transferring the fresh water back onboard the clipper with wooden buckets. I was mesmerized. The places they fished sounding more like Fantasy Island than real life. He'd bring out some old black and white pictures of tuna, as big as a man, and I knew he was telling the truth.

The stories he'd tell of being in the rack, four Calcutta poles, tied to one hook, lifting two hundred and fifty pound yellowfin as they streaked towards the surface, inhaling the squid, filled my nights with dreams of fish so big they could swallow a man whole.

"If you didn't time it just right, and they got their heads pointed away, man oh man, were you in for a world of hurt. Nothing' like liftin' fish," he'd say. The memories dancing behind his eyes.

He taught me how to wrap white chicken feathers and cow hide into perfect squid baits. He taught me how to tie the right kind of knots, for whatever we were doing. He taught me how to read the water. How to look for signs. What initially had been nothing but liquid surrounding us on our daily runs, slowly turned into a virtual landscape. Overflowing with information. Rich in texture. Teaming with life. Radiating like neon street signs. Pointing which direction to go. He showed me how to recognize temperature breaks. Currents and wind rips. He even taught me how to smell the oil herring leave on the surface after having been balled up and worked over by a school of salmon. He taught me to watch the birds. "What's going on above the water is a mirror image, reflecting what's going on below it."

And sure enough, we'd pull up on a big bird school, diving and working a bait ball, and you could see the fish flashing under the bait. Scales rippling down. "Just like an hour glass," he'd say.

But most importantly he taught me to respect the sea. To listen to what she was saying. Her rhythms and to heed her warnings. "For when she unbridles her fury, no man or ship is safe." But even more importantly, he taught me an appreciation for the cycles of life. Showing me how everything is connected. "We'll all just guests here on this big blue planet, he said, holding his arms out, eyes smiling, face to the sky, "...bobbin' around in our own little life boats," pausing, "...so treat her well."

******

Three years later, Mom passed.

The morning we scattered her ashes, there wasn't a wisp of wind. The only sound was the low, steady hum of the diesel. Hanging like a shroud around us, the fog was so thick you could hardly see the bow, but Grandpa navigated through the harbor like it was the back of his hand. Few words were spoken. Grandma held me tight by her side the whole way out. I was doing all right until I felt her shiver. I looked up and watched a tear drip off her cheek. Seeing her crying made me start balling like a little girl. Men didn't cry in Grandpa's world. I knew it, but couldn't stop. He glanced over at us without saying anything.

After awhile, he pulled the boat out of gear and shut off the main. The instant silence was overwhelming after the comforting, steady drone of big iron. It took a hundred yards for us to stop gliding across the sheet glass water. When we did, the priest, a long time family friend, said a few words. We joined him in the Lord's Prayer. Then, without any fanfare, Grandpa dumped Mom's ashes overboard. They hit the water and spread out, filtering down like a giant white cloud. *A cloud with wings,* I thought to myself, tossing a bundle of handpicked flowers onto the disappearing ashes. Grandpa gave Grandma a squeeze, thanked the priest, fired up the main, put the boat in gear and spun us around for home.

When we got back to the dock and got the boat secured, Grandpa looked me in the eye. "You still hankering to move back onto this ol' boat?" he asked.

I was shocked. "Yes, sir," I managed to get out. "You know I am."

"Then go ahead," he said. Grandma was standing a couple feet behind him. "You've been doing a good job tending to her all these years. She's old, but she's solid. You two take care of each other."

I didn't know what to say. I threw my arms around him and squeezed for all I was worth. No one ever hugged Grandpa. I felt his spine stiffen, but he let me hold on for a couple of heartbeats. Then he patted me on the back like a dog and grabbed my shoulders. His stare could have bored holes through granite. He was one of the most respected and powerful men on the waterfront—a big, tough Swede who had fish in his blood. The few who challenged him did so only once. He ran his domain with an iron fist and, in my case, a well-cured leather strap that made its acquaintance with my young ass on more than one occasion. In his world, there were no excuses, no second chances. Do it right or pay the price. Just like the sea.

He nodded slowly before speaking. "Go ahead. Get your things and move back here. But if I hear so much as a rumour about you missing a day of school or causing any problems, it'll be your ass. You understand?"

"Yes, sir." There I was, sixteen and being told I could move back onboard. I loved my grandparents, but living on the boat alone…life didn't get any better than this! "Thank you," I said, offering my hand. His grip was uncompromising. "I won't let you down."

Grandpa nodded and reached into his pocket, pulling out the keys to the old '51 Ford pickup I'd been driving around the cannery for the past three years. "You earned this," he said with a satisfied nod, handing me the keys. "You worked hard…never asked for anything and never complained. I'm proud of you, son."

I didn't know what to say. Tears started to well up and my chin started quivering. I had to bite my lip to keep from crying again.

"Work hard. Be true to yourself," he told me. "Everything else'll take care of itself."

He paused, looking out across the harbor into the fog. "Moving back onto the boat, you'll be on your own. You got work at the cannery if you want it, but I'm not going make you come in. If you find something better after school, or you want to play ball—fine. If not, you've been working deck and cutting fish now long enough. You know good grade the instant you see it. If you want, you can start buying or run one of the boats. Up to you."

"No shit, Grandpa?" I blurted out, without thinking.

He frowned at my language, but a smile managed to slip out. "Like I said, son, you've earned it."

Be yourself. Especially, do not feign affection. Neither be cynical about love, for in the face of all aridity & disenchantment it is as perennial as the grass.

Chapter 2

The three of us had grown up together—a couple of dock rats and the homecoming queen. An unlikely threesome if there ever was one. Karyn was from an esteemed, respected family who lived high up on the hill, way past my grandparents' house. Shane and I, born and raised on boats, sons of the sons of fisherman. When we were only kids, no one seemed to pay us any attention…or didn't seem to care if they did notice. But as we grew into adolescence and were seen doing everything together, people started talking. "That sweet young thing, always surrounded by those boys. She's developing into such a beautiful young lady. She shouldn't be spending all her time with those boys from the docks. It's not right."

We were certainly not the type of young men an outstanding family like Karyn's wanted to have courting their only daughter. But all the fuss was in a world we couldn't care less about—an adult world that seemed miles from our own.

Weekends were heaven. Exploring the sights and sounds of Seattle, we roamed the open-air markets of the waterfront. For as long as each of us could remember, we had been inseparable. In our youthful innocence, we thought nothing would ever change that—until gangs of raging hormones made their way into our young bodies. Before we knew it, they started dominating our world. It was only a matter of time before either Shane or I would get the girl—one of us tasting the sweet nectars of love, the other left alone to discover just how important a young man's right hand really is.

We'd all been clamming in the flats during one of the lowest tides of the summer. The late summer afternoon was hot. By the time we'd filled up our buckets, we were a mess. The ensuing mud fight was inevitable. By the time it was over, we were covered in sticky black goo from head to toe. Shane and I had been in a wrestling match, which ended in a draw with both our faces pressed into the mud. Laughing hysterically, we trudged back towards the shoreline through the ankle-deep muck. Shane's mom driving by just as we reached the road. She shook her head at the three of us, but smiled. She needed his help with something, so he climbed into the back of their pickup, leaving Karyn and me alone.

"My house is closer than your boat," she said. "This mud is starting to dry, so let's go there and clean up."

"Your parents will kill us if they see us like this," I said, holding out my arms for emphasis.

"We can sneak in the back gate and use the pool house."

When we got to her house, we rinsed off with the garden hose so we wouldn't track mud all over the place, but our clothes were still a dripping mess.

"Here!" Karyn tossed me one of the two big beach towels she'd snagged from just inside the pool house door. "Wrap up in this and leave your clothes out here."

"I'm good," I said as I finished rinsing off.

"I want to shampoo this stuff out of my hair and you should, too," she insisted, turning her back and pulling off her top. She wrapped a towel around her waist before manoeuvring her pants and panties down to her ankles. Her little wiggling motion froze me in my tracks. Turning around, she gave me a mischievous smile that set my loins on fire—an uncontrollable erection instantly on its way. When you're my age, if the wind blows hard enough, you get a hard on. Seeing her undress right there in front of me was way too much.

"Are you coming?" she whispered softly, stepping out of her panties and sliding past me.

Embarrassed, I didn't know what to do. So I just stood there, frozen in place like an idiot, trying to hide a full hard-on. Glancing over her shoulder—seeing the bulge under my towel—she smiled again before disappearing into the pool house. A few seconds later, I heard the shower running. I could see her silhouette through the bathroom window as it started to steam up. The images of Karyn naked in the shower just a few feet away drove me crazy. I couldn't help it. I reached down and came within seconds after touching myself.

I was sitting on the padded wicker couch, still in my wet trunks with the beach towel securely draped over my lap, when Karyn came out of the shower, her skin glowing. A towel was wrapped around her, tucked in just under her arm to cover her breasts but barely covering her thighs. Her head was tilted to one side and she was wringing her hair. She was the most beautiful thing I'd ever seen. The sun had dropped down, just tipping the top of the trees surrounding the pool. The light reflected off the water, shining through the windows and bathing the room with soft, golden light…the beginning of an incredible summer sunset.

She sat down next to me. I couldn't look her in the eye. I was completely overwhelmed by her presence. We sat there, neither of us saying a word. Finally, as she finished towel drying her hair, she leaned over and gently brushed the corner of my mouth with her lips. I couldn't move. She lingered there, her face just inches from mine. Reaching over, she touched my cheek and tilted my head up so our eyes met. I saw a smile in her eyes. She radiated life. Barely letting her lips touch mine, she kissed me again.

This was the first time I'd been kissed by a girl. And this wasn't just any girl—it was Karyn. I could feel her sweet warm breath on my face. The world began to melt away, leaving only the universe within our souls. Our bodies quivered as our lips met again, but this time she pressed down hard enough to force my lips apart. Her tongue slipped inside my mouth, sending a new wave of chills down my spine. Closing my eyes, I surrendered to exquisite sensations—her soft lips, her warm mouth and gentle touch, her fingers around the back of my neck. As our kisses grew more passionate, our bodies hungered for more. She pulled me closer, pressing our mouths together even harder. Arching her head back, she gasped for breath. My lips slid down her neck, soaking up her skin in a never-ending kiss. Her towel had loosened. Holding my head with both hands, she gently guided my lips toward her young breasts. I could feel her heart pounding under her soft velvet skin. Her palms covered my ears, muffling all sound; her fingers clutched my hair, controlling my every move. Slowly guiding me across her chest, she kept my lips just inches above her breasts. With every breath, her chest swelled and her nipples rose, barely grazing my tongue. Finally, she lowered my head, allowing my aching lips to make contact with her nipples. She moaned and then pulled my head away, holding me there, just inches from her heart. Then slowly, she lowered my head again. I ran my tongue along the underside of her pure white breast. Her heart was pounding. She guided my mouth back to her perfect nipples that had hardened as I engulfed them. She moaned louder as my kisses turned into suckling.

"Oh, God," she whispered, "that feels so good." Suddenly she yanked my head up. Biting my ear, she moaned, "Make love to me, please. I want you inside me so much it hurts." We both were breathing in short, hard gasps. Our hearts pounding. "Please," she pleaded. "Please!" Her towel fell completely open, revealing the soft tuft of her light-blonde pubic hair. Spreading her legs, she took my hand and guided it toward her young vagina. It was warm and moist. My fingers slid inside her effortlessly.

"Oh, God," she whispered breathlessly. "Kiss me there," she pleaded between moans, pushing my head down from her stomach. Arching her back and bending her knees slightly, she opened her legs a little wider, completely exposing herself. My lips touched her there. Delicate juices exploded in my mouth. I'd never tasted anything so intoxicating, so sweet. It was incredible—a taste of life itself.

She tried holding her body perfectly still, but could restrain herself no longer. She'd dreamed about this moment for a long time. Her legs began quivering as she allowed her hips to slip into a rhythm of their own. My mouth was barely caressing her swollen, pulsating opening. She arched her back, pushing herself harder against my mouth. My tongue slipped insider her. She moaned. I let myself go, becoming one with her pulsating rhythm as she became one with my mouth. My tongue was everywhere. Caressing, sucking, probing.

Suddenly she arched up. Grabbing my head, and screamed, scaring the crap out of me. I froze, thinking I'd done something wrong. Her hands became vices around my head, holding me perfectly still, my mouth covering her womanhood. "Oh, my God! My God!" she shouted. "Don't move!"

I couldn't if I tried. I was petrified. My mind was searching for a reason, for answers it couldn't possible know. Questions swirled around inside my brain. *What happened? What did I do wrong? I'm sorry. I'm so sorry. I love you.*

She kept whispering over and over again, "Oh, God. Oh, God."

Slowly, her hands relaxed around my head. She leaned forward, her lips resting delicately on top of my head, barely touching my hair. The warmth of her breath sent a new wave of chills down my spine. I didn't have a clue what had just happened, but was still too afraid to move. She held me perfectly still, trying to catch her breath. I'd been kneeling on the floor between her legs. Slowly, she slid down off the couch and slid underneath me. I was still rock hard, but moments after her mouth found my penis, it exploded. She continued sucking while I came. The next thing I knew she was on her knees, straddling me. I was still hard. Effortlessly, she guided me inside her, lowering herself down until she completely engulfed me. We both stopped breathing. When our eyes met, I saw a tear running down her cheek.

"I love you," she whispered. "I love you so much." She leaned over and we kissed. A deep, slow kiss, growing in intensity. I could feel her pulse beating along the full length of my penis. Her quick, intense squeezes started our bodies moving again. She pushed herself up off my chest. Her beautiful breasts stark white against her golden tan, her nipples firm and tight. I arched up to kiss them.

She moaned again. Her hips started undulating, faster and faster. "Oh, God, I'm going to come again!" she screamed. Her head flew back. I could feel every contraction of her being. Her orgasm mushroomed around my penis. Her legs quivering, her entire body vibrating. She sat motionless, pulsating with passion. Her eyes closed. Breathing hard. Beads of perspiration glistened off her body. Eventually, she eased off me. Rolling over and sliding onto her stomach.

"I want to feel you come again," she whispered. Spreading her legs, arching her smooth white ass off the carpet. Presenting herself to me. I slid effortlessly back inside her from behind. "Oh, my God. That feels so good," she moaned.

Looking down at her beautiful little ass was the most erotic thing I'd ever seen. Her rich golden tan highlighting the places where the sun couldn't reach—the secret, sacred places she'd kept hidden from the world. Until now. Her beautiful flaxen hair, still wet from her shower, lay tangled across her back. Her soft moans, the heat radiating off her body, her taste, the delicious sweetness of her being… completely overwhelming me as we moved in perfect harmony. The feeling of being inside her from behind was so different from having her on top of me. For the first time since she'd kissed me, I started to feel a sense of control over what was happening. Having already come twice, I wanted this moment to last forever. Whenever I'd feel myself starting to cum, I'd slowly pull myself almost all the way out, leaving just the tip of my penis, touching the inside of her lips, she'd hesitate for a moment and then push backwards, forcing herself against me, surrounding me with pulsating warmth, passion and pressure.

"Don't tease me," she pleaded, shaking her hair. "Don't tease me like that. I've wanted you inside me for so long. Don't stop. Don't ever stop loving me."

And I'd surrender, pushing into her as deeply as I could. Looking down, I saw her vaginal lips, swollen and crimson. My penis glistened from her moisture as it slid in and out of heaven. The feelings were unbelievable. After awhile, I could feel my entire body getting ready to explode again. "I'm going to cum!" I screamed.

Her body responded instantly, tightening around me, demanding. We came together in perfect unison. I collapsed next to her and rolled onto my side, still inside her. My arms were round her chest, holding onto life itself. Our bodies, a perfect fit, were locked together in total bliss. She held me inside her, her heartbeat surrounding my every nerve. We lay together, slipping into eternity—breathless, exhausted, bathing in the afterglow that only love can give. The sun, had dipped below the horizon long ago. The room was all but dark, yet a light still shone in her eyes.

"I love you," she whispered.

"I love you, too, Karyn. More than anything in the world."

"I know," she said, nestling her head into my chest. "I know you do."

I could have died right there and my life would have been perfect. I didn't know that such feelings of absolute peace and contentment existed. Lying together, holding one another, the world could have come to an end and we wouldn't have cared. Our souls were at one with each other. Neither of us uttered another sound for the longest time. Nothing needed to be said. Our bodies, our hearts, our souls were saying it all, celebrating the pure essence of love. We'd been best friends since we could remember, and now we'd crossed a threshold into a new world.

Lying there, I knew that for as long as I lived, I'd never forget a single moment of what we'd just shared... the way she looked coming out of the shower... her radiant skin, glowing, wet from the hot water...her beautiful hair rolled up in a loose bun. And that look in her eyes—a look I'd never seen until that night. The look of love...the look of a woman in love. Gone was the girl I'd known all my life. Gone was the boy I'd been until that moment.

The soft light of the moon poured into the room and covered us with a blanket of warmth, protecting us from the world outside. I chuckled, thinking how perfect it was, when only hours before we'd been in an all out mud ball war in the tidal flats. I had no idea anyone could feel like this, that two people could make each other feel this way. I lay there wondering, thinking, *Why me? Why am I the luckiest person in the world?* I don't know if she sensed it or if the thoughts actually escaped my lips, but she knew what I was thinking. She lifted her head to look at me. She smiled and the room lit up around her.

"What?" I asked.

"Didn't see this coming, did you?" she asked, smiling at our entwined bodies. Her voice had a new tone to it—something strong and permanent, a knowledge and depth I'd never heard before that night.

"No, I didn't," I answered honestly. "I'm still half afraid I'm just dreaming."

"Oh, trust me," she said, her smile broadening, "you're not dreaming." Her kiss sent chills down my spine again.

"Why me?" This time I heard the words come out.

She waited a long time before answering. I didn't care. I could have laid there with her forever. "I've seen you checkin' me out. Looking when you thought I couldn't see you. Glancing at my breasts or looking at my butt when I bend over." I wouldn't have dreamed it possible to feel embarrassed after what we'd just shared, but I did. "It's okay," she said reassuringly, gently brushing my hair back. "I like it when you look at me like that."

"You're so beautiful…I can't help it." I was still embarrassed and couldn't look her in the eye.

"But you never tried anything," she said. "You never once even tried to kiss me. Not once."

I didn't say anything, but God knows I'd dreamed about doing a lot more than just kissing her. A thousand nights I'd lay awake unable to sleep. She was all I could think about. Her radiant smile. Her perfect body. Those incredible breasts that had blossomed right before my eyes. Catching a glimpse of white under her blouse or seeing the outline of her panties through her shorts made me crazy. Her quick wit and golden hair. Her gentle way with people. Her eyes. Oh, God, I loved her eyes. She was all I thought about whenever I played with myself before going to sleep. But she was right—I'd never uttered a word to her about the way I felt. Even if I had the balls to tell her, I wouldn't have known what to say. So I'd just kept my mouth shut.

"I knew you wanted me," she continued with intuition beyond her years and way beyond mine. "I could see it in your eyes." I turned away. "Don't be embarrassed," she said, gently pulling me towards her and kissing my forehead. "It's one of the reasons I love you so much." She paused, the smile never leaving her eyes. "But you never tried anything. At first I thought maybe it was because you didn't like me."

I started to interrupt, but she touched my lips with her finger. I kissed it, and for a moment all thought processes came to a halt. "But then I'd see the way you looked at me and I knew you felt the same about me as I did about you. After awhile, I realized you were just shy. I thought it was cute. I wanted my first time to be perfect. With you, I knew it would be."

"This was your first time?" I blurted out without even thinking. She'd been so in control…had known exactly what to do. I was shocked. It felt like she'd made love a thousand times. A shadow crossed her face. I felt like an idiot. "I didn't mean it like that," I said, trying to apologize. "It's just that…it's just that you were so good. I mean you made everything so perfect. I thought, because you seemed to know exactly what to do, that you must have done it before." My words trailed off limply. "I'm sorry. I didn't mean that the way it sounded."

The smile returned to her eyes "What? You think guys are the only ones who play with themselves?" I was shocked. I had no idea...never dreamed that girls jerked off. "Trust me," she said with a coy smile. "Maybe not exactly the way you're thinking, but we do."

"Unbelievable."

Laughing out loud, she said, "If we waited around for you guys to figure out what to do, mankind wouldn't even be here today. Trust me, we want it as much as you guys do...if not more." Her hand was inching its way over my stomach. "Here, let me show you..."

Lowering her head, she took me in her mouth again. Time ceased to exist as we made love again. We'd created a universe of our own, wrapping ourselves in a cocoon of love. Our souls were entwined for life. By the time we finished, it was well after midnight. We kissed each other goodnight for the umpteenth time before she left the pool house and slipped through the back door of her parents' house. For a few moments, I waited outside the gate to make sure she made it up to her bedroom without waking her parents.

Walking home along the quiet, deserted streets felt more like floating. I don't think my feet touched the ground once. I was in love, head-over-heals. The world around me was in perfect harmony...until I got home and climbed on board. Shane had come over after finishing the chores his mom had for him. He'd fallen asleep on the back deck and awoke a little startled as I sat down across from him.

"Where have you been?" he barked. Looking me over, he immediately knew something was different. "What the hell?" he said gesturing with his chin. I hesitated, not answering him. "You've been with Karyn, haven't you?" he asked, an accusing tone in his voice. When I didn't answer he snapped, "That little bitch!"

Springing up, I was in his face before he even knew it. "Take that back, you asshole."

"Easy, Rider!" he said, holding up his hands. "I didn't mean anything by it."

"Take it back!" I demanded.

"Okay, okay" he said laughing. "She's not a bitch."

I relaxed as I backed away from my friend, but I was still pissed. *How could he say that about her?*

"You fucked her tonight, didn't you?" He had no idea what love was. "I knew it!" he said, getting all excited. "I knew it. I could see it the minute you woke me up. You devil," he continued. "I've been trying to get in her pants all summer."

"You what?" I snapped back at him.

"Relax, cowboy," he said, holding up his arms innocently. "She wouldn't have anything to do with me. Managed to kiss her a couple of times, but she wouldn't even let me get to first base."

"You kissed her?"

"Don't look so shocked, amigo," he said smiling. "She's hot. Why wouldn't I give it a shot?"

"You never told me," I said lamely.

"Why would I?" he said. "Nothing happened. I kissed her a couple of times. No big deal. Tried to get into her panties, but she wouldn't give it up. Said she was saving herself for the 'right guy.'" He laughed. "Looks like you're the lucky one."

After having just had the most incredible experience of my life, I hated listening to him talk like that. "It wasn't like that," I said.

"Then tell me. Was she hot or what?"

"Fuck off!" Now I was pissed. "It wasn't anything like that."
"Sex is sex," he announced. "They're all tramps."

"You're fucked up," I said. Shane and I had been best friends since we were kids, but this was breaking new ground. A part of him I'd never seen before was coming to the surface, like a really bad zit. His take on women was bullshit. "Where do you come up with this crap? I'm tired. I'm going to bed."

"It's true. Women are all the same."

As if you know anything about women. We'd been spending the night on each other's boats since forever, so having him sleeping over was no big deal. But that night, something changed. I felt different about him being there. I wanted to be alone. Actually, I really wanted to be lying next to Karyn. But as I lay there, listening to him doze off and start snoring on the bunk next to mine, I realized our worlds had shifted and would never be the same again.

As far as possible, without surrender, be on good terms with all persons.

Chapter 3

Four years later.

The clear, balmy June afternoon couldn't have been prettier. It was the weekend following our high school graduation ceremonies. Our fairy tale wedding made news in the local papers. "The Perfect Wedding" read the front-page headline in the social section of the *Seattle Post*. "Corey Phillips marries into the Lake family, taking the hand of the charming and talented Ms. Karyn Lake, only daughter of Mr. and Mrs. Robert Charles Lake. The wedding took place under clear blue skies on the terrace of the exclusive West Bay Yacht club. Among the notable in attendance were...."

After our night in the pool house, Karyn and I were inseparable. We did everything we could to keep her parents from finding out about us having sex, but we didn't fool them for long. Mr. Lake threatened to kill me if I touched his daughter again. It was like a scene from the movies...I ran for my life out of their house...Karyn screaming she loved me and pulling on her father's shirt...her mom crying hysterically. It would have been comic, except for the fact that Mr. Lake would have killed me had he caught me.

Following that little incident, the Lakes did everything in their power to keep Karyn and me apart. In her sophomore year, they sent her to an all-girls boarding school outside Shaker Heights, Ohio. The day after they dropped her off at the headmaster's office, she booked a first-class, one-way ticket home (using the American Express card they'd given her for emergencies only). They gave in. Mrs. Lake devoted her time to socialite spin control. They hadn't wanted us to get married, but were making sure the world they lived in saw our union in the right light.

"Corey Phillips, the eldest and only grandson of Seattle's own R. J. Walters, President and CEO of Walters' Processing and Shipping, the largest purveyors of sea food on the west coast.... Sweethearts since childhood, Karyn and Corey looked ready to take on the world today, and all of us here at the *Post* wish them the very best. Good luck, newlyweds." Those were the last words of the article in a newspaper Mr. Lake supported annually with major advertising dollars. All the while, Mrs. Lake was silently thanking God that Karyn wasn't pregnant under her wedding dress for the extensive photo spreads.

Despite the Lakes' offer to help us with the down payment on a house for our wedding gift, Karyn and I decided we wanted to live together on the houseboat. We loved it down there. She transformed the boat into a delightful floating home. In spite of themselves, by summer's end Karyn's parents enjoyed spending Sunday afternoons with us. At first, they'd refused to set foot on board the boat, but after awhile, seeing how happy their daughter was, they couldn't resist. Sundays became a tradition—barbequing fresh salmon on the back deck, a big pot of crab legs steaming on the old oil stove, and the mouth-watering smell of Karyn's home-made sourdough bread filling the air. We were becoming a family. With her mom's home-grown garden salads and a couple of bottles of White Zinfandel from their private reserve, life was good. After dinner we'd sit on the back deck, enjoying the quiet beauty of a summer's day drawing to a close.

"You still like working at the cannery?" Mr. Lake would inevitably get around to asking.

"Daddy, you know he does. Why do you ask us that every time we see you?"

"I just want him to know there's a spot for him if he ever wants it. That's all."

"Appreciate the offer, Mr. Lake, but I like what I do." I'd had offers to crew as well, but didn't want to be away from Karyn for weeks at a time. So even though the money wasn't great, I kept my job as a buyer. Being home every night was worth it. We couldn't have been happier.

With Karyn and me being married, Shane was odd man out in our little threesome. Shane and I made it though a rocky spell after Karyn and I first hooked up. But being as athletic and good looking as Shane was, it didn't take long for him to feel he was the lucky one—with all the trim he was getting. When we were alone, he couldn't stop spewing the intimate details of his endless nights of romance.

"How can you just hang with one chick?" he wanted to know. "Karyn's cool and all, but dude, there's nothing like fresh pussy."

"Maybe," I'd say humouring him. "But what else can I tell you…I'm in love."

"Love, you say." He jumped down my throat. "Why are you always talking about love? I ain't talkin' love, man. I'm talking sex. Pure sex. About getting into as many pairs of sweet young panties as I can. Every chick has her secret, my friend. Every one of them. And trust me, its there, right there between their legs. Everything else is an afterthought."

"You're sick. You know that?"

"Heaven on earth, baby. Heaven on earth," he'd say, laughing and punching me in the arm. "I'm telling you, you're blowing it, only making love to one chick."

"I feel sorry for you."

"You only live once."

"You're a bad cliché," I said, shaking my head. "No wonder women grow to hate men."

"You're just jealous you're not getting any of the fresh stuff."

Never for a split second did I feel as if I was missing out on anything by being with Karyn. I knew I was the luckiest man in the world. As much as Shane tried to convince me otherwise, I was at one when I was in her arms.

******

But then the war came home. I don't know if it was because of Vietnam or the fact the world just started spinning a little off it's axis, but for three kids growing up listening to the boys from England, believing peace did stand a chance, we were about to be thrown into a world of napalm and bombs that didn't give a rat's ass who you were…or what you believed in. Nixon was elected President in 1968 and had criticized the draft in his campaign. The first draft lottery since World War II was held December 1ˢᵗ, 1969; it determined the order for conscription into the Army for men born between January 1, 1944 and December 31, 1950. In the fall of 1971 having your number picked didn't mean winning the lottery—it meant a one-way ticket into hell. If you were an able-bodied, all American male, 18 to 38, and your number was called, you were basically fucked.

Being single and not in college, Shane was USDA prime beef, 1-A draft status. Of the three hundred sixty-five birth dates selected for the draft that year, Shane's came up forty-third. He filed for status as a conscientious objector, but was rejected. A few weeks later he was standing in line in his underwear, along with a thousand other inductees, turning his head sideways and coughing while some medic held his nuts. Told to urinate in a cup, was stamped 1-A, and shipped off to Fort Ord for basic training.

The night we found out Shane was headed to basic training; I announced during dinner, "If you're going, then so am I."

Karyn and Shane both looked at me, but neither one said anything. Finally Shane reached over and grabbed my shoulder. "Listen up, amigo," he said, looking me in the eye. "I know what you're saying and I appreciate it."

"Bullshit," I said, sensing where he was headed. "I'm going."

Shaking his head, he squeezed my shoulder hard. His grip vice like. It hurt. "I love you like a brother," he told me. "You know that." I nodded as he continued. "But you're married. You have Karyn to think about…to take care of."

"But…"

Karyn was hanging on his every word, but remained silent.

"No buts about it. You're staying here. You've got responsibilities. I promise you…I'll be all right." I looked away. He squeezed harder, forcing me to meet his eyes. "I promise," he said staring into my eyes, until he saw my look of surrender. "Not all of us are destined to be warriors," he said softly. "Not this time around, anyway."

Karyn reached over and put her hand on my knee.

Shane gave me a little squeeze before letting go of my shoulder. "Besides, I not going to have time to look after your sorry ass over there. You'd probably end up getting us both killed."

Springing out of the chair, I flew at him with an open arm tackle, tipping his chair over. We both went tumbling to the floor. "I'll show you whose sorry ass needs looking after." Pinning me in seconds, Shane had me begging for mercy.

Karyn's laughter rang in our ears as she started clearing the table. "You guys'll never grow up."

******

After three months in basic training, Shane's platoon was given a four-day pass and he flew home for the long weekend before being shipped off to defend our nation against the all-powerful North Vietnamese. Those were the last days of life long friendships.

For the first time in history, the mayhem of war was played out in living color every night on the six o'clock news. The effects on the country were mind numbing. By the time Shane finally came home after three tours, he and America were changed forever. Other than a few bumps and bruises, he'd escaped unscathed. Decorated with honours for bravery and heroism, he stood erect and proud, but his eyes were deep orbs of darkness and depression. The horrors he'd seen had manifested into a vicious cancer that was eating him alive from within. He was a hollow shell of the proud, young man he once was.

Without a second thought, he moved in with Karyn and me, taking over the same stateroom we'd shared as kids. The three of us were reunited. The post-war Shane didn't talk much, and when he did, it was never about the war. As far as I could tell, he didn't sleep much either. One afternoon while Karyn was at the market, I asked him if he wanted to talk about what had happened over there. He stared at me with unblinking eyes. Shaking his head slowly, he said, "You don't want to know."

I held his gaze. Searching his eyes but finding only darkness in the blank emptiness of his stare gave me goose bumps. "Don't ask me again, okay?" he said. That's the last time we ever talked about the war.

From day one, he cautioned Karyn and I never to come into his cabin at night. "Can't sleep much," he told us after being back a few days. "What rest I am getting is only skin deep. So, please, for your own safety, don't ever come into my cabin without knocking." Karyn and I nodded, thinking we understood. We didn't. "And most importantly," he added, "wait 'til I say it's okay before you open the door."

Karyn and I nodded again and exchanged glances. Seeing our confusion, he added. "I might react without thinking," he explained, pausing before drifting away again. We waited. Growing accustomed to his disjointed conversations. He was never fully present.

"Especially at night, when I'm in the dark, when I'm sleeping…don't come in on me, okay…" It wasn't a question.

The weeks passed by. I went off to work every morning, leaving the two of them to take care of things around the boat and handle the chores. They'd shop for fresh vegetables, home made breads and pastas on Market Street or pick up lunch and bring it down to me at the docks. The time they were spending together, walking our old stomping grounds, seemed to be slowly helping Shane ease back.

One afternoon I came home early, needing a file that I had stored in his cabin. I'd been using Shane's cabin as a home office before he moved in. He and Karyn were out when I got to the boat, so I just went in to get the file. What I found instead scared the crap out of me.

When they came home, I was sitting on the back deck, holding his loaded 9 mm in my lap. They both saw the gun as they stepped on board. Before Karyn or I could say anything, Shane stated flatly, "I sleep with it, locked and loaded, on my chest. Can't close my eyes without it." Karyn and I looked at him as he continued. "I've been trying to wean myself off it. Like today," he said, looking at Karyn, "forcing myself to leave it here when we go out."

"Do you mean you've been carrying that thing around town with us?" Karyn asked, astonished.

"Afraid so," he said flatly.

Karyn was speechless. "I've got to put these groceries away," she said heading inside.

Shane's eyes never left the gun. I handed it back to him. "Thanks," was all he said, taking it and following Karyn into the salon. For the first time since he came back, I realized I didn't want to know what happened over there. Ignorance was my bliss; Vietnam his hell.

That night as Karyn and I climbed into bed, I asked her if she'd been able to talk to him at all about the war or what had happened to him over there.

"Not really," she said. "Sometimes in the mornings after you go to work, we'll sit together, sipping our coffee. We mostly just sit, listening to the stereo. But sometimes he'll open up a little."

"And say what?"

"Nothing really. He loves the music. Wants to know all about the artists—Joni Mitchell, Crosby, Stills and Nash…especially Dylan. Says if it wasn't for the music, he doesn't know what he would have done over there. Says it was the one thing that kept him from going insane."

"Really?"

"Yeah. Says if he had it to do over, he'd go to prison before letting them use him like they did."

"Really. Does he ever talk specifics?"

"No," she said, snuggling her head under my arm and onto my chest. "Sometimes I get the feeling he wants to, but then he gets this glazed look and shuts up." She paused. "I don't push it."

"Did you know he sleeps holding a loaded gun?" Karyn lifted her head and gave me a look I couldn't decipher. "What?" I asked her.

"Nothing," she said, looking down. "He'll be all right. It's just going to take time. He certainly doesn't need you or anybody else pressuring him."

"That's the last thing I'm doing," I said defensively. "I'm just trying to help."

"He'll ask for your help if he needs it. Until them, just let him be," she said curtly, rolling over, away from me. "Go to sleep. You've got another early day tomorrow."

******

5:00 a.m. came as it did every day. The faint buzzing from the alarm somehow found its way into my grey matter, activating a series of involuntary electrodes to start the transition from dreamland to reality. By the time I hit the snooze control my brain was kicking in. It was time to get up. I left Karyn alone in bed, like I had to do every day since our honeymoon. The fish market never closed, so neither did our cannery. The mornings of her rolling over, barely conscious, reaching out with her eyes still closed, begging me to stay and make love, were long gone. She no longer even groaned at the sound of the alarm.

Once the steaming hot water started to work its wonders, I was able to shake the cobwebs out. The morning would then start to grow on me, especially summer mornings. The tranquility of a new dawn; the quiet stillness on the water; the peace of mind that settles in while going through familiar routines; the comfort of knowing that things are as they should be; the mirror steaming up from the hot water; the fresh aromas that fill the room after stepping out of the shower; the clean scent of shampoo lingering in the heavy air; knowing my love was just past the door, tucked securely under the thick warm down comforters, sleeping like a baby. But not today.

Leaving Karyn was never easy, but when it was raining it was twice as hard. We'd had such a wonderful summer, especially because Shane was home. During the past few days, while we'd been prepping the boat for winter, we'd started to dread winter's arrival. The only interesting part was watching old man Wilson salute at Shane whenever he saw him. Shane would stop whatever he was working on, stand up straight and salute back. The night before, we'd watched the storm track on radar together during the late news. Even though I knew it was coming, I just wasn't ready for the start of another winter. Especially not this morning.

The whole time I was getting ready for work—listening to the wind and rain pounding against the windows, knowing how damn cold it was going to be once I stepped outside—all I wanted to do was climb back into bed and wrap my arms around my wife. But I had to settle for giving her a soft kiss on the cheek. She barely moved as I whispered, "I love you" before I headed out. That first storm sent a cold chill down my back as I lowered my head to make my way up the dock to work.

Karyn thought nothing wrong with the fact that her talks with Shane now included some holding and comforting. Shane was a friend and there was nothing wrong with nurturing him. She thought nothing wrong with giving to a friend what he so desperately needed. In her heart, she felt Shane not only needed her love, but deserved it. She couldn't deny him what he needed to become whole again, knowing none of the old high school flames he'd been seeing could give him what he really needed. And even though she was infuriated when he'd come home some nights reeking of their perfume, she held her tongue. How could anyone blame her for giving him the one thing she knew would make him whole again?

But as tears continued to pour from his scarred soul, simply holding him was no longer enough. Karyn became driven by a primal instinct she had no control over—an instinct so powerful, so strong, it was driving her beyond reason, beyond rational thought. Men go to war; women pick up the pieces. Men kill; women nurture. The tattered anti-war poster hanging next to the back door had taken on a whole new meaning since Shane's return. *Make love, not war.*

So, without thinking of consequences, Karyn allowed her body to give in a way only a woman can. The boundaries of right and wrong blurred and melted away. What began, as a selfless act of giving, driven only by compassion and friendship, became a fire burning with such strength that denial was no longer an option. She gave herself completely, over and over again. She withheld nothing. Their needs engulfed them in a fire so powerful nothing in the world could have kept them apart. Moments of tenderness would be swept away, leaving them gasping for breath. With their lovemaking lasting all day, everything in her life—except Shane—became meaningless. One veteran's healing had begun.

As their days of making love turned into weeks, then months, somewhere within the deepest reaches of their collective consciousness, they knew their actions would have far-reaching consequences. A price would eventually have to be paid. Because within the balance of nature, for every action, there's an equal and opposite reaction. She knew she was saving the life of a man she had known all her life. Little did she realize that in saving one man's life she was destroying another's.

She knew what had started out as controlled compassion was now an obsession raging out of control. She couldn't help herself. She wanted Shane's touch more than she'd ever wanted anything in her life. Her body ached for him. She'd lie awake in those pre-dawn mornings, pretending to be asleep, waiting for me to leave for work, knowing Shane would be inside her the instant I left. Her body longed for his touch, almost hurting with anticipation. With each passing day, their love erupted with more passion. As they clung to one another, covered with sweat, the steamy scent of their love hanging over the bed, they knew it was only a matter of time. They were beyond caring if they got caught; they threw pretence to the wind. Getting busted would be a relief.

Even when the signs are all there, the one whose heart is about to get ripped apart always seems to be the last to know. I remember when I first began sensing something was going on between them, resisting those subtle alarms. Primal, survival instincts firing off warnings deep within my soul. *There's no way. The two of them together?* Those thoughts went against every fiber of my being. It felt so surreal, as to not even seem possible. *They're my best friends*, I muttered to myself, driving to work. *For Christ sake.* Visualizing her lying there in bed, curled up on her side in her favourite fetal position, all warm and toasty under our thick comforter... her golden hair tousled with a few stray strands gently lying across her forehead...her slow, deep breathing as she slept...her soft skin, her slender long legs and beautiful breasts...so inviting...so alone...

A horn blasted behind me, jarring me back into reality. Dazed, I eased away from the traffic signal. I hated myself for even imagining them together, for even thinking something might be going on. *You're an idiot. If you don't start paying attention here and concentrate on driving, they're going to be scraping you off the pavement.*

I was about half way to work, when I realized I'd forgotten the sales summary I'd been working on the night before. Hanging a U-turn at the intersection, I headed back to the boat to pick it up. *If you'd pulled your head out of your ass, you wouldn't be getting soaked for the second time this morning,* I scolded myself, as I ran back down the dock in the rain. I leaped on board, threw open the door to the salon...and ran right in on them making love.

I stood frozen, unable to move. They didn't even hear me come in. I couldn't breath, as I watched my wife, straddled on top of my best friend. Their orgasmic screams of ecstasy ringing in my ears.

Avoid loud and aggressive persons; they are vexations to the spirit.

Chapter 4

The next thing I knew I was behind the wheel of the old truck. The rain never stopped. I just kept driving, for days on end. Sleeping in the cab when I couldn't keep my eyes open any longer, eating junk whenever I had to stop and get gas. Everything became one giant soggy blur. I never left the 101. Catching glimpses of the rugged coastline through the rain and clouds somehow kept me from going insane. After crossing over the Columbia River and continuing south, I pulled into an old motor lodge along the outskirts of a little town right on the coast, called Manzanita. I was a mess. Looking in the cracked mirror of the neat, but tiny rented room, I hardly recognized myself. I hadn't showered or shaved since I'd left. How the elderly couple running the place found it in their hearts to rent me a room must have come from pure pity, because I looked worse than Charles Manson. Too tired and too damned depressed to do anything about it, I stripped off all my cloths and fell into bed stark naked. Thankful sheer exhaustion dragged me into oblivion.

Early the next morning I drove to the nearest gas station, which thankfully doubled as a little 24 hour convenience store, bought a couple of John Deer t-shirts, a new pair of jeans, socks and some toiletries. Slinking back into my motel room before anyone else was awake, I soaked in the steaming hot shower until there was no more hot water.

Showered, shaved and clean for the first time in days, I felt like a new man. The sun actually broke through the clouds for the first time as well, so I decided to stay and look around. In the manager's office, I rang the little bell sitting on the counter top. When the elderly lady appeared from around the corner, at first, she didn't even recognize me.

"Mr. Phillips," she commented, "you're looking quite handsome this morning."

"Thank you, Ma'am. Sorry for the way I looked last night. It's been a rough trip."

"Now don't you worry about that," she said in a kind, motherly fashion. "The important thing is you've got yourself all cleaned up and looking mighty spiffy this fine morning."

"If you don't mind, I'd like to stay another night or two."

"No problem," she said smiling, pushing her reading glasses up off the bridge of her nose, focusing in on the ancient pages of their registration book and carefully making a notation under my room number and name. "Will you be paying in cash again?" she asked politely.

******

Later that morning, I found myself walking along a quiet, residential street a few blocks from the motel. The street was lined with beautiful, classic old Victorian homes, most with full wrap around porches. Huge trees hung over the cracked, concrete sidewalks. Well-manicured lawns with potted plants and ivy clinging to the well-worn brick exteriors gave the neighborhood a warm, lived-in, feeling. It reminded me a lot of my grandparent's house. Of Seattle... I waited for it, but for the first time since the 'incident,' I was remembering something from there without the acute pain I'd become accustomed to chocking off my breathing. It was nice to being able to breathe again, if only for the moment. I was enjoying the quiet when out of nowhere I heard a child's voice call out.

"Hey, mister. You want to buy a puppy? They're only twenty dollars."

Before I knew it, two of the cutest little girls I'd ever seen thrust a wiggling bundle of fluff in my face. The girls, who couldn't have been more than six or seven years old, were talking a mile a minute. Looking over their blond heads and past the puppy, I saw their mother sitting on the top step of their front porch, observing as only a mother can.

"It's their birthday. They're eight weeks old today. We want to keep them all, but Mom says we have to find 'em good homes. Do you have a good home, mister?" one of the girls asked. "Do you like puppies?" the other asked. They had a cardboard box full of the most adorable golden retriever puppies in the world.

"Well, I don't know about a puppy," I said, taking the wiggling bundle they'd thrust at me and giving it a kiss. There's nothing in the world like the smell of a puppy's breath. "Having a puppy is a lot of work," I told them.

"No, they're not," the girls countered instantly, in unison. "They're easy. We can teach you how to take care of 'em." Fighting to be heard over one another, the girls bombarded me on how to feed them, when to feed them, how to brush them, when to brush them… "The only bad part is having to pick up the poo. Gross!" They said, giggling.

The last thing I was thinking about was getting a dog, but there are few things in the world that can transform your emotions as holding a puppy. They melt in your arms and when they make that little whimpering, half grunt sound…they melt your heart. Inhaling the sweet smells of puppy breath put me over the edge. I couldn't resist.

The girl's mother came down the herringbone brick walkway leading from their tin- covered front porch. "They're pretty cute, aren't they?" she asked when she arrived.

"Yes, Ma'am. I haven't held anything like this in a long time," I said, lifting up the puppy whose tail was going so fast it was shaking its entire body. "This little guy's the cutest thing I've ever seen."

The girls shouted together. "She's not a *he*—she's a girl."

Sure enough, the he was a she, and she was about to be mine. "You know, you're right, girls." I apologized. "My mistake. She is beautiful, isn't she!"

She's my favorite," one of the girls proclaimed.

"No, she's not. She's *my* favorite."

"All right, girls," the mom said. "Stop it and ask the gentleman if he has a good home and if he'll promise to take good care of your puppy. Just like we talked about."

The realization hit me that I'd been living out of my truck the past few days, if you can call what I'd been doing 'living.'

"Yes," I said, looking over at the mother, but avoiding her eyes. "I have a really nice little house, with a huge backyard. I work out of my house, so I won't ever have to leave her alone. How does that sound?" I added asking the girls. (Okay, I was lying through my teeth. But I knew that I'd cherish this little animal and it didn't matter that I no longer had a home.)

"Perfect," one of the little girls answered immediately.

"Do you want her?" the other chimed in.

"Absolutely," I said with a big smile. "How could I not want her?"

About this time, the puppies' mother came bounding from around the corner. She stuck her nose in the box for a quick inspection and then came right over to me. She looked up at the one I was holding and went to work sniffing my pant leg. I squatted down so we were face-to-face. She gave me the once-over and moved closer to sniff my face. I lowered my eyes and bowed my head down for her. After a few moments, she gave my face her resounding vote of approval with a big, wet lick. The deal was sealed. I handed the little girls each a ten-dollar bill and promised to be the best dad any puppy ever had. I thanked them and their mom and gave her my name, the phone number of the cannery and its address in Seattle. They wanted to keep track of their babies, said the girls.

She looked at it. "You're not from around here."

"No, just visiting. But I love your town. It reminds me of home."

She smiled. "Yeah. We're lucky to live here. Oh, by the way, she's only had one shot, so be sure and get her to a vet in the next couple of weeks."

"No problem," I assured her. The girls gave me a few last minute instructions on feeding and handed me a small brown bag containing some of her food. "Thank you," I told them again, and we were on our way.

For the first time since leaving, I had a reason for living. *Thank God for little girls and puppy dogs.* While I was walking back to the hotel, the clouds started to roll back in. Tucking the puppy safely inside my jacket, it fell asleep. The sun had only poked its head through the clouds for a few hours, but it had been long enough to convince me to stay, take a little walk, and as it turned out, long enough for me to find a friend. Winters in the Northwest are cold and wet...period. No getting around it, but I was sick of it. So with my newfound companion, I decided to leave.

Figured the old couple running the motel deserved to keep the money I'd given them earlier for the additional couple of nights because they'd let me in when few proprietors would have, looking the way I did. We got into the truck and headed south, towards Mexico, as far away from the memories as I could get on the little money I had left.

******

Motion changes emotion, so we kept moving. Stopping now every couple of hours, and being sure to pull well away from any traffic, so she could do her business, which after, turned into unbridled playtime. We slowly wound our way along the rest of the beautiful, rugged Oregon coast. Through Crescent City, down Northern California, into the Redwoods, over the Golden Gate. Always hugging the coast, staying on PCH as we made our way through Montery and Big Sur, down the coast past Malibu and Hermosa, through Laguna before eventually dropping into a little town called Ocean Beach.

OB, a place that welcomes stray dogs, nude sunbathers and wandering souls with open arms—a perfect blend of huge old shade trees, blonds in bikinis, dilapidated beach shacks, and busted Volkswagen vans. With its skateboards, beach cruisers, fish tacos and juice stands, OB is an out of the way community that doesn't give a damn about anything east of the boardwalk. It's sunshine, surf and sunsets, beach fires and good music, veggie burgers, guacamole and tofu, getting tan, getting tubbed, and getting laid. Squeeze some fresh OJ in the morning and hit the beach. The breakfast of champions—Sun Flakes and surf.

We were getting low on funds, so before we melted totally into a beach life of having to collect empty soda bottles for refunds, I knew I'd have to find some work.

If it hadn't been for Sierra, I may have never discovered *The Dew Drop Inn*. We were sitting on the tailgate of *Little Green*. Okay, I confess. I named my truck. I know it's gay, but what can I tell you, it's a five window '51 Ford. My grandpa taught me how to drive it when I first started working the cannery, and it runs like a charm. Sierra's ears perked up and her tail started wagging. Sure enough, within a few seconds, an older gentleman walked up and stopped just short of us.

"Young man, it looks to me as if you've got yourself two of the most important things a man could ever want in life." He paused, as he looked us over. I didn't interrupt his thoughts. "A devoted dog and a good truck."

His simple summation of my existence made me smile. Couldn't help but smiling whenever Sierra did some of her puppy stuff, but this was one of the first times I'd actually smiled at another human since leaving Seattle. "You'll get no argument from me, sir." I answered, extending my hand. His grip was strong. "Corey Phillips."

"You're not from around here, are ya?" he asked.

"No, sir. Up north." Nodding toward Sierra, I added, "We've only been here a little while."

He looked around and paused again. "It's not what it used to be, but it's still a pretty good place to live."

"Yes sir, it's a beautiful spot."

He sat down next to Sierra and affectionately patted her on the head for a couple of minutes.

"You like burgers, Johnny?"

"What?" Thinking the old man was going senile.

"You know, hamburgers. Lettuce, tomatoes, pickle, and all beef patty on a sesame seed bun."

Now I knew he'd lost it. Humming the McDonald's theme song.

"I think you'd like this place around the corner. It's called The Dew Drop Inn, but it doesn't have a sign out front or anything. You just got to know it's there and be looking for it in the trees." With one last affectionate fluff of Sierra's head, he said goodbye. Before he continued his walk, he added, "They even let dogs in." Just as quickly as he had appeared, he was gone.

Funny how the universe works.

******

Just like the old man said, the place was tucked way back off a shady side street. Covered with vines and shrubs, it was half hidden by huge overhanging fichus trees. If you hadn't been looking for it, you would've thought it was just another old beach house—one that housed a family with lots of friends. The worn, faded brick pathway leading to the open Dutch door was relatively well traveled, but a mossy texture about its edges gave it a feeling and look that fit the place, neatly blending into the freshly mowed lawn. As you got closer to the house, the scent of the freshly cutgrass gave way to even more powerful aromas. The fresh baked smells of old-fashioned home cooking wafted over to us and overwhelmed our senses like a spring morning.

"Come on in," a warm voice called out from behind a bushel of flowing auburn hair. "The dog's welcome, too … as long as you aren't with the County."

"Thanks," I said, opening the door.

"Sit anywhere you'd like," she added, gesturing to the wooden tables and chairs scattered around the room. "I'll be with you in a minute." The place wasn't crowded. Several old oak tables and captain's chairs were vacant. We moved across the worn, uneven wooden planks to a small booth in the corner that looked out toward the street.

"I didn't hear you drive up," another friendly voice announced approaching the booth. I was still looking out across the front yard. "Lots of parking this time of the year. Just wait a few months and you won't be able to park within a mile of this place."

I turned and my breath caught in my throat. The face behind the voice was breathtaking. I had known a beautiful woman, much to my pain, but this one was an angel.

"I ride my bike in most of the time, anyway," she continued.

I lapsed into speechlessness.

She continued to work her magic on the dog without seeming to notice I couldn't speak. "Come here, baby, and give me a kiss." Sierra didn't need to be asked twice. "I bet you're hungry, aren't you, girl? You're the cutest thing in the world." More kisses. "Come on. Let's see what we've got in back." And with that, they both disappeared around a corner towards what I could only guess was the kitchen.

My heart was racing. I closed my eyes, glad to be alone. I had no idea what had just happened. We had only made eye contact for a split second, but in that moment I saw something in her eyes. Maybe the way she looked a me. I don't know. But there was something there. I slowly shook my head, trying to clear my thoughts. *Relax,* I told myself. *What are you thinking?* I had no idea, but my heart pounded in my ears. There was something about her. I picked up a menu and tried to focus on something else, but her image lingered on the pages between the hash browns and scrambled eggs.

"You in the mood for breakfast? You've been looking at that page for the past couple minutes. We've got great eggs. Raise the chickens out back. 100% organic feed. "

I didn't know what to say. I felt so stupid. Staring at the face of an angel and not being able to form a sentence.

"Take all the time you need. Sierras in the back yard. We rustled her up a little something to munch on. Just let me know when you're ready to order."

"How did you, ah, know her name?" I finally managed to get out.

"It's on her collar."

I nodded.

"I'm Jennifer," the angel said, extending her delicate hand. "You must be Corey. Either that, or you've kidnapped one of the coolest dogs I've ever met." Her charm was effervescent and cascaded effortlessly from her like a gentle waterfall.

Instinctively, I stood up and took her hand. Her touch sent chills down my spine. Our eyes locked. I was still speechless. Time stood still. Her eyes didn't flinch but looked deeply into mine. Searching without asking. And there it was again … dancing to the surface … that spirit inside her. She smiled from within and I melted. I have no idea how long we stood there, but eventually she placed her other hand on top of mine. I looked down feeling her touch.

"How about I bring you some OJ to start with?"

"Fine," I heard myself answer from somewhere in the distance.

******

Jennifer held the half-orange in her palm against the whirring juicer.

What was that all about? She thought to herself.

She cut another orange in two and watched Corey from the pass-through to the dining room.

Sierra's friendly. That's for sure, but she's just a pup and I've never met a Golden that wasn't friendly. But still, good dogs come from loving owners.

On cue, Sierra came bounding in through the back door. Running full speed through the kitchen, past Jennifer, directly toward my table. But on the hard wood floors, when she put on the brakes, all four legs went sprawling out from under her. If I hadn't bent over in time to catch her, it would have been a crash landing into my chair. But as it was, she was in my arms, all kisses and wiggles. Her tail wagging so hard her entire body was moving, oblivious to the averted disaster, acting as if she'd planned the entire sequence.

A dog's world, Jennifer continued thinking to herself, *totally in the moment. Not a worry about what might have been, or what's going to happen next... just happy she's in his arms... He treats her right, that's for sure, and she definitely loves him...They're pretty cute together.*

She juiced two more oranges and filled an old oversized jelly jar covered with hand painted hibiscus and palm frowns.

So what's different about this one?

She picked up the glass.

******

One minute I'm walking into a restaurant, thinking about ordering a burger and the next minute I can't even say my name. I kept my attention focused on Sierra, for fear of another meltdown, as Jennifer brought over the OJ. "Thank you," I managed to get out.

"My pleasure," Jennifer said. Then, addressing Sierra, "When he's ready to order, why don't you just come and get me. What do you say, girl?"

Glancing up in time to see Jennifer smile as she turned away from the table. *There was something about her.* I wondered how many restaurants would allow a dog inside to begin with, and then actually treat the animal as if it belonged there. I liked the place immediately, long before I ever tasted the food or fell in love with my waitress.

Somehow I'd managed to order. After finishing the best burger I'd ever eaten, the bronzed, silver-haired proprietor, Douglas, came out from around back and wanted to know whose pup Sierra was. Given that there were only about a half-dozen other people in the place, and most of them he already seemed to know, I owned up. "She's mine."

"Don't recall seeing you in here before."

"First time. Great burger by the way."

"Thanks. Organically fed. Makes all the difference. Mind if I sit down."

We continued talking. I got around to telling him we were from Seattle, left in a hurry. "Been on the road for few couple months. Took a while for to find our way out of the rain."

He nodded. "It doesn't get much better than this," he said. Looking out the window. "Don't mean to be pushy, but we had one our of cooks quit a few days ago, and I've paid my dues behind that grill. You wouldn't be looking for any work, would you?"

I thought about it as he continued.

"Anyone with a young pup like this one," he added, swooping Sierra off her feet and into his arms, "is someone I wouldn't mind having around. You interested in flippin' a few burgers?"

Drop Inn for a meal—stay for a lifetime.

Ever wonder if what ultimately happens in our lives, what creates our destiny, comes down to the simplest choices we make?

Every minute of every day, that's really all we do, is make choices. Most are mundane and seemingly insignificant, made on autopilot. In and of themselves they appear to have little or no consequence in our lives. Stopping at stop signs. Going to the market. Getting a haircut. But every once in awhile, the seemingly insignificant choices we make, sometimes, end up changing the course of our lives forever.

It's when you look back at these presumably random choices and realize that they've taken on a life of their own, that's when I start to wonder who's really in charge. As much as I'd like to lay claim to being the architect of my own destiny, somehow, being hungry and in the mood for a hamburger, just doesn't seem to qualify as a life-altering decision. But the simple act of walking into the *Dew Drop Inn* changed my life forever.

Just then, the beautiful auburn-haired waitress came around the corner and chimed in, before I'd had a chance to answer Douglas. "If you don't stay, at least leave this adorable pup here with us. I'm in love with her." Sierra slid out of Douglas's lap and wedged herself between Jennifer's beautiful, tanned athletic legs.

"We come as a matched pair." I said, surprising myself.

She flashed another smile.

My second meltdown didn't surprise either of us.

******

I started work the next morning. Friendly people, good food, lots of cold drink and of course, Jennifer was there.

The days liquefied into sunsets, the nights into weeks, and the weeks into months. After work, Sierra and I would walk the beach or drive over the hill to Point Loma. During the winter the landings and shipyards were mostly deserted at night, so we'd walk along the boardwalks. Occasionally we ducked under gates or around half-torn-down chain link fences to get out onto the docks. Sometimes we'd startle a blue heron or an errant harbor seal that had claimed a dock finger for the night.

There was nothing like being down by the water. The rough commercial docks and sport boats held an interest for me that's hard to describe.

There's magnetism about workboats and the people who run them. Those men and women are a unique breed. As I kid, I looked at the captains and crews of the commercial boats as if they were Gods. My dad, in particular, was bigger than life. He was at sea for weeks at a time, riding out the most vicious storms hundreds of miles from nowhere while I lay trembling in my little bunk, scared to death that our houseboat, tied to the dock, was going to sink right out from under us. How they survived out there was beyond my wildest imagination. They could only be Gods.

So Sierra and I walked the docks at night, looking at the boats, listening to their stories.

It had been six months since I started working at the Inn. Years ago, the garage behind the Inn had been converted into a studio, and when the couple that had been living there moved out, Sierra and I moved in. It was set off from the rest of the house by an ancient wisteria hedge that covered the patio and worked its way along the overhead lattice in a seamless twisted system of thick vines and rich green foliage. When in bloom, it filled the air with an aroma so sweet it melted your senses. A large opaque skylight built into the roof of the old open beamed ceiling allowed soft filtered ambient sunlight to fill the room. It was simple and clean. Facing the far side of the garden, and hidden from both the ally and rest of the house, a bathroom had been framed into the corner. The shower opened to the garden. Showering felt like standing under a waterfall in the mists of a tropical rainforest.

The only drawback was that whenever someone didn't show up for work, Douglas knew my commute was a no-brainer. I was on call 24/7, a small price to pay for free rent. Besides the beach and my long walks with Sierra, working at the Inn was my life. There was enough social interaction to feel connected, but not threatened, so I had no complaints. In fact, it even started to feel like home.

Evidently, Karyn filed for divorce as soon as I left. Guess she and Shane had some big plans for the future. "Fuck 'em," I had told Grandpa during a phone call when he informed me the papers had been delivered to the cannery months earlier because no one knew where to reach me.

"She wants everything," he said. "Your boat, the furniture ... everything you guys had ...." His voice trailed off.

"She destroyed everything we had." I took a deep breath and waited for the pain I'd been running from to re-surface. Surprisingly, it didn't. "She can have it all. I don't care. I'm done with the both of them."

Grandma got on the line. "We've been real worried about you, sweetheart, when are you coming home?"

I shook my head without answering. Grandpa and Grandma had lived in the same house for over 50 years. It would always be the center of their universe, but I knew if I went back up there, I'd be lost forever. "Grandma don't worry. Everything's going to be fine. I love you. Bye."

I'd been talking on the pay phone outside the back door of the kitchen and hadn't heard Jennifer come up behind me. When I hung up, she was right there.

"Overhearing part of that conversation," she said, holding me with her eyes, "I just learned more about you in sixty seconds than I've learned in the past six months." The penetrating, unwavering look in her eyes demanding more. "I want to know who you are. I've been waiting, but it's time." She wasn't about to apologize for eavesdropping.

Since the day Sierra and I walked into the Inn and first laid eyes on her, I'd felt it, too. There was an undeniable attraction between us. Other than that lame comment when we first met about Sierra and I coming as a matched pair, I'd done my best to voided her — averting my eyes whenever we worked together (which was almost every day). She would brush by me in the kitchen, her scent leaving me light-headed. Reaching in for a condiment or something over my shoulder, she'd touch my arm, the electricity surging between us.

At the sight of her, my heart leapt into my throat, choking off anything clever I might have come up with, so I'd just kept my head down and let Sierra do all our talking. But now she wanted more. I didn't know what to say, so in typical chicken-shit male fashion, I turned and walked away, leaving her standing there, glaring at me as I headed toward the sanctuary of the kitchen where I found Douglas. "Hey, Boss, I need some time off."

He nodded and swirled a damp cloth over a little spot of spilled Thousand Island dressing. "You can run, but you can't hide," he told me, not looking for a response as Sierra and I headed out the door.

Shaking her head, Jennifer wiped her eyes. The adrenalin from the huge wave still surging through her body. *What a rush.* It was getting late, so instead of waiting for another set, she decided to catch the next small wave. Riding it long after it broke, staying ahead of the white water, all the way into the beach.

"Nice ride," one of the locals told her as she walked by carrying her board.

"Thanks," she answered, with that smile of hers. Nodding in agreement. "It was an incredible wave. Held up for long time. I was lucky to be out there."

"Wish I'd had a camera," the other guy chimed in. "Would have made the cover of *Surfer*, for sure. You were in that barrel for- 'ever.'"

With a friendly nod, she kept walking up the beach. The drive back to OP from La Jolla only taking a few minutes. PCH hardly had any traffic. Sierra and I had been gone now for over two weeks. If it hadn't been for the water, she wasn't sure what she would have done. The ocean was her sanctuary. Her bliss. She'd gone over those last few minutes over and over again in her mind. Trying to figure out what she'd done to drive me away. It was killing her. It had been so long since she'd even allowed herself to feel anything for someone, and poof, just like that, I was gone. Gone before we'd even....even had a chance. *Why do relationships always have to be so fucking hard?*

******

Change comes easy for some, hard for others. For me, it was a nightmare. I hated it. The betrayal. The pain. The emptiness. I would have died if it hadn't been for Sierra. But I was slowly and painfully beginning to realize the only constant in life, is change.

So deal.

Eventually I had to, because I was running out of money, again, and had to get back to work.

The second we pulled up in front of the Inn and Sierra saw Jennifer coming out the front door, she leapt out of the passenger side window and raced across the front yard directly into her waiting arms. We'd been gone over two weeks. Watching them together, as I finished parking and shut off the motor, was like watching two best friends who hadn't seen each other in years. They rolled around on the grass like a couple of kids. Sierra's tail wagged a hundred miles an hour as she tried to lick Jennifer all over the face. Jen's hair was flying everywhere and she was laughing hysterically. I walked around the front of the truck, leaned against the front quarter panel and waited. After a while they just collapsed, breathing hard, Sierra's head on Jennifer's chest. You could actually see the smile on that dog's face.

Finally, Jennifer spoke to me. With her eyes still closed and her face towards the sun, her voice was soft, but her words iron. "I should kill you for taking Sierra and dropping off the face of the planet like that. You're such an asshole." Her words hung in the air. "The only thing I haven't been able to figure out is how a self-centered, emotionally retarded pendejo like yourself could raise a dog like this. It defies logic." Sierra rolled toward Jennifer and demanding more attention again. "Keeping my baby away from me like this." She ruffled Sierra's ears. "You're no different than the rest of them. Come on, girl. Let's go inside and see what we've got for you. I bet you're starving. You look so skinny. Did he even bother to feed you?"

They headed for the front door, leaving me standing there by myself. Her words hanging in the air. I'd never heard her talk like that. Never heard her curse before.

It was late afternoon. The place was deserted. As I pushed open the screen door and looked around, Jennifer and Sierra were nowhere to be seen. *Most likely in the kitchen,* I thought. Suddenly Jennifer came up from behind, wrapped her arms around me and pulled her face into my back. She held me there, squeezing hard, not moving or saying a word. I started to turn towards her, but she squeezed tighter, holding her ground, not wanting me to face her.

"Don't move," she whispered. "Don't say a word." I could feel her warm breath through my T-shirt as she confided, "I just want to hold you."

Her touch consumed me. It had been so long I'd forgotten what a woman's touch could do to your soul. I stood transfixed, soaking it all in, allowing her embrace to absorb my every thought. The world around us slowly came to a stop. I reached back, gently pulling her around, her head now against my chest. No eye contact. Neither of us spoke. We just held one another. Holding on to what we were both so afraid of losing.

Finally she murmured, "Don't ever do that again." I immediately let go, thinking she didn't want me holding her. The moment she felt me let go, she spun around and walked away, hissing at the floor, "Men are so fucking stupid."

Baffled, I didn't hesitate, following her through the kitchen and out to the garden. She sat on the side of the cement planter with her back towards me. "What are you so mad about? What did I do?"

"If you can't figure it out, then just go fuck yourself," she said without looking up. "It's probably what you do best anyway?"

"Jennifer—"

"Don't Jennifer me, you prick! You disappear for weeks…take Sierra…you don't say good-bye … you don't call. Nothing. You just up and vanish. I didn't know if I'd ever see you again. You never even said good bye."

"I told Doug I needed a little time off."

Her eyes on the ground, she slowly started shaking her head. As if she'd come to a painful conclusion. I thought I saw a tear hit the grass.

"Then you came strolling back like you'd never even left … like nothing ever happened. Like it was no big deal." She tried to force down her tears, but couldn't.

"Jennifer," I pleaded, my heart aching seeing her cry.

"Don't say anything. Just leave me alone."

I was baffled. "I don't know why you're so upset."

"Get away from me. Just leave me alone."

"Jennifer," I pleaded, stepping closer to her, "I'd never do anything to hurt you. You're one of the only friends I have."

"Friends!" she snapped through clenched teeth, starring at me for the first time. "Is that all I am to you?" Astonishment blurring her pain. "I mean it!" she hissed. "Get out of here and leave me alone!"

She buried her face in her hands, turning away, sobbing. Her pain shot through my heart. I dropped to my knees and reached for her. She didn't resist. It felt as if she'd given up. Her tears pushed me over the black abyss I'd been so afraid of. Without a second's hesitation, I pulled her into my arms, squeezed her against me, and held her for all I was worth. Neither of us moved as time stood still. Her tears eventually slowed, our breathing calmed, but our hearts still raced. We were both so afraid; instinctively knowing that whatever happened next would change our lives forever.

Words were not an option.

Silently... ever so cautiously... we allowed our bodies to do what our minds couldn't. We allowed our souls to touch... to entwine... ever so slowly, we began breathing in one another's being.

The soft afternoon light gently filtered through the giant Chinese Elm covering the garden. Random rays of sunshine barely catching the highlights of Jennifer's sun-bleached hair. The sweet smell of wisteria filling the air. A dove's cooing blended with the faint sounds filtering in from around us. Nothing else mattered. We were together. So afraid to let go, and still... too afraid to speak.

After Seattle, I didn't ever think I'd say the words I heard myself whispering, but there they were. Without a second thought, without effort or a moments hesitation. They flowed from my heart. "I love you, Jennifer. I love you and don't want to ever spend another minute without you." Before I knew what was happening, tears streamed down my cheeks. Without warning, breaking the dam I'd been hiding behind for so long wide open. "I love you," I whispered again over and over through my tears. The next thing I knew we were lying on the grass. Jennifer had me cradled in her arms, rocking me like a child, whispering softly, "I love you so much." The only other sound I could hear was the steady beating of her heart. The pain I'd been running from.... had kept buried so deep inside... was dissolving with every beat. In its place feelings of overwhelming contentment and peace were flooding in. Secure in her arms, I felt safe again. No longer alone. A sense of belonging ... of oneness … swept over me, filling me with the knowledge that love had somehow found its way back into my life … into my heart … into my very being. Totally surrendering... we transcended time... and found ourselves in a place that comes only to those who are willing to give themselves totally.

Somehow, we managed to find our way from the Inn to her beach cottage a few blocks away. We must have walked, but I can't remember a single step. Everything was a blur. I know we made love for hours because I remember gaining consciousness just long enough to realize it was pitch dark. At some point Jennifer must have lit candles, which were still burning, but now paled by the first rays of sunlight creeping into the room. Dawn's light awakened our bodies long enough for us to melt into one another again. We couldn't get enough of each other. Surrendering all thought, our bodies had taken control. We were now one. It was if our bodies were saying to us that living apart was no longer an option. We joyously surrendered to the unquenchable thirst of our souls. The more we made love, the more we wanted one another. With every new touch, our passion burned hotter and hotter … total and complete surrender … our bodies leading the way to oneness. We'd both been waiting our entire lives for this moment, without any assurances it would ever come.

I'd tasted love before, but nothing I'd ever experienced before, even came close to this. Everything paled in comparison. Seattle seemed like a distant childhood dream. This was all consuming, complete and absolute. A love beyond words. A oneness beyond union … beyond mere mortals. This was communion with God.

The morning light continued filling the room with its warming golden gift, gently filtering through the lace curtains, teasing our eyelids.

"I was afraid this was never going to happen," Jennifer whispered tenderly, her head resting on my chest. Our legs entwined, our bodies finally at rest. "God knows, I prayed it would." Her voice trailed off. "But you were so far away."

She was right. Ever since my life had been shattered in Seattle, I'd been scared shitless. Totally shut down. Function, dysfunction and compensation. Our bodies built in self-defense system. Born out of survival. Out of raw fear. I'd shrouded myself in a suit of armor.

But last night, somehow, Jennifer had melted that armor away. I could actually breathe again. "Thank you," I whispered.

"Thank you," she whispered back. Pausing, "When we first met, I thought, maybe ...." She shook her head slightly. "But then... I realized, there was nothing anyone could do. I just had to wait."

"If I'd had any idea you felt like this," I teased, reaching up under her breast and pulling her closer to my lips, kissing her forehead, "do you think I would have waited?"

She pressed my hand against her heart. "God knows I wanted to tell you how I felt ... to hold you ... to feel your arms around me. There was nothing in the world I wanted more than to pull you out of that train wreck. I could see it in your eyes ... feel it your voice. The fear. The pain. It was right there, just below the surface. I could see it in the way you moved, except when you were playing with Sierra. Seeing how much you loved that dog gave me hope."

I felt a tear drip off her cheek, landing right smack dab in the middle of my soul.

She continued in a softness just above a whisper. "But you never let on, or said a word. You just smiled from behind your sad eyes and kept going. Kept up a friendly front, doing your job. I knew someone had to have ripped your heart out and it was all you could do to hold on. If you were ever going to crawl out from whatever hole you were hiding in, you were going to have to climb out on your own. As much as I wanted to dive in there and pull you out, it would have never worked. You weren't ready for me, for love, or anyone for that matter."

Her tears flowed warm against my skin, but her voice remained steady... "Watching you with Sierra everyday is what gave me hope."

Something so special, just a great joy, just to hear you laugh and to see the smile in your eyes. ~jamie l.p. moore

Chapter 5

The smell of bacon frying was too much for my sleeping senses to ignore. I mustered all the energy I had to make my way into the kitchen. Seeing Jennifer standing in front of the old gas-burning Gaffers & Sattler, wearing a white cotton Oxford shirt, open and tied at her waist, with nothing on underneath, took my breath away. Hearing me come in, she half turned, innocently exposing part of her beautiful breast. Her eyes dancing.

"How about a little breakfast for dinner?" she asked.

Before I could answer, we were in one another's arms again. We'd been in bed for 24 hours straight, and yet we still couldn't get enough of each other. I lifted her onto the edge of the kitchen counter, and our bodies effortlessly blended together. Her legs wrapped around my waist, gently pulling me into her. The room glowed from the evening sun as it poured in through the farm-style curtains she had tied open over the deep trough porcelain sink. The insatiable urgency of last night had subsided, giving way to gentle desire. Our bodies rejoiced in their union. In contrast to the intense heat and fiery passion of the night before, our lovemaking built now with its own sweet rhythm. Our bodies—way ahead of our minds— knew we weren't going anywhere because we were already there.

By the time we sat down to eat, it was dark outside. A nearly full moon made its way over the eastern hillside behind her house and casting a soft blanket of light over the evening. We ate, showered together, and afterwards I brushed her hair—long, strong, healthy strands turned a rich, natural golden color from her days on the beach. Her entire being radiated life. I could almost hear her purring, as the last tangles gently broke free. Now I was able to get full, deep strokes with the brush as her hair shone and cascaded over her bronzed shoulders. We melted into the moment as our lives once again fused.

The weeks following were the happiest either of us had ever known. We were as much in love as any two people had ever been. Simple things, everyday activities, took on new textures and new meaning doing them together…from washing dishes, to walking Sierra. She even tried teaching me to surf, but that was a disaster. Never heard anyone laugh so hard watching me pearl time and again. Being together was all that mattered.

Brushing Jennifer's hair became one of those little routines couples find themselves doing without really thinking about. It became an evening ritual that we both looked forward to. We'd sit together on the worn wooden steps of her front porch—Jennifer on the lower step between my legs—and I'd gently work through the tangles. We'd watch Sierra in the front yard running out to greet neighbors and strangers alike as they strolled along the sidewalk. We'd talk about the day or explore new ideas. Jennifer was one of the most intuitive people I'd ever met— well educated, yet equally street-wise. I often had trouble keeping up with her. It didn't matter because wherever our conversations took us—from politics or far off lands to civil rights, religion or fame—we'd always ended up thankful for one another and our love. Some evenings we'd sit quietly, without words, watching the sun as it slipped into the Pacific, simply enjoying the world. Content in what we'd found in ourselves, an unbreakable trust building between us. Fortifying our love, filling us with self-confidence and strength the likes of which neither of us had ever known.

******

As much as I had always been a fisherman before I took to slinging hash, Jennifer had been an artist. Several of her pencil and charcoal sketches were neatly framed and hung in the short hallway between the bedroom and living room. Their simple, black wooden frames with gray matting directed your attention perfectly to the drawings on the off-white rice paper.

One sketch of an old fishing boat caught my attention the minute I laid eyes on it. It looked like something that had been built in the late thirties. She had drawn the boat from a perspective off the port quarter. The stern and rails running up to the bow blending into the fog were crowded with anglers standing shoulder to shoulder. A couple of the anglers were holding bent or tangled rods; one was leaning between the rails dipping a gunny sac; another angler was pulling what looked like a small calico over the rail. The captain was watching out of his wheelhouse window.

A deckhand was standing on the bait tank, a torn net by his side; another was reaching out for the calico. The wooden planking along the hull was buckling and worn. Obviously, her days were numbered, but not today. Not for this group. They were fully engaged and she stood proud. The water around the boat was flat calm. She was anchored up just outside a kelp line, which was barely visible in the foreground.

Stirring something deep within me. For the first time since my Dad had been lost at sea, standing there, looking at her drawing, I felt a yearning to be back on the water.

"What ya' thinking?" she asked, sensing something.

"How long it's been."

"Since, what?" she said putting her arms around me, "Since we made love."

Her gentle kisses melting me, melting away years of repressed fears.

"When I was younger, I used to fish with my Dad," I began to explain. "A long time ago. Your picture made me remember how much I used to like being on the water."

"I actually drew that from memory off an old photograph I saw at a place called the Crab Cooker in Newport."

"It's an amazing drawing."

"Thanks," she answered humbly. "Do you miss being out there?"

"Haven't until now."

For the first time since we'd been together, I felt her withdraw. Ever so slightly, but we'd become so in tune with one another, I noticed it immediately.

"What?" I asked.

She hesitated, before confessing, "I don't want to be without you. Not even for a moment." Exposing her fears, unashamed, her eyes open and honest.

"What do mean?" I asked, a bit confused. "I love you. I'm not going anywhere."

"But you just said you missed being on the water, missed fishing with your Dad."

"Oh honey," taking her in my arms. "He's dead and there's no way I'm doing anything without you."

"I'm so sorry. What happened?"

"We got caught in a storm off Saint Matthew Island. The boat rolled over. Everyone got out except him. I haven't been back out on the water since that night."

"I'm sorry."

"It was a long time ago."

"But that's horrible. Seeing your Dad die. I can't even imagine."

"I was just a kid and I really didn't see him die. Everything was insane. The wind, the waves, everyone yelling. As soon as we rolled, the main died and a minute later, the generator quit so we lost all our lights. Everything went black. I was asleep in the wheelhouse, in my Dad's bunk. He was on watch. All I remember is him grabbing me out of the bunk, jamming my arms through a life jacket and pulling the straps so tight I could hardly breathe. I was completely disorientated because the boat was lying on her side. Looking down I was standing on one of the side windows, when suddenly it imploded. The wheelhouse instantly filling with freezing cold water. I remember my Dad kicking open a door on the ceiling, which I later realized was the opposite side door of the wheelhouse, and pushing me up and out. One of the deckhands was running up that side. He grabbed me and in one motion, flung me over the side. I landed right next to the life raft that he'd been leading up the side of the boat. Everyone else had made it into the raft. They pulled me in right as the boat turtled. The guy that had tossed me over dove off the side trying to get to my Dad. He kept driving down, again and again, but we never saw my Dad again."

Jennifer remained silent. Moments passed as the memories of that horrible, freezing cold night faded. "If we hadn't been fishing with one of our code boats right next to us, we would have all died of hyperthermia."

******

In love we were content spending our days flipping burgers and slinging hash. Nights we'd go to a movie, build a fire, either in her river rock fireplace, or on the beach, or we'd just stay home, watching TV or reading. Sometimes we'd take a ride, and tonight we found ourselves driving along Harbour Boulevard, heading toward the tuna docks around G Street when the fog started to roll in. We drove under the Coronado Bay Bridge, past the Naval base along Cummings Road all the way down to Terminal Avenue. We were pretty much at the end of the road. We got out and made our way over to the boardwalk. It was a seedy part of town, a place we'd never been before, so Jennifer was holding onto my arm a little tighter than usual as we headed into the abyss. Sierra even was staying close, instead of her normal lead distance ahead of us. The thick eerie fog continued to roll in off the harbor. It was getting so thick we could barley make out the sparse weeds scratching a living out of the cracked concrete beneath our feet as we cautiously made our way along the ancient waterfront. Had we been walking in familiar surroundings, the thick silent mist engulfing us would have been romantic. But we were nowhere close to familiar.

Even though we were out of our element, it was still exciting exploring new territory, especially because we couldn't see more than twenty feet in front of us. We made a game out of trying to figure out what the next shadow was lurking in the distance as we got closer and closer to it. All sounds around us were deadened. It was a little spooky as each new image emerged from the fog, taking on proportions larger than life. There was no one else around. The last people we'd passed were a half-mile behind us.

We were right along the edge of the harbor and a slight tidal surge was pushing along the crumbling seawall. Other than that, everything was virtually still. We were parallel with National Avenue, which was a few blocks inland but may as well have been a continent away. With the exception of the distant foghorn sounding off the light on Point Loma, you couldn't hear a thing. The world by the water's edge, past the naval shipyards heading towards National City, was deserted. All along that stretch were long piers designed for huge ships—nothing like the crowded docks around the marinas. Down here between the fingers were vast areas of open water.

"Let's turn around and head home," Jennifer said.

As she spoke, something caught my eye just ahead. "Mind if we check this out first?" I asked, pointing ahead.

"Okay," she slowly agreed, "but after that, let's go home. I'm getting scared."

"We can turn around right now," I said, stopping. "No problem."

She hesitated, sensing something. She gazed into the dense fog ahead. "What are you thinking?" she asked.

I shrugged my shoulders. "Nothing. It's no big deal. Let's go home and make some popcorn."

"Wait a minute," she said. "I can tell something's got your attention. What is it?"

"Nothing, really. I don't know. Just a feeling. Curiosity is all," I said dismissing the feeling and starting to turn around. "I just wanted to see what was next."

"Then let's go," she said without a moment's hesitation, giving my arm a little squeeze and leading the way. "What do you say, Sierra?"

Sierra wagged and pranced out a few paces ahead of us, but not too far. It didn't take long—maybe only another minute. As we kept moving south, there it was, just ahead of us, mysteriously shrouded in heavy fog, but taking shape before our very eyes.

As we got closer, she loomed larger and larger in the fog. The tide was in, so she was riding high over the seawall. We stopped. Our breathing became shallow. Something about that boat reached out and touched me. We'd stumbled onto something I couldn't resist.

Most people don't know boats have souls, and the few who do, don't talk about it much. It doesn't matter if it's been carved out of ironwood, cedar, spruce or white oak, welded from half-inch steel plates or aluminum, glued together with layers of marine plywood, cold molded, injected, hand laid or laminated. Once a boat's keel has touched water and she's sailed from her safe harbor, she takes on a soul of her own—a soul as real as anything on earth. If you're one of the fortunate few blessed enough to be able to hear them talking, then you know. You've listened to their stories of waves as tall as buildings and winds that blew so hard they took the top of the ocean with them. Stories of storms so fierce they reshaped coastlines, taking lives and ships with them. But by the grace of God, the boats recounting such tales—the ones that somehow managed to ride out the fury and stay afloat, delivering their crews safely home—are the ones whose tales of heroism, bravery and tragedy shape the lives of those who work the sea for a living. Every vessel, large or small, has her story and we were about to become a part of one.

We inched closer to the edge of the seawall. She must have sensed us before we saw her. She was now only a dozen feet away—broken, abandoned and covered with guano, but still holding on like a trapped animal—too wounded and exhausted to run away, too proud to cower. Her dull, lifeless paint was blistered in random, ugly blotches. Jagged pieces of half-inch glass protruded from her cracked and broken wheelhouse windows. Her uneven teak decks were warped, buckling, split and black with fungus and neglect. Rust stains streaked her hull. She was listing hard to port, sitting well below her waterline. Looking at her powerful, bold lines standing out against the fog, I could only imagine how proud she must have once been. Strong, classic lines, but definitely a lady in distress. We stood and listened, but heard not a whimper. No cries for help. Only silence. She'd been beaten hard and put away wet, but she wasn't dead. How much life she had left was anyone's guess, but from the looks of things, she didn't have much. Yet, in spite of everything, she still held herself with pride and dignity, as if she'd accepted her fate and was going down with class.

"How come she's chained to the dock?" Jennifer asked.

My stomach lurched at the injustice. "I don't know. "

We moved along the broken chain link fence a little further. Jennifer spotted a rusty sign hanging off the barbed wire on the rim of the fence.

WARNING
OFF LIMITS TO ALL BUT AUTHORIZED PERSONNEL
SAN DIEGO COUNTY SHERIFF'S DEPARTMENT

HARBOR DIVISION
KEEP OUT

"She's in jail," Jennifer said chuckling. "Wonder what she got busted for?" I took my eyes off the boat just long enough to give her a sideways glance. "What?" she asked, holding her arms out to her side playfully. Looking back at her again from the fog, her eyes dancing. I couldn't help but laugh with her. Pausing, she asked again, "What is it? You've got a look in your eye."

I answered helplessly. "I think I'm in love."

"You'd better be," she said immediately, throwing her arms around my waist and pulling me close. She got up on her tiptoes to half bite and half kiss my lower lip.

"You know how much I love you," I said after a full kiss, dispelling any jealousy that might have been creeping into her brain.

"More than anything?" she asked.

"More than life itself." We kissed again. "But I wasn't talking about you. I was talking about her."

She smiled as both our gazes returned to the old boat. After awhile, Jennifer nestled her head against my chest. "I've always wanted to try a threesome."

If you compare yourself with others, you may become vain and bitter; for always there will be greater and lesser persons than yourself.

Chapter 6

We had the day off, so first thing the next morning we returned to the harbor. Jen had been right—all the impounded vessels were in jail due to their involvement in some form of illegal activity. Some had been confiscated for drugs, others had been abandoned. By the time they made it down there, most were considered beyond repair. The unofficial consensus was to just 'tow the whole lot out to sea and sink 'em.'

"Yeah, they'd make great target practice. Don't see why the Navy doesn't just pull 'em out there and blow 'em to smithereens," suggested one of the old-timers we asked about the boat. He was one of three old men who were sitting in row. Their chairs leaning up against the cargo carrier that served as the locked sheriff's substation. They looked as though they hadn't budged for years...but they hadn't been there last night.

"You don't know squat," one of the old-timers scolded the first. "There's not a boat in the bunch that would stay afloat long enough to get a shell in her. Once they hit the swells, they'd sink all by themselves. Some targets they'd make!"

"Hell, as soon as you untied them they'd sink," chimed in the third. "The damned docks are the only things keeping most of them afloat."

And so the banter continued. They were worse than a bunch of old women. We headed back to the truck, but not before we wrote down the number to call posted on the outside of container's door. On our way home, Jennifer asked, "What exactly are you thinking?"

"Well, I'm not sure," I told her honestly. "So far, it's just a feeling." She nodded that she understood. "There's just something about that boat. There's something there...like she's calling to me...asking for help. I don't know...." I glanced over at Jen to see if she was laughing at me.

She wasn't.

"I could tell something came over you pretty strong last night."

"What do you think?" I asked her.

"I don't know squat about boats. But I trust you, and if there's something inside that's whispering to you, then I say trust your instincts." *Oh, the brave and crazy wings of youth.*

Hearing her words, a wave of appreciation washed over me. "It's been a long time since anyone's supported me the way you do."

"It's my job," she said with a big smile, "I love you." She slid a little closer across the bench seat of the truck and put her arm around my shoulder. Sierra hanging her front paws out the passenger side window.

"Let's see if we can find out a little of her history, why she's chained up."

"She looked better last night, all covered in the fog."

"That's for sure." It had been hard to tell just how bad she was in the dark, but in the harsh morning light, there was no missing the piles of shit she'd accumulated serving as a temporary home for an entire flock of local sea birds. The stench alone was almost unbearable.

With a little research we discovered that a local yacht broker handled all the SDSD's repossessions and sales.

"I'll be right back. Just let me go pull the file." After a couple of minutes the broker sat back down in front of us. "We're having a little difficulty locating the paperwork. Would you mind coming back in few minutes?"

Jennifer and I hadn't eaten, so we walked across Shelter Island Drive to the Red Sails Inn. An hour later, the enthusiastic salesman met us as we walked back into the brokerage office. "I'm sorry for the delay. I don't know how the file on such a fine vessel could have been misplaced, but we have all the paperwork here and would love to show her to you. When are you available to see the boat?"

"How much?" I asked.

"Well, let me tell you a little bit about her first—"

"How much?"

"Ah, sir, the bank's holding papers on her for just over two hundred thousand dollars—"

"Are we talking about the same boat?"

"Yes, sir." The salesmen had obviously never seen the boat. He described her as "a beautiful, custom built, 60-foot twin diesel Drake sport fisher. Designed right here in San Diego by Larry Drake. She has the same bullet-proof hull as the navy's ASR vessels."

"She's Air Sea Rescue?" I asked.

"You know your boats, sir." He was stroking me. "Same design, but originally built as a yacht. Her hull was laid up in Long Beach…let's see…in yep, here it is…in 1956. She's fiberglass over six layers of half-inch laminated marine ply."

I interrupted him again, "You're talking about the boat chained to the Sheriff's dock?"

"Yes, that's correct. She's currently moored at the San Diego Sheriff's substation, south of the Coronado Bay Bridge."

I turned to leave. "Forget it."

"Excuse me?"

"I said forget it."

"But, sir, you said you were interested in the boat."

"I am, but not for anything close to two hundred grand. You're out of your mind." I prodded Jennifer out the door.

"Well, you see, that's the amount the bank's looking to recover. The amount left on the loan is much greater, but the bank is willing to take a loss—"

I cut him off again. "I don't care what's on the books. The boat's been beat to shit, and not worth anything close to a couple hundred grand. Have you even seen her?"

"Well...no, sir, not recently, but I'm sure with a little—"

Sierra was already out the door.

"Forget it. You don't know what you're talking about. That boat's about to go down, and you're wasting our time talking that kind of money."

"Obviously, sir, you have another figure in mind?"

"Yeah, but nothing even close to six figures.

"We only represent the bank. If you'll let me explain...we serve as the bank's agent. We've handled a lot of interesting vessels over the years and would be more than happy to submit any offer. In fact, we're legally obligated to present every offer we receive. So whatever you have in mind, I'm sure—

"Twenty grand."

He gasped and his glasses slid down his nose. "Excuse me?"

"I said twenty grand."

"Are you serious? I couldn't possibly take such a ridiculous offer."

"Present it."

"But...sir." His protest caught on his astonishment.

"Listen. You just told us you're legally obligated to present every offer you receive. So write it up and I'll sign it."

He shook his head. "I couldn't possibly."

"Listen. I don't want to hear any more of your babbling. The boat's a disaster and she's probably not even worth twenty grand. She's been ignored for so long even the birds don't have a clean place to shit on anymore. The decks are rotted and buckling and I can't even imagine what her machinery looks like. I'm surprised she's still floating. I'm half out of my mind for even offering that much, but that's the number. Present it."

He stared at me with a mixture of annoyance and downright hatred. "Very well," he replied curtly. "You'll have to sign the offer and leave a deposit."

Jennifer chimed in. "I've got a checkbook and a pen."

I gave her a grateful look.

"I feel obliged to explain to you, sir, that an offer of this nature is not only an embarrassment to us, as the representing brokers, but I can tell you from my years of personal experience in dealing with things like this that the bank will be very offended. Not only will they throw out the offer, but they won't even counter."

I didn't like this guy, but I knew if we got the boat, we'd never have to deal with him again. "Do yourself a favor. Go have a look at the boat. You're going to be a rock star for bringing in any offer. This is a gift."

"This isn't an offer. It's an insult," he said under his breath after we'd signed the offer and were on our way out the door.

Jennifer looked hard into my eyes. "Never heard you talk like that to anyone before."

"Arrogance and ignorance are two traits that don't sit too well with me, but I should have talked to you before making a crazy offer like that."

She could see the concern in my eyes, and with one smile melted it away. "Don't be sorry. I loved listening to you deal with that guy. You were so cool. Plus, it's kind 'a exciting."

******

As expected, a couple days later we got word the bank had refused our offer. I demanded to know why.

"We're dealing with a fine, classic yacht here, sir. One that originally cost close to a million dollars to build." The agent was doing his best to convince me.

"I don't care what it cost fifteen years ago. In fact, I don't care what it might have been worth last year. As it sits today, she's worth shit. "

"I'd appreciate it if you wouldn't use that kind of language here in the office."

I nodded at the same time Jennifer subtly gave me an elbow in the ribs. They were right. This wasn't the time or place. "Sorry. Have you seen the boat?"

"As I told you before…no, I have not personally seen her."

"Then I want to talk to your boss. Those idiots at the bank don't have a clue what we're dealing with here."

"Very well. I'll see if he's available."

The salesman left and returned with his broker. I didn't give him a chance to say anything, I was wound up. "The boat's a disaster, and we're willing to take her off your hands. Someone here is going to have to physically look at the boat and then inform the bank exactly what they're stuck with."

The broker countered, "Our listing shows that she was built by one of the most reputable builders in the business and has a long history of outstanding service."

"That's all in the past. What you've got now is a neglected, dilapidated old boat that's covered with shit and listing so badly she looks like she's about to go under. God only knows what's keeping her afloat."

"She couldn't be in that bad a shape," the broker rebutted, adding, "We have a cleaning service that takes care of all our listings."

"Then you're getting ripped off because this boat hasn't seen a hose or deck brush in years. She's a wreck, and unless you guys are working some insurance scam and waiting for her to sink so you can collect, I suggest we all take a ride over there right now."

"I don't know if that's possible. I've got a meeting scheduled this afternoon, and—"

"If you don't, my next phone call is going to be to the bank's insurance underwriter." My voice was hard and direct. "They just might be interested in investigating your little relationship here." I met the broker's hard stare head on. "From the looks of things, gross negligence and fraud wouldn't be too hard to prove." He didn't blink, and neither did I as I continued. "I don't know if they could nail you. I don't even know if you're doing anything wrong. But I'll guarantee you one thing. The investigators, all those attorneys, the police, franchise tax board..." I let the words trail off as I took a deep breath. "Guilty or not, they'll make your life miserable." I smiled.

He looked away. "Where's the boat?" he demanded, looking at his salesman.

"Sheriff's impound dock, South Substation."

The broker looked genuinely shocked. "What?"

"The Sheriff's dock. Down past the Bay Bridge."

"I know where the damn dock is. What are we doing with a boat that's impounded?"

The salesman shrugged his shoulders and shook his head.

"Never mind," snapped the broker as he gave his young protégé a dirty look. "You can fill me in on the way over there. Grab the camera," he ordered. "We'll follow you over in our car...if you don't mind?"

We were already halfway out the door.

******

What had been a doable project in my mind suddenly looked hopeless as we all climbed on board. The broker and salesman agreed. They couldn't believe something this fucked up could still float—the weight of the barnacles alone should have been enough to pull her under. I didn't say, "I told you so," because they realized it immediately. The boat was a disaster. A dozen 35 mm frames later, they were ready to go.

As we headed back up the ramp, Jennifer politely asked the broker, "What are you going to tell the bank?"

"That they should seriously reconsider your offer." The salesman could see his commission slipping away. "We'll get these pictures developed and over to them right away, see what they say and then we can talk. Would you be willing to go to a somewhat more realistic price?"

"Would you?" Jennifer asked.

"Yeah, well...." the broker mumbled, looking away. "I'm assuming we have your number."

We didn't expect to hear back from them.

******

Some folks say the two happiest days in a person's life are when they buy a boat and when they sell it. I'd pretty much resolved myself to the fact that the brokerage and bank were in bed together and had already figured out a way to collect on the insurance, rather than accepting some ridiculously lowball offer like the one we'd tossed at them. But I just couldn't stop thinking about her.

"What are you guys going to do with a boat anyway?" One of the waitresses asked me at the Inn the next day. Word had gotten around quickly.

"We're planning on turning it into a floating brothel," I said, teasing her. She was a little hottie and guys were always hitting on her. "Know anyone cute enough who might be looking for some honest work?" It was lunchtime, the Inn was packed and the grill was going full speed. I pushed a couple of guacamole burgers towards one of the new girls who wasn't sure what to think about our rapid-fire conversation.

"You're a perv," the hottie retorted.

I smiled, nodding in agreement.

"Dream on," she said. Both of us enjoying the light-hearted banter. "Where's my double-double, Dickwad?"

"Coming right up. Sure you don't want to think about getting a real job?"

"And give up all this," she said, adding, "Get rid of Jennifer and I might just give you one."

"You couldn't handle a real man," I told her as she grabbed her burgers and headed out of the kitchen. Passing Jennifer coming in, she added, "Your boyfriend is a sicko."

"That's only one of the reasons I love him so much."

Approaching the grill with a new order, Jennifer knew I'd been teasing the waitress. "You're going to make her crazy if you don't knock it off."

"She can take it. Here's your Cobb, dressing on the side and a chicken Caesar."

I turned my attention back to the grill, I wondered, *what the hell were we going to do with a boat, anyway?* The whole thing was an impulse. One of the things that had me thinking was how quickly I slipped back into hardcore negotiating with those brokers. I'd left that life in Seattle and was determined never to go back. But I didn't plan on flipping burgers the rest of my life, either.

"Adam and Eve on a raft, and wreck 'em," barked another waitress.

And so it went. Life at the Inn.

******

A few days later when we got home from work, the light on the answering machine was blinking. The agent had left a message for us to call him as soon as possible. "The bank got back to us about the boat, they want us to call them." I yelled out to Jennifer.

After the third ring the receptionist picked up the line. "Douglas and Douglas Yacht Brokers. May I help you?"

"This is Corey Phillips. I'm returning Bob's call about the old Drake."

"One moment, please. I'll connect you with Robert's office."

After a short pause, Bob came on the line. "Mr. Phillips thanks for getting back to us. We've received an interesting counter-proposal from the bank."

My pulse quickened, I asked, "How much?"

"As I was saying, the bank came back with a very reasonable counter offer…one that we feel is more than—"

"How much?" I repeated, louder than before.

Shakily, he continued. "Well, after reviewing the photographs we sent over for review—"

My hope turning to anger. "I asked you a simple question. How much?"

"One hundred and ten thousand."

I hung up.

Ten seconds later the phone rang. "Mr. Phillips?"

Recognizing the broker's voice, I said, "We've got nothing to talk about."

"Please, just hear me out. I think they'd be willing to listen to any reasonable counter you may have."

"I already made a reasonable offer."

"Come on," he said pleadingly. "Twenty thousand dollars for a 60-footer?"

I knew he was right. No executive board would want to have to try and answer to their stockholders (or explain to the IRS for that matter) why they let an asset once valued at close to million dollars go for twenty thousand bucks. "Okay, you're right. You're right, Bob." I loved over-pronouncing his name. "I'll go twenty-five."

There was silence on the other end, so I added, "If they accept it, fine, call me and we'll close. If not, don't call me again." A long pause followed. I waited patiently.

Finally the broker said, "I understand. I'll present your new offer and get back to you within seventy-two hours."

"Only if they accept. Otherwise, leave us alone."

The bank didn't take long to make a decision. The next night when we got home from work, there was another message. *"Offer accepted. One condition...you accept the boat as is, how is. Please call at your convenience."*

I nearly bounced off the floor, my whoop of triumph reverberating through the house.

Jennifer came around the corner. She took one look at me dancing around like an idiot, and threw her arms around me. "Well," she asked, with a big grin on her face. "Now what are we going to do?"

We'd gone back to the boat after making the counteroffer, and had spent a couple of hours going through her. Well, actually I did. Jennifer and Sierra waited in the truck after the stench had driven them both off the boat. I'd had a pretty good idea of what it was going to take to bring her back—at least I thought I did. Not in a thousand years would anyone sane ever agree to those terms. The words still haunt me. *As is...how is.* Buying a boat without complete structural and mechanical surveys is pure insanity.

Enjoy your achievements, as well as your plans. Keep interested in your own career, however humble, for it is a real possession in the changing fortunes of time.

Chapter 7

"You look beautiful," I whispered.

Morning found us still wrapped in each other's arms. Our bodies, once again, totally fulfilled and content in celebrating in the pure joys of passion.

We just couldn't get enough. Each new touch wove bonds of steel through every fiber of our beings. We lay together in the delicate morning light, as it filtered through the uneven paned glass windows on the east side of the bedroom. Jennifer's thick golden hair, a tangled wreck, perfectly framing her peaceful face. Her skin glowed. Her eyes were still closed.

Rolling toward me without opening her eyes, she moaned gently as her lean body stretched to greet the day. A smile found its way naturally onto her face.

I leaned over her and whispered, reliving one particular moment the previous night when she was straddled on top of me.

"Oh, yeah," she yawned, feigning indifference. "I almost forgot about that part."

"You're the devil in disguise," I said, pulling the pillow out from under her head and fighting to get it over her face.

After breakfast, we went to Jennifer's bank, presenting them with close to ten thousand dollars, mostly in small bills we'd saved in a shoebox in the closet, which represented all of our tip money. The balance Jennifer withdrew from her savings account. The bank cut us a cashier's check for the full $25,000. The papers were drawn up in both our names. After we signed, the broker gave us the name of the service they recommended for transferring title on documented vessels.

"We'll get everything started. It'll take about a month for the new documentation to arrive from Washington," the lady handling the transfer told us. "Here is your temporary." She ran off a couple of copies, suggesting we keep the original on board when we got it. We shook hands and she congratulated us on being the owners of a new boat—she hadn't seen any of the photos—and we headed out to look for a slip.

We got lucky at one of the smaller marinas on Harbor Island and were able to secure a temporary slip. Thankfully, they didn't ask for a picture of the boat; otherwise, we'd still be looking. Once again, Jennifer wrote the check, this time for the first and last months' rental, plus a nominal utility/deposit fee. Watching her signing the checks required a conscious effort to let go of the lingering tinges of my male ego. Seeing how excited she was helped to remind me we were in this together.

The sheriff's department wanted the boat out of their docks immediately and gave us forty-eight hours. "After that," the female deputy informed us, "it's $120 dollars a day for storage fees."

"That's $2 per foot per day," Jennifer protested.

"You got it, math genius," snapped the pinched-faced deputy behind the desk. She shook her head as if we were out of our minds. "You bought it. Now deal with it."

"Can we hose her off and get her cleaned up before—"

"No one's allowed to work on the boats." The girls locked eyes. "Insurance."

Jennifer nodded, angry but understanding.

"Besides," the deputy added, "there's no dockside water or power."

One of the male deputies leaned over. Obviously attracted to Jennifer and perhaps feeling a little sorry for her, he referred us to the tow and salvage operation the department used to move abandoned and sinking vessels. For a mere pittance of $175 an hour, we made arrangements to have her towed to the marina. Jennifer wrote yet another check in advance for the estimated four hours of service.

"Honey," I asked, "are you all right with all this?"

She nodded, balancing her checkbook. "As long as you don't short out on me about the money, I'm fine."

It was hard. I'd been brought up that it's the man's responsibility to provide, to pay for things, but Jennifer was so different. She'd been on her own long enough to know that was bullshit. We were in this together.

The tow was the last of the day, so the boat didn't arrive at the marina until well after dark. *Thank God.* She was unceremoniously backed into slip #26 on "B" dock. The marina manager had left her office long before the tow arrived. Otherwise, she would have never allowed us in. The boat was an absolute disgrace. Most everyone else had gone home as well, except for a couple of full-time crewmembers living on the surrounding boats. They couldn't believe what they were seeing. The stench was overwhelming. Knowing this, we'd armed ourselves with gallons of industrial solvent, bleach, liquid soap, four-inch blade scrapers with extended handles and a pair of hard-bristled deck brushes. We knew we had until first light to get her detoxed and cleaned up…if we were going to have a chance of staying there. The outgoing tide would carry most of the bleach and crap away. I felt a tinge of guilt for the surrounding clam beds and eel grass, but figured after a hundred years of people throwing worse pollutants than that into the bay, a few more gallons wasn't going to make any difference. *Wrong.*

"Isn't there some law about dumping solvents and stuff into the bay?" Jennifer asked innocently.

"Maybe. Yea. I don't know. I'm sure there is, but we don't have a choice. Either get her washed off tonight and cleaned up before morning, or we're screwed."

Even with the gallons of solvents and pure bleach we were pouring onto the layers of built up guano, the stench was still overwhelming. Inch by inch, we worked our way through the years of built up guano. Our backs were aching, our hands swelling and we were covered in slime. The clean up took us all night. As dawn's first gray light ushered in the new day, we'd made a good dent. Sierra hadn't come within two slips' distance. She was eyeing the entire process from her distant post, most likely wondering if she'd hitched herself to a couple of people who had gone stark raving mad. She hadn't wanted anything to do with the stench, but as we washed off the last traces of soap and bleach from the swim step, she sniffed the stern cautiously and stepped aboard.

We were totally exhausted, but our feelings of pride and accomplishment made it worthwhile. Standing there in the cockpit, still covered with slime and sweat, we couldn't have been happier. I was the luckiest guy alive, with my lady, my dog, a new boat and a glorious sunrise. Life didn't get any better. The city hadn't awakened yet, so the still, quiet dawn was all ours. A blue heron standing nearby caught our attention as he swiveled his head towards some bait. He was perched on the piling across from us, but we hadn't noticed him until he moved.

"Beautiful bird," Jennifer observed.

"It is. Beautiful morning, as well."

She put her arm around my waist. "That it is, my friend."

We watched the silhouette of San Diego's skyline take shape out of the darkness, but we couldn't enjoy it for long. Our arms and legs were filthy, our hands were throbbing and our backs were aching. For the past two hours, while I was finishing scrubbing the cockpit, Jennifer had been down below cleaning up the master stateroom so that we could sleep there.

"What do you say?" she asked, falling asleep on her feet. Pulling me feebly toward the stateroom, she said, "Let's hit the hay."

******

The dull ache deep within my knotted muscles intensified as sleep slipped away. Muscles that had gone untested for far too long were now complaining loudly. I had no idea what time it was. Jennifer was still fast asleep beside me. The boat was an absolute disaster inside. How Jen had managed to carve out enough room for us to sleep was amazing. But the decks were clean and the stench had been carried away with the outgoing tide. We slept most of the day.

Lying there, I thought about how hard she'd worked last night. Her blisters had actually started bleeding before I realized it and long before we quit. Watching her sleep, breathing in a deep easy rhythm, I thought about her waiting tables and me flipping burgers. Not a bad gig, but not something I could see us doing for the rest of our lives. Maybe we'd be able to make this boat work for us. I had no idea how. For the moment, just being on board was enough.

******

The next morning, covered with oil and grease, with a couple knuckles bleeding from being cracked open trying to turn a wrench in tight quarters, I glanced up to see Sierra, looking in at me. Her head hung partway into the engine room hatch; her body was spread out across the deck. Her tongue out, and facial muscles drooping, completely relaxed, I swear to God she was laughing at me. "What are you smiling at, you ole' dog? You get in here and do this."

Sierra didn't answer, nor did she bark, she or move, so I had no warning.

"You know, you'll be lucky if her chines aren't split." A deep, unfamiliar voice boomed in through the hatch, scaring me half to death. I was wedged behind the outboard side of the port main and had pretty much resigned myself to the fact that it was just going to be Sierra and me today. Douglas had called Jen this morning from the Inn, asking her to cover because a couple of the girls didn't show.

The voice continued, "The timber under those teak decks is rotten. You can tell by the way she's buckling here. The glass below the waterline will likely peal right off her hull when you get into any kind of weather—if you ever manage to get her running again."

I knew it wasn't Sierra talking, but couldn't see the source of the voice. Working my way out from beside the engine and toward the hatch, I emerged, heaving another wad of tangled wiring onto the deck ahead of me. The stranger stepped aside. After being in the poorly lit engine room, my pupils were closing as fast as they could in the direct sunlight, so all I could make out was the outline of a big man. I extended a filthy hand across the growing pile of debris on deck. Nodding toward the mess, I introduced myself. "I'm Corey Phillips. We just got her."

Looking at me as if I were crazed, the stranger extended a weathered, rock-solid hand and crushed mine without even noticing. "Name's Lloyd," he said as he looked over the array of old wiring, busted hoses, pumps and parts scattered all over the cockpit.

As my eyes adjusted, his face began to take shape out of the shadows below the brim of his well-worn, faded yellow CAT hat. His face was the color of dark, rich, fertile soil. Weathered and worn, with deep crevices around his eyes, he looked as if he'd spent his entire life in the sun. He had the kind of crystal clear eyes that didn't miss much...if anything. There was calmness about him; as if he'd seen it all and knew whatever was coming next would be here soon enough, so there was no need to rush. I could almost hear him thinking to himself, *so this is the wacko who bought her.*

Eventually Lloyd got around to asking me about the boat. "How come she was chained up over there?" he said, nodding toward the far end of the harbor.

"You saw her?" I asked him, surprised.

"I did. How long did they have her?
"Three years."

"Been at least that long," he said more to himself than me. "Hated watching her rot away like that. How come they had her?"

"A legal mess involving some Nevada shell corporation, tax evasion or some shit. When we bought her, the bank didn't tell us much. They were just glad to get rid of her." She was still supporting an entire ecosystem under her hull, with barnacles a foot long. It was the last thing any bank wanted to repossess, but they'd had no choice.

"No doubt," he said.

"What'd you pay for her?" Straight to the point.

I hesitated, appraising the guy, deciding if he needed to know the details, still wondering where he'd come from.

He looked back at me and for the first time cracked a half-smile. "Didn't mean to pry," he said politely. "Sorry to have interrupted your work. I'll be on my way."

"Twenty-five grand," I told him before he turned away.

He nodded. "Not bad." Pausing again, he continued to look around. "You did all right."

"You think?" I asked him.

"Absolutely," he assured me. "Now do the ole' girl right and get her back into shape. She's something special."

"That's exactly how I felt when I first saw her," I blurted out excitedly. "Something special."

He looked directly at me and hesitated. His laser eyes bored into me. I wasn't sure what he was going to do, and for a moment it looked as if he wasn't sure either. The moment hung in the air, as if some fate of the gods was about to be sealed.

Breaking the silence, I said, "You're welcome to take a look around...go through her if you're inclined. We could use some good advice." I spread my arms hopelessly at the mess on the deck.

His expression didn't change, but through the tight wrinkles surrounding his eyes, I glimpsed a twinkle deep within the dark blue that had obviously never been covered with a pair of polarized lenses—eyes that most likely had greeted a morning sun from the deck of some vessel since childhood. Everything about the man radiated knowledge gleaned from having spent his entire life around boat, from the slight tilt of his head to the quiet, precise way he moved, and the easy manner in which he spoke. They all fit—this guy knew boats.

A half-smile crossed his lips. "Do you think the timbers under these old teak decks will hold both of us at the same time?" He stepped out of the cockpit and started up the starboard side.

"Let's find out," I said, following him to the bow.

With that, the old girl found her guardian angel. If ever a vessel needed the knowledge of an old shipwright, this one did. He didn't say another word. Instead, he focused on the sounds his weight made walking forward while studying the decks as though he could see right through the wood. He circled the bow, moved aft along the port side, across the cockpit and into the hatch. With not so much as a glance into the salon, he descended into the engine room.

"You got a flashlight?" I reached inside the salon, grabbed one of the new Maglights we'd bought at the Marine exchange, handed it over and followed him into the dimly lit engine room. "Let's take a look at what she's got," he said again, more to himself than me. After thoroughly inspecting both mains, he asked, "Have you tried firing 'em off yet?"

"No."

"Good." Smelling the dipstick and rubbing the pitch-black oil between his finger and thumb, he added. "This oil is messed up; it's obvious they haven't run in a long time. Trying to light 'em off would only have made things worse."

Lloyd sat on an overturned five-gallon plastic bucket, and I perched on one of the stringers. He automatically wiped the dipstick clean on a faded red mechanic's rag he had in his back pocket before sliding it effortlessly back into the big starboard main.

"Best we drain this old oil, pour through a few gallons of fresh stuff, drain that, and then refill 'em before we try light 'em off." There was just over six feet of headroom if you straddled the keel, but the engine room was full of junk, making it crowded and hard to move around, so I stayed put as he spoke. "Best we do the same for the fresh water," he said, shaking his head. "That's what worries me most. The damn cooling system." He asked for a 3/4" wrench.

Scavenging through the almost empty, rusting toolbox that had been left onboard, I found what he was looking for. "Amazing," I said, handing him the wrench.

He placed it on a nut holding one of the internal zincs. Spinning off the nut, there was nothing where the zinc should have been. "Shit," he said. "Figured as much." Pausing, he looked around the shadowy engine room. "See if you can find any spare zincs." I started rummaging through a pile of old cardboard boxes that were piled up beside the fuel tanks.

Lloyd kept talking, "CAT builds the best damn motors in the world. They still got oil in 'em, so we might just get lucky. Look, here," he said, breaking off some white and green powder that had formed a thick crust around the raw water pump. "The seal is shot, for sure. No use trying to even start 'em until we pull these pumps and go through 'em all. Heat exchangers, the works."

"You said *we*."

In the dim light from the flashlight and the single 100-watt open light bulb I'd rigged earlier to hang from an "S" hook in a ceiling beam, I saw the old man smile. His eyes sparkled as his entire face lit up. "What am I supposed to do?" he asked with a twinkle in his eye. "Leave you alone down here? Who knows, you might have tried to start 'em without even bleeding 'em out first. That'd screw up any chance in hell we might have of saving these babies." He shot me another smile. "We've got a lot of work to do."

Not knowing what to say, I nodded.

"So, why are you still just standing there? We've got to get all the old fuel siphoned out, dump it and get these tanks polished. They're stainless, so they should be fine. We got 'a pull the injectors and replace them. Filters, belts and all these hoses are cracked and shot to hell. Grab something to write on. We'll start pulling numbers and making a list."

"Yes, sir. "

"Like I said, they're CATs…." He was in his element. Giving one of the 8" stainless steel exhaust pipes a loving pat, he continued. "These 343's were built to last a lifetime. Best engines CAT ever built. Let's take care of what we know needs tending to, then see if she wants to run." He paused. "You ready?"

With a nod, a friendship was born. It's hard to explain, but when people commit to something outside of themselves, they transcend time and space. Sometimes you catch a glimpse of it watching a championship team on TV. There's a chemistry that can't be defined by words. One of the benefits about working on a boat is it gives you time to think. Lloyd and I spent the rest of the day in the engine room. When it was time to quit, we were covered in oil, grease and sweat. Standing on the deck, I reached out my hand. He took it, once again leaving my fingers numb.

"Thank you," I said. "What do I owe you?"

He looked over at me, shaking his head. "Did I ask you for anything?" he inquired politely.

"No."

"Then don't worry about it."

"Can't do it. Can't have you working all day for nothing."

"Who said it was for nothing?" he asked calmly.

"Well, if you don't want any money, what do you want?"

"Let me worry about that."

"That ain't fair," I told him. "Wasn't brought up like that. An honest day's pay for an honest day's work."

"Good motto to live by," he agreed.

"Then let's settle up."

This time he took a deep breath before speaking. Turning to look me in the eye, he said, "Do you want me to help you, or not?"

"I do. Yes sir, you know that. We got more done today than I would have been able to do in a week."

"Then you trust my work?"

"Completely."

"Fine. Then trust me, too. I'll let you know if I need anything." He paused. "You quit worrying about paying me, or any of that nonsense, and I'll be glad to keep lending you a hand."

Our eyes met again. I didn't understand where he was coming from, but decided not to argue.

I nodded, and that was that.

******

Lloyd and I spent the better part of the next two weeks below deck. "The heart of the beast," he called it. Bolt by bolt, piece-by-piece, part-by-part, we tore into the big iron. He taught me more about diesels in a week than I'd learned in my entire life. The maze of manifolds, valves, injectors, lines, pumps, hoses, fittings and filters slowly started to make sense as we worked to simplify the systems. Each independent part working as part of the overall system. Each system supported and interdependent with the next. I was learning from a master.

"Hold it! Hold it!" he shouted. "Think about what's going to happen if you button that down all the way." I was working on one of four bolts holding the salt-water pump Lloyd had rebuilt the night before. I paused to think for a moment. He smiled patiently at me. "Just like we did with the valve cover. You want to apply the pressure evenly, one bolt at a time. Snug it up, and then move to the next one. Snug that one and so forth until they all have about the same amount of pressure. Then go back and run the rack again...a little tighter each time. Nice even pressure across the entire surface so the gasket 'll seal evenly. We don't want it leaking. Got it?"

I should have remembered that from earlier. "Sorry," I said.

"As long as you're learning, there's no reason to be sorry. She's trusting herself to your hands," he said affectionately, patting the motor. "You take good care of her and she'll do the same for you when you need it most." He was right. I would have had to loosen that initial bolt to get the pump properly aligned, and compromised the seal. Reading my mind, Lloyd added, "Every single detail's important. Like a domino. If one fails, it affects the entire system."

As the weeks went by, Lloyd completely redesigned the engine room. "There's only a few things that belong in an engine room," he said. "The mains, generators, the fuel manifold, filters and the tools to work on 'em. Everything else belongs somewhere...but not in here." Once so cluttered and messed up you could hardly get around the generators, the engine room was soon open and spacious. The only exception to Lloyd's rule regarding engine room equipment was a new set of deep cycle batteries. We'd built a custom battery box outboard of the starboard stringer. It fit in there perfectly. Kept the weight low and made the cable runs short. Given all its advantages, Lloyd had agreed to bend his rules.

Everything in the engine room had been meticulously thought out. Each piece of equipment in its proper place served a unique purpose. But as I lay upside down, half wedged under several tons of metal, working to break free a frozen bolt on the underside of the alternator, I wondered which rocket scientist had designed this system. "I'd like to see that asshole climb in here and do this," I complained to Lloyd. "What a moron." Lloyd chuckled as I handed him the bolt I'd finally freed.

Through it all, we were seeing significant progress. We'd managed to pump all the old diesel oil out of the four 600-gallon tanks and had them hydra-washed and inspected with remote fiber optics. Fortunately, the boat had been impounded with full tanks, so the tanks were rock solid. The fuel oil had prevented the tanks from rusting from the inside out. We were learning to count the smallest of life's blessings.

Every evening after work, Jennifer would bring us dinner from the Inn. She and Lloyd took to one another immediately. She became the daughter he never had. She loved doting on him. They made me smile. In the evening, sitting around the settee together, Lloyd would spin tales of his early days as a merchant marine, and then jump to when he crewed on a tuna clipper.

"Those four pole fish were incredible," he'd recount. "There were days when we'd be in the racks for ten, twelve hours straight. You'd be so tired by the time the bite was over you could hardly make it to your bunk."

"About the way I've felt lately," I said with a sigh.

With sparkling eyes, he replied, "This is nothing, son. I'm talking about *real* work."

And so it went. Day after day. Busting our humps, getting the job done. Always looking forward to seeing Jennifer, sitting down to each meal and spending the remainder of the evening talking.

"You guys come up with a name for her yet?" Lloyd asked one night.

"*Vintage*," Jennifer said immediately. It was the first time I'd heard it. We'd been kicking around names, but we hadn't come up with anything we really liked. A vessel's name is important. *Vintage* felt right.

"What do you think?" she asked, looking at me.

"I like it," I said, repeating the name out loud. "*Vintage*. I like it a lot."

"How did you come up with that, Jennifer?" Lloyd asked.

"I was driving over here tonight thinking about when we first found her. How we'd been walking along and it was all foggy and cold and I wanted to turn around and go home, but Corey said he just wanted to keep going a little further. I trusted him, and he trusted his instincts." She smiled. "I thought about the name *Instinct*, but it just didn't quite fit. Then, as Sierra and I were walking up to her tonight, it hit me. She's a classic. *Vintage* just felt right."

"I love it," Lloyd said immediately.

"Me, too," I piped in.

"Then so be it," Jennifer beamed. "But first let's ask her. *Vintage*," she said in a quiet voice, "what do you think?" Another boat must have run past us a couple minutes earlier. A small wake gently rocked the vessel on cue, almost as if she were nodding her head in agreement. We all laughed out loud.

"Perfect timing," Lloyd said, "but since you're going to rename her, we're going do it right" His voice became serious. First of all, we have to make sure everything on board that has her old name on it gets chucked. Everything—life rings, paperwork, pictures, the works. We can't leave a thing on board with her old name on it."

The boat had been abused so there were no photographs of her on board. We'd been through her guts for over a month, and other than a few receipts stuffed in parts boxes, hadn't found anything with the old name on it. Jennifer offered to go through and double-check all the cabin drawers and lockers.

"Good. Double check the wheelhouse as well," Lloyd suggested. "Once we finish below and get her running, we'll start on her cosmetics. When we get there, we'll sand off what's left of her name from her bow and across the stern. We'll take it all the way down to bare glass and start fresh. When we get her painted, then and only then, Jennifer will bless her with her new name."

The gentle kindness in his voice, his compassion and knowledge spoke volumes.

"We want you there when we do," Jennifer said.

"Appreciate your offer. I really do. I'd be honored to be there. Most folks don't think much of it—throw a christening party and invite their friends and make a big production out of the whole thing. But listen to me," he said in his serious tone. "She's your boat. When you're out there," he said, pointing his chin toward the open sea, "she's your life's blood, your guardian angel. Your lives are going to be in her hands. So, by my way of thinking, the blessing should be a little more sacred than a party." He paused again, looking Jennifer in the eye. "You and Corey make it a special moment. Don't worry about formalities. For the most part, the 'rules' are a bunch of bullshit anyway. Just make it special. Trust your instincts. Do what feels right in your hearts, and she'll know." With a big grin, he gently patted the teak salon table. "When the time comes, you'll know what to do."

******

One tough month stretched into two, but late one Friday, we were finally ready to try the mains. Jennifer had gotten off early and was in the engine room with Lloyd and me. *Vintage* had her start/stop controls right where they belonged—in the engine room.

"Being in sight of the machinery when she turns over, you can see any problems immediately," Lloyd had said while we installed the panels.

Our pulses were racing as Lloyd rechecked the oil and water levels, and then checked the trainee fluid for the umpteenth time. Finally, he depressed the green starter button located on the bulkhead just above the port main. The deep, unmistakable rumble of a giant awakening from a deep sleep echoed through the engine room. Within seconds, another, defining sound filled the air as the big CAT roared to life. Jennifer and I squealed like little schoolgirls. Thank God Lloyd didn't hear us! He was jammed between the forward bulkhead and the main, looking, listening, searching for anything wrong. But she just kept purring like the big old cat she was. I jumped out of the engine room and checked the exhaust. The water flow was good and true. The initial plume of black smoke was dissipating by the time I got on deck and now just a trace of steam was escaping…just as it was supposed to.

One of the crew a couple boats over nodded his head approvingly.

After she'd come up to temperature, Lloyd throttled her up to about 1500 and held her there. Inside the engine room, the noise was deafening. He was holding her steady, well below red line, but it sounded as if she was going to explode. Lloyd looked up. Seeing the terrified looks on our faces, he shot us one of his patented 'Nothing to worry about' looks. She held true. He throttled her all the way back. The roaring immediately stopped. Jennifer took her hands away from her ears as an incredible sound came out of the motor. As the deafening full power roar ended, a snarl filled the engine room, as the big main settled back down into a low purr at idle.

Lloyd was pleased about the motor's performance. "Did you hear her snarl at us? That's one of the most beautiful sounds in the world." *He loved his machinery.* "The big ol' CAT giving us a little growl at having been brought down from speed. This lady wants to get up and run. Listen to how content she is now. You take care of her the way I've been showing you, and she'll take you anywhere you want to go."

The simple pleasures of life. Three of us standing in the engine room grinning from ear to ear at one another, all because an old motor was purring happily along beside us.

"Let's see what her twin has to say," Lloyd suggested, pointing to the starboard's ignition button. "Go ahead."

I knew I'd be doing this for the rest of my life. Though Lloyd was as tough as steel, I could see at the end of each day he moved a lot slower than he did in the morning. This was his day. He'd been the one who had come along and jumped in without asking for a thing. Without him, I don't know what we would have done. This was his moment. He'd earned it. "No, sir," I said, "She's all yours."

He nodded in appreciation.

"Go on." I said, "You've got the magic touch."

This meant more to him than I'd ever expected. All the while we'd been working together, I couldn't help feeling guilty because he hadn't asked for a thing. And since our talk, I sure as hell hadn't broached the subject.

With his bear claw of a hand, he reached up again and depressed the starboard starter. Within seconds we had a repeat performance. Both mains were fully operational. We were ecstatic as we shut them down and climbed out of the engine room.

My emotions overwhelmed me. "I can't thank you enough. I don't know what we would've done if you hadn't come along."

He looked at us with confidence. "You would have managed just fine, son. You've got a knack for this. We've still got a lot of work to do...replacing the generator and going through the rest of her systems. But as long as those mains are happy, everything else will be a piece of cake. Besides, it's been my pleasure helping to bring this fine lady back on line. She's as sound as they come." He patted the bait tank. "Going to make you two a fine charter boat."

"Charter boat?" Jennifer asked. We'd been so immersed in working, running around getting parts and focusing only on the motors that we hadn't even talked about what we were planning to do with the boat.

Lloyd saw us thinking about it. "What the hell else you going to do with her? Run cocktail cruises around the bay?"

Jennifer and I looked at him without answering. To be honest, we had no idea what we were going to do with her.

He realized we didn't have a clue, so he laid out his ideas. "You've got plenty of time to decide. First, we'll get the rest of her systems on line. You're going to have to get all this old paint off, but that's no big deal. Just a lot of hard work. Strip the varnish and polish out the stainless. These decks, here," he said, kicking at the blackened teak under his work boots. "They're two inches thick and will sand out and come right back to life, good as new. There's no wood in the world like teak. All in all, she's going to be just fine." He paused again and looked into the salon. "Some new carpet inside, fresh wallpaper, linens and things, and you guys will be ready to roll. Besides," he asked us again, "how else you plan on making her pay? A boat's got to earn her keep—you know, otherwise she feels neglected."

"We haven't thought about any of that stuff," I said. "By the time we wrap it up every night, I'm so beat I can hardly eat, never mind thinking about the future."

"Pussy." He turned to Jennifer. "No offense."

******

"You were right," Jennifer said, finishing another bite in a little restaurant tucked away on a side street between Scott and Rosecrans. "This is the best calamari I've ever had."

Lloyd reached over to give her a loving pat on the arm. "Glad you like it."

We'd all worked our tails off the last couple of months. Other than the nights in the salon, when we were almost too tired to talk, this was the first time we'd all been together away from the boat.

I could tell Jennifer was up to something. She finished off her plate and caught his attention with a look.

"So, Lloyd…what gives? You show up out of nowhere, spend every waking minute working with us, won't take a dime and we don't have a clue why.

"I love boats," he said, pausing to let that simple statement sink in. "Loved them all my life. I knew your *Vintage* here when she was first launched. One of the prettiest boats I'd ever laid eyes on. Beautiful lines. She was a proud lady and served her original owners well. I knew them both. Elderly couple from up north someplace. Hollywood or Pasadena, I think. Anyway, when I ran the fuel dock, they'd come in and we got to be friends. They ran that darn thing alone. Just the two of them. Damnedest thing I ever saw. For years, they'd take her down to the Cape for the season. Then out to the islands. Took good care of her, too. Oil changes like clockwork. He was ex-Navy and did it by the book."

A look of sadness came over his face. "Don't know what happened to them, though. One day the boat was here; next thing I know, she's gone. Someone told me they'd sold it to a family from Florida and they'd run her through the Canal and left her in Fort Lauderdale. But that's all I knew until one day I saw her being towed by the Harbor Patrol. Wouldn't have recognized her if I hadn't known the boat before. She was a disaster, a total mess. Rust running down her hull, busted out windows, bird shit all over her—pretty much the way you found her. I asked around and found out she'd been impounded, but you know the damn cops…they wouldn't tell me a thing. Said she was in the middle of some legal mess. No one was the making the mortgage payments, slip fees, nothing…so they came and got her."

He took another sip of wine. I was astounded. He'd known the history of the *Vintage* all along.

He continued. "I'd been keeping my eye on her, wondering what was going to happen. About that time, I decided running the fuel dock was getting to be too much. Especially during the season when we were pumping twenty thousand gallons a day for the sport boats. I had a couple of real good guys working for me, so I just turned the business over to them. But I'd been keeping my eye on her, wondering what was going to happen to her."

"You owned the fuel dock?" I asked, more astonished.

He nodded. "I had a pretty good hunk of it. Poole owned it, but he gave me enough to let me retire and just mess around. I've got a little shop in my garage. Rebuilding pumps and starters and things. I like to keep busy tinkering, you know." If he thought what we'd been doing the last few months was 'tinkering,' then I was screwed. As far as I was concerned, it had been the most intense, difficult work I'd ever known.

"But why have you been doing all this for us?" Jennifer asked.

He swirled the wine in his glass and waited until the liquid had settled. Secrets were difficult for him from the way his thoughts must have been wrestling with each other. "I watched you guys having her towed away that afternoon," he confessed. "In fact, I followed the boat over there in my truck. Kept an eye on her all the way from the time she left the impound until you had her tied up there at "B" dock," he paused. "Fact of the matter is, the next morning when I walked down the dock, I couldn't believe what I was looking at—the amount of work you guys did that first night. I was impressed. I've scraped seagull shit off before and I know how Goddamned hard it can be. Like concrete. Pretty much decided right then and there that I wanted to find out what was going on. The way I had it figured was obviously one of two scenarios. Whoever bought her was rich and had hired a crew to do all the work, which was a long shot, because no hired crew would have done that amount of work overnight, or someone was committed to bringing her back. The fact you brought her to 'B' dock told me whoever was behind this wasn't from money. I was curious to meet you."

He lit up, looking at Jennifer. "Had no idea that someone as beautiful and charming as your lady Jennifer here would be involved as well." Jennifer blushed. As tough as Lloyd was on the outside, he was a gentleman on the inside. Holding up his wine glass, he offered a toast. "To the *Vintage*. May she serve and protect you with the grace of God."

I felt the emotion welling up in my throat and joined my wine glass to theirs with a tender click.

******

The next morning before we started sanding, Lloyd asked me if I had a operator's license.

"You don't have to have a license to drive a boat."

"You do if you're going to carry passengers for hire…if you're going to charter. How much sea time do you have?" Lloyd asked.

I didn't want to think about the life I'd run from in Seattle, but I had to say something. "Been around boats my whole life—hell, I was born on one. My dad ran a boat up north. We lived on a houseboat."

"If you can document two years sea time, all you've got to do is submit your papers and take the test." He looked at me with those unblinking steel blue eyes.

"I'm not much at tests," I confessed. "I pick shit up pretty quick…you know, watching someone do something first, showing me how…but I've always had trouble with book learning."

"I've watched you. You're a quick study." He put his arm around me like a father and gave me a squeeze. "Quit your worrying. I'll help you study. Did the same for my kid before he joined the Coast Guard."

I was surprised. "You got a kid in the Coast Guard?"

"Yes, sir," Lloyd said proudly. "Fact is he's getting out in a couple of months." He let that sink in. "You think I've been doing all this for fun?"

he said looking around the *Vintage*. "He's going to need a job when he gets out, and there ain't nobody I know that can out-fish my boy."

******

A subtle movement of the boat woke Jennifer and me up from another deep sleep. We'd spent a lot of nights on the boat since we got the interior fixed up, and were both becoming acutely aware of the slightest movements that weren't integral to the natural rhythm of the boat.

Lloyd's voice boomed through the salon. "It's just like running any other business, but about ten times harder. You're going to live, eat and breathe this boat twenty-four hours a day, seven days a week." This was a first. He'd never come on board without us being up and about on deck. I hadn't really thought about it before that moment, but he just seemed to appear every day about the time we were getting started. No particular hour, just whenever we got to moving about, he'd be there. This morning was different—he was here early and all business.

"You hear me, sleepyheads?" he hollered down to our stateroom. "Seven by twenty-four. Can you handle it?" Sierra had already scrambled up the companionway into the salon and I could hear Lloyd talking to her. "What do you think, girl? Can they handle it?" Then another bellowing challenge. "Get your asses out of the rack! We got work to do."

"You always this ornery in the morning?" I hollered back at him, pulling on my jeans. Jennifer rolled her eyes and pulled the comforter back over her head.

The next three months flew by. From that day on, every morning, just after first light, Lloyd would show up and make the coffee to get things rolling. Jennifer would get breakfast started. When you combine the aroma of fresh brew with bacon frying and muffins cooking, you've got a pretty good start to any morning.

The work never stopped. It seemed as if the deeper we got into the repairs, the more there was to do. We knew the teak decks forward were going to have to come up. When the boat had been in Florida, fresh water had seeped in between the teak and the plywood sub-deck, rotting out the supporting framework. The dry rot and damage were too extensive to try sistering the beams, so every single cross beam and lateral support brace had to be replaced. We were virtually rebuilding her decks. We wrapped the rails with blue tarps, duct-taping the bottom portion to the hull to keep debris from falling into the bay. We tore the living crap out of that boat.

I'd cut my hours down at the Inn to weekend nights to allow more time for the boat, so consequently, I wasn't producing much income. It seemed like every paycheck was already spent on materials and supplies before I'd cashed it. But Jennifer kept her hours steady and wouldn't let me worry too much. "We're fine. Don't waste time worrying about it," she assured me. "We've got money we haven't even spent yet."

Without Lloyd, I don't know what we would have done. His understanding of the boat's systems, how and why they worked (or, in the *Vintage's* case, didn't work) was amazing. As the days turned into weeks, we traced down and replaced or repaired problem after problem. By the time we'd rewired the entire boat, we'd used over twelve thousand feet of new wiring. An overwhelming sense of accomplishment started to build within each of us as the boat took shape. There's no other feeling in the world like the pride of ownership. The *Vintage* was starting to show her true colors.

The warm June sun beat down on our bronzed backs and salty sweat dripped into our eyes as we laid on the last coat of non-skid. Standing back, we stood together admiring four months of non-stop work. We didn't say a word. The work spoke for itself.

Lloyd broke the silence, "Tomorrow we'll get started on the bright work."

Vintage's wood had been neglected for years. What remained of any varnish had long ago pealed and yellowed. The unprotected and exposed teak had taken on the sad tone of faded gray ash—it looked like dead flesh. Good teak has resilience like few other woods. I was adequate with a wrench (and under Lloyd's supervision had actually become pretty competent around the machinery), but when it came to woodwork, I blossomed. Working wood felt as natural under my hands as Jennifer's body. Scraping and then sanding the faded top surfaces with course 60 grit, getting down to the raw wood…I loved the feeling of breathing new life into the wood as the grain started to surface again.

As we progressed up to 80 grit, 100 grit, 150 and eventually 220, the wood's rich texture took on the silky feel of a baby's butt—velvety smooth and soft. We stripped, sanded and varnished her handrails, boarding ladder, tackle center and trim. After each new coat of varnish, we'd go back over it the next day with some wet and dry paper, working our way up to ultra-fine 400 paper. The beautiful grain deepened with each coat, and she started to take on the look of mirrored glass. The overwhelming pride continued to grow within us. People were stopping along the dock to admire the boat—a far cry from the state of affairs just a few months earlier.

Contentedly brushing on yet another coat, Lloyd whispered to the wood like a mother talking to her babe. "Varnish. Liquid gold...a gift from the gods. A gift to make you shine." Eleven coats of hand-rubbed varnish later, she shone like a prom queen—radiant and proud.

Her stainless had all been brought back to near pristine condition. We'd rolled and brush tipped her hull and topsides with LP while in the water—no small feat. We rented an industrial steam cleaner and got the bilges spotless. Inside, there was new carpet, wallpaper and headliner, as well as new high-density foam on the bunks. We worked out a trade with an old Portuguese woman to sew us new slipcovers and drapes in exchange for promises of fresh fish once we got running. Jennifer was in charge and decided to go vintage using old Hawaiian bar cloths. With the boat's rich teak interior, the combination was breathtaking. Her interior was welcoming and warm. She looked awesome. *Vintage* was a lady again.

******

Lloyd and I decided to set aside a couple of hours every night after dinner to study for my operator's license. I was under the delusion that I had a fairly good handle on how to run a boat, but when it came to what the Coast Guard wanted, I was clueless. After helping with the dishes that first night, Lloyd got out the books. When Jennifer was finished in the galley, she sat down with us.

"I'd really like to learn about this, too," she said, gesturing to the chart Lloyd was spreading out across the table.

He beamed. "Young lady, you never cease to amaze me. I'd love it if you joined our little class, but take it easy on the screen licker, here," he said and poked me in the ribs. "We don't want him thinking he should be riding the short bus."

Jennifer learned quickly. But I was having all sorts of trouble. I could spin a boat on her axis and back her into a slip with 20 knots of wind blowing against a cross current, but wasn't able to decipher how to do it on paper. I couldn't break down the hypothetical situations. Though Jennifer had never run a boat, she immediately picked up the principles of using a spring line and counter rotating props to position a boat head-on into a swift current or strong wind. Speed, distance and time, bearings, estimated positions, set and drift…it all came to her naturally. For me, it was a nightmare.

They should have reserved a seat for me on the short bus, but Lloyd and Jennifer stayed with me, night after night, patiently helping me grasp the questions and understand the principles behind them. Slowly things started to make sense. Lloyd knew more than any man I'd ever met about seamanship, navigation and the rules of the road governing vessels at sea. The fact that he was able to transfer that knowledge to us was amazing. A Naval Chief, he'd had two ships blown out from under him during the Second World War. He held an unlimited ticket and was licensed to operate any vessel, anywhere in the world. There are only a handful of individuals who hold that ticket. It was the highest level a civilian could obtain. If he'd stayed in the Navy, he'd have been a Rear Admiral. Instead, here he was, sitting onboard a small yacht, sharing his lifetime of knowledge with us. He was able to take practical sea experiences and transform it into simple text that allowed us to communicate on paper. He was able to share his knowledge and understanding of the whys and wherefores of each and every situation the Coast Guard was likely going to throw at us.

"At sea," he'd say, "it's rarely a single incident that causes a catastrophe. It's usually a combination of little things that aren't properly handled and compound on top of each other until it's too late to avoid a disaster. Sometimes you'll only have a split second to analyze what the problems are…and act on them. Things can turn to shit in a hurry."

Lloyd was making damn sure that if we earned the privilege of being entrusted with the lives of others at sea, we'd take the helm as fully competent and capable operators. Being in his presence was an honor. We soaked up his wisdom best we could. The more we learned, the more frustrated Jennifer became, knowing that she didn't have the sea time to qualify to take the test.

"It doesn't matter," Lloyd reassured her. "When you get the time, you'll get your ticket. What matters most is that you're going to know what the hell's going on out there and what to do." We both knew he was right.

When I passed the test and got my 100-ton ticket, she was beaming. "Now we're in business," she announced, holding up the license proudly "Let's go get a picture frame and hang this baby in the wheelhouse."

I could barely contain my excitement. "You're next," I said.

Lloyd agreed. "From here on, all we're doing is counting the days until you rack up enough time."

We hung my license off center, so when she got hers, they'd be perfectly centered on the wall. That made her smile.

******

One of the top charter agents in the area was a long-time friend of Lloyd's. We'd met with him earlier when he'd agreed to book the boat once we got her ready to go and I had my license. "Congratulations," he said, upon learning the news. "But I'm not putting you on line until you've got your crew squared away."

No problem, I thought. We ran an ad in the *San Diego Log*, which got the phone ringing off the hook. Unfortunately, most of the applicants turned out to be nothing more than transient dock rats or users looking for an easy meal. There was nothing easy about setting up and running a charter operation. Without the right crew, we'd be finished before we even got started. Lloyd said he'd put the word out as well, and late one evening, as Jennifer and I were closing down the Inn, he walked in with a handsome young man.

"Corey, this is my son, Travis," Lloyd said, introducing us with all the pride of a father. "Travis, meet Corey Phillips. He and his better half own the boat I've been telling you about." Lloyd looked around for Jennifer.

Extending my hand, I felt lucky to get it back in one piece. Just like his father, Travis emulsified it with a grip like a steel vice. *Doesn't know his own strength*, I thought to myself. *Just like his old man.* "That's some grip you got there," I said, massaging my fingers.

Travis didn't seem to hear. He'd locked in on one of the pretty young waitresses the Inn was famous for, staring as she bent over to wipe down a nearby table.

"Kid just got out of the Coast Guard," Lloyd said proudly. "Four years. Chief's mate. Licensed op and certified big iron mechanic to boot."

"Really," I said, nodding my head. "Impressive."

"I was thinking he might be just the man you're looking for. Strong, a damn good mechanic and not afraid of work. Been around boats most his life." Lloyd and I smiled at the fact we were carrying on a conversation about Travis right in front of him, and he was totally oblivious. Mesmerized by the waitress. "He's been at sea awhile. Or, at least, away from such beautiful women," Lloyd added, as Jennifer walked up, instantly breaking the spell Travis was under and drawing his attention away from the waitress.

"Travis," Lloyd said, smiling at Jennifer as she gave him a hug, "this is Jennifer Comstock."

Travis hadn't taken his eyes off her. With an alarming amount of charm, he extended his hand. I cringed, watching her delicate hand disappear into his. I almost screamed, *don't*. He held it like a lovely flower. "It's a pleasure, Jennifer. I'm Travis Jordaine."

Their eyes met. She smiled, "The pleasure is all mine."

"Travis is Lloyd's son," I said abruptly, a tinge of jealously creeping up my spine.

"Then it's an honor as well," she said, withdrawing her hand and wrapping it around my waist. "Any son of Lloyd's is a friend of ours." Feeling like a king with her arm around me, my pangs of jealously were instantly gone. Jennifer hadn't missed a beat, knowing exactly what to do to make me feel secure.

"Travis has been stationed up north…Coast Guard," Lloyd boasted. "Just got released and flew home today."

"Then I bet you're ready for some good ol' home cooking. How about one of our world famous burgers?" Jennifer asked.

"Yes, ma'am," Travis said, obviously disappointed to see her display her loyalty to another man.

"Don't ma'am, me," Jennifer replied, poking him in the ribs.

"Sorry. Didn't mean any disrespect," he apologized. "The last two years I've been in Homer…Air/Sea Rescue Team."

I nodded, knowing full well how treacherous Alaskan waters are and how dangerous his job was. "Would you like to see the *Vintage*?

Travis was watching the waitress again and didn't answer.

"Her name's Cathy."

Travis smiled.

******

Over the next few weeks, new friendships started growing out of mutual respect. Just like his Dad, Travis was an expert. Jennifer and I could both tell he really appreciated everything we'd done to the boat so far. Anyone can stand back and admire a well-maintained boat, but it takes a boat lover to really understand how much work goes into making it look that way. And Travis was a boat person all the way.

Putting the *Vintage* on line as a legitimate charter boat meant we had a lot more work to do. Outfitting her for multi-day trips, we added a few new systems and upgraded what we had whenever we could. We put in a new 20-scoop bait tank to supplement her existing 30-scoop main tank. Working with Lloyd, Travis designed a raw water manifold system to service both tanks, and added dual 12-volt backup pumps in case we lost the generator.

"Gotta have a backup system," Lloyd said. "You can always run without your generator if you have to, but if you lose your bait—forget it—the trip's over."

Converting the original fish hold from ice to a blast freezer took some plumbing, but it was a joy watching Lloyd and Travis work together, seeing the father pass his tools, knowledge and lifestyle on to his son. They were a perfect team. What would have taken me days of trial and error to figure out and piece together took them only moments. They'd assess the situation, grunt a couple of times and before I knew it, they'd hand me a parts list. They'd be all over—ripping, tearing, cutting, and drilling, whatever it took. They didn't hesitate.

"She wasn't sure about this, at first," Travis said, tightening down one of the new freezer spray nozzles, "but now she's getting happy, aren't you, girl?" He was asking the boat.

Adding an outdoor electric grill to the cockpit behind the salon bulkhead was the final touch. It was Jennifer's suggestion. When we finished the installation, she loved it. "This will make fixing dinners a thousand times easier. I can't wait to start running."

She didn't have to wait long. Knowing we were close to having her ready, Larry Ward, our charter agent, had started booking for us a couple of weeks earlier. He hadn't told anyone except Lloyd, who made sure we would be ready. We were scheduled to run our first trip in five days. That afternoon, Jennifer and I sat down with Douglas at the Inn and let him know our schedule. He'd known this day was coming. We all did. It had only been a matter of time before we'd both have to quit.

"We're really going to miss you guys around here. The place won't be the same. Especially without you, Jen." Douglas gave her a long hug. "Five years is an eternity in the restaurant business."

Jennifer didn't let go. She was going to miss Douglas and the Inn as well. She started to cry.

"Wish you guys could do both," Douglas said with a slight tremble in his voice. "Run the boat and still work here. But I know that's impossible."

Shaking Doug's hand, I saw the tears in Jennifer's eyes and a flood of emotions surged through me. The Inn had been the place where Jennifer and I had met. It had been the first place I'd felt at home since leaving Seattle. Douglas had watched over us. He'd helped Jennifer through the long period when she was trying to cope with my indiscretions and fear. The Inn was more than a job; it was a part of our lives and we were all going to miss each other. Sometimes, changes come hard.

"I can't thank you enough for everything you've done for us," I said, searching for the right words.

Douglas smiled. Letting go of my hand, he gave me a big bear hug instead. "It's been a pleasure having you here," he said. "As far as I'm concerned, you guys are on a little holiday cruise. Now, don't get me wrong. I'm wishing you all the best with the boat. In fact, we all are. But if you ever need to come back, you'll always be more than welcome here. As long as I own this place, your jobs are here waiting for you." We couldn't ask for anything more.

"I've got an idea," I blurted out. "We need to do a couple shake down cruises before we start running, why don't you come with us. We'll make a day of it. Bring every one. We can run out to the islands for the day. The yellows have been snapping pretty good."

"That's a great idea." Jennifer said. "Come on Doug. We'll have a blast."

Without a moment's hesitation, he agreed. "When?"

"Why not tomorrow." I asked, looking over for Jen's approval.

"Perfect." she said.

"I'll hang a sign on the front door that says *Closed. Gone Fishing.* I love owning my own place." Looking over to one of his girls, he told her, "We're closing tomorrow. Anyone that wants to go fishing with Corey and Jen be here at….what time?" he asked us.

"I don't know. Let's leave early, be at the islands for the dawn bite. Say 2:00 A.M. At the boat."

Douglas gasped. "Are you shittin' me?" His jaw went slack. "I haven't seen dawn in twenty years."

"Then it's about time," Jennifer said, poking him in the ribs with her familiar gesture of affection.

Douglas let out a deep sigh. "Ok, then. Anyone who wants to go fishing be here by midnight and we'll drive over together."

"Midnight?" I asked.

"You think I'm going to frickin' wake up at two in the morning. It's easier to stay up all night."

True to his word, Douglas didn't sleep a wink that night. He showed up right on time with a handful of girls from the Inn. They were all impressed with the boat. Jennifer showing everyone around like a proud mother hen.

Lloyd and Travis were chomping at the bit. At first Lloyd hadn't wanted to come with us, but it only took Jennifer a second to convince him. "There's no way I'm going without you." She told him in no uncertain terms. If it weren't for you, none of this would be happening. I just wish you could run every trip with us."

"Maybe a few years ago," he said shaking his head. "If I were a little younger and you were a little older."

"Dad, you're grossing me out." Travis said overhearing the flirting.

Continuing as if Travis hadn't said a word, Lloyd told Jennifer, "These old bones have had about all they can take out there. But as soon as you guys got back from the Inn and told us the plan, I checked the weather forecast. It's calling for calm seas and no wind. I should be able to handle it."

"You ole' devil, you were planning on coming this whole time." Jennifer said reaching up and giving him a loving shove on his shoulder.

Lloyd laughed out loud. "You bet. I just like having a lady invite me anywhere these days."

I walked into the salon just then and Lloyd turned to me, "You ready to get this show on the road, Captain?"

Travis and Lloyd cast us off and we headed to the bait receivers. We loaded up with a perfect mix of fin bait and squid before heading out of the harbor on a 180-degree course toward the islands. Lloyd and Travis spent the first half hour in the engine room, looking for any signs of trouble.

"All systems are go." Lloyd proudly announced as they came into the wheelhouse. "She's running like a kitten."

He couldn't have been prouder. We all were. Months of work behind us. Calm seas ahead. It felt good. All of us in the darkened wheelhouse. Sitting quietly.

Lloyd yawned loudly. "Well I'm hittin' the rack," he announced. "Nothin' like falling asleep to the sounds of those purring CATs. Good night, you guys."

"Me too," Travis said.

They each climbed into one of the wheelhouse bunks, leaving Jennifer and I alone. Neither of us much else. Savoring the realities of our dreams coming true.

******

The run over was smooth as silk. When we got to the islands, we metered around in the dark for a while. Looking for any signs of bait. But didn't see any. So just before dawn we anchored up along a little riff that runs out at a 90 degree angle from the inside of south island. We hung the squid light over just in case, but nothing showed. Travis started a chum line in the grey and within minutes we heard some fish boiling behind the boat. All the 'passengers' were asleep, except Doug. I flipped a dean back on a 20# outfit and got picked up immediately. Setting the hook I handed the rod to Doug, "Here you go, amigo, our first fish. He's all yours."

Without warning, the line screamed off the reel. "Holly shit!" Doug said, holding the tip up. The rod bending double. "What the fuck is it?"

"It ain't no calico," Travis said.

"It's gotta be a yellow." I said.

Travis brailed a full scoop. Fish exploding on the bait.

Jennifer ran below, yelling, waking everyone up.

Lloyd was on deck. "It might be a white."

"I don't know. Eating like that on the surface?"

"Yea. You're right. I just saw a tail flash in the deck lights. They're yellows."

The fish were inhaling everything that hit the water. Every bait was instantly boiled on. We had a half dozen going in the dark. Douglas was the only one in his group who had ever fished before, so he got several to the boat. But the waitresses were a mess. Half asleep, and fighting fish in the dark, we broke off a dozen fish, only managing to land one for the girls. But they didn't care. They'd really only come out to see the boat, hang with Jennifer and spend a little time on the water.

All the fish we did land were regulation size. Averaging about twenty-five pounds. But as soon as it got light enough to see the water, they shut off. Disappearing as quickly as they arrived. But it didn't matter. Everyone was having fun. Jennifer whipped up a big breakfast and we all sat around the cockpit with paper plates, watching the sun come up with mouths full of scrambled eggs and fresh blueberry hotcakes.

"Not bad." Doug said. Thanking Jennifer as she refilled his coffee mug. "So this is what it looks like." He said nodding towards the glowing orange ball making it's way over the hills in the far distance.

After breakfast we made a couple of moves. Metering a few fish and picking off some bass, which we released. We had plenty of fish from the morning bite. The girls had fun pulling on a bunch of bonito that charged the boat and by mid day, everyone was ready to head home.

******

The next morning Doug called the dock phone and asked if Jennifer could come in and cover another shift. "It's so weird," she said hanging up. "Cathy hasn't missed a day since she started. It's not like her to not show up. Not at least without calling. Douglas said he hadn't heard a word from her."

I glanced up from mending one of our bait scoops, and caught a distant look in her eyes.

"What do you mean?" I asked, only half interested. My focus was on the net.

"Cathy and I have been working together for years. And not once, not once," Jennifer added for emphasis, "has she ever missed a shift. I was really surprised she didn't come with us yesterday. I asked girls and they said they hadn't heard from her in a few days. She's just not like that. We've traded shifts, and covered for one another a bunch of times. That's no big deal but not showing up and not calling in. It's just not like her. She would have called if nothing were wrong. I'm worried."

"Really?" I asked, still not looking up from the net.

Realizing I wasn't anywhere near involved in the conversation or paying any attention to her concerns, Jennifer let it go. She leaned over to kiss me goodbye. "Doug asked if I could come right over. See you tonight. I love you."

"Love you, too. Drive safe."

I looked up long enough to see Sierra leading the way off the boat, as she did whenever either of us left. Jennifer loved driving the truck, especially with Sierra hanging out the side window. Told me they were dude magnets. She talked about getting a bumper sticker made up that read *Big Truck, Little Tits*. Neither of which was particularly true. *Little Green* wasn't that big, and Jennifer's beautiful breasts certainly weren't small.

******

Larry came over that evening saying, "Between the three of you, it looks like you've put together a pretty good crew. But if you don't mind me making a suggestion, you might want to consider adding a pinhead."

"You think we need one?" Travis asked for the both of us.

"I do," said Larry. "Running all night, fishing all day, running home, cleaning and restocking the boat, supply runs, re-fuelling, then having to turn around and do it all over again for the overnight trips—it's brutal."

We had no idea how brutal. "Any suggestions?" I asked.

"Funny you should ask," Larry said with a smile. "I think I know just the kid."

He explained that the kid's dad owned and operated one of the top charter boats in the harbor—the *El Queso Grande*—a beautiful 80-foot Ditmar/Donalson, custom built for executive charters. Her reputation was impeccable and she was always the first boat booked for the season. Never ran anything less than two-day trips, and commanded top dollar. The problem was that the kid—Brian was his name—had been working that boat every summer vacation since he was nine. He'd reached the age where young men start to think they know more than their parents, and being confined together within just 80 feet, things had reached the boiling point. In fact, Brian's dad had privately asked Larry to help him find another ride for the summer. So, here we were…Larry's first choice.

As Brian walked down the dock, he didn't look old enough to have been working that long. "How old are you?" I asked suspiciously as Jennifer welcomed him aboard.

"Fourteen."

"Larry says you've been working over there," I nodded towards the big boats, "for the past couple seasons."

Brian looked me in the eye before answering. Not a challenging look, but a look that demanded attention. Once he had it, he continued. "Actually," he said politely, "I've been working the *Grande* all my life. My dad owns it."

"So why do you want to work for us?" I asked. "Hell, we're nothing compared to that boat."

"Size don't matter," he said, getting Jennifer's interest. "Crews are what make the boat what it is…or isn't." We were watching him closely. Travis and I both nodded slightly in agreement with what he'd just said. The kid was smart and experienced. "I've been decking since I could walk," he continued. "I can help you guys out. I just can't work for my dad another season." He was up front and honest. He didn't look down or away from any of us. He spoke clearly and with conviction. This was a kid way beyond his years. I knew immediately he'd fit in with us, but looked over at Jennifer and then Travis before saying anything. They both nodded.

"You want to take a look around? Go ahead, check things out. This is Jennifer, Travis, and I'm Corey." He shook my hand. His grip was strong and firm. Working hands.

"Do I have the job?" he asked trying to look me in the eye, yet wanting to avoid seeing any rejection there.

"What do you think, guys?" I said, already knowing their answers as I looked from Jennifer to Travis.

She extended her hand. "Welcome aboard."

A mischievous little smile came into Travis's eyes as he extended his hand to Brian. I watched Brian's hand disappear and was impressed when only a slight cringe showed through his clenched jaw. Travis was letting him know the pecking order right from the get go.

With that, our crew was set. Travis and Brian headed into the engine room. Jennifer, Larry and I headed over to the *Grande* to find Brian's dad. Larry introduced us over the transom of the big Ditmar, and we were immediately invited on board. Another massive hand soon enclosed mine for another crunching experience. *I've got to start squeezing a tennis ball or something*, I thought to myself. *This shit is getting old. What is it with these guys and their vice-like grips anyway? Can't they feel my fingers splintering like toothpicks?* But like Brian, a few minutes earlier, I kept a straight face and took it like a man.

"I've been watching you guys through the glasses just now, talking to Brian," his dad said. "Looks like you're taking him on."

"We wanted to talk it over with you first." Giving him the due respect he'd earned.

That caught the old man by surprise.

I continued. "He's your son, and we're not about to put him on without knowing where you stand."

"I appreciate that," he said approvingly. "What did you say your name was again?"

"Corey. Corey Phillips. And this is Jennifer Comstock."

"I've already talked to both Lloyd and Larry about you guys taking Brian this summer. They say you're all right. Green, but okay. They like you. Larry even thinks you might be able to pull this charter business off." He looked out at the frantic activity going on all around them. The season was gearing up and every crew was scrambling to take care of last minute details.

"That's encouraging," I said, somewhat sarcastically.

"Brian's a good kid," he said, changing gears. "Just growing up is all. He's a hell of a deck hand. Can smell fish. Good with people, too. Knows how to run a deck. I'm going to miss not having him, but figure it's best for us both if we have a little time apart."

"So you're okay with him working for us?" Jennifer asked straight up.

He glanced off toward some distant place before answering. "I'd appreciate you taking him under your wing this summer. Knowing he's working one of the boats will keep him off the streets. Like I said, he's a good kid. But you know how it is...having a father for your boss at fourteen just isn't going to cut it. Can't treat him like a kid anymore. He's becoming his own man."

"Yes, sir," I said, "I understand completely." And I did. Raging teenage hormones and authority are a volatile mix.

"I expect you to work his butt off. No slacking. Someday he'll be running his own boat, and I don't want no Daddy's Boy taking over when I retire. You understand?"

"Yes, sir," we chimed.

"He's got a sixth sense when it comes to fish. Like I said, he can smell the damn things. Swear to God he can. We've been out trolling and all of a sudden he'll run up to the wheelhouse and tell me to circle around. Nothing on the meter. No birds. Nothing. But then, sure as shit, we'll get bit. It's happened more than once. Says he can smell the oil from the bait when they've been feeding." Brian's dad shook his head slowly, lighting up another cigarette. Holding it up, he rolled his eyes. "I can't smell shit...smoking these all my life...but Brian can smell 'em. Anyway, don't do him any favors. He's old enough to pull his weight, so work him hard and true. That's all I ask."

There was a touch of sadness in his voice. He knew his son was growing up and things between them would never be the same. "If you guys ever need anything out there, don't hesitate to give us a call." With that, he shook our hands—crunching mine again, just when it had quit throbbing from the initial mauling.

Heading back to *Vintage,* Jennifer noticed I was rubbing my fingers as we walked down the dock. Larry had stayed on board with Brian's dad. She smiled. "What is it with you guys and your macho handshakes?"

"God, if I only knew," I said. "I've got to quit meeting people or I'm not going to have any feeling left in my fingers."

"Pussy," she said, giving me a shove and taking off running.

"I'll show you pussy!" I yelled, chasing after her.

＊＊＊＊＊＊

Our crew was set and our boat was ready. Fish had been taken by the long-range boats 250 miles south-southeast of the point—still out of range for us, but they were moving up the line, getting closer.

The next few days were some of the happiest I'd ever known. I thought of Jennifer, *Vintage,* and how everything had somehow miraculously come together. The endless days of backbreaking work to bring the boat back to life...seeing her taking shape...Jennifer and I growing closer with every passing day. I woke up early feeling as if I was living a dream. I lay there without moving or opening my eyes.

Sierra stretched her legs, glancing up to see if it was time to get up. Hearing her move, I opened my eyes and smiled at her. She thumped her tail a couple times, laid her head back down, closed her eyes and fell back asleep. Jennifer stirred under the quilts. None of us were morning people.

A couple of hours later I heard Travis and Brain talking as they climbed on board. "Get up, boss!" Travis shouted down the companionway. "We need to go over our tackle situation."

Jennifer rolled over, nestling her head into my chest. "You ready?" I whispered into her ear.

She moaned. "Let's go somewhere for a couple of nights. We've earned it. I want to sleep in, have breakfast in bed, make love all day, and not even think about boats for awhile."

I ached to have her all to myself all day. "You're on. I think I know just the place."

She tossed her hair back in a tussled mess and threw her arms around my neck. "Can we leave right now?"

I left her in the shower and went to tell my crew.

"What's up, boss?" Travis asked as I came into the galley. "You've got a shit-eating grin on your face."

"I'm thinking about running up to Catalina for a couple days."

"What about the tackle? We've still got to top off the tanks. And we need to make a grocery run—"

"All excellent points," I said cutting Travis off. "Let's run over to the fuel dock right now and top her off. We can pick up what we need in Avalon and stock the rest of boat when we get home. What do you think?"

"Sounds good to me," Travis said. Looking over at Brian, "we can work on the tackle on the way to Catalina."

"Let's do it," Brian said looking at me, "say when boss."

"You take her Travis."

Beaming, Travis climbed into the engine room. A few seconds later the big ole' CATs roared to life. A small plume of white smoke, followed by lots of water pouring out of each respective exhaust. They sounded good.

Travis climbed up into the wheelhouse, stuck his head out the starboard window and nodded he was ready. Brian and I tossed the bow and spring lines on board. Then untied the stern lines. Holding on until Travis gave another nod. Flipping the lines off the cleats, we stepped onto the swim step as he put her in gear.

After topping off all four tanks, Brian asked, "Do you want pick up any bait?"

"I don't think so. Let's not even think about fishing. Plus, I doubt if any of the paddies are holding this far North."

So we steamed past the receivers, out past Point Loma and made a right hand turn towards Catalina. The run up was smooth. We were in behind the island before a light westerly wind could begin to put some spray over the bow. An Avalon Harbor Patrol Officer met us, as they do all vessels, at the entrance of the harbor.

"Welcome to Avalon. Nice boat." The officer said, pulling along side of us. "You folks looking for a mooring?"

"Yes, sir. We are." Jennifer answered the officer.

"How many nights are you staying?" the handsome young officer asked, flashing Jennifer a big smile.

"Two," she told him.

He looked her over. "No problem. We've got a couple cans open right by the casino. How long is your vessel and what are your doc numbers?"

"505-099 and she's 60 foot."

"That'll be $64 for both nights. Mooring number two-four-eight. Second row in. Right next to the casino," he added and pointed toward the west side of the harbor. "Enjoy your stay," he said, pulling away after we paid him. He tipped his cap at Jennifer.

She giggled. "I think I'm going to like it here," Jennifer said teasingly. "That was one cute officer."

"So you like a man in uniform?" I asked, getting an idea.

"Absolutely. Especially one as cute as he is."

Brian started sulking.

"Hey, Brian," I asked, "think we should get some uniforms?"

"No way, Skip. We're fisherman, not cops," he said as he shook his head at the departing patrol boat. *A little jealous.*

Jennifer laughed. "You know I love you guys just the way you are. All I'm saying is that he looked handsome in his uniform."

Brian and I exchanged looks.

"She sounds mutinous," I evaluated. "What say we toss her over? See if she floats."

She gasped and backed up. "Don't even think about it."

We both turned on her, grabbing her before she could scoot away. I had one arm between her legs and one wrapped around her waist. Brian lifted her from behind with his arms under hers. "You're going over."

She squealed and laughed at the same time, trying to twist away, but we had her firm. "Don't you dare!" she managed to get out between gasps.

Brian kicked open the transom door with his foot, and we carried her screaming onto the swim step.

There were no other boats around. Conditions were safe; so on the count of three we tossed her in.

She came up laughing hysterically. "You're both going get it!" She threatened as we idled away.

I looked over at Brian. I could tell he couldn't believe we just tossed her in. "Can you handle the mooring lines?" I asked him.

"Yea, sure. No problem," he said.

Pulling off my t-shirt, I dove in after her. The water sent an instant chill through my body, but it wasn't cold. About 68-degrees. After the initial chill, it felt good after having been in the sun all day. I came up for air right next to Jennifer. A big mistake. She immediately shoved my head back down. Forcing a mouth full of salt water down my throat. I came up again gagging, backpedaling away. Waving her off.

"O.K. O.K." I pleaded. "We're even,"

"Not even close. She slid gracefully up next to me and wrapped her arms around my neck, "but it looks like you could use a little mouth to mouth."

The perfect beginning to our stay in paradise.

******

Instantly, the island became one of our favorite places. Walking around Avalon was like stepping back in time, fifty years. The quaint shops, and family-run restaurants were charming. The place had aura about it that was captivating. It felt as if time had passed it by. Leaving only the best of a bygone era. The palm-lined streets were filled with old bicycles and electric golf carts. Not the ones you'd see at a nice country club, these were working carts. Each painted or decorated in unique ways. Some had four seats, but most, where the rear seats once were, had wooden platforms and racks. There wasn't a car in sight

Our couple of days there flew by. Travis and Brain met a couple of girls in town and we never saw them again. Alone on the boat sitting in the cockpit, we watched the sun dip behind the old bell tower. The lights flickering on, as a quit stillness filled the air.

We melted into a world of our own. The reflections within our eyes danced into the night. We'd come to realize that we were no longer traveling alone. This thing called life was something we'd be sharing together forever. It was so complete. So encompassing. It transcended consciousness and left us humbled in the realization of how truly lucky we were. Making love that night, we fell asleep knowing we'd found our way home.

******

Towards the end of our run back to San Diego, Jennifer and I eventually found ourselves alone in the wheelhouse when the guys went below to get things ready for docking. As we rounded the point and headed into the harbour, we knew the trip to Catalina was just what we'd needed. A perfect couple of days before the season. The guys had gotten lucky with the girls they'd met. Brian didn't want to talk about it around Jennifer. He still had a little crush on her. Travis had too much class, but not seeing them for two nights, it was written all over their faces when they climbed back on board a few minutes before we were scheduled to shove off. Jen and I were both happy for them. Nothing like a little R & R before facing months of endless work.

I pulled her back, slowing to five knots as we entered the marina. Jennifer leaned over and kissed my cheek. "Thank you," she whispered.

"For these past couple days, but most of all, for being you."

I loved her beyond words. "I'm nothing without you."

She smiled. Her eyes filled with joy. Putting her arm around my waist she added, "Thank goodness the guys are below. If they heard us talking like this, they'd puke."

Speak your truth quietly and clearly and listen to others, even the dull and ignorant, for they, too, have their stories.

Chapter 8

Shortly after we tied up, Larry and Lloyd came down the dock. "Your timing couldn't be any better. The fish moved up and are within a hundred miles of the point...a long run for an overnight trip, but doable. It's time for you guys to go work."

On the way home, Travis and Brian had gotten all our gear ready. The tackle was lined up across the back of the wheelhouse, filling the 48 stainless-steel rocket launchers C-fab had built and installed. It was an impressive array of equipment. All Shimano.

"That looks good," Larry complimented the boys, looking up at the array of rods and reels, all full of new line. "Really good."

Brian was busting at the seams. He said proudly. "We've got everything covered, from 12 to 80 pound."

Lloyd nodded. "I've got a full truckload of supplies and groceries," he said. "Mind giving me a hand?"

"That's why I'm here," Brian said proudly. He jumped over the rail, showing off for us.

"Damn kids," I muttered jealously, at Brian's fluid, youthful mobility. How was he so young?

Jennifer laughed. "Impressive. When you turn forty, I might have to think about trading you in for a pair of twenties." She gave me a peck on the cheek before following Brian up the dock to help offload the supplies.

******

Our initial charter was slated for departure at 2200 hours. Lloyd arrived and was sitting comfortably across from the galley, watching as we finished putting the stores away. "Almost wish I was going with you, Corey."

"Why don't you ride along with us? That's a great idea."

He answered with a smile. "I appreciate the offer, but I've done my time out there. Trust me, I'll be perfectly content sitting here on the beach waiting for you every night with a fresh load of groceries."

"At least come with us on this first trip," Jennifer pleaded. Lloyd shook his head.

"Well, you know the invitation is always open," I said. "Anytime, any trip. We'd love to have you."

Travis came into the salon and caught the last part of the conversation. "What? Are you nuts? Inviting the old man is just asking for trouble." He sat down next to his dad. "You think he's tough while the boat's tied to the dock. You ain't seen nothing until he gets some swells rolling beneath his feet—turns into the original Captain Bligh." He gave Lloyd a friendly glance. "Hell, that's why I joined the Guard…just to get away from him."

"Boat looks good." Larry said, looking around. "Your group should be here in a couple hours. I've got you set up with the bait receivers. You're on 30 days net with them. Same with the fuel dock."

"Thanks, Larry…for everything."

Fishing albacore from San Diego is unlike any other fishery in the world. When the fish arrive within day range, the place goes absolutely nuts. A new concentration of fish had been located that morning about 75 miles south of Point Loma. The word spread like wildfire. Guys were calling in sick to work from here to Santa Barbara. It was as if someone was ranging the dinner bell. Southern California anglers wait for these fish all year. Albacore are simply the fish for locals. At 75 miles, the schools are well within overnight range, and on the eve of our first charter it made me think the Gods were smiling on us.

Jennifer was just putting the last of the soft drinks into the refrigerator when Larry arrived with our first charter group. After introductions, Jennifer showed everyone their staterooms. Travis and Brian helped them with their gear.

Larry pulled me aside, walking down a few slips away from the boat. "You're going to be fine. Treat them well. Let them know your game plan and keep them informed throughout the day. Don't worry about the fish. Just make sure everyone is working hard. You can't control the bite, but you can control the service. That's all you can do." I nodded, as he continued. "Most clients will understand if you don't catch fish. They'll be disappointed, but they'll understand as long as you take care of them. Do a first class job on the things you can control. Make sure they're well fed. Plenty of cold drinks and snacks. Keep a fresh pot of coffee going all day, and talk to them. Let them know what you're doing—communication and service. Everything else will take care of itself. Just do the best you can out there."

"I didn't think I'd be this nervous," I confessed.

"You'll be fine," he assured me, patting me on the shoulder. "I've talked to a couple of my other guys and they're aware this is your first trip. If you get into any trouble give them a call on 19. Other than that, stay off the horn. Just listen and learn."

"Anything else?" I asked.

"You know where you're going?"

"I was listening this afternoon for anything I could use. Looks like the bulk of the bite was just inside the double 220. That's where I thought we'd start at first light."

"The 220 sounds fine, but if you want my suggestion, follow the lights of boats like the *Prowler* or the *Pronto*. These fish can move out of an area in a heartbeat. Those boats were on fish all day. You know they're overnight boats, like you, so they have to fish within range. The last thing you want to do is to follow some multi-day boat. Then you're totally screwed. They don't know you from Adam and they don't want to know you, so you're going to have to play it smart. Stay about three miles behind them. Don't crowd 'em. If you stay behind Buzz or Allan, come dawn, I promise you'll be where they think the fish are going to be. From there, start reading the signs and work the area. At least you'll know you're in a good place to start the day. If the fish are still at 75 miles, that only gives you about six hours to make it happen. You can't be running all over the place, your start point is critical."

I was grateful. "That I know. Thanks for the advice. Anything else?"

"That's about it. Make sure you go over your safety procedures with the guests when you get back on board."

We shook hands and walked back to the boat. Larry wished everyone a good trip as we fired up the mains and eased the *Vintage* out of the slip. It was exactly 2200 hours.

From the marina, it was a short twenty-minute run out to the bait receivers. I idled up to the line up of boats. More than twenty sport boats were already tied up, scooping bait, and another dozen sport boats and a couple dozen yachts were in line. I glassed through the dark, looking for the *Prowler* or the *Pronto*. I couldn't find either boat. A rush of anxiety surged through me. Travis and Brian were in the wheelhouse with me. Jennifer was below with the clients. *Just breathe through your nose*, I told myself. The scene was electric. The best sport fishing boats in San Diego, grouped together in a tight mass, jockeying to hold position. A few of the early arrivals had already topped off their tanks and were heading out of the breakwater, their aft deck lights fading in the distance. I felt another wave of anxiety.

"What if the *Prowler* and *Pronto* are in that group?" Travis asked.

I had told Travis and Brian what Larry had suggested on our way out to the bait receivers. They both agreed it was good advice.

"Then we'll find our own fish," Brian said, without looking away from the scene in front of us.

Bright deck lights reflected off the water. Dozens of anglers looked over the rails as crews worked hard brailing bait. It took about a half hour for a space to open up where we could slide in for our turn. Brian suggested we bucket the bait instead of using the nets. We were going to need about 30 scoops of anchovies. Using the buckets takes about three times as long as using the nets, but the bait never leaves the water, doesn't get compressed and lives better. The problem was that we were holding up space.

One of the guys working the bait dock was shaking his head as he approached us. "You can't do that shit with all these boats in line," he barked.

We were almost done. They'd been so busy with all the other boats that it had taken him that long to get to us. Because we'd slid into a spot at the far end of the inside receiver, we'd almost gone unnoticed with all the sports in line. I handed my bucket to Travis and told him to keep bucketing. Walking towards the dockhand, I said, "No problem. Appreciate you letting us do it this time." Extending my hand, I handed him a Franklin. "I'm Corey Phillips."

He took a good look at the bill before stuffing it into his pocked. His tone instantly friendly. "Anytime," he said. "I'm Zach."

He looked over the boat. "Heard you and some girl were bringing her back. You guys did a nice job. Listen," he said, looking back along the packed dock, "I've got to get back to it, but if you guys want to keep bucketing, next time try sliding in after the rush."

I nodded, thinking we might not be able to get bait if the supply ran short.

"Don't worry," he added, sensing my concern, patting his jeans pocket where he'd stuffed the hundred-dollar bill. "I'll make sure you're covered. If we're light, just hang back. I'll call you in. If need be, we can poach some of the good stuff from the long-range boxes. I don't want everyone to start using buckets. We'd be screwed."

This looked like the start of a very mutually beneficial relationship. The good stuff Zach had referred to was bait that had been cured—bait that had been caught and placed in the receivers for at least a week. The longer it had been since being caught and transferred, the better the bait. Normally only the high liners—the high profile long-range boats—had access to the good stuff. The fresh bait was passed off on the overnight boats and yachts. Our hundred-dollar tip had secured us prime bait for the future.

"Nice move," Travis commented, finishing up the bucket brigade.

The *Prowler* pulled up for bait, as we were finishing.

"Perfect timing," Brian said.

Holding onto the bowline, Brian stayed in position until I leaned my head out the wheelhouse window. Travis was on the stern line. "All right," I told him, "let 'er go."

With the flick of his wrist, Brian undid the final half hitch he'd left around the cleat and flipped the bowline up and over the rail. He slid along the side, joining Travis at the stern cleat. I kicked the bow out and away from the receiver. The stern close enough for them to easily step onto the swim step.

"All yours," Travis said, stepping onboard. I took the boat slowly away from the receivers and over the north side of the channel, and waited for Buzz to finish baiting up and run past us. We were just clearing the point when he passed us. Following Larry's advice, slowly bringing *Vintage* up to speed, I allowed Buzz to get a couple miles ahead and stayed well off his stern. He was on a 165 degree heading, right for the double 220, a high spot about 78 miles from San Diego. I smiled, guessing where he was going to start. At 10 knots, we'd be on the same spot at gray light.

Jennifer had our people settled in for the night. As we cleared the point, she joined us topside. We were charged, excited to be running our first trip. None of us could sleep. Jennifer gave me a little squeeze on the shoulder and said she was going to hit the sack. I wanted to stay at the helm until we had cleared the Coronado Islands. "Travis, I'll take first watch. I'll wake you up at 1:00. Get Brian at 3:00, and Brian, you get me up at 5:00. That's two hours each."

"What about me?" Jennifer demanded to know. "I can take a watch." We all looked at her. "What? I'll take a watch. Just like everyone else. I can do it."

"We know you can, but you've got to work the galley all day tomorrow by yourself. You'll need your sleep."

"So what!" she snapped back. "I'll take a watch, just like everyone else."

"Fine—you'll get no argument from me. Jen...midnight 'til 2:00; Brian...2:00 to 4:00; and Travis...4:00 to 6:00. Pointing to the twin deck lights a couple miles ahead of us, I added. "Everyone...we're trailing the

Prowler. Stay this far behind her. Unless she changes speed, we're synced up. No one on the radio, please. Radar is set for six miles. I don't want any targets coming within a mile of us. Understand?" Everyone did. I pointed to a spot on the chart. "Travis, this is where I want us to be at first light."

"Got it," Travis said, looking over the chart. Brian and Jennifer indicated they understood as well.

"Check the engine room every shift. The alarms are set, but I want visuals."

"Understood," they all chimed together.

"Just be damned careful when you go down there alone. I want visuals after you've got your relief up. Understand? Don't go wandering around the boat without someone else being awake." Nods all around. "Last item…the most important thing to remember…while you're on watch, you are responsible for the lives of everyone on board. If you can't stay awake, don't try and be a hero. Wake me up. No one falls asleep on watch. I mean it. Not on board this boat. Don't even close you're eyes when you take over. If you're starting to nod off, wake me up."

"You want me to wake you when we get there, or just put out the jigs and start trolling?" Travis asked.

"You'd better roust me. We should be on the spot right at dawn. Jennifer, we'll get you up as well to start breakfast."

"This is going to take some getting used to," Jennifer said, giving me a hug and climbing into the only double bunk in the wheelhouse.

Travis said goodnight as he took off his deck boots and slid into one of other bunks. Brian climbed under the dashboard into the honeymoon suite. Only the faint glow of the red instrument lights illuminated the now quiet wheelhouse. I had the VHF on at low volume, listening for any last minute dope. Most of the sports worked in code groups. It was a nightmare trying to chase them through their secret channels. A few of the boats had two meters (which Lloyd had insisted we install), so we were in the game if I could keep up.

"Manny, you there?"

"Yeah, Rich. Switch to the other one." In an instant, they'd be gone. Even with the scanner, I couldn't keep up with all the traffic.

A few minutes later. "Buzz?

"Good evening, Alan. Drop down a couple."

Yeah, now we were cooking, I thought to myself.

"You there?"

"Yeah."

"Switch to the other side."

What the hell does that mean? The other side? I was trying to track these guys through 88 channels when Travis bellowed from his bunk, "Shut that damn thing off. I can't sleep."

So much for finding out any dope on the VHF about where the fish were going. When you're out there every day, you get into a rhythm with the fish. You develop a feeling for what they're doing…how they're feeding…how the wind and water conditions are affecting them…the direction they're moving in…what they were feeding on. Moon phase, time of day, current breaks—it all figures in. But this was our first night out, and we were more or less running blind.

During peak season, the overnight fleet averages over 60 sport boats and another couple hundred private yachts—all leaving the harbor about the same time. But it's amazing how quickly all those deck lights spread out and disappear in the vast darkness. If you're rested, night watches can be a good thing. If you're not, they're hell. It's just you, the boat and the sea. When everything's running smoothly, you have time to think. The hardest part is staying awake. Even with all the adrenaline running through me this first trip, the last hour was brutal. I started seeing things on the radar screen and on the horizon that weren't there. Just inside south island, we ran into an area of concentrated phosphorous. I was watching the bow wake when all of a sudden a couple of dolphins streaked out from under the pulpit, leaving behind a trail that looked like torpedoes.

At midnight, I woke Jennifer up. She moaned, rolled over and reached up to pull me into bed with her. I stood back.

"Come on," she whispered, still half asleep, "hold me."

"Come on, baby, you've got to get up. It's your watch." I hated forcing her out of bed. It was unnatural because all I really wanted to do was climb in with her. *I need to rethink this watch schedule, so we can have a few hours in bed together, instead of having to roust her.* "Come on, honey," I whispered again in her ear, giving her a little kiss at the same time, "you've got to get up."

"Kiss me again," she moaned, still half asleep.

"Can't—it's your watch."

"Grump!" She said, pulling a sweatshirt over her bare breasts.

She was so beautiful. Standing up, she pulled on a pair of sweatpants over her lace panties. It was all I could do to keep my hands off her.

"You're so beautiful," I said as I watched her flip her hair back and twist it into a single mass of golden strands. "This sucks."

She agreed, giving me the eye as she finished tucking her hair into a bun. "And to think...." she said, sliding seductively past me into the helm seat, "that was only the beginning of what I had in mind." She paused for effect. "You blew it, bucko."

"Maybe we should switch the watches around," I whispered.

"You think?" was all I got back.

"Keep an eye on those lights," I said, pointing to the *Prowler*. "I want to be close to him in the morning."

Jennifer settled in and checked the gauges. "Did you check the engine room before you woke me?"

"Roger. Make sure Travis and Brian do the same when they take over."

"No problem, El Capitan," she said, saluting. She was not a morning person and this wasn't even close to being morning.

122

"I can't get that picture of you standing there in your panties and pulling up your sweats, out of my mind," I told her, climbing into the bunk. "I could hardly keep my eyes open until them. Now all I want to do is pull your sweats down and kiss every inch of you."

Fully alert now and on watch, she said, "Knock it off and go to sleep!"

But there was no way I was going to be able to fall asleep now. "How about I help you with your watch?" I suggested. I got up, slid in behind the helm seat, and put my arms around her.

"You're so bad," she whispered.

Softly kissing the back of her neck, nibbling on her ear, I felt her initial resistance slipping away. The salt spray mixing with her hair smelled so good. Shiver bumps shot up her spine. She cringed as I bit a little harder. I knew there was no stopping now. I grabbed a quick glimpse at the radar screen, making sure there were no targets before slipping my hands under her sweatshirt to find her nipples. They instantly hardened at my touch. She moaned as I caressed them. I turned the seat around, pulled up her sweatshirt, and surrounded one of her perfect breasts with my mouth. Passion flooded us in waves. Pulling her sweatshirt over her head in one quick motion, she cupped my head, guiding me from one nipple to the other. Arching her back, letting go of my head, she reached down to pull off her sweatpants and panties.

Her hands were instantly back around my head, directing my mouth from her breasts down her flat stomach into the waiting warmth of her womanhood. She was pure nectar. Her lips were swollen, her juices flowing. Arching her hips in perfect rhythm with my tongue, she filled my mouth with liquid joy. Her initial orgasm swept over her like a gentle wave, slowly building until it reached the point where she knew she was going to come, no matter what.

She moaned softly. "I'm going to come again. Oh, God that feels so good—I love you so much."

Sending shivers down my spine, feeling her coming in my mouth was pure ecstasy. I stopped moving and stopped licking, but held my mouth perfectly still over her, letting the waves of her orgasm settle. I could have stayed like that forever.

After a couple minutes of pure bliss, she whispered, "I want you inside me."

Rock hard, I slipped inside her swollen wetness in one easy motion. Gently contracting and relaxing her vaginal muscles, she massaged me into her being. There was no other motion, just me deep inside, her senses heightened to the point of not needing anything else. I was so turned on; it only took her whispering in my ear, "Come inside me. Come with me. Now. Please come with me! Oh, God, I love you so much."

Those words echoed in my mind as she tucked me into the bunk. I also vaguely recall her whispering, "Get some sleep."

******

I heard screaming. It ripped through my dream like bullets. "We're bit! We're bit! Jig strike!"

Why are you shaking me? I didn't do anything. My mind struggled to make a connection.

"We're bit, Goddamn it!" Travis yelled again. "Get up, Skipper."

Still three-quarters asleep I rolled over Jennifer who, at some time during the night, had gotten back into the bunk with me. I pulled on my jeans, T-shirt and boots, and staggered down the ladder. We had a double jig strike—both rods were still screaming. The first of the passengers came running out of the saloon. Brian had already brailed a scoop of bait before I hit the deck. Fish were charging the boat, foaming on the bait.

"Forget the troll fish!" I yelled as another passenger came running out of the salon, half-dressed.

"Take this!" I yelled, handing him the live bait stick I'd just baited. Reaching up to pull another bait stick from the rack, out of the corner of my eye I saw him lean back and throw it with all his might, his thumb nowhere near the spool. An albacore boiled on the bait as soon as it hit the water. The line snapped with the sound of a gunshot, blowing up somewhere deep within the back lashed spool.

The rest of the charter group was pouring into the cockpit.

"Grab the trolling rods!" Travis shouted at them. They all went for the bent rods. "Get those other rods in! Wind like hell. You might get bit on the retrieve!"

Brian was still throwing bait. We were still sliding. Sure enough, one of the trolling rigs went bendo. We had a triple going on the jigs. Fish were boiling in our wake and we still didn't have bait in the water. I grabbed another bait stick out of the racks, and it got hammered immediately. After setting the hook and adjusting the drag, I handed it off to the nearest passenger. The reel was screaming.

"What do I do?" he yelled.

"Nothing. Just hold on!"

I grabbed another bait stick, which again, was bit instantly.

"This is it, gentlemen!" Brian yelled. "This is what we came for! Make it count."

We were bit in the grey, still five miles from the double 220, but who cared. We were in fish. Brian brailed another scoop. Instantly, the water exploded as fish crashed the corner. None of the passengers had a clue what was going on. I handed off another baitfish.

"It doesn't get any better than this!" Travis yelled, sticking the first jig fish as it came to the boat with a jubilant scream, Travis dumped it into the kill sac, high-fiveing the angler. Two of the bait fish got crossed and before either of us could get there, we lost both fish.

"Stay in front of your fish, you guys!" I shouted. "Don't just stand there and pull! If your fish moves, move with it!" We needed more help on deck. It was a madhouse. Every bait that hit the water got bit instantly, but at the rate we were dumping fish, it wasn't going to last. "Jennifer! Jennifer!" I screamed. "Get down here! We need help!"

Travis guided a novice angler down the stern, following the fish around the corner. Brian kept a constant stream of threes and fours on the corner. Baiting another rod, I threw it on the spot, but no bite. I handed it off to another one of the passengers.

"Keep your thumb lightly on the spool. Let the line go as the bait swims away. If you get bit, flip the lever." I glanced over to see where the jig fish were. "Don't try to stop the fish with your thumb. It'll never happen."

Before I could show the guy where the lever was, he got bit. He burned his thumb as he applied full pressure to top of the spool, trying to stop the fish. He pulled away instantly, back-lashing and breaking off yet another fish. "Ouch! Goddamn it!" yelled the angry angler, shaking his hand and glaring at the white-hot streaks on his thumb. "Shit! That hurts."

The second jig fish came to gaff, but the one we'd hung on the retrieve wrapped another baitfish, burning through the 20 pound like butter. Brian was putting the chum right on the spot. We hung one more baitfish. But with so many fish breaking off and streaking for the depths, we couldn't hold the school. Travis stuck the last fish, and it was over as quickly as it had begun. It was one of the most aggressive bites you'd ever see—fish crashing the boat, eating everything in sight—but we ended up with only a handful of fish on the boat. We should have had at least a couple dozen. I was pissed…Fishing 101.

******

"Travis."

"Yeah, boss."

"Would you jump up top and spin us over this area in a couple of figure eights?

"Roger."

"All right, listen up, you guys." I focused my attention on our passengers. "That was tuna fishing—it doesn't get any better than that."

"Where did the fish go?" asked one of the guys.

"They sounded. We dumped so many fish; it put the rest of 'em off the bite. Brian did a good job holding 'em as long as he did," I added, giving

Brian a nod of approval, "given we were dumping fish as fast as we hooked 'em. Next time, you guys have to be ready."

"If there is a next time," Brian griped. He hated losing fish.

"We talked you guys through the drill last night," I continued, "but let's go over it again. When we get bit, first guy out takes the rod that's bit. The rest of you pull in the jigs. Who got bit on the slide?" I asked. One of the guys raised his hand. "Good job on the crank, man."

"That was my first albacore ever," he said, grinning from ear to ear. He was ecstatic. Two other guys said the same thing and high-fived each other.

I realized they were pumped. To them, the stop had been a huge win. Having no idea how close we were to a bonanza, they were happy just getting their first albacore. Taking a deep breath, I relaxed, realizing all eyes were back on me. I took another deep breath. This trip would not be about the numbers…it was all about the experience.

"Okay, okay," I said. "For a first stop, you guys did all right." High fives again. They were still on the rush. "Like I was saying, first guy out takes the bit jig rod. The rest start winding in the other rods. I looked at the guy who had caught his fish on the slide.

"What's your name?"

"Scotty," he said immediately.

"Like Scotty here did last time."

Another one of the passengers high-fived Scotty, having no clue how badly we blew that stop. Another deep breath. There was no reason to pop their bubble. "Next stop," I said looking over at Brian, "he'll be throwing bait while Travis and I get you set up with bait sticks. You've got to learn to just barely keep pressure on the spool until you get picked up. That way, the anchovies can swim. You want the bait to look as natural as possible. If you put too much pressure on the spool while they're swimming, you'll keep jerking them back. Chances are, they won't get bit."

Looking for the guy with the burned thumb, I kept going. "And when you do get picked up, let the line run off the spool, count to five and then put the thing in gear… like this," I said, showing them how to do it. I demonstrated the simple action a couple more times. "At some stops, we'll only get one shot at these fish, so you have to be ready, and you have to move quickly."

"Everything happened so fast," said one of the passengers.

"Yeah! That was crazy," added another.

"That's tuna fishin'," I said again.

"It was awesome!" Scotty exclaimed.

"We can troll for hours without a bite, but when it happens, you've got to be on it." They were all nodding like they understood. "Just remember, your thumb is God when using conventional gear."

I helped Brian get the last of the jigs back in the water. "From the smell of it, guys, it looks like Jennifer's got the bacon frying and breakfast started. So eat up."

They were ecstatic.

"Brian. I'm going topside to see if we can round up another jag of fish."

"That sucked, boss," Travis said as he slid out of the helm seat, allowing me to take over.

"No shit," I agreed. "I can't believe how many fish we lost. What a cluster fuck."

"Those guys are clueless," Travis continued. "Those fish wanted to die."

"I know. They were there."

"We're just going to have to hook and hand everything from here on out. Don't hand off a rod until you're hooked up."

"Roger. That was nuts."

"Yeah, it was." I was staring at the up and down. "Any marks?"

"Nothing."

"Didn't think there would be, but it was worth boxing."

"Agreed. What did you guys put out?"

"Same as what you started with. Black and purple Zuckers on the outside. Yellow and green, Mexican flag and a cedar plug down the middle."

Brian came into the wheelhouse. "We got bit initially on the flag, then one of the outside rigs. Then that guy on the slide got picked up on the plug."

"Got to love black and purple. Let's stay with this pattern for awhile and see what happens."

"Sounds good," Brian said. "You want me on deck, skipper?"

"What do you think?" Respecting his judgment.

"Absolutely."

We were in an area where we could see half-dozen boats within about a two-mile radius. We got bit again fifteen minutes later—a single jig fish and a couple of bait fish. Nothing like our first stop, but we continued picking off a fish every twenty or thirty minutes. They were biting the feathers as well as the plugs. With an occasional baitfish thrown in, we were building a pretty good count for the morning. Most importantly, our group was having a good time, and that's what really mattered. They were pumped up...and thankfully the fish were cooperating.

After Scotty landed another fish, he high-fived Travis joyfully. "This is the best trip of my life."

"Glad you guys are having fun," Travis answered him, adding, "and it sure helps when the fish bite like they're doing this morning."

On deck, I'd been soaking another bait for a few minutes, but knew the stop was over. "Wind 'em up," I told everyone. "Let's see if we can find a bunch that wants to bite a little better."

Scotty was chattering in Travis' ear. "It's not just the fishing. It's everything you guys are doing, and that little honey you got in there cooking. Jesus, she's hot. When she smiles, you just want to rip her fuckin' shorts off." Travis looked over in time to see me flinch. I wanted to tell the guy to watch his mouth, but Jennifer was inside and hadn't heard him, so I didn't say anything.

Travis had my back and stayed cool. "Yeah, I know what you mean," he said, turning away from the guy to set the jigs.

"She's the best looking thing I've ever seen on a boat. And…can she cook! What a delicious breakfast."

Taking another deep breath Travis said, "Well, that's why we hired her."

"Man I'd have hired her even if she couldn't boil water. She's smokin'."

"And, she's spoken for," Travis said, turning to face him, "so be cool. Show a little respect."

With Travis looming over him, the guy got the message. Backing up a step, he said, "Didn't mean anything, man. No offense. Just wanted to let you guys know that you're doing a great job."

"Thanks," Travis said, following me up the ladder, leaving Brian to watch the jigs.

"Everything going to be all right down there?" I asked Travis as he came into the wheelhouse.

"Yeah," Travis said, shaking his head. "He's wearing a gold necklace for Christ sake. What a wingnut. Figure this is as close to a beautiful woman as he's been in awhile."

"At least one he hasn't had to pay for."

"So true," Travis nodded in agreement.

"Don't worry, boss. Jen can take care of herself."

"I know…."

We picked off a few more fish under a single bird, making a tight circle while Brian threw a lot of bait, but that was about it. An hour later, Jen came up with lunch. "Here you go, my Captain," she said, handing me the plate.

I thanked her. "Why so happy?" I asked.

"Everything," she said, giving me a little hug. "Nothing…I don't know…just being out here." She looked around. "Being with you…working the boat…catching fish…I don't know. It's our first day. Everything's going well and I'm just happy."

"Those guys giving you any trouble?"

She shot me a sideways glance. "No, not at all. They're fine. You know, just guys being guys. They're having a great time."

"Good," I said, avoiding her eyes. "If anyone ever gives you any shit down there, about anything, you let me know, okay?"

"Why? What's up?" Her instincts sensed something.

"Nothing," I said, shaking my head. "Nothing."

But she wasn't biting. "Come on. Something's up."

"Really. It's nothing."

Reading me like a book, she waited. I knew I had to tell her, but tried to say it in a way that didn't make me sound like a total jerk. "It's just you're down there alone with all those guys. And, well, you know…like you said, guys are guys."

"Are we a little bit jealous?" she asked with a big smile, putting her arms around me again.

"No, it's not that."

"It is!" she said, beaming. "You're jealous. I love it! That's so cute. I like you being jealous."

"It's just that I don't want anyone taking advantage of you. You're so outgoing and friendly. I don't know…maybe one of those guys might get the wrong idea."

"You're so cute." She gave me a kiss.

"I just want you to know that you don't ever have to take any shit from anyone down there, okay?"

"Listen up, buddy boy," she said, balling her hands into fists, assuming the worst looking impression of a heavy weight contender I'd ever seen. "Don't you forget, I've been slinging hash for years. I've dealt with every type you can imagine—from drunks and addicts, to GQ's and arrogant rich pricks that think their money or good looks can buy them whatever they want. Trust me…I can handle myself." She threw a few air punches and challenged me. "Come on, give me your best shot," she joked, continuing to pummel her invisible opponent.

Her energy was so good, so full; she dissolved whatever worries I was having. I found myself being drawn into her magical spell. "You're on, baby," I said, accepting her challenge, "and may the best man win." I spun out of the helm chair in mid-sentence, catching her completely off guard. Before she could react, I had my arms wrapped around her waist, lifted her off her feet and in slow motion, body slammed her onto our double bunk. Simultaneously screaming and laughing hysterically, she couldn't catch her breath. Tickling her sides, she was all mine. "Take that, you wench! How dare you challenge my authority? This is mutiny. Punishable by death. Death by tickling."

She was barely able to stop laughing. "Stop! Stop! You win," she shouted. "I give. I give."

"You are hereby ordered by the captain of this fine ship to be tickled until dead."

"Please…please stop. I give…you win," she begged through her hysterical laugher. The next thing I knew, her lips were around mine. She was still grasping for breath as she sucked the air out of my lungs. "I love you so much," she said, still catching her breath. Her tongue caressed the area between my teeth and the inside of my lips. "I love you. I love you. I love you."

Her kisses melted me. Our bodies fit perfectly together, and I relaxed into her embrace. Suddenly, grabbing my balls and squeezing just hard enough to let me know she was in total control, she proclaimed, "Now you're mine! Your ass is mine!" She was cracking herself up, tightening her grasp ever so slightly.

"Whoa! Easy!" I pleaded. I couldn't move. She had me.

Grinning from ear to ear as she stared me down, she asked with a twinkle in her eyes, "Give?" A slight pause brought just a fraction more pressure, and we both knew it was over.

"Okay, okay," I said, surrendering. "I give." For admitting defeat, I received another big kiss, as I felt her let go, I whispered meekly, "But you cheat."

"All's fair in love and war," she said, grinning. Still laughing, she sprang up and extended both hands over her head triumphantly. "Champion of the world!"

Being the poor loser I am, I couldn't help myself. "You just got lucky, that's all."

"Any day. Any time. Any place," she challenged. "You're mine...all mine." She bent over and kissed my crotch through my jeans. "Those nuggets are mine!"

"If this is losing, then I never want to win again." Running my hands through her hair, and feeling her hot breath through my jeans, I couldn't believe how lucky I was to be loved by such an incredible woman. "I love you, lady."

"I know," was all she had time to say.

One of the reels suddenly screamed, as the line ripped off the spool.

"Jig strike!" Brian screamed from below. "We're bit! We're bit!"

Vaulting up, I pulled back the throttles and put the boat in neutral. Turning to Jennifer, in my most stately voice, I announced, "There's just no substitute for knowing how to read the signs." It was a blind strike.

We both knew I had nothing to do with it.

"Yeah, right!" she said sarcastically. "If I hadn't distracted you for a couple of minutes, you probably would have turned the other way and run right past these guys."

Leaping in front of me, running toward the stairs and grabbing the handrails, she disappeared down the ladder. Her feet never touched the stairs. Following right behind her, I stopped in amazement as she grabbed a bait net and brailed a scoop across the stern in a perfect fan. She looked like she'd been doing it her entire life. In fact, she'd only watched Brian do it this morning for the first time. She nodded, more to herself than anyone else. Smiling, she turned back toward the bait tank and pulled out another scoop for a repeat performance.

"Go to threes and fours," I instructed her, seeing the fish behind the boat. She smiled and nodded.

After the pick we'd had all morning, this jag of fish really wanted to go. They charged the boat, eating all the trolling jigs on the slide. They were foaming on the chum. We were in the middle of a wide-open bite with fish boiling everywhere. Every bait that hit the water was bit instantly. Jennifer reacted instantly in rhythm with the fish. Going from threes and fours to throwing ones and twos, the fish were exploding on the spot. She had them eating out of her hand.

Every one of the passengers was hung. As soon as one fish came in, we'd hand them a fresh one. You didn't even have to cast—just flip a bait on the spot and you were bit. It was one of those incredible bites that never seem to end. Looking up, I saw the *Prowler* off our starboard side about a half a mile away. Catching a glimpse of white water in its wake, I saw it was still trolling. Though Larry had said to say off the horn, I ran up to the wheelhouse and grabbed the microphone. "*Prowler…Buzz…Vintage.*" I waited. Short pause. A slightly hesitant voice came back.

"*Prowler* returning."

"Buzz, we're into a wide-open bite over here. It looks like these fish are staying with us. You're only a couple minutes away, and if you'd like to slide in on this, I think these fish will transfer over."

There was no pause this time, as Buzz, the owner-operator of the Prowler, came right back. "Is that you? The yacht, just below us?"

"Roger. About a half-mile inside your starboard."

"Gotcha. How long have the fish been up?"

"About twenty minutes," I told him. "They're still going WFO. You're more than welcome to give it a shot."

"Don't want to screw things up for you," Buzz said, turning towards us.

"Can't," I assured him. "Even if they sink out, our guys have had plenty, so come on in."

"Okay. We're headed your way. Appreciate the call."

"No problem," I said, double-clicking the microphone.

"Vintage."

"Returning."

"What's your name?"

"Corey...Corey Phillips."

"Thanks again for the call. See you in a few."

I heard Buzz double-click and headed back down to the deck. It was still pandemonium in the cockpit. Travis and Brian both had gaffs in their hands. Brian was reaching for a fish; Travis was standing by with bent rods on either side of him.

"Jennifer, we've got another boat coming in."

Looking up, she asked, "You call them in?"

"Yeah."

"Sweet move."

"When they get close, start brailing again. Try and hold them up."

"Got it," she said.

"Gaff! Gaff!" screamed one of the passengers along the rail mid-ship. Grabbing a gaff and running up the rail, I stuck the fish. The angler screamed with joy. I led the fish back to the stern, and dumped him into the kill sac, just as the *Prowler* slid on scene.

"*Vintage...Prowler* calling," crackled the muted radio from inside the wheelhouse.

I leapt up the boarding ladder two steps at a time. "Yeah, Buzz," I said into the microphone.

"Where do you want us?"

"How about going stern to stern?" I suggested. "Lay in on the high side and just slide on down."

"Roger!" The excitement in his voice reverberated through the speaker. "We've only been able to scratch a few fish. It's been a tough day for us so far."

"Get in as close as you can. Doesn't look like these fish are going anywhere."

Buzz skillfully maneuvered his boat perfectly into place, less than half a boat length off our port corner. The deckhand on his tanks started brailing. The fish didn't even flinch. Every rod on the *Prowler* went bendo as soon as the bait hit the water. It was too cool for school. Fishing just didn't get any better than this. We continued hanging fish as well. With both boats keeping up a steady stream of chum, the fish were foaming. We were getting close to limits.

"Brian, you got any idea how many we have?" I asked.

"I've been too busy to count, skipper," he said, "but we must be getting close."

"I'm scraping the bottom of the tank," Jennifer chimed in. We were down to our last couple of scoops.

"Travis, how many in bag before this stop?"

"Twenty-two," Travis answered instantly. "We've dumped in at least another two dozen," Looking down at our feet. "Plus all these fish on the deck. The bag's plugged."

The last dozen fish had been unceremoniously dumped on the deck. We were awash with albacore. Our saltwater wash-down hose was running along the inside port quarter, keeping the decks from becoming too slippery to fish.

"Counting the ones on deck, plus the…let's say forty already in the bag…we're there."

California limit is ten albacore per person. We were fishing Mexican waters where they didn't give a shit how many you killed, but we were an American vessel, offloading in San Diego—so we ran by their rules. With a party of six and a crew of four, we were legally entitled to a total of a hundred fish for the day. I wasn't worried about going over because, as far as the six passengers knew, our limit was sixty. I told them before we left that on this boat, crew didn't count for kill limits.

"We've got seventeen on the deck, skipper," Travis announced.

"Okay, guys!" I shouted at the passengers. "Three more fish and we're limited out. Make these last ones count!"

Three of them had already stopped fishing. They were exhausted. These fish can kick the crap out you. The three were leaning against the tackle locker, cold beers in hand, watching their buddies getting worked. Looking over at them, I got the thumbs up. They were exhausted and smiling, with satisfied looks on their faces.

"I've never seen anything like this in my life," said one of the older gentlemen with a distinctive mid-western drawl. "Back home, the biggest fish I'd ever caught was only about twelve inches. I can hardly move my wrist."

"Me, too. These things kill ya'," another one chimed in. "I'm dead. I can hardly hold my beer." There was laughter all around.

"Me, too," said the tired third angler. "Hey, skipper, can we go home now?"

"As soon as these guys get their fish in," I assured them. "We're a little over seventy miles from the point, giving us an ETA of about 7:30 tonight."

"Coming down!" shouted one of the guys with his rod bent double, half in the water, half out as he followed his fish around the corner. Travis was by his side.
"You're doing a great job. Keep your rod tip pointed down as you go around the corner," Travis coached him.

"Keep it down?" the exhausted angler muttered. "I couldn't get it up if I had to."

"Aw, come on. You've almost got him," Travis coaxed.

"I'm dying," the angler said. All his buddies laughed. He looked over his shoulder just as the fish took off on another run. Immediately snapping his focus back to the water.

"Get around the corner, quick!" Travis yelled. "Come on. You've got to pay attention. The fish turned and you've got to go with him. Fiberglass beats mono every time. Don't let the line rub under the boat."

There's nothing like fishing albacore. When they go off, it's incredible. The fish had already dragged the exhausted angler completely around the boat a couple of times. That was one tough fish. As they disappeared again up the side rail, I turned back to his buddies. "As soon as they get this last fish in, we'll fire up the barbecue for the ride back. How does fresh albacore and steak sound to you guys?"

"I hate fish," said the guy with the midwestern accent, "but those steaks sound good."

"We've got plenty. Just let Jennifer know how you like 'em."

"Charred, blood rare," he answered. "Is there any other way to eat meat?"

Travis stuck the last of the fish, giving us our limit. Jennifer had tossed out the last few deans. By this time, the *Prowler* had drifted off our corner about thirty yards. Fish were still boiling off her stern. We'd been able to pass off the school exactly the way it was drawn up in the manuals. I was savoring the moment, when the Charter master—the same guy who had been drooling over Jennifer's ass—and the last guy hooked up and blurted out, "They stole our fish!"

"We've got our limit. It's time to head for the barn."

"Yeah, but that's bullshit! They came in here and stole our fish." He'd been so busy pulling on his last fish that he'd only just noticed the other boat.

"I called them in," I said.

"You what?

"I invited them in. We're plugged, man. Look around you. We've got our limit." He didn't say anything. "We're over seventy miles from home and we've got to get rolling. This way, instead of just pulling off the school and leaving the fish, we were able to help those guys out by passing off the bite."

"I think it sucks!"

Mister Personality, I thought. I took a deep breath through my nose. The day was too perfect to let a jerk wad like this guy screw it up. I continued to reason with him. "What if it had been the other way around today? What if we were the ones not getting bit? Wouldn't you want them to call us in?"

"Fuck 'um," was all he said, turning and stomping into the salon. I could hear him telling Jennifer that he wanted a cold beer.

"What an asshole," Travis muttered softly.

We looked at each other, shaking our heads. "To quote his immortal soul," I said, "fuck 'um." We both started laughing.

No one could have asked for a better day. Perfect conditions, grease calm water, no wind and plenty of fish. I headed up the ladder as Travis helped Brian pull the fish out for filleting.

The ride in was uneventful. Travis and Brian were cleaning and bagging fish for two straight hours before they could scrub down the boat. They were both exhausted when they came into the wheelhouse. We were all tired, but I told them to catch a few hours.

"ETA to the point is 7:20. It's noon now. Travis, I'll wake you at 3:00. Get Brian up at 6:00 and roust my ass before we get to the point…say, around 7:15. Okay?"

"Roger," was all Travis said, kicking off his boots and lying down. They were both asleep before their heads hit the pillows.

Jennifer came up a little while later, after cleaning the galley. "All the passengers are asleep. You okay, or do you need me to take it for awhile?"

"I'm fine," I told her. From behind the helm seat, she put her tired arms around my shoulders and rested her head against mine. "That was a great lunch. Thank you. Grab a nap. We're not running tomorrow, so I'll be okay. I'm waking Travis at 3:00."

She gave me a kiss on the cheek and crawled into our bunk… instantly asleep.

Alone on the helm after one of the best days fishing I'd ever seen in my life, I was feeling pretty damn good. I loved running the boat. I loved feeling her purring contentedly under me. Despite being physically exhausted, I was wide awake, my senses alive and acute from the adrenaline high that still lingered from the last stop…the soothing, steady sound of the CATs humming below deck…the bow waves washing off the hull. With everyone else on board asleep, I could just settle in and feel the boat. The afternoon westerly had started to push up a little wind chop. Nothing much—just a little top to what had been grease all day. *Vintage* arched up over the small wind swells, making slight corrections on the pilot as she came down, tossing her bow proudly, arching toward the next swell. She was like a puppy playing at the water's edge, a young colt prancing across a spring field. She was running happy. Our first day out, and everything had gone according to plan. Relaxing for the first time all day, I took another deep breath and let the rich salt air fill my lungs. I glanced over the gauges before sitting back to enjoy the ride home.

That evening, when we were nearly finished scrubbing the boat down, Larry stopped by to see us. Even though the charter master had been a dick, they tipped us $400 dollars and evidently gave Larry a glowing report about what a great trip they'd had. I didn't give a shit about that prick's opinion. People like that think being a big tipper makes up for being an asshole.

Larry could see I wasn't listening to him. "You paying attention? I've got an important one for you guys tomorrow night." He made eye contact with me to make sure I was paying attention. "A group of lawyers from L.A. and some bigwig judge and his kid. These attorneys must be trying to impress this guy because they faxed me a shopping list of stuff they want on board."

"Like what?" I asked.

"Nothing fancy." He said, "They just want to make sure you've got plenty of cerveza in bottles and lots of mixers. They're bringing their own booze."

"I'll make sure Jennifer takes care of it."

Larry handed me their shopping list. "Nice job with Buzz," he added. Word traveled fast on the docks.

"Glad it worked out," I said, trying to sound nonchalant. "Seemed like the right thing to do."

"I guess!" Larry said. "Buzz was pretty impressed. He said he almost didn't come back when you first called 'cause he didn't have a clue who you were."

"I could hear the hesitation in his voice. Can't blame him."

"Yeah, well, anyway," Larry, continued, "he said for a new kid, you did good. Might even have potential."

"That's nice to hear."

"You listen to all the weekend warriors out there squawking on the box, wanting to know where the fish are, never giving anything back or thinking for a second that some of us are actually trying to make a living out there." Pausing, Larry pulled off his worn, sun-bleached Chargers cap and scratched his head. "You did good, kid. Just keep quiet and before you know it, they'll bring you in. Maybe not this season, but soon enough. How was everybody?" he asked, referring to the crew.

"Good. Everyone did good."

"Boat run okay? Any problems?"

"No. Everything was good. She ran fine. We're just beat. Haven't gotten used to the hours and sporadic rack time. It was hard getting up this morning." Larry shook his head and smiled. "What are you smiling at?"

"Hell," he said fondly, "I bet it was."

"Was what?" I asked him, not getting it.

"Hard," he said, laughing out loud at his own clever play on words. "Who wouldn't be, bunking with Jennifer?"

Our friendship was forming in typical male fashion. "And this whole time I thought you were gay," was the best comeback I could think of.

"You wish," he said, both of us laughing out loud.

"You're a lucky man, my friend," he said, his voice turning serious. "A very lucky man."

"I know."

"Don't blow it," he said, looking toward the city lights. "A lot of women tolerate being fish wives, but would never do what Jennifer's doing for you."

"I know. She's something special."

Jennifer came out of the salon just then. She stopped and looked at us. "What are you boys doing? Just standing around here, gabbin' like a couple of old hens? Snap to. We've got work to do." She was holding a trash bag of dirty linens from the staterooms.

"Here's a list of things the charter wants for tomorrow night," I said, taking the bag and handing her Larry's list.

Glancing over the list, she smiled. "No problem. Larry, can I get you a beer or coke or something?"

"I'd love a Coke. Thanks."

"Coming right up. Honey, do you need anything?"

"No, thanks. I'm good."

"I'll say," she said, heading back into the galley for Larry's drink.

"I'd better be getting over to the other boats," he said. "Have one more multi-day leaving at midnight."

"Why so late?"

"They wanted to spend some time downtown at the strip joints before leaving." He rolled his eyes. "About the last thing I'd want to do is hang out in a nudie bar before climbing onto a boat with a bunch of guys for three days." Jennifer came out and handed him his coke. "Thanks," he said taking his drink. "I'll see you guys tomorrow night. Take care." He shook hands with me and started to leave.

"Hey, what about a hug goodbye?" Jennifer asked.

At first he hesitated, not knowing what to do. She walked over to him, reached out and gave him a big hug. He was a bit surprised, but loved it nonetheless. Slowly, he stepped back and looked at her. "Thank you."

"My pleasure," she murmured, giving him one of her infectious smiles. As Larry walked away, she came over and took my hand. "I like him. He's a good man. You can feel it."

"I liked that you gave him a hug. You could tell by the way he reacted it had been a long time since a beautiful young woman had wrapped her arms around him."

"I know. I've got a feeling he's been through a lot. His friendship won't come easy," she reflected, "but if does, he'll be one for life."

Our first official charter was in the books. Lloyd arrived to pick up Travis. Since we had the next day off, they decided to head home for the night. Brian did the same. Jennifer and I were alone on the boat. After everyone left, we leaned against the railing and watched the activity going on around us.

Most of the charter boats running that night had already left. A few crews on the faster, private yachts were still hustling around, busily taking care of last-minute details. There were still a fair number of people scurrying up and down the docks. The bite was on and albacore fever was high. Listening to the deep rumble of diesels firing up around us, the sounds blending with the other boats—many of them likely running hard for the receivers—we appreciated the fact we had the rest of the night off.

"Has it dawned on you just how fortunate we are?" Jen asked without looking over at me. "I mean, do you realize how truly blessed we are?" She wasn't looking for a response. She didn't need one. She knew I knew how lucky we were to have one another. She was just letting her thoughts run free. I put my arm around her shoulder, pulling her into me. "Watching Larry walking away alone, it really hit me," she continued thoughtfully. "I'm so lucky to have you. All my life I've been pretty much self-sufficient. Hell, growing up with a couple of older brothers, I had no choice. But as time went on, I guess it became more of a habit than anything else."

"What did?" I asked.

"Being alone, being independent. Doing stuff on my own. Living alone and learning how to take care of myself. After awhile, it just became kinda automatic."

We'd never had one of those past girlfriend/boyfriend talks. Neither of us had felt the need to. I could tell that something was brewing inside her, so I kept quiet, allowing her to continue formulating her thoughts.

"It's not like I've never had a boyfriend or anything. I've had my fair share, but none of them ever made me feel like this." She leaned her head on my shoulder, wrapped her arm around my back and pulled me close. "I've been in love before, a couple of times—but never like this.

This is so much more. I can't explain it, but I can't imagine living without you."

Her words flowed with her thoughts. I leaned down and gave her a long, soft kiss on the side of her head. My lips lingered on her hair, content never to move.

"It's not like I planned on being alone," she continued. "At first I didn't think anything of it. After awhile, you just are." She let out a long, deep sigh. Her words hung in the air. "Then you came along and changed everything." She looked up, holding my gaze with her intensity. "Promise you'll never leave me."

Looking back into her eyes, she was so experienced... yet still so innocent. So pure...so full of knowledge, of life, of passion. Her soul shone through her fears—completely open, sublimely vulnerable.

"Never, not in a thousand years will I ever leave you. You're my life."

"Did you ever see Zeffirelli's *Romeo and Juliet*?" she asked.

I shook my head.

"We'll have to get it. One of the best films of all time," she continued explaining what happened. "When they first met and fell in love, Romeo had climbed a tree up to her veranda and was professing his love for her when they heard someone coming. Juliet told him he had to leave, and he said, 'O, wilt thou leave me so unsatisfied?' And Juliet asked him, 'What satisfaction canst thou have tonight?' Romeo says, 'The exchange of thy love's faithful vow for mine.' And this is where it gets really good. Juliet looks at him and says, 'I gave thee mine before thou didst request it: And yet I would it were to give again. I wish but for the thing I have. My bounty is as boundless as the sea. My love as deep, the more I give to thee, the more I have, for both are infinite.' Most romantic lines ever written," she stated unequivocally. Her face radiated a huge smile. "Touching souls," she whispered softly. "Feels pretty good. Wouldn't you say?"

"I could never go back."

"To what?" she asked.

"To living without you. I don't want to ever take another breath without you beside me."

A couple of guys rambled by pushing a dock cart loaded with rods, tackle boxes, duffel bags, ice chest...the works. "How was the fishing today?" one of them yelled at us.

"Pretty good," I told him.

They stopped. "Oh, yeah? How many?

"Limits."

"No shit!" the other one blurted out. "Where were you?"

"Seventy miles. Just north of the double two-twenty.

"Thanks, man," they said together, pushing to get their cart back in motion.

"Good luck," Jennifer added as they moved off.

After awhile she said, "I've learned something. Thoughts are important, because they determine what you do, and what you do becomes your habits, those habits make up your life."

"Never thought about it like that, but it makes sense."

"I thought so, too."

"I've always figured a person is what he gives."

"Exactly," she said. "And what controls that? Our thoughts. We are what we think."

"Only to a point. Without actions, thoughts don't mean squat."

"But they do. Without the thought behind the action, there wouldn't be any activity."

"Agreed."

"So that's when I realized that the stuff I had been telling myself about my fear—you know, of being rejected, being hurt again, whatever—was keeping me from doing what I really wanted to do."

"And that was…?"

"Telling you how attracted I was to you…how much I wanted to get to know you."

"But you did."

"Finally," she said, rolling her eyes. "It only took me forever."

"Thank God you did."

She laughed. "God only knows if I'd waited for you to make the first move, we'd still be alone." I nodded in agreement. "But it scares me to death to think I'd gotten so used to being alone that, at one point, I was thinking of just letting you walk. That's the thing about thoughts—they can take on a life of their own, and if we're not careful, before we know it…we become what we're thinking without even knowing it."

"I never thought about it like that.'

"My point exactly." She looked out at the lights reflecting off the water, nodding to herself.

"Don't sweat the little stuff...but those little things add up."

"Exactly."

We didn't say anything else for a few minutes. Sierra came out of the salon and curled up at our feet. Content, she fell asleep. It had been a long first day for her as well. For some reason she felt as if she had to lick every fish that hit the deck. We all cracked up watching her trying to paw those fish and get them to stop flopping around long enough for her to lick 'um. We figured it was the retriever in her. Bottom line...she was dead tired.

"Your timing was perfect," I said after awhile. "Absolutely perfect. It couldn't have been any other way. I was done with women. Getting my heart ripped out and stomped on. I'd pretty much resigned myself to just getting laid once in a while without any attachments, no commitments. But after awhile, those encounters leave you pretty empty."

She looked at me knowingly.

I continued, "You obviously didn't know why and were smart enough not to ask. But you knew something was wrong. You trusted yourself, listened to your instincts." I squeezed her a little tighter. "And thank God you did. Look where we are now."

"Come with me," she whispered. "I want to give you something." Taking my hand, we stepped over Sierra and she led me into the salon. "Sit here," she instructed, indicating the couch, "and take off your boots." I started to ask her why, but she touched my lips with her finger. "No more talk tonight. Just trust me."

"I do with my life," I answered softly, as she hushed me.

Turning off the lights, she headed across the salon into the galley. As I took off my deck boots and socks, my eyes started to adjust. I could barely make out her silhouette against the reflection coming from outside the galley windows. Leaning back to the sound of running water, I closed my eyes. A few moments later, I felt her gently lifting my foot, then slowing lowering it into a pot of hot water.

"Shush…" she whispered before I could speak. "Shush...." Caressing my foot, she began cupping the hot water in her free hand and spreading it over the top of my foot until I got used to the temperature. As she caressed, she lowered my foot deeper into the hot water until it was up to my ankle. Then she began massaging my foot…long, slow, gentle strokes. The muscles in my foot surrendered to her touch. The more I relaxed, the more pressure she applied. Thoughts slipped from my mind and the pleasure became all consuming. Just when I thought it couldn't get any better, she lifted my foot out of the water and slowly began pouring something onto it. It was coarse, but didn't hurt. At first, I had no idea it was salt. She began to massage my foot again, working the salt between my toes, around my heel and up my ankle.

"Oh, my God," I murmured.

"Shush," she whispered again, kneeling in front of me. She continued with the salt rub until I lost track of time. Eventually, she dipped my foot back into the now warm water. Rinsing off the salt, she wrapped my foot in a towel and gently patted it dry. My thoughts began to focus again. I thought she was finished, but I couldn't have been more wrong. She kissed my foot, whispering, "Now for the good part."

Resting my foot in her lap, she squeezed lotion into her hands and began massaging again. The contrast between the salt and the silky smooth lotion was beyond description. My foot felt weightless by the time she wrapped it in a towel and lowered it to the floor. Picking up my other foot, she began again. I'd forgotten I had two feet. By the time she'd finished, I could have walked across water. My entire being felt as light as a feather. Like a newborn baby.

"Thank you," I whispered before she shushed me again.

"Shh," she said, unbuttoning my jeans and slipping them off me. Lifting her blouse over her head and undoing her bra before slipping out of her shorts and panties, she stood motionless for a moment, naked against the soft back- lit reflections of the night. Her beautiful silhouette radiating love. A tear formed and slid down my cheek. Overwhelmed by her grace... her beauty... her complete surrender and unbridled giving. My soul weeping in gratitude for her gifts beyond words.

She pulled up the blanket lying over the arm of the couch and lay beside me. The warmth of her body filled me with more love than I'd ever known possible. Our lovemaking was soft and tender, unhurried and complete. The previously unquenchable fires of our burning passion quietly and peacefully surrendering to the inner knowledge we both shared—we were going to be together forever. No longer was our love driven by need and unfulfilled hunger. We were bathing in pure bliss, total contentment, and absolute fulfillment. Grace filled our hearts with love, and our tears melted together as we came. I hadn't cried this since the day she first held me, but I didn't care. I'd never known such love.

Kissing the tears off my cheek, she laid her head down on my chest and listened to the steady beat of my heart. Heartbeat for heartbeat, we lay in each other's arms. We slept, cradled in the wings of an angel, surrounded by the pure joy of being in love.

Exercise caution in your business affairs, for the world is full of trickery. But let this not blind you to what virtue there is; many persons strive for high ideals, and everywhere life is full of heroism.

Chapter 9

The morning dawned with a strong southern wind from a tropical storm blowing off the tip of Baja. Tugging at her dock lines like a rambunctious colt, *Vintage* woke me out of a blissful sleep. Jennifer was still out. I closed my eyes again, settling into harmony with the boat's rhythm, letting the memories of last night wash over me like warm rain.

"What are you grinning at?"

I must have been lying there with a shit eatin' grin on my face when Jen opened her eyes. "Just reminiscing."

"Umm," she said, scooting closer, one hand sliding across my chest heading south, her lips nibbling on my ear. Shivers shot up my spine.

"You'd better behave yourself," I pleaded, cocking my head in a feeble attempt to escape, "or—"

"Or what?" she challenged, half-blowing half-whispering in my ear, her hand finding my hardening penis.

Sensory overload…it was too much. I spun into her. I forced my shoulder and exposed ear down into the sheets, rolling away from her now aggressive onslaught of desire. Nothing makes for good sex better than good sex…and last night had been incredible. She'd awakened hungry for more. Grabbing a full hand of her luscious mane, gently but with enough force that she had to respond, I forced her head down to expose the back of her long neck. Before she knew what had hit her, my mouth had a firm hold on that sensitive area just below and behind her ear. She squealed in an uncontrollable mixture of pain and pleasure as I worked my way toward her spine, half-biting, half-sucking. She was squirming to get away, but my body was on top of her. The harder I sucked, the harder she squirmed and the harder I got. In a matter of just a few moments, we were both totally turned on.

"Fuck me," she pleaded. "Please. Right now." With her face in the pillow, she spread her legs, arching her beautiful little ass up just enough for me to slide into her with one motion. She was completely aroused, soaking wet, her vaginal lips flushed crimson with desire. "My God," she said, breathing hard, "you feel so good." It felt as if we hadn't made love in months. Her cheeks absorbed my every thrust. Penetrating in and out as far as I could. Her contractions were instant. She grabbed my penis, her vaginal muscles demanding I come with her. I was already ejaculating deep inside her before she begged, "Come with me. Oh, God!"

I collapsed next to her. Both of us tried to catch our breath. The whole thing had taken less than a few minutes, but we were breathless.

"God, I love you. Thanks for that." Taking a couple more rapid breaths, she said, "I'm starving. Feed me...now that you've had your way with me."

******

Whitecaps were topping the ever-increasing wind chop in the harbour, making it look like a giant bag of popcorn. It was pretty, except for the fact that we were running another trip that night. "If it's this bad in here, it's got to be miserable outside," Jennifer said on our way back from breakfast. She loved driving the ol' truck with Sierra sitting contentedly between us. Looking out across the harbour from the passenger window of the truck, I agreed. I didn't say it, but knew it was only get worse. If the wind kept up, which it was supposed to do, the trip tonight would be a rough one. By the time we got back to the boat, Travis and Brian were already there. We made the short run to the fuel dock, where we topped her off and stocked her up with the extra supplies mentioned on Larry's list, which Travis had picked up the night before. We really didn't need the extra fuel, but I with the weather starting to kick up, I actually wanted the extra weight on board.

I hated the wind and it hadn't let up all day. By the time our charter group arrived, it was blowing a steady 20 knots inside the harbor. I didn't even want to think about what it was like outside.

"From the looks of things, it's going to be a little bumpy out there tonight," I told them as they gathered around the cockpit. They didn't seem too interested. I felt like I was talking to myself. "Life jackets are under the salon couch, as well as inside the wheelhouse. This isn't an E ticket ride at Disney, so watch yourselves. Once we leave the receivers, I suggest you stay inside, but if you do come out here into the cockpit, do it with a buddy system."

"Can I get another beer?" one of the guys barked at Jennifer.

"Yeah, me, too."

"Make it three."

"Anyone else?" Jennifer asked politely before fetching their beer.

"Anyway, we'll get you up at first light," I added.

None of the passengers even looked at me. Travis gave me a smirk and nodded as I told him and Brian to cut us loose. I remembered Larry's final words: *A bunch of lawyers are kissing some judge's ass. Evidently, he's a big shot, so be careful out there tonight.*

We pulled out of the slip at exactly 2200 hours. Loading up at the receiver, we were on our way to the grounds 45 minutes later. As soon as we cleared the south jetty, the full force of the angry seas grabbed us like a toy, slamming into our bow and covering the wheelhouse with a sheet of water.

"Oh, this is going to be fun," Brian said dryly.

Figuring the wind had to be pushing everything up the coast, I decided to shoot high, a full 20 miles north of the numbers we'd left the *Prowler* on the day before. "I'll take her down past the islands, make the turn west and once we clear South Island, I'll wake you up. Okay, Travis?" He nodded in agreement. We wouldn't be following any lights tonight. "Jennifer, you're next, and then Brian."

The four of us were sitting in the wheelhouse together. Only the dim glow of the radar lit the interior. No one was very talkative. Rough weather does that to a crew. Everyone settled in as best they could for the unpleasant night ahead, knowing that sleep wouldn't come easily, if at all. The winds were still blowing a steady 20 knots out of the south, knocking the tops off the 8-to-10 foot swells we were plowing directly into. Thick patches of rain dotted the radar screen, as we worked our way around the Coronado Islands.

The pilot was having trouble keeping up, so I handled the wheel as we passed South Island and made the dogleg turn to starboard, toward the spot some 60 miles south/southwest of Point Loma. The going was wretched. A constant sheet of water covered the wheelhouse. The low cloud, combined with the rain and the fact that we were running under the dark of the moon, made visibility virtually nonexistent.

Thank God for radar, I fought to keep my balance. I was seated and holding onto the wheel with both hands. *This sucks.* I knew the *Vintage* had been through a lot worse. She was a proven veteran, an extremely sea kindly boat, so I wasn't overly concerned about the conditions. I just dreaded the fact we were in for a long, miserable night. Little did I know that our little charter was about to turn into one of the worst nightmares of my life.

Jennifer had told us that she learned the bigwig was a Superior Court Justice of Appeals for the State of California. "Evidently one of the most politically powerful men in the state."

I was glad I'd been especially careful going over the safety procedures and rules with the passengers before we'd left the slip, even though it appeared they weren't paying the least bit of attention. Playing games to keep myself awake, I went over my little speech again in my mind. *There's a pretty good breeze blowing on the outside. It's going to be a little bumpy on the ride out, so please, no one on deck alone after we leave the receivers. I'd prefer it if you didn't even go out on deck during the night, but if you have to, do it with a buddy. Okay?* I got nothing back from the suits except a couple annoying nods, as if to say, 'Like, who the fuck do you think you are to be talking to us like children?' In hindsight, I should have locked them all in the salon and thrown away the key.

Albacore, like any tuna, are always on the move. Sometimes they'll hold behind a temperature break or stay with a pocket of bait for days, but when the water rolls over—like it was doing tonight—it's anyone's guess what the fish will do. Being in the dark of the moon was a plus, but trying to figure out the effects of the warm water being pushed up the storm was tough. Sixty-four degrees—that was albacore water—but the stuff coming up with the storm could be as much as 10 degrees warmer—not good for albacore, but it could hold some exotics, like yellow fin, split tales, dorado and stripers.

There was very little radio talk. Each boat was working its way out through the slop. Rough water makes for a very quiet wheelhouse and no sleep. I could see Jennifer twisting and turning in her bunk, trying to wedge herself into the corner to keep from getting pitched out.

To get to the area where I wanted to start fishing in the morning meant that we'd either have to shoot between North and South Islands or dogleg around South Island. Under the poor conditions, I opted for the longer, safer route—head south past the island, then make the turn west, clearing South Island by a mile or so. The decision would add about thirty minutes and five miles to the run, but the course would keep us clear of any high spots and keep us from getting blown into harm's way if we ran into any unexpected trouble. It seemed like the prudent thing to do. We'd changed fuel filters that afternoon, but with all the washing around inside the tanks, anything could happen on a night like this.

I had no way of knowing that sometime during that part of the run, either just before or just after making the dogleg turn, our Superior Court Justice had decided to get up and relieve himself by pissing over the transom. He never alerted anyone to the fact he was going out on deck.

Suddenly, one of his buddies came bursting into the wheelhouse, scaring the shit out of me and screaming at the top of his lungs, "The Judge's gone! The Judge's gone!" The guy was in a total panic.

"What the hell are you talking about?" I spun around, yelling back at him. I couldn't understand a word he was saying.

"The Judge's gone!"

"What? Slow down and speak clearly!" I demanded.

"The Judge is gone!" And then, as if in a trance, he added, "He must have fallen overboard."

I almost shit my pants. "What the fuck are you talking about!"

"He's not here. He's not on the boat."

I immediately pulled back the throttles, leaving her in gear to help maintain headway. I flew down the ladder, ripping open the stateroom doors, turning on all the lights, counting heads, waking everyone up, and screaming for the Judge. He'd bunked in with his fifteen-year-old son, who hadn't heard him get up to leave their stateroom. Everyone else had been trying to sleep as well. No one knew that he'd gone outside. The bone chilling reality was that the Judge was no longer on board.

Racing back up to the wheelhouse, I was shocked to see how far the wind had already pushed us off our bubble trail in just the thirty seconds it took me to search the staterooms and heads. Jamming her throttles back to full rack and spinning the helm hard over, I immediately swung the boat back around 180 degrees to put us on a reciprocal heading. Once we were lined up and heading back the way we'd come, I reached for the mike. "MAYDAY. MAYDAY. MAYDAY. This is the fishing vessel *Vintage*. Repeat. This is the FV *Vintage*. We have a MAYDAY. MAYDAY. MAYDAY." Travis, Brian and Jennifer were all up, holding on, standing beside me at the helm.

"What do you want us to do?" Travis asked.

I don't know. My heart was pounding so hard I thought it would burst right through my chest. I prayed that another boat following us might have seen him in the water, and then realized that in these conditions, there was no chance of that happening. I called in the Mayday and reported our situation and position to the Coast Guard. In the middle of the night, rough seas, high winds, and no moon, there was little the Coast Guard could do until dawn. And by then, it would be too late. Even a healthy individual in good shape and equipped with a life jacket would have a hard time holding on in these conditions. It was like a washing machine with 20-knot winds. Sixty-four degree water won't kill you, but it'll take its toll in a hurry—sapping strength, energy and resolve as your core temperature drops. I couldn't even imagine the sheer terror of falling overboard with the boat leaving you in its wake, running full rack...hitting the cold churning prop wash...coming up and seeing the deck lights—your only link to life—disappearing in the distance, leaving you totally alone, surrounded by darkness in the middle of nowhere.

I hoped one of the few boats running around the island would hear our Mayday and circle around and help in the search, but I knew most of the fleet had split the islands. Looking ahead, there were only two sets of distant running lights coming our way. I also knew most the fleet ran at night with radios turned way down or completely off—definitely not on channel 16. Way too much chatter to keep the crews awake, and sleep was more valuable than gold.

"What you thinking, Skip?" Travis asked again.

"We'll run up a little further, idle back and swing the light." Looking over at Travis for the first time, it shocked me to see the entire charter party had come into the wheelhouse.

"Sounds good," Travis answered in a hushed voice.

"What did he say?" barked someone from behind me.

"Get them out of here!" I snapped. Desperate to do something, Travis and Brian whirled on the tightly packed group.

"You heard the skipper. Everyone get below. Back into the salon!"

"That's bullshit!" complained someone in the group.

"What's bullshit is that none of you listened to a single Goddamned word he said before we left. He told you not to go outside!" The tension rose.

"He never said anything like that," one of the lawyers snapped back. Turning to one of his colleagues, he demanded, "Did you hear him say anything about that."

"No."

Spinning from the wheel, I yelled at the gaggle of law fuckers. "Get out of my wheelhouse! Right now!" Everyone paused. "Now, Goddamn it!" That did it. Brian and Travis herded them out the door and below.

Within those few minutes, the two boats that were behind us passed by. We were now totally alone. Jennifer hadn't said a word. She was in the port corner staring straight ahead into the blackness. I could actually feel the life draining out of me, the despair pulling me down with the drowning judge. The swells were now directly behind us, picking up the stern, forcing the bow down the face of each wave before it passed under the hull. With every wave, we yawed to one side or the other, gaining speed as we came down its face. Our bow was pushed into the troughs, making it hard to hold course. I couldn't tell how much to compensate for the twenty-plus knots of wind pounding us from behind. The compass was swinging as much as 20 degrees to either side as I fought to hold her true.

If we were ever going to see the judge alive again, I knew we had to retrace our path exactly. *There's no fucking way*, I told myself. With the howling wind ripping the tops off the waves in every direction, our sight lines were almost totally blurred...virtually non-existent. We couldn't see shit. And here we were, trying to find a speck in the middle of nowhere. It was all I could do to hold any semblance of a course. Travis and Brian came back into the wheelhouse, but didn't say a word. No one had to—we all knew it was hopeless.

I'd been fighting the wheel since I'd brought her around, trying to hold her steady, but the harder I fought, the worse it got. Admitting this wasn't working, I forced myself to relax and think. Since finding out the judge had fallen overboard, I'd just been reacting. With no distant lights or fixed bearings, the only thing I had to go on was a gut feeling. Fighting the compass was an act of futility. Forcing my hands to relax on the helm, I closed my eyes and tried to feel the boat. Once I quit fighting her, she settled into as close a course as possible to where I wanted to go. In a few minutes, I had a pretty good sense of how much I had to compensate for the wind. Instead of looking at the compass, I focused on the water just ahead of us and let the boat pick her own headway.

"Give 'er her head," my Dad told me one day when he'd gotten into a blow. "Trust her, she'll know what to do." *But this is different. We're not just riding out a storm; we're looking for a man overboard.*

Reaching up, I pulled back the throttles and we idled to a crawl. Within seconds, we were rolling violently in the trough—worse than before. You couldn't even stand up, never mind look around for a floating head bobbing around. Luckily, Travis had marked our position when I had spun the boat around. At least we had a reference point. "What do ya' think?" I asked him.

"This is all we can do. Run up a couple hundred yards, pull her out of gear and drift over the spot."

"We don't know," I said, confessing one of my doubts, "When he went over. Was it before we made our dogleg turn, or after?" There was no way of knowing. If I guessed wrong, we'd be searching waters that were miles from where he'd gone over. *Chances are we're already miles away. This is insane. The fucking guy's dead.*

We tried pushing ahead for a few minutes, lighting up the boat with all the deck lights, swinging the searchlight around, and sounding the horn, making as much noise as possible. Then we'd go black and silent, shutting down the mains so maybe we'd stand a chance of hearing him calling out if he wasn't already dead. Move, look and listen. With the wind howling, you could hardly hear yourself think. But maybe that same wind would carry the judge's cries for help…if we were downwind, that is.

We repeated the procedure for what seemed like an eternity. In reality, it was a little over an hour. At one point, we thought we'd heard something different from the wind and waves. We all froze, praying it was him, but after a few more minutes, there was no other sound and we didn't see a thing. We boxed the area in an ever-widening pattern and came up empty. It was a hard decision to leave the area, because it was the only possible contact we'd had since we'd started searching, but we hadn't found anything. It's amazing how twisted things can become when your mind starts playing tricks—willing you to see or hear something, anything, besides the water, the wind and the spray. The longer we searched, the worse it got. We were all standing across the console in the wheelhouse. As the minutes ticked off, desperation started creeping in. Fearing we'd lost him, no one said a word.

Suddenly Travis screamed, "There's something! There's something right there!" He pointed to a spot at the furthermost range of the searchlight just off our starboard bow. All eyes were riveted on the area.

"What was it?" Jennifer blurted out.

"I don't know!" Travis answered without blinking or taking his eyes off the spot. "I just caught a glimpse of something."

Time froze. I pushed her into gear and then right out—just enough thrust to inch us closer. Another minute passed. Nothing. Again, I bumped us in and out of gear. Then Brian screamed, "There it is! There it is!"

Sure as shit, the light caught on something foreign, something unnatural. Something was bobbing between the cresting whitecaps and the spray. We pushed ahead. Then, and only by the grace of God, we saw him. His head was just above the angry sea, his white hair plastered to his face. His white hair must have been what caught the light. Travis and Brian were already halfway to the bow. Without hesitation, Travis threw him the life ring when he reached the end of the pulpit. It was a perfect shot. It landed within a few feet from the judge and it drifted right to him, but he let it drift by.

"Grab it, Goddamn it!" I screamed from the wheelhouse, the wind muffling my voice. Without hesitation, Travis kicked off his boots and dove off the bow. Fully clothed, he swam as hard as he could toward the judge. I pushed the boat port main back in gear to bring the bow around. We were being pushed down and away from the two men. Travis hadn't taken time to put on a lifejacket and his clothes were weighing him down. Brian was pointing…Jennifer kept the search light on them.

One of the passengers suddenly appeared, clinging to the handrail halfway up the bow.

"Goddamn it!" I screamed again. "What the fuck are you doing!" He was looking over the side, along with two other passengers. All three of them were squatting down, holding on for dear life as the boat rolled violently.

As I glanced down, Jennifer let the light swing away from the judge. Another jolt of panic shot through me. "Jennifer!" I screamed. She looked up. Immediately realizing her mistake, she brought the light back up. There he was. We shot each other a quick glance. I leaned out the wheelhouse window, screaming, "Get the hell back into the salon!" Reversing direction, they inched their way back towards safety. *What the fuck were they thinking.*

Jen kept the judge dead center in the radius of light. Travis finally managed to reach him. As he put an arm around him for support, the judge instantly went limp, his head sinking below the surface. Brian pulled in the life ring while Travis swam and made another perfect toss. Travis grabbed for the ring with his free hand and struggled to get both the judge's arms through it. The judge was dead weight, barely conscious. The waves were breaking over them and the line started to go taught. I pushed the boat back into gear to keep the line slack. It was all Travis could do to keep him from slipping away. He waved his arm for us to come and pick them up. I was already powering forward, but the boat was bow on, downwind, and totally out of position to attempt a pickup. *Vintage's* bow is over 10 feet above the water line. We would have to take them stern on. In the storm, I had no control of the boat's drift. I knew we'd have to spin around, get the stern pointed upwind, and try quartering directly back into the wind for the pickup. The trouble with backing down in those conditions, against the wind and waves, is that a ton of water and anything else in your path gets sucked directly into the props.

"No matter what happens," I told Jennifer, without taking my eyes off the two men, "don't take your eyes off those guys! Keep that searchlight locked on them! I've got to spin the boat around, so you'll have to follow them as we turn. Understand?"

"I got it!" she assured me.

Finding a bobbing head in the ocean on a clear, flat calm sunny day can be tough. These conditions were anything but ideal. As spotters, Jennifer and Brian's roles were critical in saving now, not only the judge's life, but Travis as well. We were drifting fast, the distance between us increasing every second. Taking my eyes off them to get back on the wheel was one of the hardest things I'd ever done. I glanced at Jennifer, now entrusted with their lives, her eyes were locked on the two half drowned men.

Forcing the boat around, I was amazed at how much throttle I had to put to the mains to get the boat to quarter into the wind. The big CATs roared to my demands without hesitation. The entire boat shuddered as she came around and got pounded by the waves as she settled in an unnatural position. Solid blue water began crashing over the stern, filling the cockpit. Brian jumped off the walk around into the knee-deep water sloshing violently around the cockpit and held onto the wheelhouse ladder rails to keep from getting knocked over.

"Hurry!" I heard him scream from below.

It wasn't going to take long before the cockpit was completely full of water. Backing into the swells, the scuppers were actually acting as scoops. Facing this direction, there was no way for the cockpit to drain. If she filled all the way up to the combing, I wasn't sure she'd be able to recover.

"Come on, man!" Brian screamed again. "We're sinking!"

I maneuvered the boat closer inch-by-inch...starboard in forward; port in reverse...both engines under load. The props were spinning so fast they would have instantly churned the men into mincemeat if a swell hit us at the wrong angle and tossed the stern sideways. Travis and the judge would be sucked into instant oblivion.

Travis was exhausted trying to stay afloat while keeping the limp judge from slipping out of the life ring. He screamed for us to hurry. I could hear the panic is his voice, but couldn't go any faster. The last ten feet were pure agony. After riding up a wave, the boat would come crashing down the back side, the swim step smashing into the water with enough force to split a man's skull wide open. A couple of times the boat rolled over far enough for the high-side prop to break free—screaming, red lining the main—only to come crashing back into the angry water, grabbing full force, all four blades sucking up everything in their path.

The timing had to be perfect. If it wasn't....

We were less than five feet away. As we rode up the next swell, I knew this was it. We were out of time. The cockpit was almost completely full. Travis was beyond exhausted. There was no other option. The boat shook violently as I poured coals to her, forcing her up the front side of the cresting wave. Coming over the top, I pulled the throttles back and she slid down the backside of the wave. The swim step crashed into the trough, burying itself into black water. The two men slid up and over the swim step, into the fully flooded cockpit. In one fell swoop, we had them both on board.

The combing was at water level; we were sinking. Brian had been pulling the bitter end of the life ring line inch by inch, as we had gotten closer to them. Otherwise, the slack could have easily gotten sucked into the props and we would have been royally fucked. As it was, we were still in grave danger. Jennifer leapt into the cockpit to help Brian. They were all awash, level with the sea. It was all they could do to keep from getting sucked back overboard. Jamming the port into forward gear, I pushed both throttles to the hilt. Nothing happened. With her cockpit completely flooded, she couldn't move. Her mains were grinding with everything they had, but she just sat there, stuck in the hole I'd forced her into, screaming past red line. As the props spun at full speed the noise was deafening. The unnatural vibration sent shockwaves through my feet and up my spine. She was tearing her guts out, trying to pull herself out of the death grip. Paralyzing fear shot through me. There was nothing more I could do...nothing any of us could do. We watched in horror as another cresting wave reared up behind us, it's angry white capped fangs leering down at us. The devil himself was poised to crash down in one last backbreaking assault.

After that, everything started to move in slow motion. It was like watching a movie. Frozen in fear, we held our collective breath. Miraculously, *Vintage* managed to pull herself up, away from the wave. Feeling the props tearing at the water, clawing for power and grabbing every once of liquid they could, a ripple of hope surged through me. *But it's taking so long.* She gained strength with every revolution, shuddering to her core, defying the odds. She was reaching out, pulling herself up by her fingernails. *Come on girl,* I whispered. *You can do it.* Inch by inch, she willed herself to move forward, to find strength that defied logic. Ever so slowly, she gained speed as she forced the sea to accept her raging fury. Her raw power churned the water behind her into a boiling white mass of foam. She inched away from the wave. It broke with a roar, crashing down with a fury of its own, just missing the transom. Spray filled the boat.

She'd broken free of death's grip and was now running for her life. *She'd saved ours.* Her bow started cutting a path, clearing a way for her hull to follow. Settling in, picking up speed, she left the angry wave behind us. Running down swell, the scuppers were able to do their job of draining the cockpit. As we came up to plane, I backed off the throttles, allowing her to settle down a bit, closer to her familiar cruising speed. I threw her into autopilot, locking us on a down swell heading. I took a deep breath and patted her on the dashboard. *Thank you, girl. You did good. Real good.*

After I left the wheelhouse, I leaped down into the cockpit. Jennifer immediately threw her arms around me. She was soaking wet and her entire body shook. "I thought we were going to die. That wave was huge. It looked like it was going to break right on top of us."

"I know, I know." Having her in my arms never felt so good.

******

It took a few minutes for the cockpit to drain completely. Travis and Brian checked the engine room bilges and lazaret. The heavy teak hatches, though not water tight, had done what they were built to do. There was very little water below deck, especially considering how much we'd taken on board. The ol' girl had done good.

Jennifer got the judge out of his wet clothes and wrapped him in blankets. Travis and Brian climbed topside and changed into dry clothes. Jennifer boiled a kettle of water for hot chocolate, warming her hands over the burner. I took over the pilot, and headed for home. Once the judge was settled into the couch and had two cups of hot chocolate in him, Jennifer made her way into the wheelhouse to get out of her wet clothes, too. I asked what she'd been able to find out.

"Evidently the judge had been drinking all evening before they stepped on board."

"I smelled the booze," I said, "but figured he'd just had a couple of drinks with dinner."

"So did I. Anyway, one of the guys said as soon as we got outside into the rough water, the judge went into his stateroom and passed out. At some point during the night, he got up to take a leak over the rail and fell overboard. Everyone else was in their bunks. No one heard a sound."

"His pants were still down around his ankles when we got him back on board," Brian added.

"How the hell did he stay afloat all that time without being able to kick his legs?" Travis asked.

"It's beyond me," I said. "I would've had a frickin' heart attack watching the boat steam away."

We all looked back as two of the lawyers entered our sanctuary. I hadn't said a word to them since I'd kicked them all out of the wheelhouse. I gathered they had come to thank us for saving their friend. Instead, they announced, "The judge is feeling fine, so we've decided we still want to go fishing. Turn the boat around and head back towards the grounds."

I couldn't believe what I was hearing. A couple of arrogant, duch-bags were standing in my wheelhouse telling me what to do. "No way," I said softly, without looking at them. "We're heading in."

"We all talked it over. The judge said he's fine and wants to go fishing."

"We're going home." The Coast Guard, sheriff's department and paramedics were all waiting for us at the Harbor Patrol dock. "I don't care what he says. The man's in shock. He needs medical attention."

"Bullshit!" snapped one of the lawyers. "We chartered this boat and we want to go fishing. Now turn this Goddamned thing around!"

"Fuck you!" I screamed back at the prick. Pent-up stress and adrenaline exploding. I spun around right in his face and through clenched teeth, "We're going to the Harbor Patrol dock," I said, pausing. "And you're getting the fuck out of my wheelhouse right now!"

"We're going to sue your ass," one of them shot back over his shoulder, heading out the door.

I turned around and stepped back in front of the helm. "Fuck 'em. They're a bunch of pricks. Their friend takes a header and almost dies. We save his life and they want to sue us." I shook my head in disbelief. "Goddamn lawyers."

******

We saw the unmistakable flashing red and blue lights of the police vehicles and ambulance well before we pulled into the Harbor Patrol dock on Shelter Island. As soon as Travis and Brian had secured us, the paramedics were onboard, examining the judge. Also greeting us were all the harbor patrol units, a half-dozen police, and a couple of Coast Guard officers. It was a circus. I'd radioed Larry when we were about an hour out and told him what had happened. He and Lloyd were both there when we arrived, but they weren't allowed on board. "Official police business," one of the cops said.

Other than still being somewhat intoxicated, there was nothing wrong with the judge. The paramedics wrote up a report and left, but not the cops or Coast Guard. They all had their little notepads out, asking everyone the same questions. After an hour, they seemed satisfied.

The charter master pulled Larry aside and told him they wanted to go back out. "I'll have to check with the skipper." Larry said. He climbed the boarding ladder to the wheelhouse to ask me privately. "What about just running out to the islands?"

"There's no fucking way, Larry! Those guys are the biggest pricks I've ever met. Not one of them has even thanked us for saving that asshole's life."

"I know, I know," he said shaking his head. "But the problem is…what you guys did out there tonight…saving that guy's life…it'll never come out in a courtroom."

"What the fuck are you talking about?"

"I've been through this kind of shit before. They're down there pointing fingers at you, claiming negligence."

"Bullshit!" I screamed. "The mother fucker was drunk. He didn't stay inside like we told him to do, and fell overboard taking a leak."

"I know," Larry said, trying to reassure me.

"I can't believe this shit!" I said in disbelief.

"Believe it," he said. "This shit can get real ugly, real fast. Especially with this bunch. They're all fucking attorneys and he's a Goddamn judge, for Christ sake." Larry pointed his chin toward the gaggle of pricks standing in the cockpit huddled around the judge. "I'm going to tell them you haven't had a wink of sleep and that you and your crew are exhausted. I'm going to offer them their money back, and pray it ends there."

"Bull shit! Don't be offering them their Goddamn money back. They fucked up, not us."

"Corey, listen to me," he pleaded, "If you're lucky, they'll take the money and let it go. If they push this thing and go after you legally, they'll break you. Do you realize how much power those guys can wield?"

"Fuckin' pricks," I said, shaking my head. "We didn't do a Goddamned thing wrong. We saved his life, for Christ's sake."

"I know that and you know that. So does everyone on board. But by the time they get done spinning this thing, all the jury is ever going to hear is how you 'allowed' the guy to fall overboard. You can't win. You won't win. Trust me, I know," he pleaded. "I've been through this shit before."

He took a deep breath and continued. "I didn't always operate a charter business. I used to run my own boat. Fifteen years ago, I lost a guy overboard—it was an accident." He paused. "I didn't do anything wrong then, either." He looked me in the eye. "But we never found him and the family sued me." He paused again, taking another deep breath. "I lost everything—my license, my boat, everything—so please, let me talk to them. Offer to refund their money. I'll set them up on another boat. Let me see if I can make this go away before it turns into a real shit storm."

"I don't want them on my boat ever again," I said.

"I understand…completely."

"In fact, don't ever book another fucking lawyer on my boat again."

"Let's pray you still have one to book."

I shook my head in disgust. Larry cracked a half-smile. "I'd never book another lawyer period, if I could, but they've got the bank."

"Their money's no good on this boat."

"Roger," he said. "I understand. And by the way, you guys did a hell of a job out there tonight. I don't know exactly what you did, but whatever it was, you did good. Real good.

"We got lucky," I said, a wave of fatigue and emotion washing over me. "We just got lucky."

"Head on back to the slip. Get some rest. I've got you booked for tonight."

"Okay," I said. As he started to turn and head back down, I reached out, touched his shoulder and extended my right hand. "Thanks, Larry. I appreciate your covering our back."

"No problem," he said, gripping my hand tightly. "Let's pray this is the end of it."

Larry had the charter off the boat and loaded into his van before I left the bridge. He flashed his lights as he drove away. I hoped that was a good sign. The Coast Guard officers told us they wanted to see us all tomorrow downtown, but had everything they needed for now. I thanked them for their help and support during the Mayday calls over the radio. "Just having someone there to talk to helped," I added.

"Skipper," one of them said, extending his hand, "that was an amazing rescue. You and your crew saved a man's life tonight. Get some rest, but we'll need you to come in tomorrow."

"What time?"

"Eleven hundred hours. Our office's on Shoreline Drive," the officer said, handing me his card before stepping off the boat.

Brian and Travis were standing by with the lines. "Cut her loose," I told them, leaning out the wheelhouse window. "Let's go home."

******

The preliminary Coast Guard investigation the next day determined there was no negligence on behalf of the crew or myself. In fact, the officers commended us on an extraordinary rescue. I thanked my lucky stars the guy hadn't gone down on our watch, but had a nagging suspicion this thing wasn't over.

That evening, we had a group from the valley that had never been on an overnight. My safety speech before we left the slip had an added mandate, not a request. "No one's allowed on deck after we leave the receivers." Everyone nodded. "If you wake up early, make yourselves at home in the salon, but do not go outside under any circumstances. Understand? One of us will be down tomorrow morning when it's time to start fishing."

The story of the rescue was all over the docks. Larry had already told them about it, so they had no problems with the new rules. Normally, we stowed the life jackets under the bunks in the wheelhouse, but that night l asked the boys to bring a half-dozen down for the safety speech. We showed them how to put them on, assuring them there was very little chance they'd need them. I must have scared the shit out of them, though. The next morning, I was the first one off the wheelhouse. When I looked into the salon, half-dozen faces were anxiously peering at me through the windows. Each one wearing a bright orange life jacket.

Two days later, the Coast Guard called us all in for further questioning. They talked to us one at a time. I was last. After being questioned, Travis, Brian, Jennifer and Larry were each shown out a side door. I had no idea what the Coast Guard was after, but knew in my heart we hadn't done anything wrong.

"Mr. Phillips, they're ready for you now. Please follow me." An Ensign escorted me into a large open room. A long wooden table was perfectly centered at the far side of the room. Behind it, with their backs to the wall, sat three high-ranking United States Coast Guard officers. I couldn't tell what ranks they were, but they had a shit load of stripes and braids on their uniforms. None of the officers who had interviewed us at the Harbor Patrol dock was present. This was the 'A team.' I had on a clean but faded denim shirt, a pair of shorts and topsiders. *So much for first impressions*, I thought.

"Mr. Phillips, please sit down. We have a few questions for you about the incident of this past 22 July on board the Fishing Vessel *Vintage*."

Two and a half hours later, we'd gone over ever detail at least twice— even coming back to a few particulars and going over them second by second. A stenographer took down every word. Throughout the interrogation, they would periodically stop the questioning to whisper amongst themselves. Finally, they seemed to be in agreement and brought things to a close.

"Captain Phillips," the ranking officer said, "our official findings will be made available soon, but we all agree—from the information we've gathered over the past couple of days, including interviewing all your passengers, reviewing the tapes of your Mayday transmissions, and talking to the paramedics and Harbor Patrol officers that met you on scene—that it appears nothing you've done constitutes an illegal act. Nor, in any way, can your actions be construed negligent."

A sigh of relief escaped through my parched lips. The other two officers gave me curt nods in return.

"Quite the contrary. Your seamanship is to be commended. That was a one-in-a-million rescue, especially under those conditions. You and your entire crew should be proud of yourselves. That man owes his life to you, captain." He extended his hand. "Nice job."

I was shocked. I'd figured for sure they'd find me guilty of something and yank my ticket. Instead they were standing there shaking my hand. "Thank you, gentlemen." I heard myself saying. I was having a hard time fathoming what was happening. The energy in the room had taken a 180-degree turn—from military decorum and hard questioning to congratulations.

"We run man overboard training drills in good conditions—daylight, calm seas—and there have been times when our own crews have lost track of target and have had to use aerial surveillance to relocate the target. What you did out there was truly amazing."

"We were very lucky," I said modestly.

"That may be true. But nonetheless, you did everything right. He's one hell of a lucky man to have had you at the wheel. One suggestion…you might want to assign a crewman to deck watch during the night."

"Right," I said. *We can barely stay awake on wheel watches as it is and you're suggesting one of us sit in the salon all night and baby-sit. No way*, I thought to myself. Before I could say anything else, one of the officers must have been reading my mind.

"We understand you run with a limited crew. It's only a suggestion. Certified sports are required to have a deck watch posted at all times."

That was news to me. Once the boats cleared the receivers, every deckhand I knew who wasn't on wheel watch hit the rack. "Makes sense when you've got 50 or 60 passengers on board," I said, "but with only four of us running the boat, we just don't have the manpower. Once we bait up, we make the cockpit off limits."

"But without a crewmember below, how do you know if someone does go outside? None of you knew the judge was even awake, much less on deck. "

"I know," I said, "That's why now I'm laying down the law before we leave. I'm going to tell them if anyone is seen on deck at night after we leave the harbor, the trip is over. Period. We'll turn the boat around, and when their buddies wake up, we'll be back at the dock sitting tight while the one who screwed up explains it to the others."

"Might work," said one of the officers. "At least it's worth a try."

Travis and Brian had gone back to the boat after their interviews, but Jen and Sierra waited outside all day. When they saw me coming out of the building, they ran to greet me.

"What'd they say? Is everything all right?"

"We're cool."

Sierra's tail was wagging at full speed. "Hey, girl," I said, kneeling down, fluffing her ears. "How you doing? Want to go to the beach?"

Looking up at Jen, "How does that sound?"

"Fine. Sounds fine. But what did they say?"

"They went over every detail…times, sequence of events, who did what, when. What I was thinking when I decided to do this or that…what happened before we left…had we observed them drinking…what happened immediately after we knew he'd gone overboard…what we did when we found him…how long Travis was in the water. It was endless."

"What did they say afterwards? Larry's been real worried."

That surprised me. "Really?"

"Yeah. Told me he'd been through something like this before. He's worried." I hadn't told Jennifer about Larry losing his license.

"We're O.K."

"Larry's worried this is only the beginning. If they rule that you're negligent, it could get really ugly."

"Seriously?"

"Yeah. I've never seen him like this."

I had no idea. I figured it was like they said when they called us in—standard operational procedure following a Mayday call and rescue.

"You're so cute when you're naïve," she said, giving me a little kiss. "Sweetheart, nothing's standard when it comes to this kind of thing. A man was almost lost at sea. The boat almost sank during the rescue. You're the captain. It's your ass."

"They actually complemented us on the job we did."

"Who are you kidding? It was all *you*. You were the one who found him. I'm still amazed at how you did it."

"Don't kid yourself. It took all of us."

"But you were at the wheel."

"That guy just wasn't destined to die on our watch."

She smiled and put her arm around my shoulder as we headed toward the truck. "The beach sounds good, but we've got to call Larry and the boys first and let them know they cleared you."

Walking in the sand was just what I needed. "Best therapy in the world," Jennifer said as she spread her arms, threw her head back and twirled in a circle, allowing the water to wash up over her tanned legs. The storm had blown itself out over the past couple of days. The waters off southern California were back to normal. A gentle shore break kept the sandpipers busy as they searched the wet sand for morsels. We walked for over a mile. Sierra was in heaven. It was just what the doctor ordered. By the time we got back to the truck, we were refreshed and content.

Driving back to the harbor, I became aware of a nagging vague thought at the back of my mind, just hanging there, outside my grasp. I figured it was some leftover residue from everything we'd been through the past couple of days, so I tried focusing on what was ahead. The season was gearing up fast. I knew we'd be slammed for the next several months. This would likely be the last afternoon Jennifer and I would spend together on the beach until the fish moved north in the fall. Feelings of nostalgia swept over me. I pulled her closer and gave her a kiss on the cheek.

"I like it when you do that," she said.

When we got back to the boat, the boys wanted to know every detail of the investigation.

Travis said. "They grilled us all pretty good."

"That's for sure," Brian added.

"We're a team, aren't we?" Travis asked.

I nodded. "Absolutely."

"What happened out there happened to all of us, not just you. We either trust each other, or we don't." He paused. "If we don't...we've got nothing." He was dead on. We all knew it, and respected him all the more for saying it.

"All right then," he said, the seriousness in his voice gone.

"Oh yea, Larry's been over here twice since looking for you guys. One of the boats needs a cook for a three-dayer. We're not booked, so he was hoping maybe Jennifer would cover."

"Which boat?" Jennifer asked.

"*Dorsal,*" Travis answered. "They need to know right away. They're scheduled for 10:00 tonight. He asked if you'd run down as soon as you got here, find him or one of the guys on the boat and let them know." He finished, looking at Jennifer.

"Three days?" I asked. "Doesn't he think we might book another trip by then?"

"Don't know." Travis shrugged his shoulders.

"What do you think?" Jennifer asked me. "Should I go?"

"No. I don't want you gone for three days."

"Yeah. Me, neither," she said. "I don't want to do it. Maybe an overnighter…but not for three days.

"Then you'd better go tell them. It's getting late," Travis, said, looking at his watch.

Before we could get off the boat, Larry showed up. "There you guys are," he said. "Corey, Jennifer, this is Joe Hunt. He runs *Dorsal* and they're in a jam."

"Yeah, we heard."

Extending his hand, Joe started right in. "Wouldn't even ask, but Max, our regular cook, got a call this evening from his wife. His little girl got hit by a car."

"Oh, my God!" Jennifer gasped. "Is she all right?"

"Haven't heard. His wife was hysterical when she called from the hospital. He was a wreck racing out of here."

"That's horrible…I can't even imagine…" Jen's voice trailed off.

"Jennifer, if you could cover for him, it would really help us out," Joe pleaded. "I wouldn't even ask…"

Reacting as if it would somehow help the kid, Jennifer immediately said she'd do it. "Sure, anything I can do to help."

"Thank you so much," Joe said.

"Their group is going to be here any minute," Larry said quickly.

"Is there anything I can help you with?" he asked Jennifer.

"No, but thanks anyway," Jennifer said. "Just give me a couple of minutes to get some of my gear together. I'll be right over."

"Thank you so much," Joe said, shaking her hand.

"Is the boat stocked?" she asked.

"Yeah. Max had everything ready to go before he got the call. All we need is you."

And just like that, it was done. Jennifer was going to be cooking on a stranger's boat for the next three days. I was miffed. Everything had happened in a flash. She reacted without even thinking, as soon as she heard the little girl had been hurt.

"We'll be waiting for you," Joe said, as he and Larry left to meet the charter group.

I followed Jennifer up to the wheelhouse. She started gathering the things she'd need for the trip. "Honey...you sure about this?" I asked.

"No." She stuffed some clean clothes into her backpack. "I have no choice. That little girl got hit by a car. I have to help."

"But we don't even know those people. We've never even met 'em. It's not like you can do anything for that little girl."

Stopping, she turned to face me. "They're no different than we are...just trying to run a boat. If I can help by covering for that little girl's dad, then I'm helping her." She gently brushed a lock of hair away from my face. "Listen, I don't want to go either. I don't want to be away from you for a minute...but they need me. What if the tables were turned and we needed help?" She was right, but it didn't feel right.

"You're climbing on board some boat and heading out with complete strangers for a three-day trip. I don't like it."

"Look," she said as she started packing again, "Larry wouldn't have asked if he didn't know I'd be fine. *Dorsal* is one of his top boats. I'll bet you he's known Joe for years. I'll be fine."

I couldn't argue with her rational thinking. Anyway, it was obvious she'd made up her mind the second she learned about the accident. Her compassion for a kid she'd never known touched me. It reflected the core of who she was and why I loved her so much. "I'm really going to miss you," was all I could say.

Finished packing, she threw her arms around my neck. "Tell me how much you love me."

"More than life itself," I said, squeezing her tightly.

"I love you, too. You're not going to miss me half as much as I'm going to miss you." We kissed. "Now walk me over to the boat."

Before we stepped off the *Vintage*, Travis gave her a hug. "Take care, lady. Don't worry about your boy here," nodding in my direction. "We'll take good care of him for you."

Brian's eyes were downcast. He didn't want to see her go either. "See ya, Jennifer," he mumbled.

She wasn't going to let him get away with that, and surprised him with a big hug of her own. I thought he would faint. Letting go, she added, "Larry told me you were going to spend the next couple of days with your mom."
Brian nodded.

"I'd like to meet her."

Brian's mom was waiting for us at the top of the ramp. Brian handled the introductions. "Hope he hasn't been giving you any trouble," she said in a pleasant voice, as she fluffed his hair like only a mother is allowed to do.

"Oh, Mom!" Brian said turning away, embarrassed.

"Not at all," I assured her. "In fact, I'm not sure where we'd be without him. He knows his stuff."

"That's for sure!" Jennifer said. Brian smiled.

"Well, he's been on the boats since before he could walk. I'm glad to hear he's been a help."

"He's more than just help—he's an important part of our crew." Now Brian was beaming.

"I'm glad to hear it," she said sincerely. "You ready to go, son?"

"Yeah."

"Is that any way to answer a lady?" Jennifer asked him.

"Sorry," he said, embarrassed again. Watching his emotional roller coaster would have been almost funny, except I knew how hard it was being a teenager. "Yes ma'am," he said, looking to Jennifer for approval. She gave him another hug, which once again sent him on a high. We said goodbye. Jennifer and I headed back down the dock.

Dorsal was one of the nicest boats in the fleet. A custom built 85-foot Ditmar, she was all planked and solid as a rock—a strong, seaworthy vessel. The boat was immaculate and beautifully maintained. Jennifer and I were impressed as we climbed on board.

Joe, a veteran charter captain, ran a four-man crew and a tight ship. "The biggest difference between running a boat like this and being an owner/operator is simple," he said as he welcomed us on board. "With you guys, every dollar counts, whereas we're owned by a corporation. This entire operation is a write-off. They set the boat up as a business, so as long as we run trips and show income, everything becomes a write-off. The accountants do their thing and everyone's happy. They don't care how much things cost. It makes it nice."

"I guess," I said, looking at Jennifer. Unlike them, we counted every dime.

"Go figure," Joe continued. "They pay me to take care of her, to make sure she's got what she needs. They want things done right, and we do," he said proudly, glancing around the pristine cockpit. He smiled, seeing the looks Jennifer and I were exchanging. He'd been in the business a long time and knew how hard it was for owner/operators to make ends meet. "Doesn't seem fair, does it?" Knowing he didn't need an answer, we didn't say anything. "But I'll tell you, there's nothing like the pride of ownership. I've seen what you guys did for your boat over there. You should both be very proud."

"We are," Jennifer said. "Thank you.

"No…thank you," Joe told her, "for helping us out on such short notice. We've got a back-up cook, but she's out of town. This was so unexpected…Max's kid getting hit and all."

"Have you heard anything more from the hospital?" Jennifer asked.

"Nothing yet." He paused, taking take off his faded SHIMNAO cap and running his fingers through his hair. "Can't even imagine. We're just praying the kid's okay." You could see the pain in his eyes. Putting his cap back on, and taking a deep breath, he added, "Figure no news is good news." We nodded in agreement. "Come on, let me give you a quick tour."

Every inch of the boat was perfectly maintained. When Joe led us into the engine room, I was speechless. There wasn't a drop of oil or grease anywhere. You could've eaten off the engine room floor. Seeing the look on our faces, Joe smiled. "We've got a steam cleaning crew that does the engine room and bilges twice a month," he confessed.

"Very impressive," Jennifer said, climbing up the ladder to the deck hatch leading back up into the cockpit. "Where should I stow my gear?"

"Cook's quarters are forward," Joe told her, leading us back into the salon. "You'll bunk alone. The rest of the crew is topside." As Joe showed us below, Jennifer asked about her turn on wheel watch. "Not on this boat. Your job is hard enough without getting rousted in the middle of the night to help us do ours."

I was really starting to hate this guy—unlimited funds, cleaning crews, private quarters, and now he was going to spoil my girl with no wheel watches.

"Sounds too good to be true. A full night's sleep and I even get my own cabin. A girl could get used to living like this," Jen added with a sly smile. Joe left us alone in her new cabin. "Now," she continued, looking around the comfortable quarters, "this is living."

"When you get back, I don't want to hear about it," I said, tossing her backpack onto the doublewide bunk.

Raising her eyebrows, "Who says I'm coming back?"

"You've got three days, missy," I said, pulling her to my side. "If you're not back in my arms in exactly 72 hours, then look out, because I'm coming after you."

"You'd better," she said, lifting herself up on her tiptoes, wrapping her arms around my neck and pulling me to her warm, soft lips. A deep stirring kiss left us both a little weak in the knees. "I love you," she said softly, her eyes radiant and smiling.

"I love you, too, Jen. I'm going to miss you."

Dorsal was scheduled to leave shortly. We said our goodbyes, so she would have a few minutes to get her gear stored away before they pulled out. As I was stepping off the boat, their charter group showed up. Instantly, that nagging sensation in the back of my brain clicked in. Something wasn't right. They didn't look anything like a fishing charter. Two middle-aged guys with slicked-back hair and shiny polyester slacks, button-down silk shirts (opened half way to their hairy navels), thick gold chains around their necks, black leather jackets and expensive black loafers. They would have looked perfectly normal walking into a club, but strolling down a charter dock, they stood out like a sore thumb. I thought people only looked like this in the movies. They definitely weren't dressed for fishing.

Four very attractive young ladies were with them. The whole group reeked of cigars, alcohol and perfume. The girls were all giggly and looked stoned. They'd obviously been drinking and were dressed for a night on the town with their low-cut necklines, backless short evening dresses, seamed stockings and high heels. I wondered what the hell four women who looked like they belonged in an exclusive Las Vegas penthouse were doing climbing on board a charter fishing boat.

This whole thing sucks, I thought to myself, but I didn't say a word. Instead, I jumped off the boat, giving them room to climb on board. The girls had to take off their pumps before even attempting to negotiate the teak swim step. Lifting one leg at a time and bending over, they held onto the men for support. Pairs of briefly exposed young breasts flashing and lace panties peaking through hiked up skirts put an instant stop to all other activity along the dock. Everyone was watching the show, but the girls didn't seem to notice. It was all they could do to keep from falling over as they laughed hysterically, pumps in hand. The crew gladly assisted the ladies on board. I didn't look back and couldn't even watch as *Dorsal* pulled away from her slip. Three days without Jennifer.

******

We'd been keeping an eye on the problem for a couple weeks. Repairs were on our "to do" list, and with Jennifer gone and no trips scheduled, it was a perfect time to attend to them. Our starboard turbo on the main had sheered off a couple of bolts right at the flange to the exhaust. It wasn't a big deal, but it was messy and you definitely didn't want to repair it when it was hot. Travis and I got on it. Fortunately it would provide enough work to keep my mind off the fact Jennifer was gone and, from the looks of things, working on board a floating brothel for the next 72 hours.

"Shit!" Travis shouted. "Just hold the damn thing in place, will ya?" he complained because I wasn't paying attention.

"Just turn the handle and quit your whining." I knew he was right. Working on the exhaust system was a messy job. Neither of us wanted to be down there getting covered with soot, and I wasn't helping matters. I couldn't concentrate…knowing the only thing those two pricks were going to be fishing for was land tuna.

"Come on," Travis pleaded as I let the wrench slip off the backside of the bolt again.

"Did you see those guys?" I asked him.

"Who?"

"The guys that Jennifer's fishing with."

"No," he said, "but I heard about the chicks."

"Exactly. But why a fishing boat?" Granted, the *Dorsal* was high-end. "Why not just get a hotel room somewhere?"

"Who knows."

"It's buggin' me, that's all."

"Jesus, she's only been gone for a couple hours and you're already worthless. Here," he said, "Give me the damn wrench. I'll do it myself." He shook his head as I climbed out from under the exhaust. "Women," he muttered under his breath.

"What the hell do you know about women, anyway?"

"Enough," he shot back. "Hand me that seven-eighths." Taking the wrench from me. "You want to go get something to eat after this?"

Without Jennifer here looking out for us, we were a couple of inept, greasy slobs, getting hungrier by the minute. At least, I was inept. Travis put the turbo back together just fine without my help. "Yeah, I'm starving."

"Good," he said. "Me, too. I know just the place. "

"Where?"

"Trust me. You'll love it, " he said, flashing a big grin. His focus back at the job at hand he announced, "That's got it. But we're going to have ask C-fad to fabricate a couple of braces for these exhausts. Even with the new fiberglass tubes, they still weigh too much to leave them hanging here like this off the turbo. That's what caused these bolts to snap in the first place." He was pointing out the obvious and I was mad at myself for not seeing the problem earlier. "We were lucky only a couple snapped. This thing could have busted clean off...especially when you were pouring the coal to her the other night."

He was right. We hadn't talked about the rescue other than the Coast Guard results. Or about the fact I almost sank the boat. We both knew we were lucky to be alive. "She did good," I said, patting the exhaust and collecting the rest of the tools. I handed them to Travis and he put them back in their proper drawers in the tool chest.

"That's a fact—she did real good," Travis agreed. "Tomorrow we'll get to work building those braces, but for now, let's get cleaned up and go eat."

******

Even though *Vintage* had hot water and decent water pressure, there was nothing like getting pounded by the endless supply of steaming hot water at the marina's dockside shower facilities. We grabbed our shaving kits; some clean clothes and headed up there. The facilities at Cortez Marina are first rate—clean, spacious locker rooms for both men and women, white tile floors, private showers, a large common area with sinks and plenty of counter space.

It's amazing how good a hot shower feels after spending time in the engine room. There's nothing like it. Standing there with my back to the hot water, eyes closed, I remembered the first time Jennifer and I showered together…the water cascading over her silky smooth skin…the beautiful contrast of her firm breasts and her perfect, tight little white ass against the rich golden tan of the rest of her body…the intoxicating scent of her freshly shampooed hair.

I remembered the incredible sensation of shock and pure arousal when she asked me if I'd like to shave her. Kneeling down between her legs and applying the shaving cream, I looked up to see her smile. My hands actually started trembling. I couldn't do it. I was afraid of nicking her. Laughing with the innocence of a child, she pulled the blade out of her lady Gillette. "Practice once without the blade," she suggested, handing me back the razor. Practicing without the blade was fun. Gently guiding the razor along the inside of her thighs, working up, I started getting hard. Seeing that, she smiled. "Let's do it for real," she said, reinserting the blade. "I've never done this before. It feels naughty." Closing her eyes and tilting her head back under the shower spray, she whispered, "Be gentle."

Misty steam covered her. Arching her pelvis forward to keep the water from washing away the new shaving cream, she lifted one foot up onto the edge of the shower stall and spread herself wide so I could get between her legs. Her golden, delicate pubic hairs—soft and wispy like a newborn baby—offered no resistance to the sharp blade. Slow and carefully, I ran the razor up the inside of her thighs, and then worked down from her pelvis, toward the top of her slit. Her vaginal lips were swollen as I worked, ever so gently, around her opening, leaving nothing but velvet smooth skin. She was as aroused as I was. My face was only inches away from the most beautiful sight I'd ever seen in my life.

We didn't say a word after she put the blade back in. She rinsed off the residual shaving cream. When she turned back around, the water glistened off her hairless mound. She was as pure as the virgin snow. It was the most erotic thing I'd ever seen. Glancing up, I saw her radiant face flushed with desire. Her eyes were half-closed. Still on my knees, I wrapped my hands around her bottom. Firmly cradling her buns, I pulled her into my mouth. She moaned as my lips gently touched hers. Without any hair, the sensations were overwhelming...my lips and my entire being was intoxicated. Nibbling, caressing, my tongue explored every crevasse of her womanhood, rejoicing in her pleasure. Her erect, swollen, throbbing clitoris begged for more attention, but I couldn't help myself. Passionately aching to know all of her, my tongue delved between her delicate folds, cherishing, swallowing the delicacy of her nectar. It ran along her inner lips up to her swollen clitoris once again. I slid along her full outer lips, kissing, gently biting, following the natural curves of her body, between her legs, down under and around her buns. I paused ever so slightly before caressing her ass with my tongue.

The intensity was electrifying. She was so aroused, her juices flowing so freely, and my finger was well lubricated as I ever so gently began sliding it inside her ass. She moaned, "My God." Her legs began quivering. Unsure, I didn't move. But she did...lowering herself further onto my finger. "That feels incredible," she said. Within moments her rhythm was natural, flowing. Moaning, she reached down and spread her legs a little wider, pulling my lips onto her swollen clitoris. She no longer wanted gentle caressing. She held me firmly in her, demanding to be fully engulfed in deep, strong, succulent motions. The fingers on my free hand slid inside her throbbing vagina in perfect rhythm with her. I could feel them sliding between the thin linings separating her insides. It was too much for her to control any longer. Her entire being exploded as she came in uncontrollable waves of pure ecstasy....

******

"You going to just stand in there all night, or what?" Travis's bellowing voice shot through me from the next stall like a firecracker, scaring the crap out of me. "Come on, asshole," he yelled, "you're worse than a girl."

"I'm coming," I said, recovering.

"Yeah. You're just in there jerking off, you fag. I'll be outside. Hurry up, will you. I'm starving."

The short ride along Rosecrans was typical San Diego—a pleasant mix of naval personnel, commercial and recreational fisherman, locals and tourists—all getting along together without so much as a lick of trouble. San Diego is an incredible place. I liked becoming a part of one of the finest cities I'd ever seen. Travis was driving. Seemed like everyone liked driving the old truck, which was fine with me. Sierra was between us, stretched out across my lap with her front paws hanging out the window.

Travis's choice for dinner was a place called the *Hot Dog Stand*. I'd never heard of it. Tucked in behind a big industrial warehouse, it was a wonder anyone ever found it. But when we pulled in, the parking lot was packed.

NO ONE UNDER 21 ALLOWED. ID REQUIRED.

"What is this place?" I asked him, as we headed for the front door. "I thought we were going to get something to eat?"

"Trust me," he said.

Entering a small reception area with closed inner doors, we were greeted by a scantily clad young woman behind the ticket cage and one of the biggest men I'd ever seen.

"Hey, Travis. How ya' doin', man?" asked the mammoth, extending his hand.

"Good, Bear. How about yourself?"

"Couldn't be better." Evidently, Travis didn't know the girl behind the counter.

"This here's Corey Phillips. My boss."

"No shit. Didn't know you had a boss."

"He doesn't," I interrupted. "We work together." I extended my hand, anticipating another bone-crushing squeeze. Instead, Bear met me with solid, but not overwhelming pressure. "Nice to meet you," I said.

"Pleasure's all mine," he said pleasantly, opening the padded double doors behind him, "Come on in."

"Thanks, amigo," Travis said, shaking Bear's hand again before leading the way in.

I followed Travis into the darkness, looking back at Bear. I ran into Travis, who had stopped, waiting for his eyes to adjust. "Sorry."

"No problem."

Another beautiful young lady came into focus under the lights, highlighting a golden pole running from floor to ceiling in the middle of a stage. She wore a white Oxford shirt tied at the waist—the way Jennifer liked to wear her shirts when we were alone. Her legs were wrapped around the pole, as she hung upside down, her breasts just hidden behind the cotton blend.

"I'm hungry, Travis, not horny. Let's go somewhere we can get a good meal."

"I'm telling you," he said, walking around the stage, "you're just going to have to trust me on this one." Feeling foolish just standing there, I followed him.

"Hey, Travis, good seeing ya', cutie," said a petite blond with nothing on but a lace teddy and g-string panties. A little peak of white along the sides of her full breasts showed through her thin lace top. Other than her breasts, she had a rich, golden tan from head to toe. Bouncing up, she threw her arms around him. "I missed you."

"I missed you, too, Jaz," Travis responded enthusiastically, lifting her off her feet and wrapping his arms around her. "You look prettier every time I see you."

"You're such a charmer," she said.

"Only for you, my love," he assured her. "Only for you."

"Yeah, right." They hugged for longer than a normal greeting.

I waited. Looking away, my eyes now fully adjusted, I could see the place was brimming with beautiful women. An Eagles song was playing, but not too loud. Several men were perched on stools around the stage, and everyone seemed really relaxed. No one was smoking. The dancer, lying on the floor, had her fanny up in the air, exposing her full white cotton panties under her pleated schoolgirl skirt. She reached back and spanked herself.

"Who's this?" the waitress asked.

"My boss," Travis answered. "Boss, meet Jasmine. Jaz, this is Corey Phillips."

"My pleasure," she said with a warm smile, extending her hand from around Travis' neck.

"It's all mine." And it was—her energy was infectious. "Quit calling me boss," I whispered to Travis.

"Okay, Skipper." That was even worse.

"You guys hungry" Jasmine asked, "or just here for the entertainment?" Leaning back in Travis's arms, she looked into his eyes.

"What do you think?" he asked her.

"Both." She knew him well. "You wouldn't be here if you weren't hungry and a little horny." She kissed his ear. "Put me down and let's get a table so I can take good care of you boys."

Jasmine lead us through the club, past the intimate, rectangular-shaped center stage with its polished hardwood floors, surrounded by the slightly raised, padded bar with a row of dimly lit recessed lights underneath. The lights cast a warm glow on the girl performing as we walked by. Other than her bobby socks and hush puppies, she was now completely naked. Her hush puppies were propped up against the bar, and her legs were straddling the head of the guy seated directly in front of her, giving him an up-close-and-personal view that left nothing to the imagination. She barely moved her hips. What was moving stopped the guy's breathing as he stared, transfixed. Suddenly, with cat-like ease, she spun around effortlessly and slid on her belly to the opposite side of the stage to face another mesmerized patron of the arts. Smiling, she lowered her head, arched her back and turned to present her ass to him. Immediately, a five-dollar bill appeared on the padded bar just inches away. She seductively ran her hand down the underside of her belly between her legs. Spreading her fingers, she held her hand there, barely covering her clean-shaven vagina. She let her fingers linger, slowly sliding them along her swollen lips before curving her middle finger inward to caress herself.

I plowed into the backs of both Travis and Jasmine. They had stopped walking when they noticed that I was barely moving and not looking where I was going. "Jesus," I said, startled and trying to regain my balance. "I'm sorry." They both laughed.

"Not bad, huh?" Jasmine asked, looking at the girl on stage.

"I had no idea," I said. Travis shook his head.

Jasmine took my hand and led us to a secluded booth at the back of the darkened room. "You'll be able to see everything from here, and we won't have to worry about you mowing any innocent pedestrians down."

I'd never been inside a strip club before. I was amazed at how many beautiful girls were working the floor. They weren't sleazy-looking skanks. These girls were young, healthy-looking, and very attractive...like the girl next door. I was speechless. Some of them didn't even look old enough to drive. "How old do you have to be to work here?" I asked Jasmine as she seated us.

"Eighteen," she said with her charming smile. "Want to see my driver's license?" Her eyes sparkled with mischief.

"No, I'll take your word for it."

"But the sign says you have to be 21."

"To get in...not to work here."

"Really?"

"Yeah. Management doesn't want a bunch of punk kids in here. The sorority pukes are bad enough." Sure enough, the mostly male clientele appeared to be middle-aged or older. "Can I get you guys something to drink?" she asked, as we settled into the soft leather seats. "We've got some great home-made lemonade. Since we can't serve alcohol, we've got to do something to keep the customers happy." Again, that twinkle. "Freshly squeezed."

"Sounds good. I'd love one," I said. "Thank you."

"Make it two, and how about a couple of Philly sandwiches and fries?" Travis added.

"Want onions?"

"Grilled," Travis said.

"Mine too, please," I said, as she looked over at me without repeating the question.

"I'll be right back." Just like that…she was off like a wisp of wind.

"She's adorable," I told Travis.

"I know," he said.

"Cute as a button."

"And smart as a whip. Can't seem to get enough of life."

"She's definitely full of energy."

"She's got two speeds—full on or sound asleep. I've never met anyone like her." I shot him an inquiring glance. "I can only handle her for so long. She plumb wears me out."

"So you've been seeing her for awhile?"

"Yeah," he nodded, but didn't get into it. I didn't pry.

Jasmine returned with our drinks. She moved so gracefully, it was almost like she was floating. The lemonade was delicious—a perfect combination of sweetness subtly blended with a bite of bitter lemon.

"God, I must be getting old. Here I am, sitting here in a strip club, surrounded by beautiful women, talking about how good the lemonade tastes."

"It's good, isn't it?" Jasmine said, taking a sip of Travis' lemonade.

"The best I can remember ever having," I said.

Travis smiled. "Just wait 'til you taste the food."

"If it's as good as this," I said, taking another sip, "I don't know if I'll be able to handle it."

"Which…the food or the women?" Jasmine asked, seeing me stare at another beautiful blond walking by.

"Don't believe a word he says," Travis cut in. "All he can think about these days is his girlfriend."

"True?" Jasmine asked.

"Yeah," I said, nodding my head. "Guilty as charged. I am 100% head over heals in love with her."

"That's so sweet," she said. "I like hearing a man say that, especially in here. It gives me hope, instead of seeing some guy trying to hide his wedding ring."

Travis wasn't biting. I was getting the feeling their relationship might be a little more than just friends.

"Being in love is the most incredible thing in the whole world," she added.

"You'll get no argument from me," I said, supporting Jasmine's claim.

"Yeah, maybe," Travis countered, "but look at all you're missing out on." He gestured toward the stage where another strikingly beautiful brunette was tantalizingly playing with her panties, bending over, and showcasing an ass that would make any cheerleader proud.

"There are millions of beautiful women out there," I countered, "but when you're in love, being with that one person, is a thousand times better than any one-night stand."

"A million times better!" Jasmine confirmed. "One of these days," she said, poking Travis in the ribs, "if you're lucky, you'll know what we're talking about." Travis was looking away from her. She reached seductively under the front of his shirt and slid her hand over his chest, then teasingly tweaking one of his nipples.

"Ouch," he said, grabbing her hand. "Prove it."

"You got fifty bucks, mister?" she challenged.

"On a good day, you might be worth twenty."

"That's going to cost you," she said, laughing.

Before I knew it, they were up and headed for a private VIP room. Travis looked back over his shoulder. "I'll be back, so don't be eating my sandwich."

A single man sitting alone in a strip bar stands out like a neon sign on an ATM machine in the middle of the night. Less than 30 seconds after they left, I heard a soft voice. "Want a private dance?" The voice belonged to a striking brunette with long, flowing hair and deep green eyes. She was dressed in a dark blue business suit...minus the shirt and pants...just the tie, jacket and a pair of men's designer underwear.

"No, thanks. I'm just waiting for a sandwich," I offered lamely.

"That can be arranged," she said seductively. "No problem."

Embarrassed, I said, "Not that kind of sandwich."

"I know," she assured me with a trace of laughter in her voice, "but if you change your mind, my name's Amy." Her hand was as smooth as silk. I started to stand up to shake it. "No, don't get up."

"I'm fine, but thanks anyway."

"Just let me know." She bent over and gave me a little kiss on the cheek. Her perfume lingered in the air as she walked away. Another very attractive young lady brought over our sandwiches.

"Thank you."

Looking me right in the eye, she said, "You let me know when you're ready to eat the real thing." With that, I got a soft, half-blow, half-kiss in my ear, her tongue darting in for added effect.

Alone with a couple of hot Philly cheese sandwiches, grilled onions and fries. It was sensory overload. I never knew places like this existed. Travis and Jasmine returned about a half-hour later. I'd managed to finish off my sandwich and both orders of fries.

Travis slid in opposite me and noticed his fries were missing. "You pig," he announced. "Surprised you didn't inhale my Philly as well."

"I'll get you some hot ones," Jasmine told him. Looking over at me, "Didn't any of the other girls come by?"

"Oh, yeah. It was hard to even eat."

"Sorry we left you alone. That was rude of us."

"No worries."

"I had to give Travis a little taste of what his life could be like if he'd pull his head out of his ass."

"Yeah, yeah," he said, joking with her in a deep macho voice. "Just get me my fries, woman."

"He's hopeless," she said, ignoring him. "A hopeless, lost little boy."

On cue, Travis took a big bite of his Philly. A drop of sauce dripped down the corner of his mouth. "You're disgusting," she said, leaning over to lick the sauce off his chin. "Mm, that's good," she said, smacking her lips. Travis held the sandwich up for her as she took a bite. I was amazed, watching the two of them interact. Travis hadn't uttered a word about her, but it was obvious they really liked each other.

"Where's your lady?" Jasmine asked when she finished chewing.

"She left him," Travis jumped in.

Jasmine seemed generally concerned. "She left you?"

"No, no. Not like that," I said.

"Yeah, she did."

"Shut up, Travis," I said. "She's working for a few days on another boat. That's all."

"Oh, man," Jasmine, replied. "If I ever had a man fall for me the way you have for her, I wouldn't leave him alone for a second!"

"You guys are making me sick," Travis chimed in. "Give me a break, will ya? I'm trying to eat over here. She's only going to be gone for a few days. Jesus."

"He's such a chauvinist." Jasmine said, shaking her head. "Scared to death of love. "But, hell," she said. "What can I say...he's a great tipper."

"You wish," he said.

"I'm not talking to you." She smiled at me.

Another hot, young blonde came over. "Need a fourth?" she asked Jasmine.

"It's up to the boys. This one's in love," Jasmine said, gently touching my hand, "so I doubt it."

"Thanks for asking, but no," I said.

"Told you," Jasmine smiled. "He's head over heels."

"That's so sexy," said the blonde. "There's nothing more attractive than a man in love." Travis shook his head and washed down a bite of his sandwich with a big gulp of lemonade. "I get off dancing for men that think they're in love. What do you say? A couple of harmless little lap dances? Maybe rock your world a little?"

I would have thought saying no to an offer like that from a beautiful girl would have been harder, but it wasn't. "Appreciate the offer, but no thanks."

"But this one, on the other hand," Jasmine said, putting her arm round Travis's neck, "is a pig...so maybe. What do you say, Travis? Want her to join us tonight?" I was shocked at this beautiful young thing, whom obviously liked Travis, asking him if he wanted another girl to join them. I sat motionless, waiting for Travis to respond. He took another bite of his sandwich, chewing it for moment. Before he had a chance to answer, Jasmine added, "See. I told you he was a p.i.g."

"Got to keep up my strength," he said finally, looking from Jasmine to the blonde. "Not tonight, but we know where to find you."

"Count your blessings," Jasmine told the girl, elbowing Travis in the ribs. "He thinks he's this big time lover when he really doesn't have a clue." Everyone laughed, including Travis. Even I saw how flushed Jasmine was when they returned to the booth. She was glowing and that doesn't come from being frustrated. "And he doesn't even know what the word 'tips' means."

"To Insure Personal Service," Travis offered, still chewing.

"Charming," Jasmine said. "You want him...you can have him."

The blonde shook her head. "He's all yours."

"Bitch," Travis said jokingly to Jasmine.
"I'll show you, bitch," Jasmine said, climbing on his lap, making him drop the last bite of his Philly.

The blonde leaned into our booth with both hands on the table, revealing a pair of the most beautiful breasts I've ever seen under a sheer, low-cut, lace blouse. Her nipples were erect. "You guys are fun," she said looking at me, "sure you don't just want to party a little bit?"

It was tempting, but I told her no.

"A man is only as faithful as his options," she whispered, straightening up, her breasts slipping back under cover. "Heard that on a radio talk show. Looks like you're the exception to the rule."

"There's an exception to every rule," Jasmine was back in the conversation. "Just met him, and I already love him." She scooted off Travis' lap and slid over next to me, snuggling up and nudging her head under my arm so it went over her shoulder. "Now, this is my kind of man," she said, looking at Travis.

Travis wiped the last remnants of his sandwich from the corner of his mouth, took a deep breath and smiled in agreement. "You can have her."

Without looking at him, Jasmine voiced the obvious. "You're just scared."

That hit a nerve. Travis didn't say anything for minute.

The blonde left. We sat in silence.

Finally, getting serious for the first time all night, Travis said, "You're right. You're absolutely right." We both looked at him...waiting...this was getting real. "But not about what you think. I'm not afraid of love— what I'm afraid of is screwing this up."

Jasmine instantly slid over to him. "I love you," she said, taking his face in her hands and looking him in the eye. "I love you."

Travis gently touched her cheek. "I know," he said, "and that's what I'm afraid of screwing up."

"How?" she asked. Her eyes intense.

"By not knowing how to love you back."

"You already are. You don't have to do anything different. I'm in love with you...with who you are. Can't you see that?"

"I don't know," he said, shaking his head.

She wouldn't let him go. She forced him to focus on her eyes. "And you think by allowing yourself to love me, you're going to screw things up? Are you serious?"

"Yeah," he said. "As long as it stays free and easy, no one gets hurt."

His words cut to the core of her being. Lowering her head, she let her arms go slack. "You really don't get it, do you?"

"Get what?"

Tears were in her eyes as she looked into his. "The only way you can fuck this up is by doing exactly what you're doing right now."

"And what's that?"

"By not trusting yourself...not trusting me...us. This is what it's all about. It doesn't get any better than this. There's no magic carpet ride. There are no princesses in ivory towers, or knights on shinning white horses coming to rescue them. Its just people like you and me doing the best they can with what they've got. And when two people are lucky enough to find something special, something like we have...to let fear destroy it...." Her words trailed off.

Travis looked at her, almost pleading with his eyes, wanting to understand. She continued bravely. "All we have is what we're able to give. If we're afraid to give our hearts, then we have nothing." The radiant glow washed from her cheeks. She looked at me. "Would you scoot over so I can get out?

"Wait a minute," Travis pleaded, reaching out and touching her shoulder. "Don't go."

"I can't..." she said, not looking up. "I can't do this any more."

"Please," he whispered. "I love you." She stopped and stared up at him through her tears.
Travis reached out. He held her face, looking into her soul. "I love you," he repeated.

"Oh, Travis," she said, "I love you so much." She threw herself into his arms, half crying and half-laughing. The thrill of hearing him say those words to her for the first time instantly replaced the sorrow, but hadn't given her tears time to turn off. Now she was laughing out loud, still crying. "I love you. I love you. I love you," she said, smothering him with kisses.

"Jesus, woman." The old Travis was back. "Give me a break, will ya."

"Never," she said, smiling from ear to ear.

"Oh, God," he said, letting out a deep sigh.

The music changed. "I love this song," Jasmine said. "Let's dance." There was a small dance floor, but no one was dancing except the girls on stage. "Come on," she pleaded.

"I don't dance," Travis said.

"Just this once?"

"I'm a total klutz."

"You're such a baby," she said. "But you're my baby. Corey, will you please dance with me since I'm in love with a man who won't dance?" I hesitated. "Come on," she pleaded, "let's dance."

Travis nodded and said with a mock western drawl, "I'd be obliged if you'd dance with my woman."

Before I knew it, Jasmine and I were face to face, slowly moving to an old Elvis hit from the fifties. She danced like her feet weren't even touching the floor. Light as a feather, she moved effortlessly in my arms. We ended up dancing to a half-dozen more tunes. It was the first time I'd danced since my wedding. "How long have you been working here?" I asked as we headed back to the booth.

"Started the day I turned eighteen," she answered proudly. "Was working at McDonald's before that. The day I turned eighteen, I walked up to the manager and told him I quit. He said, "You can't quit." I said he should just watch me, and left him standing there in his little cap and apron. An hour later, I was up there on that very stage, naked as a jaybird."

"Weren't you nervous?"

"Hell, yes! Scared to death. Just about peed my pants. But I just closed my eyes and went for it. Earned more money dancing to my first three songs than I made in a week serving Happy Meals."

"Really?" I asked, astonished.

"Absolutely—the money is unbelievable."

"I guess."

"After my first time on stage, I ran into the bathroom and threw up."

We sat back down. "What are you guys talking about?" Travis asked.

"About dancing naked," she told him. "My first time here, how I got started." Travis had ordered another round of cold lemonades. Jasmine and I were both thirsty.

"Thanks," I said, holding up the glass and tapping Jasmine's. "To love."

"To love," she said, before downing half the glass.

"I couldn't do it," I said.

"Do what?" Travis asked.

"Dance naked in front of a bunch of women."

"Who'd want to see your fat ass anyway?" Travis said, laughing.

"He's got a really cute ass," Jasmine smiled, sliding over next to Travis.

"How about you?" I asked Travis.

"In a heartbeat."

"Bullshit." It was Jasmine's turn to counter-punch. "You don't even like leaving the lights on when we're making love." That embarrassed him. "I was so nervous, I was shaking," she continued, "but the other girls were so supportive. They said they all felt the same way at first. You get used to it. No one's allowed to touch you. It's not like you're having sex with them. You're just putting on a show. Now it seems as natural as brushing my teeth. No one hassles you here. Guys just want to look and fantasize. It's human nature. Dancing here is almost like going to the gym and getting paid for working out." She paused. "That's why we had the pole installed. The guys think it's all sexy, seeing us sliding up and down it, but most of us actually have a workout routine when we're on stage."

"No shit?"

"Absolutely."

"Incredible..." I added shaking my head. "But what about the VIP room?"

"It's there if you want to use it. Some of the girls make their living in there. Some of us don't."

"But even the lap dances out here are full body contact."

"Only if we want them to be. It's totally up to us. The guys aren't allowed to put their hands on us unless we tell them it's okay. And we all keep our outfits on. It's all fantasy, nothing but great lighting, smoke and mirrors."

"What about five-o?"

"The cops? They're cool. As long as we aren't soliciting and don't get out of control, everything's cool. A bunch of them are regulars. Use the VIP room all the time." The energy in the place was amazing. I could see why someone would rather work here than over a hot grill. "Bottom line," she said, "the money is unbelievable. I've been here two years and already have my own condo. Plus, I'm putting myself through State all on my own. No help from my parents, who by the way had a cow when I started working here. Threw me out of the house." She laughed. "Then they just about had heart attacks when I bought my own place. You should have seen the look on my dad's face when I told them. He couldn't believe it. It took a long time, but I finally convinced my dad to come in and see for himself."

"No shit! You brought your dad in here?" Travis said. Looking around. "He's not here now, is he?"

"No, silly. I brought him in during the day, when things were slow. Made sure the other girls knew he was coming and made damned sure none of them asked him for a private dance. Showed him all around the place. Introduced him to the owner and bouncers. He was so nervous. It was so cute. After everything we'd been through—him kicking me out of the house and all—I fell back in love with him that day when he hugged me, telling me how hard it had been for him, but how proud he was of me now. I realized he's just looking out for me. You know, protecting his little girl."

"You're an amazing young lady," I said, genuinely impressed. "Were you nervous about bringing him in here?"

"A little bit, but not really. I wasn't worried about the club, just about how he'd react."

"You didn't dance for him, did you?" Travis asked.

"You're sick! Of course not. It was my day off. I just wanted him to know that there was no prostitution going on or anything like that. I wanted him to see for himself that I wasn't a whore or having sex for money. After a while he seemed to kind of accept it. He didn't want me shooting any movies or posing nude for Playboy. Like they'd have me!"

I was surprised by her lack of self-confidence. "What? Are you nuts? You're a goddess, for Christ's sake."

"Flattery will get you everywhere," she said. "You should take some lessons," she added, looking at Travis.

He nodded without taking his eyes off the new girl on stage. Teasing her, he said, "I'm busy." This didn't bother Jasmine at all.

"You've got to be proud about buying your own place."

"I am. I love having my own place. Like I was saying, the money here is unbelievable. I think the fact that I bought my own place convinced my dad that working here wasn't so bad. He's old school, all about the money," she added. "Pretty typical for his generation. With everything they went through."

"How much do you make?" I blurted out without even thinking. "I'm sorry." I apologized for being so rude.

"No problem," she said reassuringly. "It all depends. Days I average about a thousand. Nights…weekends…." She paused for a second. "Oh,

I don't know," she said thinking. "Double sometimes triple that."

"Two or three grand a night?" I asked, amazed.

"On average," she said, nodding her head. "Not bad for a city girl, huh?"

"I'll say. Do you ever have any trouble with the clients?"

"Every once in awhile, a few guys will go out drinking before they come in. They're messed up when they get here. They start grabbing you. But the boys are all over their asses. Like I said, it's our show. The boys protect us like their own. As far as I know, no one has ever had any real issues in here."

"Smoke and mirrors."

"You got it," she said. "Like taking candy from a baby."

She had the place wired.

"Most of the men who come in here are all right," she went on, "they just want to look. Fantasize. Get turned on a little, then go home afterwards and make love to their wives, girlfriends, whatever. Most the guys that come in here are married."

"Really?"

"Absolutely." She looked around the room, before continuing. "I had a regular for a while. Cute guy. In a wheelchair. Said he'd gotten hurt playing ball. He was paralyzed from the waist down. His girlfriend bailed as soon as she found out he couldn't walk."

"That's cold."

"No shit," she said. "Still in the hospital…and you're lady bails. That's bullshit." She shook her head in disgust. "He never once said a bad word about her. Anyway, after awhile he'd come in during the day when things were slow and we'd talk for hours. Told me he hadn't been with a woman, or even had a date since he'd gotten hurt."

"That sucks," I said, shaking my head.

"Yeah, no doubt. I looked forward to him coming in. He was a cool guy."

"What did you do?" Travis asked.

"Treated him like he wasn't in the chair."

"And?"

"He told me I made him feel whole again."

"Really?"

"Yeah," she said. "It was pretty incredible. Made me feel like I was doing something special. You know, making a difference in someone's life. He made me feel special."

"Tavern or temple," I said.

"What?"

"Doesn't matter where you are—a tavern or a temple."

She understood immediately. Obviously. She was living it. "You're right on the money. It doesn't matter where you are. What does matter is how you treat people."

"And how you live your life."

"I like this guy," she said to Travis.

"Yeah," Travis agreed. "He's all right."

"It's getting late."

"You guys just got here."

"I got my dog in the truck. She doesn't mind waiting an hour or two, but I need to check on her."

"What kind of dog?"

"Golden."

"Oh, my God!" Jasmine squealed. "I love Goldens! Let's go see her."

"Okay. I can grab a cab with the dog. The boat's only a couple miles down, if you guys need the truck."

"No, I'll get a ride with Jaz," Travis said, looking at her. "You get off in a little while, don't you?"

"I get off just looking at you," she said, giving him a big smack on the lips. Now, let's go see that dog of yours. What's its name?"

"Sierra. Sure you don't need the truck?"

"No. Since we weren't booked, Jaz and I made plans for when she gets off. I'll see you in the morning."

"All right."

"How much we owe you?" I asked her as I got up and reached into my jeans. "You never brought us the bill."

"It's on me," Jasmine said.

"No way."

"Way," she said, doing her Valley Girl imitation. "Besides, I get a great employee discount…so smile, be gracious, say thank you." I did. "I'm up next," she announced. "Sure you don't want to stay a little longer?"

"And see you on stage?"

"Yeah," she said proudly.

"Call me old-fashioned, but it looks like we might all be hanging out together. I'd feel better just saying goodnight now."

"You're so cute," she said, giving me a peck on the cheek. "Let me see if I can trade turns…I want to meet your dog. I'll be right back." She headed towards the locker room. I slipped a $20 under one of the plates.

"You got yourself quite a woman there," I told Travis.

He agreed. "I know. She's cool."

"Love her attitude. So full of energy."

She came bouncing back. "I've got 10 minutes. Let's go. You coming out with us?" she asked Travis.

He looked from her to the stage. "Beautiful nude girl…" He held out his hands weighing his options. "Or dog. Tough decision. I just don't know."

"See you tomorrow, amigo," I cut in, shaking his hand.

"See 'ya in the morning, boss."

Jasmine instantly fell in love with Sierra. They played in the parking lot until she had to get back inside. "I'm looking forward to meeting your other two girls." She'd lost me. "Come on," she prompted. "I was starting to think you were a pretty sharp cookie." Stepping back, she held up her index finger. "One, Sierra. Two, your girlfriend, Jennifer—"

"And the third?" I still didn't get it.

"Your boat."

"Oh…I wasn't thinking."

"Most men don't after they've been inside there for a while," she said nodding back towards the club.

"That's true."

"Anyway, I'm looking forward to meeting Jennifer and seeing the boat."

"You're welcome on board anytime. When Jennifer gets back, we'll do dinner together. I think she's really going to like you."

"Sounds like fun."

"It really has been a pleasure meeting you," I said, extending my hand.

"The pleasure's been all mine," she replied, sliding past my hand to give me a full body hug. None of that A-frame crap—a full contact wrap-around hug that sent a surge of energy shooting through me. Leaning in the window, she gave Sierra a kiss goodbye before heading back to work. "See ya'," she said, smiling over her shoulder before disappearing through the front doors.

"You ready for a little walk?" I asked Sierra, firing up the truck. She wagged her tail and gave me a lick. Life was good.

******

The next morning, Travis and Jasmine showed up at the boat before I was awake. I heard them rattling around in the galley, but it was the smell of bacon frying that finally motivated me to roll out of the sack.

"Good morning, Sunshine," Jasmine said, beaming as I followed Sierra into the salon. I wasn't sure if she was addressing the dog or me. With all the affection Sierra then received, I realized she was talking to the dog. "Get a good night's sleep?" she asked, looking up in my direction.

"I did…and you?"

"Absolutely. Slept like a rock.'' Her smile was far too radiant for this early in the morning. She was flushed with the look of love. "Freshly squeezed," she said, handing me a glass of OJ.

"Thanks. Where's Travis?"

""Below. Said he wanted to check the engine room before we ate." I sat on the settee around *Vintage's* varnished teak table opposite the galley. "Looks like you got him pretty well trained," she commented, glancing towards the open engine room hatch just outside the salon.

"Not me. All the credit has to go to his old man. I've never met anyone who understands boats better than his dad."

"Lloyd's something special, isn't he?"

Surprising me. "You know Lloyd?"

"Since I can remember. We're next-door neighbors. My parents still live there."

"How long have you've known Travis?"

"Since we were kids."

"I thought you guys just met."

"Like twenty years ago. I've had a crush on him since I was a kid. He's seven years older than I am, so he always treated me like his kid sister. When he went into the Coast Guard, I wasn't even old enough to drive. We didn't see each other the whole four years he was gone."

"And when he came home?"

"I wasn't a little girl any more."

I had no idea what she looked like as a kid, but she had definitely blossomed into one of the most beautiful young women I'd ever seen. "So what happened?"

"What do you mean?"

"How did you and Travis get together?"

"I bought my place last year, so I wasn't around when he came home. One day, while I was talking to my mom on the phone, she mentioned he was back in town."

"She knew?"

"Well, yeah—moms know everything. She knew I had a crush on him when I was younger. They love him. I think she was hoping I still had some feelings for him. It had been years, but she let me know he was back in town. You know…girl talk."

"Obviously the crush was over?"

"He never had a clue. I thought about him a few times while he was gone…more as a friend than anything romantic. Certainly wasn't expecting anything like this," she said, holding out her arms and smiling. "I just wanted to see how he looked…you know, say hello. Curious more than anything else. I asked Mom to call me if she saw him hanging around. A few days later, she did. I drove over and played it a little coy."

"What did you do?"

"It was a sunny Saturday morning. I put on a pair of cut-off shorts and a little halter top—made sure he couldn't miss me while I was washing my car."

"I can only imagine," I said, picturing her with a hose and bucket of suds.

"After awhile he came out. Couldn't believe it was me." Jasmine flashed me a look like the cat that eaten the parakeet. "And, as they say, the rest is history."

"Looks like history in the making."

"True. Romance is never easy, but so far, so good," she said as she broke a dozen eggs into a big mixing bowl. Despite the fact it was the first time she'd been on board, she moved effortlessly around the galley. She sautéed a finely diced sweet Maui onion in a big iron skillet before pouring in the whipped eggs. The tantalizing aroma of bacon and fried onions kicked my taste buds into overdrive.

"I had no idea."

Turning towards me and holding the wooden spoon she'd been scrambling the eggs with, she spread open her arms and did a deep curtsy, as if taking a curtain call. "No way you could have known he'd fallen in love with the girl next door. I don't think he even knew until last night when we were all talking."

"That was pretty intense."

"Sometimes you've got to just play the cards you're dealt."

"Most people don't. They won't make the call. Can't go all in. Figure the little they have is better than nothing."

"That's why I laid it on the table last night. Life is simply too short."

I couldn't have agreed with her more. "From what I've seen so far, he'd be a fool to let you go."

"It's not easy. I know I'm not very old, but I know what men want...or at least what they think they want. Deny 'em, and the relationship is doomed." Realizing she was getting a pretty philosophical, she smiled shyly. "Sorry I was going off there."

"No. By all means, please continue."

"Most mothers don't teach their little girls the truth. They make up these fairytale fantasies we end up believing in, hoping for things that don't even exist. It's no wonder there are so many unhappy marriages and divorces. Any woman who learns and understands a man's needs is way ahead of the game."

"And you think you understand us?"

"Better than most of you understand yourselves."

"You've got my attention."

"Primal instincts, baby. Primal instincts."

"Come on, that doesn't tell me a thing."

She hesitated, assessing my investment in the conversation. "Okay," she said. "It's so simple, few get it."

"Get what?"

"How to take care of a man's most basic needs."

"That's easy...sex."

"That's the mistake most everyone makes—thinking it's just the sex."

"Then what is it?"

Locking her crystal clear green eyes on mine, she held me there.

"Surrender...total surrender." She paused, allowing the words to sink in. Glancing at the skillet, she smiled more to herself than at me. "When a woman let's go...I mean, let's go of everything and holds nothing back...when she's willing to let go of everything, every fiber of her being and totally surrenders...then she creates an opportunity for unlimited possibilities. There's nothing in the world as powerful." She noticed my forehead wrinkle, trying to follow her train of thought, so she continued. "When a woman totally surrenders...gives her entire being...she creates a vortex of unlimited creation."

"Like the gift of life. Having a child."

"That's obviously a part of the creation I'm talking about. It happens every day. Women get pregnant all the time, but never surrender anything more than their vaginas. But that's not what I'm talking about. Children are beautiful, don't get me wrong. I'm looking forward to raising a family. But what I'm referring to is the pure essence of surrender. Even if the man doesn't consciously realize what he's being given, his soul intuitively knows, and believe me, that changes everything." She paused. "You don't have to answer this, but I think you know what I'm talking about. What's it like when you and Jennifer are together, making love?"

I hesitated. Trying to figure out where this conversation was heading.

She waited patiently. So I decided to go ahead and answer truthfully.

"Transformational...all consuming...being with her is the most incredible thing I've ever experienced in my life. Sometimes when I wake up, I don't even know where we've been, but it's out there. I've never felt closer to anyone in my life."

"I knew it." She said. "I can see it in your eyes. She's giving you her entire being."

I nodded. "So what are you saying? Women should just give themselves over to us?"

"Not even close. You're missing the point. Only the most courageous women can do it. O.K. What happened when you guys met?"

"I ran for the hills."

Jasmine started cracking up. "You're all the same. Big babies. Afraid of being hurt."

"Getting your heart handed to you on a silver platter sucks."

"No doubt," she said. "And every time it happens it gets harder and harder to risk it again. Before you know it, we're all walking around hiding behind our fears." She paused, "What makes it so hard, is the fact most of us first fall in love when we're young, and all the guys are looking for is sex. So we get our hearts ripped out before we even know what hit us. Eventually, we figure out ways of getting what we want without being vulnerable, without surrendering. Then it becomes a game…manipulation for control. That's what really sucks."

I nodded.

"We've all been hurt. Anyone who has ever loved has been there."

"Even with all the feelings I had for Jennifer when I met her," I admitted, "I was too scared to do anything about it. I didn't think I could go through it again."

"You wouldn't be in love right now if you weren't willing to risk being hurt again. It doesn't work any other way. You only get what you're willing to give."

"I agree."

"She makes you feel complete because she's given you everything—heart and soul. Yet she's the strongest woman you've ever met. Right?"

"Yea, you're absolutely right."

She smiled again as she finished scrambling the eggs. "It's all about letting go…."

"Well, how do you see yourself?"

"Don't think you're asking me what I see when I look in the mirror," she answered, gently probing, testing the waters.

Her reflection was dazzling off any reflective surface, but we both knew that wasn't what we were talking about. So I continued, "At your being, at us as human beings? Do you think we're created at birth, live, die, suffer, prosper—whatever. Like they say, from dust to dust?"

"Like who says?"

"You know, the righteous, the chosen few. Or do you think there's something more?"

"As a race, or as individuals?"

"Fuck the human race." I answered immediately. "We suck. Dead-last every time."

Her contagious laugh filling the salon, as I continued. "Fat, lazy and the biggest bunch of dumb asses in the world. Slowest Goddamned learners of any species ever created. Nothing but a bunch of screen lickers. Can't seem to get it right no matter how many times we try."

"So you think we get more than one shot at this thing?" she asked, looking me directly in the eye.

"Absolutely."

"I agree," she said thoughtfully, "no doubt." As she gently brushed a stray strand of golden hair away from her face, she added, "Gave up the race, or at least my faith in humans, a long time ago." She paused, her eyes in shadow. "But as individuals," the sparkle returned, "we're incredible."

I nodded in agreement. "Beyond words."

"What's beyond words?" Travis asked coming back into the salon.

"Nothing," I answered.

"What are we having?" Travis continued.

"Scrambled eggs with fresh avocado, sautéed onions and jalapeno cheese, toasted English muffins, crispy bacon just the way you like it, and freshly squeezed OJ." Jasmine set down a couple of steaming plates of the best looking breakfast I'd ever seen.

"Everything's good below, Skipper," Travis said, sitting down across from me in the settee. "God, it smells good in here. I'm starved."

"How is it?" she asked.

"Delicious!" I answered through a mouthful of bliss. "There's a taste in here I can't put my finger on? A spice or something...," I said, taking another bite of eggs.

"I squeezed a little fresh lemon on the avocados," she said, boxing Travis in and sitting down with her plate.

"That's it," I said. "Great breakfast. Thanks."

"My pleasure," she smiled, sitting down with us and digging in.

"Why haven't you told me about this lady?" I asked Travis.

"Haven't you figured him out yet?" Jasmine asked me.

"I'm still working on it."

"He's the strong silent type. Didn't even tell me he dove in and saved that guy's life. I had to read about it in the *Log*."

"Are you kidding me?" I asked Travis.

"I told her," he said dryly.

"Yeah," Jasmine said sarcastically. "You told me you guys had to save some jerk who fell overboard. You made it sound like it was no big deal."

"Yeah, well...."

"Travis," I said, "that guy would have died if it hadn't been for you. You saved his life."

I stopped chewing for a minute. "We did it together. Remember?"

"Like I said," Jasmine added, "He's my John Wayne."

******

The boat was pretty well dialed in. Steve came down from C-fab and measured for the new brackets. Said he'd have them installed within twenty-four hours. That was the only thing left on our list, so with no charters booked, we decided to take the day off. After cleaning up the galley, we pulled out the beach chairs, cranked up the stereo and headed up to the bow—or, as Jasmine called it, the beach. It felt great to do nothing but bake in the sun and enjoy the day.

Jasmine fell in love with Sierra. She gave her a bath and then spent most of the afternoon brushing out her coat. Sunshine and good tunes. Clear blue skies and a gentle summer breeze blowing across the bay made for a perfect day. *Perfect...except Jennifer wasn't with us.* Late that afternoon, Jasmine had to get ready for work, which I assumed was just a matter of showering and shampooing...not much of a wardrobe to worry about. "You have no idea," she said. "You'd be amazed."

"You work naked," Travis added.

"Yeah, eventually. But what we wear before we get there sets everything up. It's all about the tease, boys," she said with a seductive smile, twirling a light Hawaiian print sarong around her bikini-clad body, draping it over her shoulder and partially hiding her breast. Slowly she let it slide off her shoulder, over her breast and down her hip. Travis and I didn't take our eyes off her. "See what I mean?"

She was right. We'd been together all day and didn't think twice about her being in a swimsuit that was barely legal. But when she hid behind the sarong and started revealing herself, we were mesmerized. She laughed out loud at our reactions. "Guys are so easy."

"If you could bottle that smile of yours, you'd be rich," I told her.

"I'm already rich," she beamed. "Wealth beyond money. Got to go, honey. You coming by later?"

"Definitely," Travis said. "I'll walk you up the dock."

"See you later," she said, giving me a hug before mauling Sierra.

"She's something else, isn't she?" Travis said when he got back.

"You'd better believe it. And all this time I thought you were just whoring around down there."

"At first, but then Jaz and I started hanging out. The more time I spent with her, the less I want to see other chicks."

"I know how you feel."

"I don't know…we'll see," Travis said. "She's so different. Most of the women I've dated start getting all possessive. You go out a few times and before you know it, they start closing in, like they want to own you. But it's so different with Jaz. I don't get that at all from her. In fact, just the opposite."

"She's one smart lady."

"It's hard to explain. It's like she's totally content just loving me." I smiled, thinking about the conversation we'd had that morning while Travis was below. I let him continue without saying anything. "It's like she doesn't have to have my love in return. It's so weird. It's not like she's detached or anything. It's actually feels like the opposite. She's happy just being with me. It makes me want to be with her all the more."

"I know what you mean. Jennifer's the same way."

"Like last night," he continued, thinking out loud, trying to figure things out for himself. "When that chick asked us if we wanted her to join us, Jaz was fine with it. She left it totally up to me."

"Have you guys actually done any threesomes?"

"We've tried it a few times," he said.

"No shit."

"Oh, yea…at first it was erotic as hell. Seeing the girls together …being in the middle. It was serious overload. Half the time I didn't know what was going on, or who was doing what to whom. It was insane."

"I can only imagine."

"But," he confessed. "The funny thing was…I missed Jaz. With the other girls there, it was a totally different experience. It's hard to explain. Erotic as hell. The sensuality was overwhelming. It was just plain nasty. But after a few times, I really started missing the closeness Jaz and I share when we're alone." I nodded as Travis continued, trying to put his feelings into words—not something guys are very good at or do very often. "I got a feeling she was doing it more for me than for herself. She was cool with it, said she'd always wanted to see what it felt like being with a woman, but I think after the first time, she'd gotten what she was looking for. After I asked her how it was and she said she was a trisexual."

"A what?"

"Trisexual. That she'd try anything once. But after that first time, I felt as if she was just going along with what I wanted. It's funny. Just the fact she's willing to try shit like that is enough. It makes me not even want to do it again. Makes me want her even more."

Momentarily catching one another's eyes, he added, "And don't be fucking telling her or anyone about this," he demanded.

Holding up my palms, "Promise."

"I don't know…it's weird. What do you think?"

Looking away, I didn't answer him right away. Knowing he was the only one that could make that decision. "That's up to you, Trav. It's your call."

He nodded, but I could feel he wanted more. "Is she seeing anyone else?"

"I don't think so. Haven't asked, and she hasn't said anything. We just started hanging together. She's so easy to be around. Like today…she just fits in. It's hard to explain."

"I know what you mean. It's nice having her around. Easy to talk to, intelligent and yet she sat there for hours without saying a word. Are you seeing anyone else?"

"No. Like I said, I don't even want to. And that's never happened to me before."

"Maybe you're falling in love."

"Shit," he said, shaking his head. "I'm too young to be in love."

"You might want to rethink that."

Travis nodded.

We'd been working together for weeks, and this was the first time we'd ever talked like this.

"I wouldn't trade Jennifer for the world," I confided in him. "I've never felt anything like this in my life. I don't know squat about soul mates and all that crap, but I'll tell you one thing—she means the world to me. I wouldn't know what to do without her."

******

The next evening, I caught up with Larry as he was working his way down the dock. "Any word from *Dorsal*?" Calling in daily fish reports is standard, even on multi-day trips, so I was taken back when Larry told me he hadn't heard from them since they left. "That's a little weird, don't you think?"

"No, not really," Larry answered causally, as we kept walking. "Most likely they're just outside radio range. Couldn't reach us."

"What about the side band or relaying?"

"They may have tried calling. It's no big deal. I was out most of the day. Probably just missed their call." Larry wasn't even remotely concerned.

"Nothing on your answering machine?"

"No."

"Larry, would you do me a big favor. We don't have a sideband on board, but when you get home tonight, will you try raising them? I'm a little worried because no one has heard from them in 24 hours."

Dismissing my worries. Larry patted me on the shoulder like a father. "Don't worry, they're fine. But if it'll make you feel better, I'll give them a call as soon as I get home tonight. I'll call you if I get a hold of them, okay?"

"Thanks. I'm just worried about Jennifer, that's all."

"Don't be. They're fine. Joe's one of the best skippers I've got. If there'd been any trouble, the entire fleet would have heard about it by now. No news is good news. By the way, looks like I've got you guys booked day after tomorrow."

"We're ready to rock."

"Maybe you should make the grocery run for tomorrow night and have the boat stocked when she gets back," he suggested.

"Promise you'll call me when you talk to them."

"I promise," he said, stepping on board the *El Jeffe*. I headed back down to *Vintage*.

"What do you say, girl?" She looked up with those big brown eyes and smiled, wagging her tail. Sitting on the transom doorstep, she laid down on the swim step under my legs. We just watched and listened. Life at the marina never comes to a complete stop. There's always something going on…boats heading in or pulling out…baitfish puddlin'…birds hunting for a meal under the lights… there was plenty to watch until it was time for bed.

Fragments of horrible dream-like images ripped through the recesses of my brain, waking me up but then disappearing just beyond consciousness. Normally I'm out like a light, but tonight was different. In the morning I woke up exhausted with a pounding headache. I hadn't heard from Larry. I lay there for a while, but couldn't go back to sleep. I got up and called Larry. It was a little before seven. I could tell by the scratchy sound of his voice that I had woken him up.

"Hello. Cortez Charters."

"Larry. This is Corey. Sorry to wake you, but I didn't hear from you last night. Did you got through to *Dorsal*?"

He was still half asleep. "Who?

"*Dorsal*, Larry. I'm worried about Jennifer."

"Oh, Corey. Okay. Yeah, is that you?"

"Yeah, it's me. Did you reach *Dorsal*?"

"No, I didn't." My heart skipped a beat as he continued. "I tried calling them a couple of times, but didn't get any response." He started to tell me to quit worrying, but I cut him off.

"Larry, something's wrong. I can feel it. Something isn't right."

By now he was awake and pissed. "Listen," he snapped. "I told you last night to quit worrying. I can't believe you woke me up over this. Boats go out all the time and don't radio in. It's no big deal. We should hear from them this morning when they're on their way home."

"How do you know?" I pleaded.

"Goddamn it," he barked. "If something was wrong, we would have heard about it. Everyone is supposed to radio in, but if they don't get a count, half the time I don't hear from them until they're almost back to the harbor. It's not like the landings. Our boats don't depend on fish counts. It's just a courtesy. You know that. I like to be able to tell the next group how their boat did, but that's it. I'm telling you…it's no big deal not hearing from them. Relax, will ya? You're driving me nuts."

I heard him light up and inhale his first cigarette of the day. Exhaling, he continued. "Their side band might be down, for Christ sake, who knows. You're driving me crazy with this shit."

"Sorry, Larry," I said, "I can't help it."

"I'm not running a Goddamned babysitting service. I'm hanging up now. Goodbye."

Listening to the dial tone made me feel even worse. *Maybe he's right. Maybe I'm worrying over nothing.* But that haunting feeling lingering at the back of my brain just wouldn't leave. *Trust your instincts.* "But what am I supposed to do?" I asked myself out loud. Sierra stood there looking up at me. "What do you think?" She just wagged her tail. "You're no help," I said, reaching down and patting her head. "Want to go for a little run?" She perked right up and headed for the transom. "Hang on. Let me get my shoes on."

The morning jog along Harbor Drive was just what the doctor ordered. Put the body in motion and amazing things happen. Works every time. Sierra was in heaven. The longer we jogged, the better I started to feel. Harbor Drive runs along the bay with a long flat patch of grass separating the asphalt from the breakwater, making it a perfect place to jog with a dog. I ignored the leash laws, even though I'd been warned a couple of times. I figured one of these days we'd get tagged, but not today.

An aircraft carrier moored across the bay was busy. Looked like she was getting ready for deployment. Except for a workboat, the portion of the bay before the Coronado Bridge was empty. Unusual, but nice. A few birds mid-channel were working a small bait ball that looked like it was getting pushed up by mackerel, or maybe bonito—couldn't tell for sure—but the silver and black flashes eliminated my first thoughts that maybe some bass were working below. A 737 on its final approach to Lindbergh Field skimmed over the tops of the downtown high-rise buildings. All in all, it was a beautiful morning. Running ahead, Sierra would pick up some interesting scent, let me pass her, and then come racing up from behind, only to start the routine all over again, always giving me the subtlest of head bobs as she passed.

Breathing hard, my heart pounding, it felt good to break a sweat. By the time we got back to the boat, my headache was gone. After showering, I drove over to the market to take care of the shopping list for that night's trip. I loaded up on staples, anticipating a run of charters. The boat had plenty of storage below deck. Having a couple dozen extra cases of drinks and non-perishables on board presented no logistical problems. One of our two fish holds served as a deck freezer, so I went ahead and loaded up on meat, bacon, chicken and frozen goods. I filled up seven shopping carts. At that time of the morning, the 24-hour supermarket wasn't too busy, but they opened up a register for me when I was ready to check out.

"Looks like you've got enough groceries to last a month," the box boy told me on our way out.

"At least a couple of weeks," I replied.

It took two hours to get everything onboard and stowed. I fed Sierra, fixed myself breakfast, cleaned up the galley and then topped off the fresh water tanks, adding a splash of bleach and a box of baking soda. This combination kept any odours out of the system, particularly the hot water heater. With nothing else left to do, I started worrying about Jennifer again, despite telling myself not to. *So much for my mental prowess.* Fortunately, Travis and Jasmine showed up before I slipped into a complete funk.

"What do you think about Jaz coming with us tonight?" Travis asked. They both looked a little apprehensive. I didn't answer right away. "She can take a watch and help Jennifer out with the meals. She'd be working, and you know we could use her with Brian being gone."

He was right. Brian had called yesterday. His mom was making him go visit his grandparents in Shasta. I could tell he didn't want to go, but he said he had to. "I'm really sorry to leave you shorthanded," he said, "but Mom's making me go."

"I understand," I said. "How long are you going to be gone?"

"A week. I'm really sorry."

"It's okay. Don't worry about it. We'll miss you, but we'll be okay."

"You know I'd rather be with you guys, don't you?"

"I know, but your mom's right. Your grandparents aren't going to be around forever."

"Yeah, but why can't I take time off school instead of work?" he pleaded.

I could hear his mom in the background telling him to quit whining. "Don't worry, Brian. We'll be here waiting for you when you get back. Make your mom happy. I'll mean a lot to your grandparents getting to see you."

"Okay, Skipper," he said. "Say hello to Jennifer and Trav for me, okay?"

"Will do. Take care, amigo. We'll see you in a week."

"Okay…thanks! See ya."

With Brian gone for a week, we were going to be a man short. I'd never thought about having another woman on board.

"Well, what do say, boss? We could give it a try and see how she works out," Travis persisted.

"Do you actually want to help work the boat, and not just ride along for a trip?" I asked Jasmine.

"Absolutely," she said. "I don't get seasick and know my way around a kitchen."

"Galley," Travis corrected her.

She rolled her eyes, "Okay…galley. You just had a taste the other day," she continued, building her case. After my cold cereal and burnt toast this morning, the memories of her delicious breakfast flooded my taste buds. "I work hard, and I'm a quick study." She hesitated, looking me in the eye. "Plus, I'd really appreciate the chance to do this. I'm getting a little burned out at the club."

"What's up?" I asked her.

"Nothing really," she said. "It's just lately I've been getting called in at the last minute to fill some shifts that aren't getting covered. Some of the girls haven't been showing up. It's bullshit having to cover. With everything that's going on, I feel like they're taking advantage of me. That's all…no big deal. Thought it might be fun working with you guys."

"It's tough work out there," I told her.

"I realize that," she assured me. "Travis has explained how things work, but I want to give it a try. I really do."

"It doesn't pay anything close to what you're used to making."

"I don't even want to get paid."

"Everyone onboard gets a share."

They both paused, looking at me.

"Watches are a bitch, and if you fall asleep on watch, just once, you're off the boat for good."

"Yeah!" Travis said with an unrestrained pump of his fist.

"Does that mean I can go?" Jasmine asked me excitedly.

"Let's give it a try. See what happens."

She sprang forward and wrapped her arms around me. "Oh, thank you. Thank you so much. You won't be sorry. I promise."

"Let's go get your gear" Travis suggested, reaching out his hand. "Thanks, boss. We really appreciate it. This means a lot to us."

I watched them holding hands on their way up to the parking lot. *We weren't the most talented crew running a boat, but with Jennifer and Jasmine on board, we definitely had a lock on the best looking.*

Larry showed up with our charter group early—around six o'clock—because they'd all flown in from out of state. He'd picked them up at the airport, taken them out to dinner and was now dumping them on us because he had to take care of a dozen other groups leaving that night. Friday nights were booked solid. I hated having passengers on board early. They get all excited and want to shove off as soon as they get there. Normally I wouldn't mind leaving a little early, but we'd been on the beach the past seventy-two hours and I didn't have a clue where the fish were. I was planning on another night of playing follow-the-lights. More importantly, we still hadn't heard from *Dorsal* and I wasn't about to leave without Jennifer. I pulled Larry aside before he left. "This is bullshit, Larry."

"I had to bring them down early," he said, thinking I was referring to the group's early arrival.

"No, not them," I said, gesturing toward the charter group. "I'm talking about the fact that *Dorsal* hasn't radioed in. I've been trying to reach them all afternoon on the VHF. I even went up to the fuel dock and called using their side band. Nothing! They're due back in less than an hour and no one has a clue where they are! I even checked with the Coast Guard and asked them if they'd had any reports on *Dorsal*."

"Jesus, Corey…the Coast Guard?" Larry said, still not even remotely worried.

"Something's wrong, Larry. I'm telling you, something's not right." I couldn't believe *Dorsal's* lack of communication hadn't set off a red flag for Larry as well.

"Look," he said sternly, "I've been doing this for over fifteen years. I'm telling you, if something's up, we'd know about it."

"How?" I demanded.

"I don't know…we just would."

"Bullshit! Maybe at first, but not now. Not when they're due back at the dock any minute and you haven't even gotten a fucking fish report from them."

"Relax," he said, trying to reassure me. "You've got a group to worry about right now. Be a professional and take care of them. I'll ask the other skippers if they've heard anything—maybe on the two-meter."

"I'm not leaving until I know where they are."

"Fuck that!" Larry shot back. "You're leaving at ten o'clock! You're clients are already on board, for Christ's sake."

"I'm not leaving until I know where Jennifer is."

By now, everyone on board had heard us arguing and was listening. He grabbed me by the arm and pulled me up the dock, trying to get us out of earshot. "Shut up, man. You're acting like a jerk!"

"Larry," I said slowly through clenched teeth as I ripped my arm out of his firm grasp. "I've been patient for the past three days. I'm fried, you understand me? I'm at my wits' end. If nothing's wrong, then why haven't they called in?" I demanded.

He shrugged his shoulders. "I don't know," he said with the first hint of concern in his voice. "Maybe they had a shitty trip and don't want to blast it over the horn.'

"That doesn't explain why they aren't returning. I've been blasting calls to them off the fuel dock's side band for the past 48 hours."

"Good point."

"Plus the bite's been wide open these past few days…everyone's getting fish."

"You're right. Stay here. I'll go see what I can find out."

"I'm coming with you."

"Stay here with your people," he insisted.

"No way. I'm going with you." This thing had dragged on long enough. If Jennifer hadn't been on board, I wouldn't have given a rat's ass where the boat was. But they had my girl on board and I wanted her back.

"Okay, okay," Larry said, giving in. "Let's go." All eyes were on us as we started walking back toward the boat.

"Travis." I motioned him over. "I'll be right back. We're going to see what we can find out about Jennifer."

He nodded. I could see the concern in his eyes. He looked over his shoulder at the charter group on the deck and shrugged his shoulders. "What about them?"

"It's early. Tell to them the fish moved up the line today, so we won't have far to run. Remind them we're not scheduled to leave until ten o'clock. Tell them our cook was covering on another boat and I'm going to get her."

"Have the fish really moved up?"

"Fuck, Travis, I don't know! Just talk to them, will ya?" The stress was boiling over. I took a deep breath. "Sorry. I'm freaking out about Jennifer."

"Okay," he said. "Go see what you can find out. We've got it covered here."

Larry and I continued down the finger of the marina where the dock is virtually a full-blown commercial operation. Every major charter boat in the harbour ran out of this marina. It was awash with energy. People were everywhere. Big two-man dock carts were coming and going…crews were pushing carts loaded with fish up to the waiting cannery truck…anglers were streaming down the dock in the opposite direction looking for their rides, their carts full of enough tackle to outfit a small tackle shop. We reached the first of Larry's charter boats, climbed on board and asked for the skipper.

"Dave around?"

"Not here, Larry," said one of deckhands. "Split as soon as we got in. He'll be back soon. What d'ya' need?" Larry asked if they'd picked up any traffic from *Dorsal*. The deck hand said they'd been so busy on deck; he hadn't personally talked to them. "Come to think of it," he added, "it's been a few days. What are they on—a multi-dayer?"

"Yeah," Larry told him, "but they're due back tonight."

"Don't worry. They're fine—"

"But you haven't spoken to them." I interrupted.

"No, but maybe Dave has."

"Thanks," Larry said. "When he gets back. Tell him I'm looking for him, okay?"

"No problem."

We moved on down the line. Still no word from anyone. Finally, the *Tranquility*, a beautiful custom 54-foot Hawthorne, said they had talked to *Dorsal* a couple of days ago.

"When?" I blurted out. "Where were they? Were they okay?"

The skipper, whom I'd never met, looked at me as if I were a wacko. He blew me off, ignoring my barrage of questions and addressed Larry in a cold, controlled voice. "What's going on?"

"Paul," Larry said. "This is Corey Phillips. Owns the *Vintage*. His cook filled in on a three-dayer. He's worried about *Dorsal* because they haven't checked in."

Concern immediately crossed the skipper's face. "You haven't heard from them since they left—not even a fish count?" he asked.

"Nothing," Larry said. "Not a word. When did you talk to them?"

"Three days ago, maybe. Let me think." The skipper paused. "Yeah, it was three days ago. Must have been their first day out. Joe called me on the two-meter. Said he had a couple of guys who'd brought some hookers on board and had no interest in fishing. Told me they just wanted him to head south and anchor up somewhere calm."

"Fuck, I knew it!" I blurted out.

"Joe said he was going to slide into the lee of San Martin and just hang out. Told me his deckhands were worthless with the girls onboard. He sounded a little pissed, because the fish were going off, but he sounded fine. What did he call it? Oh yeah…said they were going to be a floating brothel for the next few days."

"Anything else?" Larry pressed.

"No. Didn't think anything about it. You say they were due back tonight?"

"Yeah. At seven."

"It's almost eight now. Something's wrong." I said.

Looking at me now for the first time since being dismissed, Paul shook his head in agreement. "You might be right. They might be having some trouble, but there hasn't been a word on the horn—nothing on 16, the two-meter, or the side band."

"I've already talked with the Coast Guard. As of a couple of hours ago, nothing there either," I told him.

"What do you think?" Paul asked Larry.

"I'm going to be pissed if I find out their radios are operating and they haven't called in. I'm thinking maybe they had an electrical problem or something and they're okay but they just can't get word out."

"Then why are they late?" I asked anxiously.

"That's a good question," Paul said. "Let's give them another call." We all climbed up to the *Tranquility's* wheelhouse. "*Dorsal, Joe. Tranquility.*" Paul said into the microphone. "One, two, Joe? Pick me up?" Nothing. He switched to the two-meter and set it to one of their code frequencies. "Pick me up, Joe. One, two, *Dorsal.*" Still nothing— not on the side band or on channel 16 when he tried the VHF again. Leaving all the units on frequency, he said, "I think we might have a problem."

"No shit!" I said. "I've been saying that for the past 48 hours. Goddamn it."

"Listen," Paul said looking at me, "what's your name again?"

"Corey."

He looked as if something just clicked. "Hey, aren't you the one who saved that guy overboard awhile back?"

"Yeah, that was us. But what about *Dorsal?*"

"Nice job. That must have been hell."

"Nothing like this," I told him. "Sitting around here worrying. It's driving me nuts. I don't know what to do."

"You guys are starting to get me worried," Larry said.

"'About time!" I snapped back at him.

Paul, the veteran skipper, picked up the microphone set on channel 16. "Coast Guard Group, San Diego, returning, *Tranquility* channel one six. Coast Guard…this is *Tranquility*. We may have a problem here."

"Is this a Mayday situation?" Coast Guard asked, inquiring if an immediate threat to life or vessel existed.

"Negative, Coast Guard. Not with *Tranquility*. However, we want to report an overdue charter vessel."

"Roger, *Tranquility*. Please switch to channel two-two, alpha. Over.”

Once on Channel 22, they went over the details—departure date and time, vessel description, passenger manifest, captain and crew names, scheduled ETA…the works. If the *Dorsal* hadn't been a vessel for hire, they might not have been so concerned, but the word was out now. One of San Diego's top charter vessels had been reported missing.

Paul thanked the Coast Guard, and turned back to us. "As soon as we shove off, I'll get back on the horn and let everyone know. Have you checked with the sports?” he asked Larry.

"No," Larry answered, "but they'll all hear you on 16.”

"There will be over 200 boats running tonight," Paul added. "Within the next couple hours, every boat in the fleet will be looking for her.”

"I'm heading to San Martin," I said, the iron in my voice keeping Larry from whimpering about canceling my charter. Realizing we had a far more serious problem on our hands. I knew he cared for Jennifer and felt responsible for everyone else on board *Dorsal*.

"Keep in touch with me," Paul said. "I'll do the same if I hear anything on this end.”

"I will," I said as we shook hands. "Thanks."

"We'll find them," Paul said with conviction in his voice. "Skipper's been doing this for longer than you've been alive. Don't worry, we'll find them. Could be a thousand things."

Jumping off *Tranquility's* swim step, I ran back to the *Vintage,* leaving Larry in the dust. A smoker, he started breathing hard just climbing the ladder to *Tranquility's* wheelhouse. I leaped on board *Vintage.*

"There's an emergency," I told the group as I looked for the charter master. "I'm sorry, but we have to cancel your trip. We have a missing boat and we're going to look for it."

"Why can't we go?" the charter master asked innocently. "Doesn't look like any of the other boats are canceling their trips."

"I'm sorry," I said keeping my voice under control. "I really am. I know you guys have come a long way. But this could be a life and death situation. We just don't know. So please, gather up your things and leave the boat. Larry is right behind me, and he may another boat for you guys."

I turned to Travis as I headed below to fire the mains. "We're leaving right now. Get Jasmine off the boat and let's go." When I came out of the engine room, Travis had cleared the passengers off the boat. They were standing on the dock, arguing with Larry, who had by this time made it to the back of the boat but couldn't catch his breath. Seeing me come out of the hatch, he nodded his approval. "Let's go," I told Travis. Glancing back at the dock, I didn't see Jasmine. "Where is she? Did she get off?"

"She wants to stay with us."

"Travis, we don't have time for this shit." I flew up the ladder, two steps at a time. Sliding open the wheelhouse window, I saw Jasmine standing mid-ship with the spring line in her hand. The bowline already tossed onboard.

"You're free on the port side," she said.

"Fine," I snapped back. "Leave that spring line on the dock." Checking aft, she'd already freed the stern line as well. "Let her go," Jasmine tossed her line on the dock as Travis freed the starboard stern line and stepped onto the swim step. "You're clear!" he yelled.

Once in gear, the props instantly bit, pushing us out of the slip. We pivoted around and headed out the finger toward the harbor. I goosed her up to speed before we'd even cleared Harbor Island. Travis and Jasmine came quietly into the wheelhouse. About fifteen minutes later, as we passed the bait receivers, Travis broke the silence. "What's the plan?"

"Paul, the skipper on *Tranquility*, told us that he'd talked with them their first day out. Said they were headed for San Martin."

"San Martin?" Travis asked. "What for? Yellows, calicos. The albies are all on the outside."

"Said they weren't going to be doing any fishing. They just wanted a nice place to anchor up with their dates."

"What?"

"I don't know for sure. The guy who's running *Dorsal* told Paul that the guys had brought hookers on board and had no interest in fishing. All they wanted to do was find a calm cove somewhere so they could party."

"Jesus. Why down there. Why not Avalon or even the Coronados?"

"I thought the same thing. I saw the group the night they were leaving. Remember, when I was over there saying good by to Jennifer?" He nodded. "They were so out of place—a couple of slimy looking guys with chicks under each arm."

Jasmine broke in, "How old did they look?"

"I don't know, early 50's."

"I meant the girls?" she said, "How old did the girls look?"

"I don't know. Young. Your age. Definitely a lot younger than the slime balls they were with."

"Was that the night we first met? The night Travis brought you into the club?"

"Yeah, that was the night they left."

"Jesus," Jasmine muttered to herself.

"What?" Travis asked.

"I'm not sure," she said thinking out loud. "It's probably nothing."

"What are you thinking?" I asked her.

"It's probably nothing, but that night—when you guys came in together—two of the girls had been dancing for couple of guys that looked like they were from Jersey or somewhere. Slimy looking. You know—definitely not from around here."

"Go on."

"It was no big deal, but after they'd been with them for awhile, both the girls begged off, saying they were sick."

"And...."

"They left at the same time those slimeballs did. It was pretty obvious they were going to hook-up outside. A little while later, a couple more girls called in sick. They were all part of the same little clique. I didn't care...."

"So what are you thinkin' that you might know these girls...the ones on the charter?"

"I don't know." Jaz said shaking her head. "Probably not. I don't know what I was thinking...it happens all the time."

"What does?"

"Girls calling in sick. But I remember thinking it was weird that all of a sudden we were four girls short. Someone calls in daily with some lame excuse. They actually schedule a couple extra girls every shift because it's so common. But that night, we were *four* short. It was just a little weird."

Grasping at straws, I asked her, "had you ever seen these guys before?"

"No, they were definitely out-of-towners. They gave me the creeps, but they were throwing around money like it was nothing."

"Have you seen any of those girls since?" I asked.

She thought about it for minute. "No. I haven't. Not since that night."

"Is that unusual?"

"No, not really. Like I was saying, four girls all at one time. I remember Howard, the manager bitching about it, saying it was bullshit. Normally, he's cool, but he was pissed because we ended up four short that night. I don't know them that well, anyway…didn't think twice about it." You could see the wheels turning in her head. "But the next night—you know, after we spent that day on the boat—a couple of those girls were scheduled and didn't show up. They didn't even call in, which is a big no-no. Howard got really pissed and threatened to start firing anyone who didn't cover their shifts."

I didn't have a scrap of evidence to support how worried I was other than the fact that *Dorsal* was a few hours late returning from a multi-day trip and hadn't called in. But that was enough. My gut told me this thing was sour from the beginning. "Can you think of anything else about those girls?" I asked Jasmine.

"No, not really. It wasn't any big deal. Girls bail all the time. It's the nature of the business." That's why Howard's usually really cool; he's seen it all. The job certainly isn't for everyone, so he gives us a lot of slack. But I can't help thinking now that it's kind 'a weird that the same night Jennifer leaves on her trip with a couple of Guido-looking guys, four girls from the club go M.I.A. as well."

Looking at Jasmine under the soft glow of the red instrument lights in the otherwise darkened wheelhouse, I pressed her for more information. "Can you remember anything else? Like from earlier that night…before we got there. Or from some other time when girls didn't show. Anything." I let out a deep sigh. I was grasping at straws.

"Before the girls left, I was doing a private a couple of booths over. While I was standing on the seat, I was high enough to see down the row. I was looking around while the guy was staring at me. We do that all the time—crack ourselves up making faces at one another in the mirror. But I remember seeing those guys in the mirror and thinking how one of the girls looked like a white porcelain doll against the guy's jet-black hair and black leather jacket."

"That's them," I said. "I'll bet those are the guys!"

"Even if it is, boss, so what?" Travis asked, his point hitting home and blowing our momentary excitement, thinking we'd had a breakthrough. "Even if it was them, you probably got a better look at them on the dock that night than Jasmine did in the club."

"You're right," I said, wondering what difference it made.

"But maybe there's a connection here," Jasmine added.

I picked up the radio mic and called the marine operator. I gave her Larry's number and asked her to put me through to him. He picked up after the first ring, "Cortez Charters, Larry speaking."

"Larry, it's Corey."

"Have you heard anything?" he asked immediately.

"No, but listen. We might have come up with something here. Travis has been dating this chick from the *Stand*."

"Was she the one that left with you guys tonight?" Larry asked.

"Yeah, yeah, that's her. But listen…the night *Dorsal* left, a couple of girls from the club split early and haven't been seen since. And two more of their girlfriends haven't shown up for work since that night either."

"So?" Larry asked, "What does that have to do with *Dorsal*?"

"Probably nothing…but we've been talking it through. Think about it—those guys had chicks with them that night, remember?"

"I don't know," Larry said. "I'm running a couple dozen boats. I can't remember every passenger."

"You couldn't forget these girls. Remember, when they bent over to take off their pumps, giving everyone on the dock a show."

"Oh, yeah!" he said a trace of a smile forming. "I remember." Visualizing their impromptu peep show. "All decked out—short skirts, heels, low-cut tops. They didn't even flinch. Panties flashing, breasts peaking out. They weren't even embarrassed."

"Yeah, those are the ones. They looked like hookers." Jaz slugged me on the arm. "Ouch," I said, turning toward my assailant.

"We're not hookers," she said defensively.

"I know, I know," I told her. "I'm sorry. I didn't mean you. They were just acting like hookers that night."

"What are you talking about?" Larry asked, overhearing our conversation because I still had the mic cued.

"Nothing. Have you ever chartered to those guys before?" I asked him.

"No."

"So you've never seen them before?"

"I don't meet half my clients until their first trips," Larry informed us through the radio speaker.

"But Larry," I pleaded with him, "those guys weren't fisherman. They were wearing Gucci loafers, for Christ's sake. It was obvious they didn't give a shit about fishing. I'll bet you the girls they had with them were from the club."

"So? Who cares what they wanted to do? Their money is as good as the next guy's."

"I wouldn't give a shit either, except Jennifer is with them and now the Goddamned boats missing."

It felt like Larry still didn't want to admit to himself there was a problem. "What do you suggest?" he asked.

"What do you know about these guys? Don't they have to fill out a form or something before they book?"

"Yeah," Larry said defensively. "Normally I get a deposit, contact numbers, addresses, all that stuff."

"But?"

"But when these guys called to book the boat, all they wanted to know was how much. I told them, and about an hour later, there was a delivery service at my door. The courier handed me a sealed envelope for the total amount, plus tip, in cash."

"Didn't you think that was a little weird?' I asked

"No, not at all. I get cash all the time. I won't let a boat leave the dock unless the trip is paid for in full. No checks or credit cards either, except for early deposits that I can clear before departures. On the night of departure, it's all cash or certified bank funds."

"So you don't know a thing about these guys?"

"Not really. All I got was a name. After they called, before the money arrived, I'd blown them off. Figured I'd never hear from them again. I get calls like that all the time and most of them never amount to squat."

"After the money arrived, what did you do?"

"Nothing. I didn't even have a phone number for them. Only a name."

"Only a name?" I said astonished, "That's all you have?"

"That's it," he admitted. "They paid in full, so I went ahead and booked the boat. I had their money. If they didn't show, so what. It happens more than you can imagine. People book and don't show. Normally they call, either to get their money back or to reschedule. But as long as we have 50%, I don't care. There's nothing I can do about it."
I couldn't believe what I was hearing. "Can you find out the name of the delivery service?"

"Corey, you've been watching too may cop shows. You're driving me nuts with this shit. The boat's going to show up any minute."

"Pull your head out Larry," I said. "I know we don't have anything concrete, but Jennifer's in trouble." I felt sick to my stomach.

"If your girlfriend wasn't onboard, you won't give a shit about the situation. We've already alerted the Coast Guard, the entire fleet is looking for them, and you just pulled away leaving your group standing on the dock. I ought to ace you off the list right now!"

"Fine." I said, clicking off and switching to another channel. "Marine Operator, *Vintage*, Whiskey, Yankee, Victor, 2717, could you please put us through to the Stand in San Diego?" I requested.

"Do you have a number, *Vintage*?"

I started to say "Negative," but before I could finish, Jasmine was telling me the number. As the marine operator was putting us though, I handed Jasmine the microphone. "Find out if any of the missing girls have shown up for work." She looked at the mic. "Just hold down this switch here when you talk." I showed her the switch on the side of the microphone "When you're finished talking, let it go."

"The Stand," said a voice at the other end.

"Willie, is that you?" Jasmine asked, immediately recognizing his voice.

"Yeah. Who's this? Sounds like you're in a cop car."

"No, Willie, it's me…Jasmine. I'm on a boat."

"No shit? What's up?"

"I need to know if, God…I can't remember their names…you know the girls that took off early a few nights back…the skanky ones? You know…I can't remember their names…I need to know if they've come back to work yet?"

"Skanks?" Willie said slowly, teasing her. "Is that any way to refer to your co-workers?"

"Come on, Willie. This is important. Have they been back in since they spilt."

"No. None of them have even bothered to call. Howard swears he's going to fire all of them."

"He won't."

"I know. But listen, Willie. Thanks. I really appreciate it."

"No worries. So, are you really on a boat? That's cool. Where you headed...paradise?"

"Willie, I got to go. Take care."

"Hang on," I interrupted. "Ask him to call Larry if they happen to show up." She did, giving him Larry's number and clicked off. A few seconds later the operator's voice came through the speaker. "Will that complete your traffic for tonight, *Vintage*?"

"Roger, operator. Thanks for your help," I said, taking back the mic. "*Vintage* clear."

What did we really have? *Possibly.* A couple of guys pick up some chicks at a strip club and offer them good money for spending a few of days with them on a multi-million dollar yacht. Ask them to invite a couple of their friends. Not a bad gig. But why hadn't they come home? It's not that uncommon for a charter master to request an extension—especially if they're having a good time. And from the looks of things when they left, these guys were planning on having a really good time. But the Captain couldn't extend a trip without clearing it through Larry, which meant he'd have to call in. It just wasn't adding up.

"It is kinda spooky," Jasmine said.

"Maybe we're wrong about all this," I said.

Neither Travis nor Jasmine said anything.

"I'd look pretty damn stupid, if they're back at the dock in the morning, and we're still running full rack chasing shadows down here in Mexico."

I tried calling *Dorsal* again on several channels. Nothing.

Despite everything, the gentle roll of *Vintage*'s hull underway was helping to calm my nerves.

"Maybe they had some mechanical trouble and being tucked in behind the island, they haven't been able to call out and they're just sitting there, waiting for someone to come and get them."

Travis and Jasmine could see right through me. "Maybe," Travis said. "Either way, at least we're doing something."

"How far is the island?" asked Jasmine.

"About a hundred and sixty miles. Why don't you guys hit the rack."

"You sure, boss?" Travis asked. "I'm fresh. No problem taking first watch if you want me to."

"No, I got it. Get some sleep, both of you."

Jasmine said, getting up and squeezing my shoulder. "Try not to worry too much...we'll find her."

Instead of bunking in topside, they headed below and into one of the nice double staterooms, leaving Sierra and me alone in the wheelhouse. I monitored channel 16 on one of our VHF units and had the other on scan. No traffic relating to *Dorsal*. After awhile, I called the *Tranquility*. Nothing had been reported by anyone. As much as I wanted to believe nothing wrong, I couldn't shake that sick feeling deep in my gut. My head started throbbing.

We kept a 12-gauge shotgun well hidden up under the dashboard in the wheelhouse, because it's illegal to carry firearms in Mexico. A hidden compartment had been built into the boat when she was built. Wrapped in an oil-soaked cloth, the gun had been there ever since. You had to crawl in through a small door cut in the face of the wall supporting the dash to get to it. Once inside, it was a cluster of wires and cables. We'd organized things when we did the retrofit, but it was still enough of a mess that unless you knew what you were doing, you wouldn't want be under there. There was barely enough space to sit up. On top of the wire bundles—at the point where the bottom side of the dash met the back of the front wall—there was enough room to hide a rifle. To help keep any moisture in check we'd added a Goldenrod.

I checked the radar screen, no targets, crawled under the dash, and slid the gun out. In my hands, it felt powerful—cold and menacing. I'd never fired a gun at a living thing, but I loved sporting clays. I grew up blasting soda cans with a .22 off the back deck with Dad. But when I was twelve, he took me on my first hunt and I watched him kill an eight-point buck. He explained it was going to help feed the family through the winter. God knows, I ate my fair share of the tender venison, but after seeing those dead eyes lying there, still open…and the blood trickling out of the dead animals mouth…I never went hunting again.

There are few sounds in the world as menacing as the sound of a shell being pumped into a shotgun. It's enough to put a chill down the spine of anyone not doing the pumping. I inspected the gun. It was clean and well oiled. After loading six shells and ensuring the safety was on, I put the weapon back in its hiding place.

A moderate layer of coastal fog effectively hid the moon, so it was difficult to see even the bow of the boat. Every now and then, a couple of dolphins would jet out from under our bow's wake and speed away, leaving a phosphorous trail of bubbles behind them. The first time it happened, it scared the shit out of me; it looked like torpedoes were coming at us. But once I figured out what was going on, I started looking forward to their visits. Swish…zoom…they'd be streaking away, playing with the push off our bow.

We'd been underway for over five hours. A hundred and ten miles to go. It was just after 3:00 a.m. I figured I better get some sleep. I did another check of the engine room and woke Travis up. Jasmine stirred, but didn't' wake up. "Travis," I whispered as I gently shook his shoulder.

"I'm awake," he whispered back. "What time is it?"

"A little after three."

"Shit," he said, doing the math. "You've been up there for hours. Why didn't you get me earlier?"

"I'm getting you now."

Jasmine moaned and rolled over under the sheet, her hair falling away from her face. "I'll be right up," Travis said. A few minutes later, holding a fresh cup of coffee, he opened the door to the wheelhouse. "You okay, Skipper?"

"Fine. Just figured I'd better try and get a few hours in before daybreak. Wake me if you get tired."

"I'm good...slept like a baby."

I crawled into the bunk Jennifer and I had been sharing. I could still smell her scent on the pillow. *We're coming, honey,* I murmured as I fell asleep.

******

Rolling over...the sun hitting me directly in the eyes. *They must have seen us and fired a flare gun,* I thought to myself, still dreaming. I didn't know where I was. Squinting through the blinding light, I could make out Travis sitting at the wheel. "Is that them?" I asked deliriously.

"What are you talking about," Travis asked looking at the empty horizon.

"Never mind," I mumbled, realizing I'd been dreaming. "What time is it?"

"10:20." Travis knew I liked to know exactly what the time was whenever I woke up.

"What!" I shot up. Looking around. Nothing but water. "It can't be."

"Sure as shit. You were out, so we figured we'd just let you sleep. Jaz is below fixing brunch. You hungry?"

I was still too asleep to know if I was hungry. "How far off are we?" I asked, starting to calculate we'd run about eighty miles since I sacked out. Climbing out of the rack, I picked up the binoculars. The outline of the island barely visible through the haze.

"We've had the island on radar for awhile now. Let's see...," Travis said, looking at the screen. "We're twenty-eight off—just under three hours to the north tip. Figured you could use the rest."

"Hey, he's alive!" Jasmine exclaimed, carrying a couple of plates full of hot food. The cinnamon hit my senses first, instantly activating my taste buds. I was hungry...real hungry. We hadn't eaten last night. Jasmine handed me a plate with eggs Benedict, bacon and what looked like homemade cinnamon rolls.

"This looks wonderful, honey. Thank you," Travis said.

"Enjoy. I'm going to grab a plate and bring up some OJ. You guys need anything else?" We both shook our heads, unable to answer, our mouths already full of food.

"Glad we brought her along now, huh?" Travis said, still chewing.

"It's not that I didn't want her to come. It's just that I don't know what we're doing or what we might be getting ourselves into." I gestured toward the island ahead of us. "It could be ugly."

"How do you figure?"

"We don't have a clue what's going on?"

"I'll bet you dollars to donuts they're broken down in some cove and haven't been able to radio for help."

"Hope you're right. But unless their side band is down, it doesn't make any sense."

"I wish we had one," added Travis. Referring to the fact we didn't have a single side band onboard,

"Yea, me too. I hate falling off the grid like this. Especially down here with all the shit that's going on."

"That's for sure," he asked.

As we got closer to the island, we sighted a couple of pangas working just above the north point. Other than that, no other boats were around. We hadn't made the point yet, so we couldn't see down the backside of the island. If they'd had engine trouble, that's where they would have tried to lay in. At least, that's where we hoped they'd be. Another twenty minutes and we'd know.

As we rounded the inside point of San Martin, my heart sank—there were no American yachts anchored along the lee side of the island. We idled back and ran in close to the rocks, looking for any signs of wreckage. Nothing. No one said anything. We worked our way south along the inside of the island, then around the tip and all the way back up the outside to where we started. Nothing.

I felt the onset of raw fear and panic. Anything could have happened, and no one would ever know. "Where the fuck are they?" I blurted out, breaking the silence in the wheelhouse.

"Let's run down to Natividad," Travis suggested. It was the next island down the Baja, another 30 miles south.

"Let's talk to these pangas first," I said, pointing toward the two small, open boats we had seen when we first came up to the island. When they saw us headed toward them, they started pulling their gear. They were fishing hand lines. As we approached, they waved and held up some empty plastic water bottles. We slid in just down wind of them, and they drifted up to us. Travis reached down and took their empty bottles.

"Hola," I said. "El agua no es problema."

" Gracias. Gracias," they said. "Qué sucede?

In broken Spanish, I tried to tell them we were looking for our friends. They picked up the word amigos, but not much else. Then Jasmine interjected in perfect Spanish, explaining that we were supposed to meet up with another American yacht a couple of days ago, but we were running late. She asked them if they'd seen a big American yacht in the past two days.

"Ninguna señora bonita. Nosotros no hemos visto yates grandes de norteamericano, ni tenemos nosotros vista ninguna mujer tan hermoso como usted."

Jasmine blushed.

"What did they say?"

"Nothing," she said dismissing their complements on her looks. "They haven't seen any yachts recently, at least not in the past few days."

"Fuck it," I said. "Let's go."

Jasmine continued probing as Travis handed them back full jugs of fresh water, along with a six-pack of coke and a couple quarter-pound spools of mono. They thanked us as I put her in gear and pulled slowly away. As soon as we were at speed, I got on the horn and relayed what we'd learned.

As frustrated as I was, there still wasn't any proof something was afoul—it was all just bits and pieces. Little scraps of information, but no real evidence. The one thing we all agreed on was that if nothing was wrong, a veteran charter skipper like Joe would have called in. *Dorsal* was in some type of trouble. I pushed the throttles up a little, urging the ol' girl to give us another knot. She responded, but even at the top of the green, we were still only doing twelve knots. Travis frowned as I pushed her up to eighteen hundred. Without saying a word, he went below to take a look.

"She doesn't like being pushed this hard," he stated when he came back from the engine room.

"She can handle it," I said, not meeting his gaze but knowing what he meant. We'd never pushed her over fifteen hundred, and here I was demanding eighteen for just two more knots. I thought about it and pulled her back to sixteen. Travis relaxed a little, but still didn't like it. After the higher RPM, it felt like we were just sitting in the water, with another thirty miles to cover before we reached Natividad. We'd spent almost two hours circling San Martin and talking to the panga fisherman, so we wouldn't hit Natividad until dusk. I pushed her back up to eighteen. Travis left the wheelhouse; worried she'd come apart at the seams. I figured we had relatively calm seas and were running downhill. The extra fifteen minutes we were gaining might give us the time we needed to survey the rocks before dark. After dark, we'd have to use the searchlight, which would take much longer. A wave of new fear sent shivers through my body. My hands would have started shaking if I hadn't been squeezing the wheel.

"What if they didn't have any mechanical trouble? What if something else happened?" I asked Travis as he and Jaz came back into the wheelhouse.

"Like what?" Travis asked.

"What if they've been hijacked?"

"Come on," he said, shaking his head. "Now you're really reaching."

I got back on the horn and still was able to raise *Tranquility*. We were already too far down the line to reach San Diego Coast Guard on VHF directly. I asked *Tranquility* to relay that *Dorsal* had not been seen at San Martin and were on our way to Natividad.

"Don't you guys have a side band on board?" Paul wanted to know.

"No, it's on the list."

"Not good," Paul said. "Especially where you're headed. Not good at all. You're going to be running without any communications. I can barley read you now."

"I know, Paul, but we've got no choice. I've got to find Jennifer."

"I realize that, but heading down the Baja without any communications is asking for trouble."

"We'll try to relay whenever we can."

After a long pause, Paul came back. "Roger. Understand. I've been monitoring 2182 all day. Nothing. Nothing on the two-meter, either."

"Shit."

"Good luck, Corey. Relay whenever you can."

"Roger." My voice crackled back to *Tranquility*.

And that was that. We were on our own from here on, outside VHF range except for passing vessels.

Natividad is another small island located about a third of the way down the Pacific side of Baja. An isolated, rough rocky island, it's similar to San Martin. The island's only occupants consist of a few hardcore Mexican fishermen living in makeshift lean-tos. When we arrived, we were greeted by another group of pangas holding up empty plastic water jugs and empty five-gallon gas cans. With our water maker on board, we were glad to fill all the fresh water containers they had. But they were on their own for gas—we had only the six gallons strapped to the floor of our Achilles. We all wondered how the hell they survived out there with nothing.

Jasmine went through an array of questions regarding *Dorsal* or any other American yacht. They hadn't seen anything—not for at least a couple of weeks. They were obviously taken by Jasmine. One of the bolder young men asked if he could have a picture of her. She was flattered, but said she didn't have any pictures. Instead, she tossed them one of the *Penthouse* magazines she'd found under the sink in the crew's quarters.

"Hey! What are ya thinking?" Travis objected half-heartedly as the fisherman fought over what would be their prized possession for a long time to come.

"Relax," Jasmine retorted. "What are you worrying about when you've got the real thing?" She pulled down the left side of her bathing suit, flashing him the side of one of her beautiful breasts. That sent the Mexicans into a feeding frenzy.

"We're out of here," I said, pushing the boat into gear. Looking back as we pulled away, I saw Jasmine waving at her newfound following. The fisherman all pulled their torn T-shirts up and down over their heads. Being the fine outstanding citizen she was, Jaz responded to their requests by pulling the top of her suit off. The sight of her bare breasts sent the entire fleet of panga fisherman into pandemonium. I could hear them screaming and hollering over the sounds of the mains. They collapsed into one another's arms, laughing and yelling hysterically. It was a pretty funny sight. One thing for sure—they'd never forget us…or at least, Jasmine. International relations at their best.

Shortly after, she came up to the wheelhouse. "Miss your old job, do you?" I asked. She smiled and slid into the seat next to Travis.

"You're too much," he said, giving her a hug.

"They loved it," she said.

As we continued south, away from Natividad, towards the islands of

Benito and Cedros, it was tearing me apart imagining what might be happening to Jennifer.

******

Onboard the *Dorsal* the men had been below decks, each in a separate stateroom, each with two of the girls, since they'd told the *Dorsal's* captain, Joe, all they wanted to do was run down to the nearest island and anchor up, so they could party with the girls.

"So you sure don't want to do any fishing?" Joe asked, still not believing that his beautiful charter fishing vessel was becoming nothing more than a floating brothel.

"You saw those girls," the one guy said with a sly, almost sickening tone, "Would you waste any time fishing, when you could be fucking ass like that."

It wasn't a question.

After that, the guys took the girls below into their staterooms. To the obvious disappointment of the young deckhands who hadn't been able to keep their eyes off the young beauties.

"Did you see that one in the short black skirt? Her legs were incredible," one of the deckhands asked his buddy.

"No shit. And that blond, man her tits were perfect."

"O.K. knock it off, you guys," Joe commanded. "Go down and ask Jennifer if she'll come up here."

Jennifer hadn't been privy to the conversation between the skipper and the charter guys; she'd been below serving drinks to the girls, who were already high as kites.

"Can you believe how much they're paying us for just three days," one of the girls asked no one in particular. "Fucking ten thousand dollars each!" Answering herself as she reached into her tiny purse and pulled out a fat wad of hundred dollar bills.

"And we're going to some island, on this beautiful yacht," another girl chimed in, spreading her arms and twirling around like a prima ballerina.

"I don't care how gross those guys are," another chimed in. "For this kind of money I'd dance around this boat naked for a week."

"You and me both, baby," the first girl added, high-fiving the ballerina. "This is going to be so much fun."

The guys came down from the wheelhouse and with a disgusting wink at Jennifer, each took one of the girls under each of their arms and led them below.

Jennifer had just finished cleaning up the glasses, when one of the deckhands came into the salon, "Skipper wants you topside. We're having a little meeting."

"Sure," Jennifer said, following him topside.

"It looks like we're going to be babysitting for the next three days," Joe told everyone. "Pisses me off a little bit because the fish are really starting to go off outside." He took deep breath, before continuing. "We're going to be running down the line to San Martine and anchoring up."

"It's not all bad," one of the young deckhands said.

All he got was a sideways glance from his Captain.

"Come on, Capt. Those girls are knockouts and having them running around the boat in their bikinis for three days isn't going to be all that bad, now is it?"

"Don't be so rude," Joe interrupted. "We've got a lady on board."

"Boys will be boys," Jennifer said with a smile. "Anything special you'd like me to do?" she asked her new captain.

"I'd make sure and lock my door if I was you," he said jokingly, looking over at his young deckhands. "Especially with these knuckleheads lucking around."

Everyone laughed.

"If you weren't so old and married, you'd be as pumped about this as we are," one of the deckhands told him.

"Alright," Joe said. "Everyone hit the rack. I got first watch. Jennifer, we'll see you in the morning."

"O.K., Skipper, see you in the morning."

"Call me Joe."

"Will do. Goodnight, everyone," she added, making her way out of the wheelhouse to her stateroom below. The *Dorsal* was large enough to have both a small Captain's quarters and a crew's quarters inside her wheelhouse.

Jennifer was the only crewmember bunking below.

An hour or so later, long after everyone had fallen asleep, Joe found himself sitting there on watch, smiling, because the more he thought about it, the more he'd convinced himself, the next three days might actually be fun. Having a boat full of pretty girls, and a few days off from hard-core fishing, may not to be such a bad deal after all. *Plus I love San Martin. Great calico fishing and maybe we'll even get lucky and hang a few yellows while we're sitting there on the hook.*

The next thing he felt wiped the smile off his face. The unmistakable feeling of an ice-cold gun barrel being jammed into the back of his neck. He froze.

"That's right, don't move a muscle and everything's going to be just fine. No one gets hurt."

Joe didn't move.

"Hands up, please."

He slowly raised his hands.

"Now slowly stand-up and don't say a word."

His legs weak as he stood.

Staying behind him his assailant guided him away from the helm station towards the rear of the wheelhouse. Once there he was ordered to put his hands behind his back. A zip tie suddenly snapped his hand together. Additional pressure from the gun barrel kept him from moving his head or even asking what was going on. The last thing he remembered was a wet towel being held across his moth and nose. His eyes immediately started stinging, his throat burned, but only for an instant, as the Hydromorphone took effect. Passing out, they caught his body as he collapsed, laying him unceremoniously, but quietly to the floor. The rest of the crew received the same treatment, one by one.

The crew now, bound and gagged, the goons had taken control of the boat within just a couple of minutes and without so much as a peep from anyone.

"Like a walk in the park," said one of assailants, smirking.

"Got 'a love modern medicine," the other said securing the lid on the bottle of liquid death they'd brought on board.

"You want to get the girl tonight, or just wait until the morning?"

Let's take care of her now."

"Jennifer hadn't locked her stateroom door, in fact, she never even thought twice about it. Not that it would have made any difference. They had her gagged and bound, just like the men, before she even knew what was happening.

******

"Keep your fucking hands off me, you asshole!" Jennifer screamed at one of her captors. She was rewarded with a vicious slap across the face that blurred her vision and filled her eyes with tears. Knocked back against the galley counter, she fought to keep her balance, but wouldn't give in to the pain. That infuriated her assailant even more.

"Worthless fucking cunt!" he snarled at her, raising his hand to hit her again.

"Go ahead, mother fucker," she hissed at him through clenched teeth. "Hit me, you pussy. And then see what your boss has to say when he sees you messed up my face."

Hand still raised, he hesitated. They stood there...eyeball to eyeball...less than a foot apart. Jennifer could feel her legs giving out. She thought she was going to pee herself, but held onto the corner of the counter. The stench of his breath, the stale cigar smoke and his putrid body odor were enough to make her gag, but she didn't flinch. She saw the indecision in his eyes before he spoke.

"Think you're one tough bitch, don't you, you little cunt?" She held her ground. Not moving or saying a word, she held his gaze. She didn't blink or look away. When he lowered his hand, she started to relax. Before she knew it, with lightning speed he punched her in the stomach. She doubled over in excruciating pain. A black wave of nausea swept over her and she started to pass out. "You think you got this all figured out, don't you?" He said, chuckling. "You worthless cunt," he snarled as he stepped back. "Listen to me, bitch. You're only alive so you can feed us, you hear me? If Tony didn't think you'd be worth more clean, I'd have your head shoved into the floor and my cock jammed so far up your ass you wouldn't even know what day it is."

She knew he was right. Tony was the one in charge. But still, she was scared shitless. Deathbreath, as she referred to him, was not to be taken lightly.

"Do you hear me, cunt?" he bellowed. Still bent over, arms wrapped around her stomach, she nodded. "Fuck you," he said, kicking her over, dismissing her, enjoying her pain. "You're going down, bitch," he hissed. "I hate pushy broads. Before this thing is over, I promise you, your ass is mine." He spit on the floor, just missing her head. "Now bring us up some food," he demanded as he headed back up to the wheelhouse.

Relief flooded over her. She started shaking uncontrollably, no longer able to hold back the tears. The taste of salt from her tears mixing with the blood in her mouth. Closing her eyes, she stood alone in the galley, holding on by the thinnest of threads, fighting to keep herself together. Slowly the adrenaline began to drain out of her system... but not the fear. She knew the only reason she hadn't been drugged, raped and thrown in with the other girls was because the assholes were too lazy to feed themselves. She knew she was pushing it mouthing off like that. He'd come up behind her and grabbed her ass, squeezing hard, scaring her to death. Yelling at him was more of an instinctive reaction than anything else. Still, she'd held her own... *barley*. But, God, did those two punches hurt. The initial slap had cut her mouth. Spitting blood into the galley sink, she could feel a bruise starting to form around her eye. She thought about icing it, but figured the worse it looked, the better her chances of having Tony step in to defend her. Another wave of nausea swept over her.

Tony told the hit man he could do whatever he wanted to the others, as long as he didn't bruise them up. "Fuck 'em until they can't walk, for all I care," he'd said, "but I don't want to see a single scratch on any of them."

"But, boss," the goon had protested, "it's no fun when they're all drugged up like this." He held up a girl's limp arm. "See?" he said, letting it drop. "She doesn't even know what the fucks going on."

Tony grunted. "If you didn't have such a little pencil dick," he said mockingly, laughing out loud at his own joke, "maybe she'd feel something."

"Fuck you," the goon shot back.

"You'd like that, wouldn't you, you faggot."

The dimwitted goon couldn't think of a comeback, so reverted to the familiar. "Fuck you."

"Knock it off," Tony commanded, bored with the mindless dialogue. "We've got about three days before we get to the Cape. Get your rocks off all you want, but I mean it—not a single scratch. I don't want to see so much as a pimple on any of these bitches." The goon nodded. They'd been doing this long enough to know, the merchandise was worth more clean. "You understand me, asshole?" Tony demanded.

The goon nodded again. "I gotcha, boss. No rough stuff."

"We show up with damaged goods, it's our asses. They're expecting clean, young, white American pussy and that's exactly what we're going to deliver."

"What about her?" the goon said, nodding toward Jennifer. "She's totally fuckable and might even have a little fight in her."

Looking down at her, Tony paused, her fate hanging on his decision. Then he waved her off. "No. She's off limits."

"Come on boss?"

"She's going to be fixing our meals, dip shit. You fuck her and she could mess with our food." Tony reached out, grabbed Jennifer by the hair and pulled her head up. "You fuck with our food and after he's done with you, I'll kill you with my bare hands." He gave her a look shot sent chills down her spine—a look that told her he didn't give a shit if she lived or died. Seeing her terrified reaction, he then lowered his voice and spoke in a soft tone, as one might speak to a child, but there was unmistakable steel in his tone. "We understand one another?" Jennifer nodded. "Good," he said, letting go of her hair. "Plus, she'll be a nice little bonus. Bring as much as the other bitches. So leave her alone."

"You're the boss."

"I'm hungry. It's been a busy morning. How about some breakfast." It wasn't a question. She had been spared for the time being. "Let's go," he ordered his minion.

Before following his boss to the wheelhouse, Deathbreath looked over at her adding, "Don't even think about fuckin' with my food. If I so much as fart I don't care what Tony says, I'll cut that pretty little face of yours into something so ugly you're mother wouldn't recognize you."

She knew he meant it. She'd watched in absolute horror as they'd lined Joe and the boys, still bound and gagged, up on the swim step and executed them in cold blood. Their bleeding, lifeless bodies bobbing in the wake being blown to pieces by her captors unloading their automatic weapons on them as the boat steamed away.

Her back was to the cockpit when she heard the first sharp cracks, which initially she couldn't place. Such a foreign sound onboard a boat...*sort of like thunder,* she thought. glancing out the window at clear, sunny skies. She spun around in time to see the bodies of the crew jerking backwards, like rag dolls, from the volley of gunshots. Her mind refusing to process the horror she was witnessing. Then uncontrollable retching and blackness.

When she came to, one of the gunmen was kicking her in the ribs, yelling, "Clean this shit up. It fucking reeks in here." She couldn't do it, passing out again, face down in her own vomit.

"Clean it up, you fucking bitch! You're stinking up the whole Goddamn boat. I hate the smell of puke," his angry words falling on def ears.

She couldn't make her body respond. Her mind in denial, desperately trying to bury the horrors she'd just witnessed. Another kick to her ribs. She started dry heaving again.

In disgust, the gunman yelled, "Now! Or I'll drag your ass out there and toss you in with your friends."

Somehow, from the darkest recesses of hell, she forced her body to move. Like a zombie, she managed to raise her head off the floor. Vomit stuck to her face. Her hair soaked in bile. Finally getting her knees under her, pushing with all her strength, willing herself up, her forearms still on the floor, like a crippled dog.

The gunman smiled. "Don't move. You got 'a sweet little ass." She felt vice-like hands grab her waist.... pulling her pants down in one violent motion, ripping her panties half off. His nails ripping into her skin. Nauseating waves of crippling fear shot through her. She knew she was going to be raped...

"Goddamn it!" A second voice boomed its way into her groggy mind. The gunman released his grip. She collapsed. "Leave her the fuck alone!"

"I wasn't going to do anything," the goon insisted. "I was only messing with her."

"Yea. That's why her goddamned panties are ripped off. I told you to leave her the fuck alone." Tony was pissed. "Look at this mess. It fucking reeks in here."

That's the last thing she remembered before drifting back into the black fringes of hell.

They were both gone when the stench forced her to open her eyes. She was still lying on the galley floor, her head on its side. Through one bloody eye she saw little chunky things floating in front of her, slowly rolling in the bile with the movement of the boat, just before she started dry-heaving again...and again...until there was simply nothing left.

******

Without opening her eyes, she willed herself to reach down, between her legs. Her panties still shredded around her ankles. Tenderly feeling her vagina. Her fingers trembling…searching for any signs that she'd been raped. Everything felt typical. Then, gingerly she felt around her anus. It didn't hurt. Thankfully she feebly tugged at her torn panties and shorts. Pulling them over her bare bottom.

Somehow she managed to get herself and the galley cleaned up. She couldn't go near the stern of the boat. She couldn't even look in that direction. It took two rolls of paper towels and a ton of hot water, soap and Clorox to clean up the mess. She threw the vomit-soaked towels out the galley window. Below, she locked herself in her stateroom Steaming in the hot shower. She couldn't stop shaking. The harder she scrubbed, the more painful the memories—the vision of Captain Joe and the crew being shot. The hot water beat on her skin until it turned red. But she knew that no amount of hot water and soap was going to cleanse away what had happened.

The shower helped. She pulled out some clean clothes from her backpack and tossed the one's shed been wearing into a black plastic trash bag. She sat down on the bunk and began slowing brushing the tangles out of her hair. The familiar motion and feeling of the brush going through her hair helped calm her frenzied nerves. *Just like Mom used to do*, she thought to herself. *Like Corey used to do.* Her mind drifting in an out. Slowly she tried to grasp some sense of reality, forcing herself to think. *You're alive. So think. Where are the girls?*

Unlocking her stateroom door, she opened it a crack, expecting to see Satan himself waiting for her. The companion way was empty. She opened the door, cautiously stepped out and headed down the narrow companionway to the first closed door. Slowly she opened it—nothing. She turned, opening the door on the opposite side.

She wasn't close to being prepared for what greeted her. Another wave of nausea shot through her. She dry heaved once again. Her hell nothing compared to the other girls. Their limp, naked bodies were strewn across the stateroom like rag dolls, as if a spoiled child had gotten tired of playing and just tossed them aside. At first glance, she thought they were all dead. She stood frozen at the door, slowly realizing they were drugged, and from the looks of it, had been raped repeatedly as well. Never in her life had she been so sickened. She'd thought witnessing the brutal execution of the crew was the most horrible thing she'd ever seen, but looking at these poor girls... somehow was worse. At that moment—seeing the way those animals had left these girls—she resolved not to die like this.

She gently washed each of the girls' faces with a wet washcloth. They were a mess. Hair in knots, tangled beyond hope. She'd have to get them into a shower and apply gallons of conditioner before she could even attempt to brush out the knots. She looked in a couple of drawers below the double berths and found what must have been clothes that belonged to the crew. She got each of the girls into baggy T-shirts and shorts, and then tucked them into the bunks. The girls were so heavily drugged they barely moved.

She sat down on the edge of the bunk and tried to formulate some sort of a plan. She swore to herself that she would die before she'd let those animals get their filthy hands on her. She took one of the girl's heads into her lap and began brushing the tangled mess.

The door suddenly burst open.

"What the fuck are you doing!" demanded one of the goons.

"I'm just getting them cleaned up," she answered in a daze.

At first, the goon didn't know what to do. He just stood there, looking around the room. Everything had been straightened up. He could see that all four of the girls were still in the bunks.

Jennifer saw the uncertainty in his eyes. "I just thought that maybe... better to see the girls this way. Better to have then cleaned up, don't you think?"

Again he hesitated. "Tony told me to check on you. Didn't expect to find you in here. Yeah, I guess you're right."

"I'll leave if you want me to," baiting him.

"No, no. You get them cleaned up," he said, nodding to himself, as if he'd discovered a cure for cancer. "Yeah, Tony 'll like that." He turned and left the room, leaving the door open.

She took a deep breath. Her emotions were out of control. Waves of fear flooded over her. She closed her eyes and took another deep breath. *So the boss's name is Tony, That's a start.* She ran her fingers through the girls' hair...*just like Mom used to do.* She picked up the brush and gently, continued working it through the tangled strands of soft hair, finding a moment of peace in the familiar brushing motion.

She'd never done anything more than a little weed and a couple of lines, so she had no idea how to deal with the four drugged girls. They were so doped up; they could hardly open their eyes. Focusing was out of the question. They were on another planet. She attended to each one individually. She did what she would have liked them to do for her, had their fates been reversed. They looked much better after the runny makeup was washed off and their faces were free of the matted tangles. They didn't know the difference, but it made her feel better watching them sleep, tucked in under the covers, instead of lying strewn across the room with their legs spread apart. *Maybe the drugs are a blessing in disguise,* Jennifer consoled herself. *Maybe they won't remember what happened...won't remember they've been raped and sodomized.* Violated beyond reason. Never to be forgotten or purged. Scarred forever.

She closed the door. Climbing back toward the salon, she passed two matching staterooms located on either side of the hall. Each had a queen-sized bed and full head, beautiful teak built-ins and entertainment centers. The master—a magnificent full-width room—was just past the stairs leading up to the salon level. She cautiously poked her head in the open door. Thankfully, no one was there. She heard a noise through the ceiling—someone was above her. She quickly withdrew and headed topside towards the galley.

"Where have you been?" a gruff voice demanded as she came up the stairs. It was Tony. He had been looking into the refrigerator when he heard her approach.

"I was...." she stammered, trying to think of something to say.

"Below, cleaning up the girls," he said. "I know. We've got them so doped up they won't even know the difference."

What a scumbag, she thought. "But..." she began.

He cut her off sharply. "Are they sleeping?"

"If you could call it that," she said flatly.

"We've only got a little further to go and I don't want them totally messed up when we get there. We'll start drying 'em out."

"Get where?" Jennifer asked innocently.

He looked at her sharply. "Nice try," he sneered.

She didn't say anything else. Through the silence they appraised one another…two animals circling…trying to get a sense of the other's strengths and weaknesses. Tony lost interest after only a couple seconds, dismissing her to continue his search in the refrigerator. "Just keep cooking up the good grinds and you won't have anything to worry about."

Yeah, right, Jennifer thought. *I watched you murder four people and you're going to let me go? I'm as good as dead.*

He must have read her thoughts because what he said next, "Do you really think we'd waste someone as beautiful as you?" sent a chill, worse than death, down her spine.

Nurture strength of spirit to shield you in sudden misfortune, but do not distress yourself with imaginings. Many fears are born of fatigue and loneliness.

Chapter 10

The U.S. authorities were on alert. A vessel for hire falls under federal jurisdiction when operating in international waters, so the FBI was now involved, as well as the Coast Guard, state and local law enforcement. Larry contacted *Dorsal*'s owner to confirm that no special arrangements had been made for an extended trip. The Coast Guard launched a full-scale air/sea search and rescue. But the Feds hadn't done anything more than take a report, as far as anyone knew.

The news was all over the VHF and side band frequencies. Spreading like wildfire, everyone on the waterfront heard the story—from Point Conception on up the coast, all the way down to the tip of Baja. Different versions were circulating the airwaves, even though no one had seen or heard anything since the day *Dorsal* told *Tranquility* she was headed to San Martin Island.

Larry and Lloyd got together right after we left. They were both wrecks, but good for each other. Lloyd alerted friends of his who ran a little tackle shop called Minerva's in Cabo. The owners, Bob and Minerva Smith, told Lloyd that they'd already heard about a missing boat.

"How much fuel was she carrying?" Bob asked Lloyd over the phone.

"Hold on," Lloyd said. "Let me ask Larry."

"She's got a four thousand gallon capacity," Larry said. "I checked with the fuel dock. They told me she'd topped off after her last trip, so she was full."

"What kind of mileage does she get?" Bob asked, mostly out of courtesy to his old friend. He'd been around boats his entire life. He knew *Dorsal*, and had already calculated the answer.

"She's got a cruising range of over 2000 miles." Bob nodded his head on the other end of the line. "Plenty to bypass you guys at the Cape and head straight to the mainland."

"That's going to make it even tougher," Bob said. Most yachts heading down the Baja needed to refuel on their way. Few could make the thousand-mile run, but *Dorsal* was an exception. Without having to stop for fuel, she could be anywhere. "Do you think they've been hijacked?" Bob finally asked.

"Hijacked! Shit, Bob," Lloyd said. "We're still praying they're just having mechanical trouble somewhere up here, but no one has seen anything yet."

"Time to start facing facts," Bob said to his friend. "If they were just broken down somewhere, or God forbid, hit something and broke up, someone would have seen something by now."

"I know, I know," Lloyd said. "It's just that I can't believe someone would hijack a damn charter boat."

"She's more than a boat, Lloyd," Bob reminded him. "She's a multi-million-dollar yacht."

"But it just doesn't make any sense…just no sense at all."

Feeling his friend's desperation, Bob tried to ease his pain. "Maybe you're right. Maybe they're tucked in somewhere and the Coast Guard just hasn't spotted them yet."

"Come on, Bob," Lloyd said. "They've had planes up for thirty-six hours now and found nothing…not even at Guadeloupe."

"I was wondering about that. So they checked out Guadeloupe?"

"It was one of the first places they searched. They either sank without a trace, or someone's been running that boat hard, keeping her away from the beach."

"You know we'll call you the second we hear anything. Every boat down here is looking for them. Something will turn up. Hang in there."

"Thanks, Bob. I really appreciate it. Give my best to your lovely wife."

"Will do."

"Lloyd, if you were going to steal a boat like this, where would you go?" Larry asked after hanging up the phone.

Lloyd and Larry had fished the west coast, including Baja, their entire lives. They knew those waters as well as any two men alive. Lloyd envisioned the coastline, working his way down the peninsula and around the tip. A few places came to mind, but there was nowhere to hide a boat as big as *Dorsal*. It didn't make any sense. On the Pacific side, the only place that had an airstrip was San Carlos, and it was just a dirt strip outside a secluded commercial fishing village inside Mag Bay. Lloyd shook his head. "I don't know, Larry. I just don't know."

"Me, neither."

******

"Hey, Skipper...you hungry?" Travis asked hopefully "Jasmine's got some of that dorado grilling with a little garlic lemon butter. It smells delicious."

We'd been running past patties that were holding big-time. As we looked down at the crystal clear, dark blue water from the wheelhouse, we could see flashes of beautiful golden greens and blues darting out from under the patties as we drove by. There were days when I'd have given anything to find a single patty that was holding like these...but we weren't looking for fish. We were straight-lining it, running hard. Even so, Travis set up a couple of rigs for fast trolling. He put out only two lines—heavy 80-pound outfits—and when we ran past the next patty, they both got bit. The reels screamed as the fish leaped and shook violently, water spraying off their bodies. I didn't even slow down. Travis buttoned down the drag, trying to stop the fish. I knew he wanted me to stop, but he never yelled up or anything. He just ground it out.

He was able to land a small 25-pounder. He got its head out of the water and literally skipped it across the surface on the side of its flat body. Jasmine ran out to help him, but she never had a chance with the second much larger fish. I'd seen it jump a couple of times—a big bull that would have been close to 60 pounds easy. The sound of the line snapping after the fish spooled the Shimano Beastmaster sounded like a gunshot echoing through the air. It all happened in less than sixty seconds. Travis was pissed that I hadn't stopped the boat. He hated losing fish...for any reason.

"Son of a bitch!" he said to Jasmine as he bounced his fish, nodding towards her empty reel. "We lost everything."

"I know," she said.

Looking up he saw the look she was giving him—a friendly reminder of why we were here. The anger instantly drained out of his system. "You're right," he said. "You're absolutely right. At least we got the one."

"Cut it up and we'll have it for lunch."

Smelling the fresh, tender filets grilling on the GenAir made my mouth water. "Come on, Skipper," he persisted. "You need to eat something."

"You're right," I said, looking up from the chart of Baja. "Thanks. I'd love some." Travis nodded and started out of the wheelhouse. "Hey!" I said. Travis stopped and faced me. "I mean it—thanks." He nodded and understood it wasn't the meal I was thanking him for.

A few minutes later, Jasmine and Travis arrived with a plateful of steaming dorado, grilled to perfection. She'd whipped up a salad and some refried beans. We wrapped the dorado in fresh tortillas and added a little cilantro. The combination was hard to beat. I realized I'd cut them off and been an asshole the past twenty-four hours "That was delicious. Thank you. Sorry I've been such a prick."

With that, Travis and Jasmine started talking at full speed at the same time.

"We know. We totally understand."

"You don't have to apologize."

"We know what you're going through."

"We just want to help."

"Okay, okay, "I said. "I get it."

The relief on their faces was evident. They hated the fact that I'd been shutting them out. It was hurting us all. "It's just that we don't know what to do," Jasmine said.

"That's exactly what's making me nuts." We were still over ten miles from Benito. "I've been thinking…what if they're not at either Benito or Cedros?"

"Then where?" Travis asked.

"That's what I've been trying to figure out. At first, all I could think of was that they were in trouble…they'd hit something during the night…run over a log or something and torn up their running gear…whatever. But that wouldn't account for them not communicating. The more I think about it, the less I believe anything's wrong with the boat."

"Why not?" asked Jasmine.

"Because Joe knows what he's doing. If they were in trouble, he would have got word out immediately."

"But shit happens, Skipper," Travis offered. "You know that as well as I do—accidents happen. And they can happen quickly, especially at night. Maybe they didn't have time to get word out."

"If we hit something, and after checking out the damage, and if was serious, what's the very next thing you'd do?"

"Call for help," he answered without a second thought.

"Exactly. That's the first thing anyone would do. But there have been no radio calls, no Maydays, no debris…nothing. They didn't go down. Something else happened."

"Like what?"

"I don't know, but I'll bet you they aren't going to be at Benito or Cedros."

"Do you think they ran inside to Guerrero Negro, then?" asked Travis, drawing on his mental image of Baja. Guerrero Negro is a deep-water harbor about halfway down the peninsula. By Baja standards, it's a rather busy commercial fishing town.

"Would you?" I asked Travis.

"Would I what?"

"Head into a busy port if you'd stolen a boat?"

"That's the last thing I'd do."

"Then what are you thinking?" Jasmine asked.

"I don't think the boat's in trouble," I said. "I don't think there's anything wrong with the boat...but I do think the crew's in trouble." They didn't say anything as I continued outlining my theory. "No contact since day one, right?" They both nodded in agreement. "No calls. No Maydays. Nothing, right?"

"And there were a ton of boats out that night, so if they'd made a Mayday call, someone would have heard them," Travis added. We all agreed.

"I'm thinking the crews no longer in control of the boat."

"What are you saying—the guys who chartered the boat stole it?" Jasmine asked.

"*Dorsal* ran with a four-man crew," Travis said. "Plus, they had Jennifer. That's five to two, and you're thinking the bad guys just took over the boat?"

I nodded my head. Travis shook his, disagreeing with me. "Think about it," I said. "At night, who's awake?"

"Whoever's on watch." Travis replied. Then it hit him, just like it had hit me. "Everyone else would be asleep."

"Roger. And how hard would it be for a couple of guys, especially if they were armed, to overpower one guy?"

"It would be too easy," Travis answered. "That would be the last thing in the world you'd be thinking about on watch—getting jacked on your own boat."

"Once they had the wheelhouse," I continued, "they would have control of the entire boat, the radios…everything. Then how hard would it be to stick a gun barrel in the face of the others as they slept? One at a time…wake them up…zip tie their wrists…wrap some gaffer's tape around their mouths, and voila! The bad guys are in complete control."

"Mutiny," Jasmine said.

"Yeah, I guess you could call it that. Piracy has been going on for centuries."

"Okay. Let's say they got control of the boat. But then what? Who's going to run it?" Travis asked. "And why?"

"I don't know. They didn't look like they'd ever been on a boat before, but we don't know these guys from Adam. Larry didn't have a thing on them. Who says they don't know how to run a boat. Maybe those outfits were just for show."

"But, why?" Jasmine asked. "It's not like a car. You can't just rip it off and strip it. We're talking about a boat, a big boat, one they knew within seventy-two hours was going to be reported missing. It's not like you can hide a ninety-foot boat in a parking garage."

"They're not after the boat," I said.

"Then what?"

"The girls."

"What are you talking about?" Travis jumped in. "What do you mean…the girls?"

Jasmine was silent. As a woman, she knew. The thought sent chills down her spine. I could see it in her eyes. "Holy shit," she whispered. It took Travis awhile to absorb it, just as it had me when the idea first started to surface in the back of my brain. The more I thought about it, the more it made sense. *They didn't give a shit about the boat—they were after the girls.* If that were true, chances were that Jennifer and the girls were all still alive, but in a world of hurt.

"What are we going to do?" Travis asked slowly.

"First," I said, nodding out the forward windows, "we're going to check out these islands." Benito was dead ahead of us. "Then we'll make a run for Guerrero Negro and see if they put in there. If they did, we're fucked because they've had a big head start and obviously would have made arrangements before they left San Diego to have a plane or ship waiting for them to get the girls out of Mexico. The thing that worries me the most is the landing strip outside of town. That's the way I'd do it—by private plane."

"But if they were concerned about the Federales," Travis said, "they'd stay as far away from the beach as possible."

"Leaving where?" Jasmine asked.

"Clarion… Socorro… Benidicto…any one of those islands. Clarion has a landing strip. They'd all make perfect rendezvous points."

"But those islands are over a thousand miles from here."

"You're right, but so what? Think about it—a remote island a thousand miles below the border, hundreds of miles off Baja in the middle of nowhere—a perfect rendezvous spot."

"That means they're going to be transferring them to a big ship, right?" Jasmine added.

"Most likely," Travis agreed, and then paused. "What are we talking about? We still don't even know if the damned boat's in trouble or not." We all looked at each other. We felt something was wrong, but without facts, we had to admit it was still just speculation.

"Let's give Benito a quick look and then hit Cedros before it gets too dark. If we don't see anything we'll run .

******

As suspected, both the islands were empty. With no signs of the boat anywhere, we headed southeast toward Guerrero Negro. The *Vintage* certainly wasn't any multi-million dollar yacht, but she could hold her own. She was a beautiful vessel, especially compared to the commercial shit cans that dotted the harbor of Guerrero Negro. Her glistening white hull stood out like a prom queen, contrasting with the rusting steel-hulled gill netters and long liners that were side-tied three and four deep along the rugged fuel pier.

Most American yachts in transit along the Baja avoided Guerrero Negro. Its wharf was rough and offered no amenities. The only yachts that pulled into that harbor were desperately in need of fuel. Otherwise, they stayed away because this isolated area was known as a prime drop-off point for drugs coming up the Pacific from Columbia and headed for the States. All the illicit traffic had turned a small fishing village into a lawless frontier.

Jasmine's fluent Spanish and her raw sex appeal soon cast a spell on the hardened commercial fisherman. They were stumbling over each other to tell her they had not seen any Americans coming into port over the past week. It took only a flip of her locks and a big smile to get the driver of the fuel truck parked at the far end of the wharf to move up next to us. Normally, any foreign yacht has to receive permission from El Jefe or the Harbor Master to get fuel. Depending upon how drunk he was and how much cash you stuffed between the pages of a Swank magazine. Then he'd decide if there was enough fuel for the rich Americanos. On this particular day, El Jefe had started drinking early and was passed out in the front seat of his pickup, so we couldn't get permission to fuel up. At first, the fuel truck driver shook us off, saying we needed permission before he could give us any fuel. But after Jasmine went to work on him, he was ready to give her the whole damn truck.

With our thirsty tanks topped off, we now had a safe cruising range of nearly fifteen hundred miles. Jasmine asked some of the other dockworkers about *Dorsal*, but no one had seen a big yacht in the harbour for a long time. I'd figured as much. While Travis finished supervising the fuelling, Jasmine kept the driver focused on her instead of the fat slob passed out in the front seat of his official pickup. We needed to take advantage of being in port. "Don't either of you guys leaving the boat while I'm gone, O.K?" I asked Travis before heading off to find a land line.

"No worries, boss. We'll be right here."

I wasn't worried about Travis—he could take care of himself. But Jasmine, as tough as she talked, was still very vulnerable. And I didn't want the boat left unattended for a second. This place had a dark undercurrent that made the hairs on the back of my neck stand up. The further away from the boat I got, the worse I felt. After walking on the oil-stained pier, I headed down a dirt street toward the only phone in town. Jasmine had found out it was located inside the cantina, about a quarter mile from the pier.

Thick cigarette smoked filled the still, stale air, as I stepped into the dimly lit bar. As there were no windows, I paused momentarily at the door until my eyes could adjust to the dim light. I could feel the stares of the local patrons through the smoke and darkness. As my pupils dilated, I slowly started picking my way around the tables toward the counter. The place was surprisingly crowded. *Probably because there no other bars in this desolate hellhole.*

"Tiene usted un teléfono que puedo utilizar?" I asked an obese, greasy man behind the bar. He pointed a fat stubby finger towards the far wall. No sign, no light, but definitely a phone.

Without Jasmine to translate, I muddled my way through a call to the U.S. I didn't know nearly enough Spanish, but could count to ten, and that turned out to be enough. Waiting for the operator to make the connection, I wondered what we would have done without Jasmine. Her ability to speak the language and to charm the pants off these guys was proving to be a huge plus.

"Corey! Is that you?" Larry said over the static.

"Yeah, Larry. We're in Guerrero Negro. No sign of them."

"Shit. Same here," he said. "Nothing." My heart sank another notch.

Static hissed and crackled. "You still there?"

"Yeah. Goddamn it, Larry, this sucks."

"I know. The FBI got involved a couple days ago. Coast Guard expanded the search and has covered over 2,500 square miles so far. Haven't found anything. The papers are running a story with a picture of the boat, and the Mexican authorities have been alerted."

"Yeah…that'll help," I said sarcastically.

"Coast Guard is continuing to push their search southward along the coast, down Baja."

I cut him off. "They're not going to find any wreckage…at least not yet. They wanted the girls."

"You might be right," Larry shouted. We could hardly hear one another over all the static.

"Say what?"

"One of Lloyd's friends in the Sheriff's Department told him the Feds have set up a task force."

"What?"

"A task force."

"For Jennifer?"

"No. A task force for missing girls. Evidently over the past couple of years, lots of teenage girls have gone missing—not your runaway types, but girls from good homes. They're just disappearing. Lloyd's guy told him the Feds think it might be some kind of highly organized white slave trade."

"Are you kidding me?" I said, my thoughts racing. "I knew it."

"He found out they don't have any solid leads. Just a growing list of missing girls that shouldn't be missing. They're in the formative stages of the investigation and say the pieces are scattered all over the place. But they're on it, Corey. The Feds are on it."

"Jennifer will be dead before they figure it out."

"Don't underestimate these guys," Larry said.

"Underestimate who?" I asked. "The Feds or the assholes who took her?" After a long pause, Larry asked what our plans were. "We're headed to the Cape." I could almost hear him shaking his head over the phone before he spoke.

"Be careful. That's a brutal coastline. You know it's hurricane season down there."

"I know, but it's the only place that makes sense. Other than maybe Mag Bay or Clarion, there are no other airports or landing strips between here and Cabo. I figure if they aren't transferring them by ship, they're flying them out. Down here, no one would ever know."

"You're right. If they pulled in at night, they could get the girls off the boat and onto a plane before anyone knew what was happening. Hell, it's Baja. If I were going to kidnap someone, that's where I'd take 'um."

He was right. I knew we'd be on our own from the moment we cleared Point Loma. Standing in this shit hole of a bar, the reality became overwhelming. A feeling of total despair swept through me. "I don't know what to do."

"Get down to Mag Bay and check it out. Like you said, there's nothing that even resembles an airport there except that landing strip outside of San Carlos."

"I don't know anymore—"

"Listen, Corey," he said sharply. "You felt this thing was wrong from the beginning. You were the only one. Do you hear me? You were right. Now we just have to find them."

"At ten knots?"

"Get to Mag Bay. If they're not there, head to Cabo. We'll meet you there."

"What?"

"You heard me. Get to Mag Bay and Lloyd and I will get on a flight tomorrow to La Paz. We'll check out the east side of the peninsula, and you cover the west." He paused to do some quick mental calculations. "We'll meet at the Cape in 48 hours. If for any reason, we're not there, assume we found something in La Paz and head up there. Meet us at Minerva's. I'll call Bob and let him know our plans."

"I hate the fact we don't have any better communication."

"Welcome to Baja."

"Yeah," I said, dazed.

"She needs you," he said softly. "Don't let her down. She's out there— go find her."

******

Though I'd been gone less than half an hour, seeing the boat as I walked back down the wharf gave me a great sense of relief. Travis nodded as I climbed on board. "I have no idea how many gallons we took. Every thing's in liters."

"Just over six hundred gallons," Jasmine said, coming out of the salon. "Any news from Larry?"

"No. Said the Coast Guard was expanding their search but hadn't found anything yet."

"Figures," Travis said. "Can we get out of here now? This place gives me the creeps."

"Anything else?" Jasmine asked.

"The Feds think it might be white slavery." Jasmine's legs seemed to give out on her as she lowered herself against the cockpit combing.

"There's an ever-growing list of missing girls. Young girls, all white...girls that shouldn't be missing. But that's all their saying."

You could see Jasmine's mind revving up. The color coming back into her flushed cheeks. After a pause, her thoughts began to focus. "I've only worked at the club for a couple years, but since I started, there has been at least a dozen girls that...." She paused, as if searching for the right words. "Girls that had been working there, and then, just like that, they were gone."

"But you said that happens all the time. You said it was the nature of the business."

"That's what everyone told me. But the girls I'm thinking of, the ones I'm talking about, they never even came in to pick up their paychecks."

"That's a little weird," Travis said.

"I though so, too, but no one else seemed to think twice about it. The owners didn't care. They'd just pin the girls' checks to the schedule board and leave them there. I always thought it was so weird...those envelopes—with the girls' names on the outside and their uncashed checks inside—just stuck there with thumbtacks. Some of them had been hanging there so long they were starting to fade. The older girls said it happened all the time. You find some rich dick, and the last thing you think about is a couple measly days' pay. They were right. The real money is in the tips, and we take that home every night, so I could see their point. After awhile, it didn't really seem like a big deal. The longer you're in the business, the less that paycheck matters."

"But, still," I coaxed, "it didn't feel right, did it?"

"No," Jasmine said, continuing. "Maybe ten, twelve girls in two years. We had dozens of girls working there, some just on weekends. It was a scene. They'd come and go all the time. But still...a dozen girls gone without a trace." She was thinking this through out loud. "That's a girl every two months, and that's only from my club." Looking up into my eyes, she said, "Wonder how many girls from other clubs might be missing."

She'd hit gold. "Are we ready to go?" I asked Travis.

"Absolutely, Skipper. Let's get the hell out of here."

"Then fire 'em off. I'll be right back."

"Where you going?" he asked as I climbed back onto the wharf.

"She's on to something," I said. "We've got to let Larry know before we leave. I'm going call him back."

"Tell him what?"

"Jasmine will explain," I said, turning to run back to the bar. "I'll be right back."

The second time I entered the cantina, curiosity turned to hostility. As I made my way toward the phone, a couple of rough looking locals immediately stood up and cut me off. They weren't fisherman.

"Who da fuck are you?" one of them spat at me in broken English.

Startled, I step back and held out my arms, palms up. "Nobody."
"You're fucking DEA!"

"No! No fuckin' way. No DEA. Nada. Nada. Pesca. Pesca." I pointed toward the boat.

Evidently, news travels fast when there is none. "Tuve que informar en a mi jefe," I stumbled with my limited Spanish, trying to explain I had to report in to my boss.

Despite his size, he moved like a cat. Before I could react, he grabbed both my arms and held them over my head. The other guy stepped forward and started to frisk me. At first I didn't resist. I wasn't holding anything and figured it was the easiest way to pacify them. But when the asshole slapped my balls, I jerked my arms free, spun sideways, shoving him away. "Fucking asshole!" I yelled.

Every eyeball in the place locked on me, and for a split second I thought I was a dead man. Then a sinister smirk crossed his lips and he laughed out loud. "*El cono n tiene huevos,*" he said, holding his thumb and forefinger together like he was rolling a tiny pea between them. "*No huevos, este pinche guey.*" The whole bar started laughing. I was only able to guess what he said about my balls but it made everyone in the place crack up.

The tension was broken, but not gone, so I played along. Nodding my head, holding out my arms, "O.K, O.K.," I said stepping back a bit. I gestured to the phone. "Está bien si hago mi llamada ahora?" I said asking for permission.

They stepped aside, but as I passed the one who had slapped my balls. He reached out and grabbed my arm. Practically squashing my biceps without so much as even grimacing, he lifted me up and pulled my face towards his. "One more call," he hissed. "Then you, you're punta whore and boat leave here and never come back." Our eyes were locked. "*Comprende?*"

I understood perfectly. I nodded without looking away. He tossed me aside. "*Pelame la verga*," he said as he sat down.

I could hardly lift my hand to dial the operator. Three minutes later. "Larry? It's me again."

"What is it?" he asked.

"Ask the Feds to contact strip clubs along the waterfront that are holding paychecks for girls that never cashed them. Start with the Stand."

I gave him a quick summation of what Jasmine and I had discussed. He came to the same conclusions we had—if a dozen girls were missing from just one club, how many more could be missing citywide, or for that matter, from across the country.

"This might be something important," I added.

"I'll make the call as soon as we hang up," he said. "Shit. Now I don't know if we should fly down or not. What do you think?" Within a matter of seconds, the plan that had made so much sense when we'd talked earlier now didn't seem to make any sense at all.

"I don't know. Why don't you stay there for a couple more days while the Feds look into this club thing? That'll give us time to get to Cabo. I'll call you when we get there and then we can decide what to do next."

"That makes sense. No use in us being down there when the key might be up here. Call me as soon as you get into the Cape."

"Roger…the minute we get in."

"Talk to you in a couple of days, amigo."

"Adios."

I felt the daggers in my back as I left the cantina. They didn't like strangers. *"Fuck 'em and their fucking drugs,"* I murmured as I ran back down to the wharf. I couldn't wait to feel the swells under *Vintage's* keel. I hated murky, dirty water and the scum that festered there. Give me the blue any day.

At the boat I discovered we had other problems. The Harbor Master had roused himself out of his drunken stupor and was screaming at the top of his lungs at the fuel truck driver and Travis. His arms were flailing; foamy spit was dripping out of the corner of his mouth and his half-unbuttoned uniform revealed a sweat-stained yellowed T-shirt. *A real tribute to foreign law enforcement. What a fucking slob*, I thought to myself.

When the trouble started, Travis had made Jasmine stay inside the salon. The tide had been going out all afternoon, so Travis was standing on the back deck of the wheelhouse at eye level with the irate cop.

"What's the problem?" I asked Travis as I quickly stepped across the few feet separating the boat from wharf.

"This asshole just came up and started screaming," Travis said, gesturing toward the man who couldn't speak English any better than Travis or I could speak Spanish.

"El Capitan?" he demanded, looking at me and pointing to the boat.

"Si," I said.

He instantly directed his tirade toward me. I didn't understand a word, but the meaning was clear—we hadn't gotten permission to receive fuel, and we were in violation of some bullshit law. Fortunately, he didn't have any deputies with him, and he didn't have a radio—just a sidearm covered with an old leather flap in a dusty holster too big for the gun. Deputy Dog was pissed. Since he wasn't letting up and it seemed unlikely that he'd just have a heart attack and die on the spot, I interrupted his rant. "Un momento. Un momento, por favor." I bounded down the ladder into the salon, knowing Jasmine hadn't missed a word. "How bad?" I asked her.

"Obviously, he's pissed. More at the poor driver than us for going around him, but he's pissed. Says if we don't pay the fine, he's going to confiscate the boat to pay for the fuel...or something like that."

"What fine? How much?"

"A thousand."

"Pesos?"

"U.S.," she said.

"Fuck him. There's no way. I don't think we even have that much left, Goddamn it. Travis already paid the driver."

"We have that much," Jasmine said, looking at me, "and a lot more."

"What are you talking about? We're just about broke."

"Not since I joined this circus." She flashed that platinum smile of hers. "What do you think I was going to do with two years of tip money— stash it in my mattress?"

"How much are we talking?" I asked.

"Let's just say that I was awfully good at what I did for a living, and cash is no longer something you need to worry about."

"I'm not taking your money," I said immediately.

"Screw that," she said, shaking her head in disgust at my male ego. "And just when I was starting to like you..." Her words demanded that our eyes meet. It was all I could do to look at her. "I mean it," she said, without taking her eyes off me. She saw it in my eyes the moment I accepted her offer. Without another word, she nodded, focusing her attention on the self-anointed brigadier general outside who had just about lost all his patience. Screaming at the top of his lungs. "Usted está en la infracción y yo incauto su buque. Usted es todo detenido para robar."

Before stepping out of the salon, she told me we were under arrest and that our boat had been confiscated because we'd stolen all the fuel. At the same time, the driver was handing the general our wad of cash. Shoving into his greasy pockets, he started to scream again, until he laid eyes on Jasmine.

Following her out I said, "But it's just a loan."

"Right," she said. "You couldn't afford my interest rates. Consider me your new partner."

"Are you nuts? We're in the middle of Baja, chasing God knows who. We have no idea what we're doing, and you want to buy into this thing?" I was astonished.

"I'm already in. Have been since the minute we left."

"Let's just take it one step at a time," I said.

A shadow dimmed the light in her eyes. She looked down. "I'm not asking for anything in return. I have money, and as far as I'm concerned, it's ours—not mine. We need some now. Quit worrying about it so we can get this asshole off our backs and get out of here."

"I didn't mean I don't want you as a partner. You're an incredible lady. But I don't want to drag you into something like this."

"Fuck that," she shot back. "In case you haven't noticed, I'm already in." Turning, she headed for the cockpit. It was absolutely amazing how her presence instantly defusing the situation. Without question, she was beautiful—flowing blond hair, bright, twinkling eyes, perfect complexion, a great body and radiant smile. But it was her energy that was most captivating. She stopped traffic in the States. Down here, she froze time.

Climbing up the ladder, she greeted the general in perfect Spanish. He couldn't take his eyes off her. Without a moment's hesitation, she leaped onto the dock and extended her graceful hand like royalty. Watching him engulf it in the mutton of a paw he called a hand heightened my anxiety. She explained that her father owned the boat, that I was just a hired driver. "Nada como usted, Capitán," she flirted, reaching out and touching the insignias on his sweat-stained uniform.

Continuing to spin her web, she further explained that the driver had insisted that we not leave until you awoke. The truck driver just nodded. She went on to tell him that the driver didn't know what the 'taxes' would be, and that the assessment would be totally up to you. The general smiled at that, his authority and ego now restored. They continued to talk for a while. You could see from the gradual changes in his body language that she was winning him over. "Pero, Mi Capitán, mil dólares, es eso un impuesto justo?

"No, no," he said, now completely seduced. They continued talking for a couple more minutes. He hadn't raised his voice since she appeared, and completely ignored the rest of us as if we didn't exist.

"Un minuto, por favor me perdona." Jasmine asked when they were finished. She turned to me and explained that we owed a fifty-dollar tax, but suggested that I come back with a C-note as a token of our appreciation for the El Capitan's understanding. She told me her money was in her purse in a top drawer of the stateroom she and Travis had been sharing.

With that matter settled, we shoved off. Once underway, I looked at her and she just grinned. After winding our way around the sand bars, out of San Carlos, we cleared the northern point of Margarita Island, heading south east, directly toward the tip. Travis laid down and fell asleep on one of the wheelhouse bunks, leaving Jaz and I alone.

"How did you come up with that story so fast? And in a foreign language to boot?" I asked.

"People are just people," she said softly. "They're pretty much the same all over the place. Treat them with a little respect, the way you'd like to be treated, and most of the time you end up getting what you want."

"True, but that guy was out of control."

"Getting the fuel pumped without his permission undermined his authority. We challenged his power, and he wasn't about to let that go without a fight. Hell, it's all he's got. You saw that place. It's a rat hole…but he's the big cheese, at least on that wharf. We violated his very reason for being by going around him."

"Not intentionally," I protested. "We just needed some fuel."

"In our world, maybe, but not in his," she said insightfully.

I realized that when I get focused on something I don't care who gets in the way. I don't think about possible collateral damage. That was one thing about being underway—twelve knots gives you lots of time for reflection.

"You did a good job handling that guy," I said after awhile. "Thanks."

Jasmine smiled. "He was more pissed at the driver than he was at us. I tried to cover for the driver with that part about him trying to keep us there until his El Jefe woke up. Then I told him that you wanted to wake him up, but the driver wouldn't let you disturb him. My money is on the two of them sitting together right now, in the cantina drinking their new found tax money."

"So I was low man on the totem pole?"

"Not even on the totem pole. Just a hired driver," she said playfully. "In the end, it worked out. Luckily, there wasn't anyone else around. Otherwise, we might have been in trouble. It would have been a lot harder if there had been an audience."

"A hundred bucks," I said, smiling. "Not bad."

"We got off cheap."

She was right. We were on our way without any serious repercussions. We had a full load of fuel and Cabo was 48 hours away. *Vintage* settled into an easy southeast heading with a gentle following sea helping to push us along. Jasmine laid down with Travis and fell asleep, leaving me alone at the wheel.

Please, God, let her be all right.

Beyond a wholesome discipline, be gentle with yourself. You are a child of the universe, no less than the trees and the stars; you have a right to be here.

Chapter 11

Unknown to any of us, a warm equatorial current had been pushing its way north, hugging the Central American coast as it worked its way up past Panama and Costa Rica. Now, off the coast of mainland Mexico, it looked like an El Nino was in the works. Ahead of it, a storm coming from the northern mid-Pacific was pushing a huge cold low-pressure front down with it, as it made its way toward the coast. The cold air meeting the warm waters created what was rapidly turning into a huge tropical storm with gale-force winds. Costa Rica had been getting pounded with torrential rains and huge surf, but as the swirling mass found resistance along the coast, it turned north and was fast becoming the first Eastern Pacific hurricane of the season.

Dorsal was about two hundred and fifty miles ahead of *Vintage*, so they were the first to run head on into the storm. At first light, they'd noticed an increase in the southern swells they were plowing into on their way to Cabo, but figured they were no cause for alarm. Until now, the weather had been beautiful. Crystal clear days, beautiful sunsets, star-lit nights and calm seas had made for perfect running conditions. But during this day, the seas kept building, and the high, wispy clouds soon became thick, dark thunderheads, completely blocking out the sun's rays. At dusk, there was no sunset—only a depressing transition from gloom to darkness. As night approached, the first drops of rain hit the deck, as *Dorsal* was running into six-to-eight-foot swells. Having cleared Lazaro, they had about 170 miles to go before reaching Cabo.

Not too bad, Jennifer thought to herself as she rolled with the motion in the galley, struggling to keep the salad she was making from ending up on the floor. As she tossed the mixed greens between a pair of big wooden utensils, the *Dorsal* came off the top of a wave. The bottom dropped out, leaving the bowl a couple of feet lower than the salad she was tossing. It would have almost been comical, had it not been for the circumstances. She'd been serving the goons their meals in the wheelhouse until now, but it had gotten too rough. She'd have to go up and tell them dinner was ready, and they'd have to come down to the salon to eat it.

Rain was hitting the wheelhouse windows as she knocked and entered. Only the instrument lights illuminated the darkened interior, but she could see the silhouettes of her captors sitting motionless in the helm seats. "Dinner's ready," she announced.

"Then bring it up here," demanded Deathbreath.

"Sorry. Can't do it." Jennifer said, holding on tightly to the door jam. "It's too rough."

"Fuck that! Bring me my dinner, you worthless bitch!"

"Knock it off," Tony commanded. "If you want to eat, go below."

"You want rough? I'll show you rough, you little bitch—" Deathbreath challenged.

"I said knock it off, Goddamn it!"

Deathbreath glared at Jennifer and then looked back at Tony. "Just fuckin' with her, Boss. No big deal. What did you fix for dinner, anyway, honey?" he asked sarcastically.

"Prime rib, baby potatoes, glazed carrots and a salad," Jennifer replied, her eyes glued to the floor.

"Garlic bread?"

"Of course." Garlic bread had become mandatory at every meal except breakfast.

"I'm heading down. You coming, Tony?" Deathbreath asked. They couldn't give a shit about keeping a wheel watch. Tony wasn't moving, Jennifer noticed. In fact, he didn't look too good...a little green behind the gills. *Good*, she thought to herself. *Maybe they'll both get seasick and die*. "Come on," Deathbreath demanded, snapping her out of her fantasy. "I'm starving."

Why couldn't you be the one who's sick? She thought, turning and heading back to the salon with Deathbreath at her heels. She served him his dinner and then asked permission to take some food down to the girls below.

"Pour me another glass of wine first."

She was below when she felt the subtle change of vibration. After days of constant running, any variation in pitch immediately alerts the senses. She paused…and then it changed again…surged…then slowed and was gone. *Weird,* she thought to herself.

The unmistakable gut-churning smell of vomit hit her as soon as she opened the door to the girl's stateroom. They'd stopped injecting the girls with drugs, but the traumatized women were still not conscious. But the combination of coming off the drugs, having been kidnapped, raped and crammed into the small stateroom on a boat that was now plowing head on into an angry sea was too much. As soon as one girl vomited, the others followed suit—throwing up in their bunks, unable to get to the head. It was all Jennifer could do to keep from gagging. They were still drifting in and out of consciousness.

She placed the tray on the built in between the double bunks and headed back up to the salon, holding onto the rail with both hands as she ascended the curving steps. About half way up, the lights suddenly went out. She froze in mid-step and clung to the rail, her breath catching in her throat. The sudden and complete blackness was terrifying. Too scared to move, she stood frozen. Her heart pounded in her chest. Her eyes searched the darkness. Nothing. It dawned on her what had happened. At first, she couldn't believe it, but there was no mistaking the silence. The steady drone of the mains was gone. The motors had stopped. They were dead in the water.

Suddenly piercing the darkness, Deathbreath's voice bellowed from above. "You fucking cunt! What did you do to the Goddamn lights? Where the fuck are you?"

She tried to call out, but her voice stuck in her throat. She forced herself to move, inching her way forward, her feet feeling for the next step. She reached floor level where the handrail ended, and stopped. Her eyes were getting accustomed to the darkness, and she could make out the faint outline of the galley only because she knew it was there. She made her way into the corner of the galley where, mercifully, rough water handrails ran along the underside of the counters. She grabbed them and held on. The ride had been getting rougher all day, but when the boat lost power and stopped making headway, it only took the storm a couple of minutes to turn the boat sideways, into the trough. Out of control, the *Dorsal* was rolling wildly from side to side. The steadily increasing winds were ripping the tops off the ten-to-twelve-foot swells. It was all Jennifer could do to hang on in the blackness.

"You fucking bitch! Where are you? What the hell did you do to this Goddamned boat? I'm going to break your fucking neck!"

She didn't move. Deathbreath had no idea she was standing less than ten feet in front of him. From the direction of his voice, she knew he was still seated at the table, right where she'd left him before heading below with dinner for the girls. His words were as foul as his breath, but the all-powerful, intimidating, dominance to his voice was gone. *He's scared! Now* her instincts screamed. She felt along the countertop for the knife she'd been using to carve the meat. Nothing. She knelt down and searched the floor with her hands. Her trembling fingers touched the cold metal of the blade. She grabbed the wooden handle. With adrenaline surging through her, she started feeling her way towards the goon, the knife clenched tightly in her free hand. She paused for a second at the end of the counter, knowing she'd have to cross the aisle from the galley to the table. She knew she only had one chance. She'd have to surprise him and thrust the knife into his heart all in one motion.

She took a deep breath, but just as she was about to let go of the rail, she saw the first erratic rays of a flashlight. Tony was on his way down from the wheelhouse! Deathbreath caught a glimpse of the light at the same time. She froze and watched as he whipped his head toward the light. Instinctively, she lowered the knife to her waist. When he spun back around, he saw her standing there, but couldn't see the knife hidden below the countertop.

"You fucking cunt!" he screamed, just as Tony came through the salon door. Now that Tony had the flashlight, the fear was out of Deathbreath's voice and he became a raging bull. "You fucking cunt! What the fuck did you do down there?" She squeezed the knife. He started to stand up, but the boat rolled again and threw him back into the settee. "Goddamn it!" he screamed.

"What the fuck!" Tony exclaimed. He stumbled across the salon toward the galley, the rays of the flashlight bouncing all over the place as he tried to keep his balance. A ray of light flashed across Tony's outstretched hand. He was holding his gun. Jennifer let the knife drop to the floor, amidst all the other crap that had fallen off the unattended countertops. Tony reached the opposite side of the counter and blinded her with the beam of the flashlight. With the boat rolling, the light quickly flashed up to the ceiling, across the floor, then back across her face again. "Don't fucking move!" Tony screamed at her.

"Lou!"

"I'm over here!" was all Deathbreath got out before he was thrown back into the corner again. "Goddamn it!" he screamed, struggling to get his fat ass off the settee.

Tony watched Deathbreath trying to get up from the settee. "Goddamn it, Lou! What the fuck's going on?"

"I don't know, boss. The fucking bitch went below and the next thing I know everything goes black! She did something down there!"

Tony whipped back towards Jennifer. Only the distance of the counter separated them. He managed to aim the light directly into her eyes. She couldn't see a thing. "What did you do?" he demanded, his voice cold as ice.

"Nothing. I swear to God I didn't do anything. I just took some food down to the girls and all of a sudden the lights went out."

He was able to hold the light on her face long enough to see she wasn't lying. She was scared shitless.

"Give me the fucking light!" Deathbreath demanded. "I'll beat the Goddamned truth out of her!"

"Shut up!" Tony commanded.

"Tony, what happened?" she asked.

"You didn't do this?" Tony asked again, the light flashing.

"I didn't do a thing. I swear to God I didn't do anything."

"Shit," Tony said. "Where's the engine room?" he demanded, pointing the light down the stairs leading to the staterooms. "Can you get to the engines from down there?"

"No…I don't know," Jennifer said shaking her head. "I don't think so, but I don't know for sure."

"Fuck!" Tony said, as he lowered himself down and wedged himself into the settee across from Deathbreath. They were both holding onto the table. Tony's gun was in one hand, the flashlight was in the other, and both gun and light were wedged against the table. The flashlight now cast an eerie, fixed beam across the room. They all looked towards the light as the boat wallowed in the trough.

"She did it!" Deathbreath growled accusingly. "She fucked with something while she was down there."

"Fuck you!" Jennifer snapped back. "I didn't do anything, you asshole!" Both men instantly knew from the sound of her voice that she was scared. Obviously, she hadn't done anything to sabotage the boat.

"What are we going to do now? If she didn't fuck something up, then what the fuck happened?" Deathbreath asked Tony.

"How should I know?" Tony shot back. "I was just sitting up there trying not to puke. Then all these fucking alarms started blasting. Scared the shit out of me. Then everything just went black."

"Did we hit something?" Jennifer asked. "It didn't feel like we hit anything." The fact that she was actually talking out loud to these pricks pissed her off. Until now, she'd kept her words to a minimum, only answering them when she had to.

"We didn't hit anything, you idiot! Just shut your fucking pie-hole," Deathbreath barked. He looked back at Tony. "What are we going to do now?"

"Get into the engine room and see what happened," Tony answered with feigned calmness.

"What the fuck am I supposed to look for? I don't know shit about boats."

"How the fuck should I know?" Tony was losing his patience. "Just go see if anything looks fucked up."

"You go!" Deathbreath retorted.

You could cut the tension with a knife. Tony turned toward Deathbreath and slowly raised the flashlight to his face. Holding up one hand and turning his head away to shield his eyes from the light, Deathbreath instantly backed down. "I didn't mean it like that," he said, tucking his balls between his legs. *Bullshit*, Jennifer thought to herself. He'd backed down and Tony didn't look like he was in any condition to push it. But something had changed between them in that instant—they all knew it.

"I'll go, boss. No problem. It's just that I don't know shit about motors and crap like that."

Tony's long pause before speaking let Deathbreath know he'd fucked up, that it wasn't over, only on hold for the time being. "You've got to know more than I do," Tony finally said. "That's why I asked you to go take a look." Another long pause. The tension was still there, but no longer at the boiling point. "Do you have another flashlight anywhere?" Tony asked, looking in Jennifer's direction.

"There's one in my stateroom. And I think there's one in that drawer over there," she said, pointing toward the built-in teak cabinets where she'd seen the crew put away a couple of tools before they'd left San Diego.

Tony held the light as Deathbreath crawled across the floor to the area she'd indicated. Reaching up, he opened the drawer, felt around and found the flashlight. "Got it!" He said triumphantly, turning it on.

"I'm not sure," Jennifer offered, "but I think we've been running on the generator since we left. If it quit when the mains shut down, that's probably why the lights went out." Both men looked at her. "I think it's kinda like a car. You know, a battery starts the motors. Maybe the battery died."

"Send her down there to look," Deathbreath sneered. "Sounds like she knows more than we do."

Tony glanced over at his idiot partner. "Like a car," he said, thinking out loud. "The battery wouldn't be dead if the motor was running. But if you open the car door, the interior lights go on. There's got to be a switch somewhere." They immediately started searching the room with their flashlights. No one had thought twice about power sources—or anything else mechanical for that matter—and their negligence was biting them in the ass.

"Hey, check this out!" Deathbreath said excitedly. He'd located a toggle switch next to one of the recessed overhead lights. As soon as he flipped it, the salon flooded with 12-volt light.

A soft "Thank God" escaped from Jennifer's lips. The men immediately found several other ceiling switches and turned them all on. With the salon lit, some of the tension started to drain from her shoulders. She took a deep breath. Being in total darkness, with the boat rolling wildly in the trough, had put the fear of God in everyone. No matter how big the boat, you're still just a speck on an endless sea.

With not so much as a thought about the battery drain, Deathbreath flipped on every12-volt switch he could find. The salon was flooded with light again.

"Cool. Okay. Now we're cool," Tony said.

"Now what?" Deathbreath wanted to know.

Tony grunted. "Obviously, there's something wrong with the fucking engines. Let's get below and see if we can find what went wrong." By not ordering Deathbreath to go alone, he'd prevented another confrontation, for the time being.

"Fine," Deathbreath said through clenched teeth, "but I don't even know what we're looking for."

"Neither do I, dip shit, but we can't just sit here." Turning again to Jennifer, he ordered her not to move.

"I'm not going anywhere," she answered immediately. "I'm just praying you can get us running again." Watching the two goons stumbling as they headed out of the salon toward the engine room entrance, she felt another rush of hope. *If those assholes can't get this thing running, whatever plans they had are going to be shot to shit. Maybe I can lock them down there somehow.*

Hope was starting to creep back into her belly, when a gut-wrenching scream echoed up the stairwell from the girls' cabin. Gripping the handrail, she made her way below and ran into one of the girls who was screaming hysterically. "What is it?" Jennifer asked. She grabbed the girl by the arm and tried to brace herself against the wall. The boat rolled again and they both went crashing into the companionway wall. "What is it?"

"Debbie's dead!" the girl screamed, her wild eyes looking around hysterically. Fully conscious for the first time since her abduction, the poor thing had no idea where she was or what had happened to her. She was scared to death. The drugs had finally worn off. "Where the fuck are we?" she screamed again, looking around in the semi-darkness, trying to see in the dim light that was spilling into the companionway from the salon above. Suddenly she jumped back, as if seeing Jennifer for the first time. "Who the hell are you?" The boat rolled. Before Jennifer could answer, the girl threw-up all over her.

Being hit in the face by projectile vomit was just too much for Jennifer. She doubled over as the built-up pain and fear spewed from her mouth. She wretched over and over again and collapsed in a heap on the floor next to the other girl, who was also doubled over dry heaving. Tossed around in their own vomit like two rag dolls, as the boat rolled uncontrollably in the raging storm.

Things in the engine room weren't going much better. Tony lost it first, throwing up all over the side of the main. The hot iron instantly intensifying the rank smell. A few seconds later, Deathbreath joined him, filling the bilge with puke. They were in a world of hurt, and neither of them had a clue what a fuel filter looked like.

******

On board the *Vintage*, we felt the storm building and knew we were heading straight into it. "Let's switch over the Raycores and change filters so they're all fresh before we get into this thing," I suggested to Travis.

"Need any help?" Jasmine asked

"No, I've got it. Piece of cake," Travis said as he headed below.

"I'm not very mechanically inclined," she admitted. "Why change the filters?"

"Preventative medicine," I answered. "When things get rough, all the sediment and crap that builds up in the bottom of the fuel tanks gets sloshed around. Sure as shit, at the worst possible time, a bunch of that crud will get sucked into the filters, and when they get clogged, everything shuts down."

"Hmm," was all she said.

Sensing she still wanted to know a little more, I continued with my Fuel Filter 101 lecture. "Let's say this thing keeps getting worse and we get into some really rough seas. There's a good chance that whatever crap we have in our tanks is going to find its way to the filters. That's why we run duallies."

"What are duallies?"

"Dual inline filters. If one of the filters starts to clog, all we have to do is turn the valve to the fresh side and we never miss a beat. Then, while the clogged filter is off-line, we can change it out. That way we can keep running without rolling around helplessly in the trough. It can be hell down there trying to work around all that hot machinery if the boat's going sideways. If we stay on it, we can just keep switching filters until we burn off the problem. That's why I wouldn't own a boat without duallies."

She nodded as if she completely understood. "But what happens if all the filters get clogged up?"

"You're basically fucked." She laughed. "Bleeding the mains isn't a big deal, but it's a royal pain in the ass when it's rough."

"Bleeding the mains? You're talking a foreign language."

"Sorry. O.K. Once a diesel comes up to temperature, there are only two things that will shut it down; cut off its air supply or its fuel supply. When a filter gets clogged, it starves to death and shuts off, but not before it's tried to suck every ounce of fuel it can from the line. When lines aren't full of fuel, they're full of air, which is 'no bueno.' Once she's got air in her lines, you've got to get it out and bleed it before she'll start again."

"How do you do that?

"It's simple. Just crack open an injector line at the highest point in the manifold and bleed out the air."

"Maybe one of these days you could show me how to do it." I looked at her and she smiled. "I'm serious. I'd like to know how."

"No worries." She'd yet to stop amazing me...wanting to learn how to bleed a main. Go figure. I wondered if she liked watching football.

******

"This thing is really starting to build," I said to Travis as he returned to the wheelhouse. "We're in for a long night."

"Looks like it," he said, surveying the angry seas ahead of us.

"Everything all right below?" I inquired.

Travis just nodded. "Yeah, we're cool."

Knowing you're heading into the heart of a big blow with darkness approaching tends to keep conversation to a minimum. After awhile, Travis asked if me if I wanted him to take over. I was running on fumes and needed rest, so we switched places. "Wake me if you get tired," I said as I climbed into my bunk.

"Will do."

I was asleep before my head hit the pillow.

"What do you think our chances of finding them are?" Jasmine asked Travis after she knew I was asleep.

"Like finding a whore in church," he said, a remark that earned him a quick, but harmless jab in the ribs.

"Seriously, do you think we have a chance?"

"No, not really. This whole thing sucks." Jasmine felt her spirits sink as the harsh reality of their situation started to sink in. Travis tried to put a better spin on it. "But, hell, we lucked out and found that judge, so who knows." She looked over at him and Travis knew she wasn't buying it. "With the head start they've got on us, Jaz, we'll be lucky to even find the Goddamned boat. And the chances of finding Jennifer and the other girls..." His words trailed off. He took a deep breath as he reached out for her hand. "I don't even want to think about it."

A wave slammed into the bow, virtually stopping the boat, but only for a split second. The hull shuddered, her props dug in and she reared up like a wild horse, tossing her head skyward, fighting her way through the angry black water. She threw off a huge plume of white spray that hung over the wheelhouse like a giant shroud before collapsing to cover the boat with water.

"Who would do something like this?" Jasmine whispered.

"Scumbags," Travis said. "Asshole cocksuckers that ought to have their balls cut off, shoved down their throats and their lips stapled shut."

Travis held Jasmine all night, riding out the storm wrapped in one another's arms. They sat together in the helm seat, watching the first rays of light break through the pitch-blackness of the stormy night. At first, the color changes were subtle, almost undetectable. Then the colors intensified and pierced through the clouds, giving a faint outline to what had been the shapeless black hole into which *Vintage* had steadily plunged all night. Now in the middle of a tropical storm, dawn was a welcome site, even though only razor-thin slivers of pure crimson were able to make their way through the black clouds for an instant before being swallowed up.

And whether or not it is clear to you, no doubt, the universe is unfolding as it should.

Chapter 12

Fate played her hand by way of the tropical storm. With no sustained winds over 70 knots, she would go into the history books unnamed, but this was one tropical storm that would change the lives of all of us in its path. In spite of the winds and rough seas, *Vintage* made a good steady 8 knots over ground all night. Though no one on board had any way of knowing that *Dorsal* was floundering dead in the water, the distance between the two vessels was closing fast. Looking over the charts, plotting speed and time for distance, I marked our estimated position as being just above the Thetas Bank, 15 miles off the rugged, desolate coast of Baja.

"Why didn't you wake me up last night?" I asked Travis, who was still at the helm.

Jasmine had gone below just before I woke up and started a kettle of water boiling for her specialty of hot coffee, rich chocolate, and whipped cream over ice. It had instantly become everyone's favorite morning drink. Amazingly enough, none of us normally drank coffee, but combined with the rich dark chocolate, whipped cream and ice, it became our morning ritual.

"Jaz stayed up with me all night."

Settling into the double bench seat next to the helm, I looked over at Travis and pressed him further. "You didn't need to go all night. You guys should have got 'n me up."

"Would have if we'd needed to. You were out like a light and we were doing all right. Figured you could use the rest."

I sensed something in his voice. "What's up?"

"Nothing, man." Travis didn't seem to want to look at me.

"Come on."

"We just had...." He paused to search for the right words. "I don't know how to say it...Jaz and I...well, we just connected last night...that's all."

It was amazing. I felt like maybe they'd experienced the same thing Jennifer and I had a couple of months earlier. I knew exactly how Travis was feeling. He looked at me, caught my eye and smiled. He knew I knew. I nodded, but didn't say anything else. Men rarely do.

We just sat there, watching *Vintage* pick her way through the waves.

Jasmine returned, handing us each a cup of her delicious iced chocolate coffee.

"You guys hungry?" she asked.

"No, I'm good, thanks," I said.

Travis held up his cup. "This is good for now." It only took a second for her to slide in next to him. The three of us watched the bow ploughing through the waves in search of my missing lady.

******

The haunting echoing screams of "She's dead!" filled her fragmented nightmares all night. Jennifer knew she had to find out. Opening the door to the girls' quarters, she found herself in a war zone. Vomit was everywhere and the three remaining girls lay motionless in their bunks. She edged forward, sat on the edge of one bunk, and reached out to feel the forehead of the nearest girl. It was warm. *Thank God.* Pale white, but warm. She leaned down and put her ear to the girl's mouth and heard her shallow breathing—this one was alive. The girl next to her had wedged herself into the corner between the bunk and the starboard wall. She, too, was warm and breathing.

Moving over to the port side bunk, Jennifer sat down and touched the third girl's forehead. She yanked her hand back the instant she made contact, shock and fear catapulting her off the bunk. She stood frozen for a while, staring at the dead girl. As rational thoughts slowly regained control of her brain, Jennifer realized she had to make sure the girl was dead. She forced herself to kneel down beside the girl, feel her forehead again, and listen for breathing. The girl was cold to the touch, and there was no breath…not a sound. Death hung on her like a shroud. Jennifer didn't know what to do. She closed her eyes and said a silent prayer. Two days earlier, she'd watched in horror as the captain and crew were executed. Somehow that had been different, distant, like it really wasn't happening. This was too real. She'd never been close to a dead person before—hell, she'd never even seen a dead person before.

Slowly she became aware of her own breathing, her own heartbeat. Each breath fortified her and filled her body with life. She wasn't ready to die…not now…not here…not like this. She felt strength surging through her, a resolve beyond comprehension, a will to live. *These assholes aren't going to take my life away. There's nothing I can do about the girl.* She must have choked, gagged and drowned in her own vomit. Drugged and delirious…it could have happened to anyone.

Jennifer went back into the hall to get the other girl, and half-dragged and half-carried her into the stateroom. She couldn't put her into the double bunk with the dead girl, so she laid her on the floor, put a puke-soaked pillow gently under her head and covered her with a blanket.

Climbing back up the stairwell and entering the salon, she was amazed at what a complete disaster the boat was. It looked like a hurricane had ripped the insides out of it. Ceiling panels were hanging down; couches, chairs and even one of the built-in teak cabinets were strewn about the salon; the window shades were ripped open; books, table lamps, dishes, pots and pans were everywhere. The galley cabinet doors slammed open and shut as the boat rolled in the trough. Broken glass and bottles covered the floor.

Her sea legs were back, so she was able to walk with some degree of confidence. With the new day she could see the storm still raging, but it didn't feel as bad as it had during the night. Maybe it was waning, or maybe she was just getting used to it. Didn't matter—she had to find out where her captors were. This might be her only chance. She made her way through the salon and up to the wheelhouse. It was empty. Heading back down, she noticed that the engine room hatch was open. Tony and Deathbreath were passed out. Tony was lying between the two generators closest to her and the hatch; Deathbreath lay between the mains. Quickly she closed the hatch, but there was no lock. *Shit!*

Looking around, she found one of the long-handled aluminum nets used for loading bait. They were about an inch and a half in diameter. *If I can wedge the handle between the spokes for the hatch handle, I might be able to make it so they can't get out.* The handle just fit in between the spokes of the heavy-duty wheel that opened and closed the hatch. She jammed it in harder with all her strength, but it hardly moved. She reached up higher on the pole and pulled down with her full weight. At first nothing happened, but then the aluminum gave way, bending just above the hatch. She needed to find a way to keep the handle from turning. She grabbed another bait pole and wedged it in from the opposite direction. She reached up again and pulled down with all her weight. The second pole bent just as the first one had, so she had two poles wedged into the handle of the hatch at opposite angles. Twisting them, she was able to work the top sections of the poles together. *That's a start.* She grabbed a dock line out of the storage locker behind the bait tank, slipped the looped end over one of the poles and started wrapping them together. Pulling the handles together as hard as she could, she worked a series of tight figure eights around the two poles. She pulled out another line from the locker, secured the loops through the spokes in the hatch and then worked the second line up the poles in another series of figure eights.

She stood back and took a deep breath. Her work was a mess. She prayed that the lines would twist tighter and tighter like a Chinese puzzle if the goons tried to open the hatch from below by twisting on the handles. *It'll work if the poles don't snap.* Initially, it had taken all her strength and weight to get the poles to bend. She hoped the goons wouldn't be able to apply enough pressure from the underside of the hatch to turn the handle and cause the poles to give way.

Before this trip, she'd never been onboard *Dorsal*. She had no idea if there were any other ways in and out of the engine room but knew she had to find out. Right there at her feet were three other deck hatches—one port, one starboard and one dead center, aft of the bait tank. These steel deck hatches were heavy and watertight. She tried to open one of them, but it was far too heavy for her to lift. She squatted down over the hatch, arched her back and lifted with her legs. Straining with all her might, she still couldn't get it to budge. "Shit!" she gasped and gave up.

Taking no chances, she took advantage of the stern cleats and looped more dock lines around the spoke handles of each outboard hatch cover. Both outboard hatches led to refrigerated fish holds below deck, but she didn't know that. Once again, she twisted the lines together before running their opposite ends to the respective cleats on both sides of the boat. If they tried turning the handles from below, the lines would knot up like a towel twisted from both ends. She hoped they would become so taut it would be impossible to open the hatches. She planned to camp out on deck with one of the filet knives in case any hands tried reaching up from below to free the obstructions.

So far, so good...but the center hatch was still unsecured. Maybe she could run two lines off the center handle, tying one to each stern cleat. But there was only one line left in the storage locker. She looped that one around the center hatch handle and ran it to the port side. She remembered watching one of the deck hands store the bow lines forward after they got bait that first night out and figured there had to be more storage lockers forward of the salon. She inched her way up and along the walk toward the bow. The side decks were slick as snot and the boat was still rolling violently in the trough. She held on tight to the grab rails and inched her way forward. *My only chance is to keep those goons trapped below.*

The forward storage lockers were built into the center of the bow across the front of the house, but the handrails ended at the side of the house, leaving nothing for her to hold on to. She got down on her hands and knees and started crawling across the non-skid. With every roll, her knees slid over the rough surface. Within seconds, her blood was discoloring the saltwater sloshing around her.

What am I doing? She thought to herself. She was at the front corner of the house, looking across the vast open deck of the bow. The narrow passage between the outside rail and the house now seemed like a sanctuary. As scary as making her way forward had been to this point, it seemed like heaven compared to the vast open space she now faced. Though she'd been pitched back and forth between the outboard rails and the house, at least she'd been contained. Looking out now, there was nothing. If they were hit by a big swell, or if a wave broke over the bow rails, there would be nothing to hold onto until she hit the side of the boat. The thought sent chills through her. With the forces that were tossing the entire hundred-ton vessel around like a toy in a bathtub, her 115-pound body wouldn't stand a chance—but she knew she had to get to those lines.

Making it around the front corner of the house, she grabbed the nearest dogleg that held down the first hatch. She grabbed the second latch. In a kneeling position with her arms spread-eagled, she tried to twist both latches in order to open the hatch. Fortunately, *Dorsal* was a meticulously maintained vessel—the latches were well lubricated and twisted open easily.

She looked inside, only to be disappointed. The port hatch was full of fenders—no lines. Backing away, she let go of the hatch, allowing the heavy lid to slam closed before being re-secured, and crawled toward the center hatch. Once more, with only the latches to hold onto, she managed to get the center hatch open. A rush of jubilation—there were the lines! She reached in, trying to hold the hatch open above her head with one hand. Her timing couldn't have been worse. With one arm above her head and the other reaching inside the locker, she lost her balance when a short swell hit the boat. Her knees slid out from under her, and before she could pull her arm out of the locker, the hatch smashed down on her forearm and hand. She screamed in pain.

The wave broke over the bow and swept her toward the side. The only thing saving her from being washed overboard was the fact that her hand was still trapped under the heavy lid of the hatch. As the boat rolled back the other way, her body whipped back helplessly in the opposite direction. She almost passed out. The pain was excruciating, as bone ground against fiberglass under the weight of the heavy hatch. Reaching out with her free hand, she tried desperately to grab the edge of the hatch. Her hips, legs and feet were bleeding from being swept back and forth across the heavily applied non-skid on the bow. Her shorts were ripped to shreds and covered in blood. She felt none of this, though, because the pain in her hand was all consuming. After a momentary lull, she was somehow able to grab the latch. She rolled over on her back and forced the hatch open just far enough to pull her mangled hand free. It was a mess of bone, skin and blood. She couldn't tell if she still had all her fingers. Another wave broke over the bow, sweeping her up and slamming her against the port rail. Her primal scream echoed over the decks, but no one heard it. She felt herself being swept back across the deck into the blackness of oblivion....

Indescribable pain shot through her stomach. She'd been swept directly into one of the outboard stanchions and was hanging over the side of the boat. Feet and legs on one side, head and arms on the other, bent in half at the waist, she was draped around the stanchion like a wet towel. Another wave lifted the boat from the opposite side, dipping the side from which she was hanging deep into the water. As the boat rolled back, she came up fighting for her life, choking and gagging from the burning saltwater. Her limp body fell back onto the deck. She lay flat on her back...motionless.

When the centerline of a boat lies in the trough, the temporary pause in the endless rolling at the midpoint between swells causes a boat to stop moving. In the stillness and peace during those few precious moments, she knew she'd died and gone to heaven. *For some reason, I'm still holding onto something cold...solid. This doesn't make any sense.* She willed her hand to let go, but it wouldn't. Waves of peace swept over her. No more pain. She caught a momentary glimpse through the gates of heaven, where everything felt so still and quiet. She knew she was floating toward the silence. Then everything vanished, as another icy cold wave ripped her vision apart. She felt herself floating again, but this time she found no peace—only hard edges giving way to pain as she landed hard. Her hand was wrapped around another one of those damn cold, solid tubes. *Why can't I let go? I know if I just let go, everything will be all right.* The process seemed to repeat endlessly—blissful moments of calm, giving way to waves of confusion and pain. Again and again, she'd touch the hem of the garment and then instantly be dragged back down, away from the peace. After one final, giant cascading fall, she let go of that damned tube as her limp body was thrown over the edge. She bounced and tumbled, head over heels, over the falls and into Hell. She felt her bleeding, broken body being swept down the steps and into the cockpit.

I didn't make it. God doesn't want me. I'm going to Hell.

******

She didn't know how long she'd been lying there, but when the first painful rays of light shocked her eyelids, drawing her back from blissful unconsciousness, every cell in her body screamed in pain at being awakened. Her racked body had stiffened while she was unconscious; even turning her head sent nauseating waves of pain through her neck. Confused, she closed her eyes and tried to retreat into the darkness. Her body wouldn't let her. She wanted nothing more than to just lie there, but something deep inside forced her back, demanding that her aching body respond. Reluctantly...ever so slowly...she began to move.

Water sloshed over her, as she lay wedged in the aft port corner of the cockpit. As painful as it was, the salt actually helped by flushing out the lacerations and abrasions that covered her body, especially on her hips, knees and elbows. Those injuries paled in comparison to the pain in her disfigured, broken hand. When the hatch collapsed, it crushed the tiny bones on top of her hand and broke the middle three fingers. The hand was swollen and had turned a hyena's shade of black and blue. She had to support it with her good hand. Sitting up, she cradled it against her chest as she sat alone in the corner of the cockpit. *Alone.* Broken, bloody and exhausted, she closed her eyes as they filled with tears. *Alive.* The sun felt warm on her face. *Sun?* She noticed she wasn't being tossed around any longer—the boat was actually rocking gently.

Looking around the cockpit, her eyes locked on the unsecured center hatch. *All that for a few miserable feet of stinking line.* She silently cursed herself for trying to make it up to the foredeck during the storm. Knowing she still needed to do something to secure that final hatch, she tested her legs. With her good hand, she pulled herself off the deck. She was weak and light-headed, but with the storm gone, the walk up to the bow was like a stroll in the park. She cursed herself again for being so foolish. After pulling out the lines she needed, she headed back to the cockpit.

She tired to loop the lines around the center hatch, but with only one good hand, it was nearly impossible, trying to weave them together like she had the outboard hatches. By the time she was done, the cockpit looked like a drunken spider's web. *Was it strong enough to keep evil below decks?* She headed into the salon, pulled a bag of ice out of the freezer and sat down. Resting her broken hand on the table, she gently laid the ice over the damaged flesh. Knowing the cold would help ease the swelling; she fought through the initial pain as the ice touched her broken bones.

She took a deep breath and closed her eyes. For the first time since all the madness had started, she could finally rest. She gave herself about ten minutes before pulling a First Aid kit out from under the galley sink and wrapping her hand in an Ace bandage. Cutting a towel, she made up a sling and tried her best to stabilize her arm. It wasn't much, but it would have to do. She worked her way up the interior stairs to the pilothouse. The storm had passed. The once violent swells were now just rolling under the keel. She dialed the VHF to channel 16. Surprisingly there was still enough juice to light the dial. Cuing the mic she started calling, "Mayday...Mayday...Mayday."

The faint crackle of the broken Mayday call coming over the speaker on board *Vintage* sent my heart rate sky high. Grabbing the mic, I screamed back, "*Vintage* returning the Mayday call. Say again the name of your vessel."

Through the static, I heard her voice calling for help. "Mayday...Mayday. This is *Dorsal*. Does anyone copy? Can anyone hear me? Mayday...Mayday...Mayday."

"Jennifer! Jennifer, we're here! Copy! Copy! Can you hear me! Jennifer, we've got you!"

Hearing Corey's voice was more than she'd ever dreamed possible. At first she thought she'd passed out again and was dreaming. She tasted her tears as she yelled back into the mike, still not believing it was true, "Corey...is that you?"

"Jesus, Jennifer! Oh, thank God! I'm so glad to hear your voice. Are you all right? Where are you?"

"I don't know where we are...is that really you?"

"Yes. Yes, it's me. We've been looking for you. Where are you?"

"I have no idea."

I could almost hear the tears through her voice. *Shit.* "Can you see anything? Any land marks, mountain tops, an island...anything?"

"No...just waves. We've been in a really bad storm and the boat broke."

Panic was quickly replacing the initial elation he'd felt at hearing her voice. "Jennifer, listen to me! We can't be too far away. Unless we're picking up some wired skip, these things aren't much good over 75 miles, so we're close. Jennifer, we're close."

"I love you."

"I know, I know. I love you, too. I can't believe you're alive." Silence. "Jennifer! Are you still there?"

"Come get me…please."

"I'm trying. We can't be far away, but we don't have a direction finder, so I need you to look around. Can you see anything? Anything that might tell us where you are."

"They killed the crew," she said. "Everyone's dead except me and girls. I'm so scared, Corey. Please come get us."

Total panic engulfed me. Hearing these fragmented facts confirmed my worst nightmares. "Are you all right?"

"Corey. Hurry, please."

"Are you all right?" I repeated. "Are you all right? You're breaking up."

After a pause, she said, "I'm here, but we need help. Corey, please hurry." The last few words were heavily broken by the static. Then silence.

"Jennifer! Jennifer! Come back, Jennifer! Are you there? Jennifer, come back!"

From the wheelhouse, I screamed for Travis and Jaz. We'd been able to make way in spite of the storm. And now, hearing her voice, I cursed myself for not having found a way to purchase a direction finder for the boat. Before the season, it seemed like a luxury item we couldn't afford…but now…Goddamn it. Travis and Jasmine raced into the wheelhouse. I still had the mic in my hand. "We're coming, sweetheart. We're coming. We need your help. Can you hear me? Can you see anything? Jennifer, are you still there?"

She couldn't hear my final words. The 12V system that had been powering all the backup lights, the electronics were done. Without the generator running to power the Lewco chargers, the entire system finally gave way. The banks were completely drained. There wasn't even enough power left to operate the radio. The entire boat was dead in the water.

"Corey! Corey! Don't go!" Jennifer pleaded into the dead mic. "Don't leave me! Please don't leave me here! Corey…please come back. Don't do this to me…please don't leave me…not now…"

"Goddamn it!" I screamed, throwing down the mic, grabbing the glasses. "Where are they?"

Travis put it together immediately. "What did she say before we got up here?" he demanded.

"She said they'd killed the crew, and it was just her and the girls alive."

"Oh, my God!" Jasmine gasped.

"She said they were broken down but had no idea where they were."

"Any clues? Anything? Anything that might help?"

"No, Goddamn it! I asked her! I asked her if she could see anything and all she said was water."

"Okay, okay," Travis said, "that's a start. That's good. Then we know they're off the beach somewhere. It's a start." He moved over to the chart table.

He was right, I thought, as I started to regain control of my racing heart. Picking up on Travis's thinking, I leaned over the chart table with him. "We've been holding about 45 miles off the beach, curving slightly eastward as we made our way further south. There's nothing else out here, or for that matter between us and the Cape. They must have been headed for Cabo, just like we thought."

"So let's plot it out." Together we worked up a couple of probable scenarios based on the assumption that *Dorsal* had been headed to Cabo. "We don't know how long they've been broken down, so there's no way to figure any kind of set or drift—especially with the storm." We were frustrated trying to guess how far off course the storm might have blown the boat. "We need to know when they quit making way."

"There's no way to know when they broke down."

"I know," Travis answered instantly, but he was ahead of me. "How about we try and triangulate what would happen to us if we broke down, assuming *Dorsal* would drift pretty much the same way we would."

We already had a black wax pen plotline on the clear sheet of Plexiglas covering the chart table to mark our course from Mag Bay to Cabo. Assuming that *Dorsal* was headed to Cabo, we took the spreaders and measured off seventy miles. Around our estimated position, we drew a seventy-mile radius in red, figuring that would be the maximum distance we would be able to communicate on the VHF. The circle looked huge.

"Fuck," Travis said under his breath.

"No shit," I said, pausing. "Okay," I continued, thinking out loud, "they had to have been ahead of us when they broke down, right?"

"Makes sense," Travis agreed. "And with the storm blowing up from the southwest, they would've been getting pushed up and in ever since they lost power."

"In our direction. So let's set a new heading forty-five degrees inside of our current course. That way, we'll be able to cover about a ninety-degree spread—forty-five degrees on either side of us. What do you think?"

Travis nodded as he made his own mental calculations. "That sounds pretty good. They have to be within seventy miles...eighty at the most."

"Unless we were just picking up some fluke skip," I said, grabbing the helm and spinning the wheel to port onto our new heading.

"Or we lost her for some other reason," Travis added.

"Like what? Distance?"

"Maybe. It's true—we might be right at the limits. But I was thinking...Jennifer said the crew was all dead, right?"

This caused us all to pause. After a moment, I answered Travis, "Yeah, she said they were all dead."

"Okay," Travis said. "If they were broken down, and no one on board knew what to do, then doesn't it make sense that they might be running everything, all their systems, off the batteries?" I nodded. "It wouldn't take too long to drain 'em if they weren't getting charged."

"If the mains were down, it makes sense to assume the generator might have gone down at the same time." We both nodded.

"Maybe boss, but we're stretching here," Travis warned.

"I know. Maybe…maybe not. If they lost power during the storm, they may just have a filter problem. And if that's the case, it makes sense to assume the generator may have gone down the same time the mains did."

"Possibly," Travis agreed. "Do you think Jennifer would have known what to do?"

"No. I don't think so."

"How long do you think their 12-volt system would last? Assume they're running lights, radios, electronics…the works. No reason to think they would have been conserving the batteries if they didn't know they were going to have a problem. Hell, the radar alone would drain the batteries in just a few hours."

"You're right," I agreed.

"Let's figure they were running hard until…what…twenty-four hours ago? Thirty-six?"

"When the storm hit," I said.

"Exactly. Something screwed up when they hit the storm, so let's back it off thirty-six hours." Having already run a plotline between our current position and the Cape, Travis grabbed the spreaders. Measuring off ten nautical miles along the chart's right-hand latitude index, he started twirling ten-mile increments on the line. "We're right here, now," he said, pointing to our estimated position. "Backing up thirty six hours to when the storm first hit us, we would have been here. Figuring they were at least forty-eight hours ahead of us, they would have been here when the storm hit." He pointed to a place along the plotline about four hundred and eighty miles ahead of us. "But we've been making good for the past thirty hours. So while they've been broken down, we've made up all but about a hundred miles or so. With the storm pushing them toward us, we've been running hard. That would put them somewhere…around….here."

"I think you're right." I said, before adjusting our heading about twenty degrees further to port to line up on the mark—a heading directly into the beach.

"If they were without power in that storm and not able to quarter it, I'm amazed they're still afloat."

"That was a hell of a blow, but she's a good boat."

"I know," Travis said, "but that's not what I was thinking."

"What's your point?"

He tapped the chart table, pointing to the Baja shoreline. "They may be a lot closer to the rocks than she knows. Assuming the storm pushed them only a couple miles an hour, as opposed to what I really think it did with the winds it was packing, four or even five miles an hour isn't out of the question. Corey, they might be getting dangerously close to the beach."

We ran another triangular plot, starting where we'd first estimated *Dorsal* was when she lost power. Assuming that's what happened and where *Vintage* was at that time. Estimating a storm push against *Dorsal's* hull of five miles per hour, we multiplied the thirty-six hours we guessed she'd been disabled to get a total estimated distance traveled. The point where those three lines intersected was our best guess at *Dorsal*'s position. Plotting that EP against our current position, we were fifty-two miles away from where our best guess was they'd be—a meaningless red dot in the middle of a chart, in the middle of nowhere. The tiny dot was, however, precariously close to the desolate Baja coastline…and we were still five hours away.

I pushed the throttles up a little bit more and caught Travis's disapproving glance. I knew we were pushing her harder than we ever had before, but I didn't care. "They can take it!" I said, before Travis could question my decision to push those old CATS into the red.

"I didn't say a word," Travis said, "but if she blows, then we're all fucked."

"Jennifer's already fucked," I said, "and from the sound of her voice, every second counts."

Travis left the wheelhouse and went below to check on his precious babies. I knew he was right, but didn't pull back on the throttles. Jaz looked at me. "They'll hold together," I assured her. "They're not liking it, but they'll be okay."

Jaz nodded as she reached out and touched my hand. "Then let's go get her."

******

Losing contact with Corey pushed Jennifer over the edge. At first she didn't know what had happened. *Why isn't he answering me?* Then she realized the light dial on the radio had gone out. So had everything else on the bridge. "How could I be so stupid?" she said out loud. A boat's just like on a car? If the motor isn't charging the battery, and you leave the lights on, the battery going to die." Sure as shit, that's what had happened. They'd left everything on. The radar, instruments, radios, lights, everything—and now the batteries were dead.

She sat there for a moment...thinking. If the batteries were dead and the hatches closed, that meant the goons would be in total darkness below decks and she knew how frightening that can be. Panic shot through her as she raced off the bridge. Looking down into the cockpit, she saw the engine room hatch being forced open. Her ropes and bent poles were holding, but the goons were doing everything they could to get out.

"You fucking cunt! You're dead! You hear me! The minute I get out of here, you're dead. Goddamned cunt!"

The hatch was heavy and from below, they didn't have much leverage but still, raw fear froze her. Unable to move, she starred at the hatch as they worked to pry it open. Whatever they were trying to wedge between the hatch and the deck, slipped, slamming the hatch shut, instantly blocking out their threats. Silence. She stood motionless, still paralyzed by fear.

Then it popped right back open. Only a couple inches, but enough for their screaming to carry clearly throughout the boat. It was Deathbreath. "I told you we should have killed her with the crew. But, no...you wanted her alive. Now look at us. Trapped down here like fucking sewer rats. You Goddamned bitch! You're dead! You hear me? You're fucking dead!" The pure rage in his voice was terrifying—but not as terrifying as

303

the sight of the crowbar coming though the widening crack between the hatch and the deck. The ropes had twisted tight, preventing them from getting any more turns on the inside handle, but they'd opened it enough to get a wedge back in there. The sharp sound as they started hammering on the crowbar snapped her out of her trance. She almost fell trying to slide down the ladder from the wheelhouse. Hitting the deck hard, frantically looking around for something to try and knock the crowbar back into the hatch with. She spotted a short, wooden fish bat hanging on the side of the bait tank. Grabbing it with her good hand, but before she could swing, shots rang out. She vaulted away from the narrow opening in the hatch. She didn't know if she'd been hit... she felt something hot running down the inside of her legs. Bending over to look...expecting to see blood. It took her another moment, staring at her crotch, to realize she'd peed herself.

"Open the fucking hatch, you Goddamned cunt!" Tony bellowed from below, trying to spin the barrel of the gun around to get off another volley.

"Fuck you!" she screamed, hidden behind the hinge of the thick hatch. She swung with all her might; hitting the crowbar dead on, jamming it back into the hold. The heavy hatch slammed shut, cutting off their threats in mid-scream. "Fuck you!" she screamed again and jumped directly on top of the hatch. She could feel them pounding on it below her, but with her added weight, they couldn't force it to up far enough to re-wedge the crowbar. Elated, she threw back her head, and raising the bat in victory, let out a primal scream that echoed over the water—a scream heard only by her captives and a covey of low-flying terns.

High from the adrenaline rush, flushed with a sense of relief and power. She'd managed to stay alive and turn the tables on those murdering scumbags. *I'm going to make it...we're going to make it.* Thinking about the girls. The skies were clearing. The storm was over. The sea had ceased its endless pounding. She promised herself she'd never take another breath of life for granted. *It is truly a gift.* Tears filled her eyes. *Now, if only my knight in shining armor would come rescue me...*

She knew couldn't just stand there on the hatch all day, but for the time being, it was okay. The goons muted cursing ended, but she knew they hadn't given up. She also knew she knew she wouldn't be able to leave the cockpit—she'd have to keep watch on the hatches. Bat still in hand, she quietly stepped off the hatch and sat down on the steps leading to the salon, a few feet away. After two days of being relentlessly pounded by the storm, the still seas help calm her ravaged nerves. With slow, deep breaths the tension started to drain out of her shoulders and neck. Bat in hand, content for the time being, to just sit and wait to be rescued.

******

Their eyes alternated between probing the horizon and glancing at the sweeping radar screen for any signs of life. The Furuno forty-eight mile radar was pushed to its extreme reaches, searching for a target...any target. But so far, nothing.

"How far?" I asked, glancing back at Travis working the spreaders on the chart.

"Forty-one miles."

With just over four hours of daylight left, I prayed we'd find something soon. The waters had been laying down all day. By late afternoon, there was hardly a trace of the violence the sea had cast down upon us the past couple of days. *Amazing. Twenty-four hours ago, you couldn't even stand up. Now it's like we're riding on glass.*

"I've got a good feeling about this," Jasmine said.

"Me, too," I agreed, looking at her. "I think we're going to find them."

She smiled. "It's against all odds, but I feel it in my bones."

I just hope it's not wishful thinking, Travis thought to himself.

We continued scanning the horizon for any signs of life, knowing full well that the Furuno would pick up anything miles before we could see it. The first targets we had were the distant mountaintops that ran along the Pacific side of Baja. Checking the chart, the mountains were a couple of miles inland, but solid hits nonetheless. We were now within twenty miles of the point where we'd guessed we might find *Dorsal*. I reached down and switched the Furuno's range in half, knowing that I was cutting the scope by twenty-four miles, but also knowing that we'd be able to pick up a surface target better on the shorter frequency.

Sure enough, on the second sweep, the unit picked up something—a faint hit on the extreme ring, about 20 degrees south of our current heading. On the next sweep, it was gone.

"What do you think, skipper?" Travis asked. We'd both seen it.

"I don't know." After a half dozen more sweeps, nothing else appeared.

"A false reading?"

"Most likely," I said. "At the edges, this thing can be a little temperamental. How about we split the difference and drop down ten degrees?"

"Do it," he said without a moment's hesitation.

I brought her around, cheating in favor of the target that was no longer visible. After a few minutes, I couldn't help myself, and came all the way around, setting our new course directly at the lost target. "Sorry," I said looking over at Travis. He didn't object or ask for an explanation, but I gave it anyway. "Can't help thinking maybe we came up on a little swell at just the right moment and hung there long enough for the radar to pick up something."

"I was thinking the same thing," Travis said with a smile.

Twenty-four miles is an extremely long way for a small radar unit to pick up a target on the horizon. Even twelve miles is far, but after an hour, as soon as we closed the distance, I knocked her down another level. Sure enough…right there…almost dead ahead, we had a target.

"We've got something!" I said immediately. Both Travis and Jasmine leaped in front of the screen.

"Sure as shit!" Travis confirmed. "That's a hit!"

"Is that them?" Jasmine asked excitedly.

"No way of knowing, but it's a definite target. Still too far away to know. *Dorsal's* a big boat, but twelve miles—that's a long way for this unit. Hope it's not some freighter or cruise ship."

"Neither of those would be running that tight to the beach," Travis objected. "The good thing is that it's not solid. We keep losing her every few sweeps, which means it's not that big a ship."

"God, please let it be them," Jasmine whispered.

Another agonizing twenty-five minutes passed. We covered another six miles and still nothing in the binoculars. But at the six-mile range, we had a target that was now rock solid. A stationary target...definitely a boat...and it wasn't moving. That meant it was either a fishing boat, or... "Please God," I said, "Let it be them."

We'd been running in the red for hours. The CATS had been putting out a deafening, high-pitched scream since I'd poured the coals to them. They were pushing us at full speed, but I knew they could handle it. It wasn't often that I demanded this kind of performance from any machinery. Even though they didn't like it, they help up and did their job. *Oil changes for the both of you when this is over*, I promised, giving the dashboard a little suppositious pat.

"I got something! Dead ahead! They're dead ahead!" Travis screamed, snapping me out of my little trance. Sure as shit, the second I raised the binoculars to my eyes, I saw it, too. A tiny speck on the horizon, but no doubt, some kind of boat.

"What d'ya think?" Travis asked without taking his eyes off the distant object.

"Definitely a boat, but I can't tell yet."

"A few more minutes," Travis whispered. "Just a few more minutes." Our twelve knots seemed like a crawl. The minutes ticked by. The object was still too far off to make out, but it was getting larger as we closed the distance. "She's not moving."

"I know...could be a good sign, or it could be a Goddamned long liner."

It took another ten minutes before we could make out any distinct characteristics of the vessel. "It's a yacht," Travis stated, after mentally reviewing what he was seeing. "Definitely a yacht...white hull, white superstructure, enclosed bridge...bucket. She's a sport fisher—no doubt."

"It's got to be them!" Jasmine exclaimed.

We were glued to the binoculars. My heart was wedged in my throat as each minute brought us closer. The vessel's outline became clearer and more distinct with each passing moment. After a few more agonizing minutes, I finally nodded in agreement. We were close enough to recognize the lines of *Dorsal*. Closing my eyes, I thanked God and grabbed the mic. "*Dorsal. Dorsal. Vintage* calling. Jennifer, you picking this up?" Silence. "*Dorsal, Vintage* calling. Jennifer, we're less than three miles off your starboard quarter. Can you read this? Come back." Again, silence.

Lowering his binoculars, Travis looked over and we exchanged a look that said it all. I couldn't tell you what happened next, or even over the next hour. It was—and still is—a complete blur. All I remember is my overwhelming sense of relief seeing Jennifer standing there in the cockpit. I don't remember Travis getting the lines secured, or my jumping off the boat into her arms. Once our arms were wrapped around each other, it would have taken an act of God to pull us apart.

I could feel her tears seeping through my shirt, as she let go of the mind-numbing tension of her past few days. It was going to take months, perhaps even years, for the horrors to work their way out of her soul. Never again to bask in the innocence of youth. Life had thrown her a high, hard one…but she was still standing, safe in my arms.

"I knew you were coming...I just knew it," she whispered through her tears. Looking up into my eyes, "I love you.... so much.... never again am I leaving your side…ever."

"I was so afraid I'd never see you again…I was going out of my mind…I didn't know what to do. I'm so glad you're all right." Realizing I hadn't even hesitated before leaping on board and grabbing her, I held her at arm's length in front of me. "Are you all right?"

She looked down. "They killed the crew and raped the other girls," she whispered. "One of them is dead." Instinctively, I pulled her back to me, but she resisted, keeping the distance between us. Looking into my eyes, she added, "They didn't touch me." She stood firm. Her eyes held me, making absolutely certain I understood what she was saying. It took only a heartbeat and we connected. She saw in my eyes that I believed her completely. Knowing that was vital to her. Closing her eyes, she melted into my arms.

I'm not sure how long Travis and Jasmine had been on board but they were standing right beside us.

Jennifer and Jasmine had never met, but Jasmine couldn't control herself any longer. Gently putting her arms around Jennifer, and pulling out of my arms. Hugging her as if they were long lost sisters.

"Thank God you're all right," Travis asked softly. His eyes alert, scanning the boat. "Where's the crew? Where are the other girls?"

Jasmine felt the chill run down Jennifer's spine as she nodded toward the salon.

Travis suggested we take a look around.

"Wait," Jennifer said, as she saw us move toward the salon.

"What is it, honey?"

Jasmine knew instinctively what Jennifer was concerned about. "Trav," she said, "I think it'll be better if I check on the girls alone."

"Sure," he said as casually as possible. But before she could start toward the salon, he reached out, holding her arm, asking, "Jennifer, where are the bad guys?"

Jennifer took a half-step back from and pointed to the hatch, "They're in there?"

"What!" I yelled, startled and jumping away from the hatch as if it might explode. "They're in the engine room? Are you sure?"

Jennifer nodded, exhausted, sitting back down. "Sure I'm sure—they've been in there for awhile now."

"So that's what all this is about," Travis said, pointing to the maze of lines, bent poles and debris crisscrossing the cockpit. "Are they dead?"

"No," was all she said.

"What happened? How did you get them in there?"

"I didn't. They went in there when the motors quit running. It was during the storm—everything shut down and went black. I was scared to death."

"How many?" Travis asked without taking his eyes off the hatch.

"Two," Jennifer answered immediately. "I'm not sure what happened. It was so crazy during the storm. I thought we were going to sink."

The color drained out of her face. I pulled her back into my chest, holding her for all I was worth, whispering, "Everything's going to be all right." Her strength was amazing. She took a couple of deep breaths and began telling us about that terrifying night.

"First the motors quit. Then, just a few minutes later, all the lights went out. We were all in the salon. I was so scared I was afraid to move—you couldn't even see your hand in front of your face. It was pitch dark and so rough; we were getting the crap kicked out of us. I thought we were all going to die. The storm just kept getting worse. The boat was rolling from so violently from side to side. Water was coming in everywhere. I thought for sure we were going to tip over. If you weren't holding onto something, you'd go flying across the room. I was trying to check on the girls when we lost power." She paused as brutal visions of the night washed over her, as they would again and again, for a long time to come.

"I made it back up to galley. I had a knife. I was going to kill him." Her fragmented sentences leaving so many details out, but containing more than enough for us to connect the dots. "Then Tony came in with a flashlight." Jennifer started shaking, fighting for control.

"Whoever built this boat really knew what they were doing," she continued. "They built in handrails all along the undersides of the counters. I was holding on for life. The goons were wedged in behind the tables. One on each side. They were screaming at me and then they started yelling at each other. I don't remember how, but one of them found some switches and the lights to come back on."

"The twelve-volt backup system," Travis said, looking away from the hatch just long enough for us to exchange a glance. "Just like we figured."

"I don't know," Jennifer said, "I've never been so scared in my life, but we were all glad when the lights came back on."

"Do they have guns?" I asked her, still not fully comprehending what was going on.

"Yeah," she said, astonished at me not fully grasping the situation. "They took the crew out on the swim step and executed them in cold blood."

"Jesus," Jasmine murmured.

"And you've got them trapped in there?" Travis exclaimed, starring at the hatch.

Jennifer nodded.

"Travis, would you please jump back over to and get our shotgun," I asked

Moments later Travis leaped back onboard with the shotgun. Pumping a shell into the chamber, he nodded.

"Then what happened?"

"They went below. Right after they went down there, one of the girls started screaming, so I went forward to check. They'd been drugging the girls since we left, but they'd given them their last injections that morning, so they were kind of starting to come around. It was a mess. They were all sick. As far as I can figure, one of the girls must have choked on her own vomit and died. Because when the one lying next to her woke up and realized her friend was dead, she totally freaked. I tried to calm her down, but the next thing I remember was the girl throwing up on me...then I started puking, again and must have passed out."

"When I came to, I was lying with the other girl in the hallway." Jennifer started trembling again.

"Stop," I said, kneeling down in front of her. "You don't have to keep going."

She was gripping my arm. "I do," she said, looking at me pleadingly, as if begging me to make the memories go away. Her look broke my heart. She tried to keep talking, but she couldn't get the words out. The memory of having to leave the dead girl on the floor was too much. She started sobbing like a baby, still fighting to get the words out. "And...I had to leave her there...I couldn't do anything else...I had to just leave her in there. She was dead, and I couldn't do anything to help her."

Grasping for breath, trying to cope, to make sense of the madness. "It's alright, Jen," I whispered in her ear. "You did everything you could. It's going to be alright."

"No! It's not all right!" she yelled, jerking away, standing up. Pointing at the hatch, she screamed, "Fuck you! You fucking assholes!" Her anger and fears blending as one. "They raped those girls. They raped them and drugged them like animals. It makes me sick." Looking up at me, her eyes pleading for justice, "They're fucking assholes."

"I know. I know they are," I said, holding her firmly.

"Let's open the hatch and blow mother fuckers away," Travis said, pointing the shotgun at the hatch.

Her anger becoming her strength. Surging through her veins. She shook her head like a wild mare. Forcing her tears away. "I got you, you mother fuckers, and now you're going to pay."

Her eyes, moist and bloodshot, but showing glimpses of satisfaction in knowing she was no longer in danger. Surveying her handiwork scattered about the cockpit, she nodded her head. We didn't say anything, as we all looked over the twisted mess of lines and poles.

"What do we do now?" Travis asked.

"Not sure," I answered. All I'd thought about 'til now was finding Jennifer...

She was the most amazing woman I'd ever met. "I don't know," I repeated. "We don't have a sideband on the *Vintage*, but if we can get *Dorsal*'s operational, we could use it to call in the cavalry."

"But she's dead in the water," Travis countered, "not to mention Jennifer has the bad guys trapped below where all the equipment is...including the batteries."

"I know," I said, still having no clue what to do next. "Any ideas?

"I know one thing we're not going to do," Jennifer said without a moments hesitation or any doubt in her voice. "We're not letting those hatches open. Not even an inch." She was still scared of the venom she'd managed trap down there.

"How about we leave them down there and tow the boat to Cabo?" Travis suggested.

"Maybe," I said thinking out loud. "That might work."

Jennifer jumped in. "No way—not unless we make damn sure they can't get out."

"They've been in there since last night, right?" Travis asked.

"Yeah, they have. But earlier they got a crowbar or something wedged in there and almost got out. I've been sitting here ever since making sure they didn't try and escape again."

Travis and I looked at each other. "You've been standing guard? For how long?

"All day," she said, looking at us like we were both dummies.

"How did you stop them last time?" Jasmine asked.

"With this," she said, reaching over and picking up the bat from the corner. "I hit the crowbar with everything I had. It popped back in and the hatch slammed shut."

"Then what?"

"They tried to open it again, but I jumped on top of it. They kept trying, but with me standing on top of it, they couldn't do it." A trace of satisfaction crossed her face.

"You just stood there?" Travis asked, astonished.

"Yeah, just me and my bat." She paused. "They kept trying for awhile, screaming at me. But I had 'um. So I just stood there until they gave up and quit screaming. Then I sat down here," showing us, "and kept an eye on the hatches…waiting for you guys." *As if she knew it was a foregone conclusion we were on our way.*

"Can I take a look at your arm?" I asked.

"It's not my arm…it's my hand." She winced from the pain as she tried to lift her crushed hand out of the sling.

"Easy," I said, reaching out and gently supporting her elbow. As her hand slipped out from the sling, the sight of the Ace bandage covered in blood horrified all of us.

"Shit, Jennifer."

"It's not as bad as it looks," she said, trying to convince herself.

"Bullshit," Travis said, his Coast Guard EMT training instantly kicking in. He reached over and gently tried turning her hand. She winced and yelped. "Sorry, Jen. How did it happen?"

"The forward hatch fell on it. I think it's broken…or at least a couple of fingers are. I can't move it."

"But where is all the blood coming from?" Travis asked, inspecting her arm.

"It was during the storm. When it fell, it trapped my hand inside. I was getting tossed all over the place. It ripped the skin off my fingers."

"That needs professional attention right away," Travis said, slowly unwrapping the bloody bandage

"That settles it," I said. "We'll leave these guys right were they are, transfer the girls over, and tow the boat the rest of the way to the Cape."

"But what if they get out?" Jennifer still concerned about the goons escaping.

"I can stay on board," Travis said, holding the gun for emphasis.

"I've got a better idea. We've got a hundred pound anchor and four hundred feet of chain. Let's transfer the girls over to our boat, then we'll nose our pulpit up over the stern here, and dump it all over the hatches. That should to do the trick."

Travis agreed.

"What do you think?" I asked Jennifer.

"How much does the chain and anchor weigh?" She asked.

"I don't know for sure," I admitted, "but it's got to be a couple thousand pounds."

"At least," Travis added.

She nodded—*a couple thousand should be enough.*

"I'll go check on the girls."

"No," Jennifer and Jasmine said simultaneously. "We'll do it."

Travis hesitated. "Sure, but don't you think it would be better if you take care of that hand."

"I'm okay, Travis. Really, I am. It hurts like hell, but I'm okay. Those poor girls have been through hell. We'll go see if..." She didn't know Jasmine's name, so she paused.

"Shit. We didn't even introduce you guys," I said. "I'm sorry, Jen."

"It's O.K. I'm Jennifer," she said standing to officially meet Jasmine. But as she started toward the stairs, the boat rolled just enough for her to have to reach out to steady herself. The handrail was too far away and she almost fell. Travis and I both grabbed her. But that was all it took. "Forget it," I commanded. "Travis, go help Jasmine. Jennifer, you're coming with me."

"Yes, sir," Travis said as he bounded past Jennifer.

She seemed relieved to have been given a direct order. I took her good hand and led her toward the *Vintage.*

It had been all Sierra could do to wait onboard. She'd been told her stay after we'd secured the boats together, but seeing Jennifer coming towards her, she lost it, leaping over the cockpit to meet us. They melted. It was the first time I'd seen Jennifer smile since we'd arrived.

She stopped petting Sierra and looked up at me, tears once again filling her beautiful eyes. "Thank you," she whispered, "for saving my life."

"You saved mine," I whispered back. She smiled again as I helped her over to the *Vintage* and got her settled on the couch in the salon.

"Hey, Skipper," Travis yelled across from the *Dorsal*, "you'd better get over here and take a look at this."

"You O.K.," I asked Jennifer.

Jennifer nodded.

"I'll be right back."

"Hurry," she said, closing her tired eyes. She was exhausted, but for the first time in days felt safe being back on board *Vintage*.

I gave her a light kiss on top of her head, jumped back on board *Dorsal* and followed Travis below to the crew's quarters. *Leaving the hatches unattended.*

The goons had been listening to every sound from below. Trapped in total darkness, their acoustic senses were amped-up. They weren't missing a thing. Even though our conversations were muffled and they weren't able to make out the words, they were getting a feeling for what was going on. And little did we realize, every footstep made a distinct sound below. Like trapped animals, they waited for an opportunity to strike.

As Travis led the way through the salon, the stench of vomit combined with a decaying body was overwhelming. I almost puked halfway down the stairs. "Fuck me," I said quietly.

Leading the way, Travis didn't look back over his shoulder. "It gets worse."

Opening the door to the girls' room, we both stood motionless. How Jasmine had kept it together down there was beyond us. She had the three girls sitting back on one of the bunks. It was obvious they'd been through hell. They each had their arms wrapped around their knees, trying to hold themselves together. Jasmine had managed to get them into clean blouses and shorts, but their hair was hopelessly matted. They didn't remotely resemble the hot looking morsels we watched prancing down the dock a few lifetimes ago.

"It's okay. It's okay," Jasmine assured them. "These are my friends. They're the ones I've been telling you about...the ones who came to rescue you. Don't be afraid." Jasmine was doing her best to calm them down. Just the sight of two males coming into the room sent an obvious wave of terror through them. "It's okay. They're not going to hurt you...they're here to help us. To take you home."

Travis and I both could see the raw fear in the girls' eyes. Jaz knelt down in front of them, gently reached out and touched their arms. They stared at her. She made eye contact. "I promise. These men are here to help you—they're not going to hurt you. That's over now...the bad guys are gone, okay? Do you understand?" One of the girls nodded in a trance like motion. We waited at the door, while Jasmine explained we were going to get onto another boat to take them home. They were still scared shitless, but obediently followed Jasmine out of the crew's quarters and up the stairs. Travis offered to help, but Jaz shook him off with her head. We stepped back and let them pass.

Once they were up the stairs, Travis turned to me. "What are we going to do about her?" he asked, gesturing toward the dead girl.

"Nothing we can do, really. Maybe we could wrap her up and put her in our fish hold."

"That would be better than just leaving her in here," he agreed. "She's already getting pretty ripe."

"Let's go up and make sure Jasmine gets the other girls on board *Vintage* first. Then we'll come back and get her," I said and turned to leave the room, confident the ordeal was over.

Suddenly, a terrifying scream echoed throughout the boat. We sprinted up the stairs, raced through the salon and stood frozen at the cockpit door. One of the girls was lying on the deck, her leg stuck in a wedged-open hatch. A gun barrel pointed at her head.

"Open the hatch or I'll blow her fucking brains out!"

Jasmine and the other girls stood frozen.

"Now, you fucking cunt!" Tony screamed at Jasmine through the slight opening in the hatch. The goons had managed to pry it open just far enough to reach out and grab one of the girls as she walked by. They'd yanked her leg so hard the skin had peeled off to her knee where it was jammed into the hatch, blood oozing onto the teak deck. "Open the Goddamned hatch or this fucking bitch is dead! You've got five seconds." Time moved in slow motion as Tony started a rapid countdown. "Five, four, three, two...."

"Okay, okay! I'm coming. I'll do it, " Jasmine yelled back at Tony. She couldn't believe what was happening—none of us could—but thank God, she'd regained her composure enough to act. She started to tug at the twisted maze of lines holding the now only partially closed hatch.

"Hurry up, Goddamn it!" Tony demanded, waving the gun at the terrified girl's head. "Get us out of here, God-damn-it or I'll blow her fucking brains out, I swear to God."

"I believe you," Jasmine managed to say as she held out her arms in surrender.

"Move over here where I can see you."

She slowly moved around the girl, putting herself in line with the gun barrel.

"No!" Travis screamed and bolted through the door. I whirled trying to stop him, but it was too late. He leaped off the salon steps and tackled Jasmine in mid-flight. They both crashed to the deck. Pushing her out of harm's way, he started screaming toward the hatch. "I'll do it!" he shouted at the obscured gunman. "I'll do it! I'll get you out of there." He started to stand up.

"Freeze, you mother fucker!" the gunman screamed at Travis through the hatch. "Don't fucking move!"

Travis froze and slowly raised his arms over his head, palms out, fingers spread. "Where the fuck did you come from?" one the goons shouted.

"We were just headed to Cabo and spotted your boat drifting over here." Travis was thinking fast. Trapped below decks, the goons could have only guessed what was happening. The hatches pivoted open facing aft, with the hinges on the salon side, so they couldn't see me and had no idea I was there. I looked around for the shotgun. Travis had placed it on top of the bait tank.

"How many?" Tony demanded.

"How many what?" Travis stalled.

"Don't fuck with me, asshole! How many of you are on board your boat?"

"Just the two of us. My girlfriend and me," he said, still holding out his arms. "We're delivering the boat for the new owners."

"Bullshit!" Tony shouted back. "You bullshit me and you're dead."

"I swear to God!" Travis said. "It's just the two of us." He paused for a second. "We tried to call you guys on the radio, but when we didn't get any answer, we thought you might need some help. So we altered course and came on over. When we got here, no one answered our calls, so we came on board. That's all. We just stopped to see if you needed any help."

He was doing a good job. The talking gave me enough time to softly step down into the cockpit and slide the shotgun off the bait tank without them seeing me. Travis never took his eyes off the gunman, but I knew he could see me with his peripheral vision.

"Fuck it! Just get this Goddamned hatch open!" the other voice bellowed from below.

"Okay," Travis said, trying to buy some more time, "but you have to promise not to hurt us. Okay?"

"Listen, asshole, open the hatch this fucking minute, or I'm going to blow you, your girlfriend and this bitch away." He shook the girl's leg violently and she screamed in pain.

"Oh Fuck!" Tony screamed, feeling her warm urine running down his arm. "God! Damn! It!"

I slowly made my way around the bait tank, trying to get a better angle. My movement suddenly caught the attention of the other girls. Holding the rifle they must have thought I was another bad guy. Without thinking, they screamed.

The shots were deafening. I spun around to look at her and saw Travis being launched backwards in a spinning motion. Another volley hit the poor trapped girl square in the chest. Blood spraying everywhere. Her body jerking upwards before being yanked violently back to the deck by her trapped leg.

I dove toward the hatch, thrusting the barrel toward the opening pulling the trigger before I hit the deck. Teak splintered from around the edges of the hatch, but most the shot found its way into the black hole. Pumping the weapon, I jammed the barrel into the blackness, blindly firing into the hatch. Another volley of shots rang out from below, whizzing past my head. Pumping another shell, I pivoted the barrel, forcing the burning iron against the dead girl's trapped leg. The stench of her burning flesh immediately filling the air. I fired again, and again, fanning my shots, covering as wide an area as possible. It was only after I'd pumped and pulled the trigger several more times that I realized I was out of shells. How many times I tried to fire without any ammo, I'll never know. All I could remember was the clicking sound of the hammer hitting the firing pin, over and over...but there was no more fire coming from below either. Time stood still in the total silence following the firefight.

I pulled the barrel out of the hold, grabbed the dead girl and pulled, but my hand just slid off her limp, blood-covered body. I went tumbling backwards, hitting my head against the gunwales. I crawled back toward her, grabbed her again and was able to yank her leg free of the hatch. It immediately slammed shut.

Jasmine was at Travis' side. He'd been hit, hard. The entire left side of his upper chest was a sickening blackish red. He was out cold. He looked like he was dead. Jasmine held his limp body in her arms, screaming hysterically.

******

The remaining two girls were screaming, scrambling to get away, climbing out of the bloody cockpit onto *Vintage*. Jennifer came running out of the salon. Sierra at her heals barking wildly.

Jennifer and Sierra leaped over the rails at the same time. Both skidding across the slippery deck as they hit the blood that was everywhere. Jen screaming at me, "Are you alright?" She didn't know who had been hit. The front of my shirt was covered with blood from the dead girl.

"I'm O.K. I'm O.K." I yelled. "I'm not hit. I'm O.K., but Travis needs help."

Once Jennifer heard my voice, saw me moving and knew that I was O.K. she immediately focused her attention on Jasmine and Travis.

"Oh, my God!" she sobbed seeing Travis. "Are you hit? Jasmine, are you O.K."

Nothing. Jasmine was already in shock.

"Jasmine!" I yelled, moving toward them, my back to the hatch. Trying to reach her through the horror. "Help! Help me," I begged. "We've got to get him to a hospital. Help me get him over to our boat."

Jennifer was frozen. Pure horror shot through me as I realized what Jennifer was staring at. Knowing I was out of ammo, I spun around expecting the worse. But there was only the dead girl lying on top of the closed hatch.

"Jennifer," I said, reaching out for her, "its O.K. They're dead."

She didn't take her eyes off the hatch, "How do you know." Shock took over.

"No. Please, God, no!" Jasmine pleaded through her tears. She had Travis's head in her arms, her face against his. Blood was all over both of them.

The scene was complete chaos. It was only when Sierra started licking Jennifer's tears that she responded. Looking at the dog, then over to me, Travis and Jasmine...the blood...and the dead girl's limp body.... "Travis needs help," she said in a monotone voice.

I felt for a pulse in his neck. It was weak, but still there.

"Jasmine! Listen to me! If you want to save him, you have to help us get him into our boat." She didn't hear a word I said. Travis was solid muscle, well over two-twenty-five. I reached under his arms and tried to lift him, but with Jasmine holding on for dear life, I couldn't budge them.

"Goddamn it, Jasmine!" I screamed, grabbing her blood-soaked hair and jerking her head back so she had to look at me. She didn't even feel it. "Jasmine!" I screamed again in her face...and for a moment...her eyes focused on me. "Help us! Help us get Travis to our boat."

"He's dead," she said, in shock.

"No, he's not, but he will be if you don't help me. We have to get him to the hospital. I need your help. Travis needs your help."

That did it—at least she understood we needed to move him. When she let go, I was able to slide his body across the bloody cockpit. I slipped twice and fell hard both times—human blood is amazingly slick before it coagulates. Jasmine lifted his legs over the rail and together we were all able to get him into the salon.

The girls were already huddled together in a corner of the settee.

"We've got to get that bleeding stopped," Jennifer said, grabbing some towels out of the galley.

Ripping off the rest of his shirt, wiping blood off his chest trying see how many times he'd been hit, I could only see one entry wound. "Jam the towels into the hole," I told Jennifer. "Just pack 'em in there." But with only one good hand, she couldn't do it. Jasmine had become a zombie. I took over, pushing a clean white dishtowel into the open wound. Instantly, it became saturated with blood.

"Try another one," Jennifer said, handing me another towel. Within seconds, that one was soaked as well.

Shit! I don't know what to do. We were watching him bleed out right in front of us. Jennifer folded a bigger bath towel a couple of times to form a square, placed it on top of my hands and pushed with all her weight. The blood slowed, but didn't completely stop. "We're going to have to get more pressure on this thing or he's going to die for sure."

"What about some ACE bandages?" I asked thinking out loud.

"In the First Aid Kit," Jennifer said. "I'll go get it, " Slowly I took my hands out from underneath hers, freeing her to race to the head to get the kit.

"Jasmine!" I yelled. Nothing but a pale, blank stare. "Jasmine!" I screamed again.

"What?" She muttered.

"Listen. You're going to have to help us...help Travis. Do you understand? He needs you right now."

She just shook her head. "He's dead."

"No, he's not! Goddamn it! He needs you! You can do this!" She shook her head, but I took her hand and placed it on the towel where I'd been pushing. "At' a girl, you can do this." Both her hands were shaking as she leaned into his chest, applying the needed pressure. "At' a girl," I said again softly. "Perfect. Keep pushing as hard as you can." She nodded as if she understood, but didn't say anything. Travis was unconscious, but you could see his laboured breathing. "See," I coaxed, "he's breathing. He's alive, but we have to get him help." She nodded again. "Just keep the pressure on. Don't let up. When Jen gets back, she'll help you wrap the ACE bandages around him, okay?" She was barely there, but she understood.

We couldn't afford to waste another minute. I had to make sure the goons weren't trying another escape. I had no idea if I'd even hit them. Christ, for all I knew, I'd just blown the shit out of the bottom of the boat. I poked my head out of the salon and looked into *Dorsal*'s cockpit. All the hatches were still closed. *Maybe I did hit the motherfuckers,* I thought to myself as I sprang over the rail, keeping my eyes on the hatches. So far, so good. I picked up the dead girl and carried her into the salon. Then I ran up to the bow and released *Dorsal's* anchor. We were miles off the coast and in water much too deep for any anchor to find bottom, but I wasn't about to waste time towing them in. I figured they'd continue drifting toward the beach. The anchor would catch eventually when they got close enough, and maybe hold them off. If not, I didn't give a shit.

Working my way back toward the stern, I released the bow and spring lines that we'd used to raft the two boats together. Pulled the stern line on board *Vintage* and raced up to the wheelhouse. I spun her around and eased our bow directly up to the middle of *Dorsal*'s stern. Positioning our seven-foot pulpit past their swim step and over her cockpit, I left her in gear to keep the boats together. I ran up to our bow, and let our anchor drop... it and the entire four hundred feet of anchor chain crashed directly into the middle of *Dorsal*'s cockpit...directly on top of the hatches. As the chain piled up and spread out, it covered all three hatches.

"Try and wedge your way out of that, you motherfuckers!" I yelled over the bow. Then I cut the 7-foot piece of two-inch-thick nylon rope we'd used to secure the bitter end of the chain to the bulkhead in the anchor locker. Lloyd had taught me that trick. Never secure straight chain to the bulkhead in case you ever have to dump it, he'd said. Always splice in a short section of rope so you can cut or splice into it if you have to. *It's always the little things.*

Racing back to the wheelhouse, I threw the boat into reverse and eased her away. Spinning *Vintage* towards the cape, I pushed the throttles all the way up. She bit hard and fast, pulling herself out of the hole, leaving *Dorsal* in our wake. Travis desperately needed medical help, but listening to the mains whining at full rack, I realized it wasn't going to do him any good if I fried them, so I backed off a little—not much, but enough to hear a slight sigh in their pitch. They were wound tight...turbo chargers were screaming, but they'd be all right. We had over 140 miles to go before we reached Cabo, and every minute counted. I thought about heading into Mag Bay, but knew there wasn't anything more than a makeshift airstrip in San Carlos. Trying to arrange for a gunshot victim to be airlifted out of that little fishing village would've taken longer than running for Cabo. Once on course, I flipped on the pilot and went below to check on Travis and the girls.

"How's he doing?" I asked, entering the salon.

The room was somber. Jasmine and Jennifer were sitting on the couch with Travis. ACE bandages wrapped tightly around his chest and shoulder. The bleeding had definitely slowed but it hadn't stopped. The other two girls were balled up behind the salon table. Jasmine looked up, her eyes swollen from crying, but didn't say anything. Her hands were covered with blood.

"He hasn't moved," Jennifer said. "Isn't there anything else we can do?" She was holding a cold ice compress across his forehead.

I didn't know what else we could do. "He hasn't come to at all?"

"No," Jen said, shaking her head. "Nothing."

"It's probably for the best," I offered lamely. "At least this way he's not awake to feel it."

"He's dying," Jasmine sobbed. "I know it…he's dying."

I knelt down behind her and put my arms around her, pulling her head against my chest and holding her tight. After a couple minutes, I felt some of the tension let go as she allowed her head to rest against my heart. I knew she could feel my heartbeat. "He's tough, Jaz. He's young, strong and he's tough as nails. He's going to make it. The fact that you guys got the bleeding stopped means his body's responding. He's going to make it. We're headed straight for the Cape. As soon as we're close enough, I'll radio ahead and arrange to have an air evacuation team waiting for us. Be strong for him. He needs you to be strong."

"How long?" was all she said.

"About twelve hours."

I felt her breath catch in her throat. "He's never going to make it that long. Isn't there anything else you can do?" Her voice was pleading. "He won't last that long. He'll die before we get there."

"We're doing everything we can," I said, releasing her and standing up. "The most important thing was to stop the bleeding—and you guys did that." But looking at him again, I could see the towel was slowly turning dark red.

"Think we should change the towel?" Jennifer asked.

"No, just let it be. The bleeding has slowed down, and that's the most important thing. If we pull off the towel, it'll start again. We'll worry about infection later. For now, just keep him still. Keep the ice packs on his neck and forehead. He's going into shock and the ice will help keep his temperature down."

"Okay," she said. "Do you need anything?"

"A faster boat." I looked at the other girls. Their eyes dropped to the table before we made eye contact. They were still scared to death. I grabbed a bottle of water out of the refrigerator and headed back up to the wheelhouse. "Let me know if there are any changes."

It was getting dark, so I flipped on the overhead lights in the salon before checking the engine room. Everything looked fine. I climbed back to the wheelhouse. Now that I was alone and had done everything I could think of, waves of nausea replaced the adrenaline that had been pumping non-stop through my body since the gunfight. I swallowed hard and tried to control my breathing, but barely made it to the rail before retching. I hung onto the top rail until there was nothing left. The dry heaves lasted another few minutes before giving way to a mind-numbing headache.

Why didn't I jump in to save Jasmine? Travis didn't hesitate for a split second. He just reacted, while I stood there analyzing the situation... I kept replaying the scene over and over in my mind. *And when I finally did do something it was too late.* I felt the pounding between my temples with every heartbeat. Nothing could change what had happened. I had dragged my friend into this, and may have gotten him killed. A feeling of total helplessness and despair enveloped me. Switching off the pilot, I took the helm so I'd had something to focus on, but it didn't do any good. A day that just a few minutes before had been the happiest in my life, finding Jennifer alive, had suddenly turned so ugly I couldn't think straight. Total darkness was upon us as the sun dove below the horizon...a cold, moonless night taking its place.

I'd started making Mayday calls the second we'd pulled away from *Dorsal*. I knew there was only a remote chance of raising anyone, but I was going to repeat the distress call every five minutes until we made contact. Best guess was we wouldn't raise anyone until just before dawn, but I kept trying.

Below, Jennifer suggested that Jasmine lay down and get some rest.

"There's no way I can sleep," Jasmine said. "Why don't you lie down awhile? I'll wake you if I need you. Aren't you exhausted?"

"I am," Jennifer said, admitting how tired she was.

Jasmine changed Travis' ice pack and settled in next to him on the couch. She must have dozed off because she was startled when Travis suddenly kicked violently. He was still unconscious, but his body went into convulsions. He was shaking and covered in sweat. Earlier, he'd been hot to the touch, but now his skin was ice cold. Jasmine freaked. Thinking he was in his death throws, she screamed for help. Jennifer was already halfway into the salon, as I flew down the ladder.

"He's dying!" Jasmine screamed. "I fell asleep and he woke me up jerking like this!" Travis' head was arched back as his body convulsed in wild spasms. His legs flailed and kicked wildly. One arm jerked up and down. His other arm—the one on the side of the wound—hung limply. Jasmine was crying as she attempted to keep him from sliding off the couch.

With all the shit I'd seen on TV since I was a kid, I thought I would have been better prepared to handle the situation, but I had no idea what to do. Seeing Travis in convulsions stopped me cold. All of a sudden I felt faint. The last thing I remember is reaching for the doorframe of the salon. The next thing I knew, Jennifer was kneeling beside me. "You all right?" she asked softly.

"That was weird," I said. "What happened?"

She smiled and kissed me on the forehead. "You sprang toward the door like a knight in shining armor, but then—"

"What?"

A grin on her face. "But then you just stood there, looking at Travis."

I nodded, remembering that part, but nothing else. "Then what happened?"

"Well," Jennifer said, pausing, "you pretty much turned white and passed out."

"Shit," I said, shaking my head.

"It's alright," she said, bending over to give me another kiss. "You're still my hero."

A wave a fear shot through me. "How's Travis?"

"The convulsions stopped almost as quickly as they started."

"What do you mean? What did you guys do?"

"Nothing. Jasmine was trying to hold him down and then, all of a sudden, he took a deep breath and stopped jerking."

"Is he all right?"

"Yeah. We think he was having a bad dream."

"No shit!" I said, sitting up. "This whole thing's a bad dream."

******

We were closing in on sixty miles to the Cape. I knew we wouldn't be able to reach anyone in port this far out, but thought we might raise another vessel and maybe start a relay.

"Mayday. Mayday. Mayday. This is the American Fishing Vessel *Vintage*. Whisky…Yankee…Fox trot…Twenty-seven, seven-teen. We have a Mayday situation. Latitude 111.04 degrees north, 23.38 degrees west. Repeat. Mayday…Mayday…Mayday. American Fishing Vessel *Vintage*. We have a Mayday situation. Any vessel. Over."

"*Vintage*. This is the cruise ship *Odyssey*." The return call blasted in like they were sitting beside us, making me jump. "We're reading you loud and clear. Please reconfirm your position again and the nature of your distress. Over."

I nearly fell out off my chair. I couldn't believe anyone could have heard us. "*Odyssey...Vintage.* Our estimated position is 111.04 degrees north, 23.38 degrees west. We have a seriously injured crewman on board who is in immediate need of medical assistance. I repeat. We have a man down who is in immediate need of medical attention. Over."

"Roger *Vintage.* We copy. What is the nature of the injury?"

I didn't want to put it out on the radio that we had a gunshot victim on board—not in Mexican waters—so I made up something. "*Odyssey*, he fell on a gaff. It appears he may have punctured a lung. He's been bleeding for over six hours and needs immediate assistance. Repeat. He's been bleeding from a chest wound for over six hours." I was praying the cruise ship was operating under the American flag. I asked, "Do you have a doctor on board? Over."

"Roger, *Vintage.* We have professional medical personnel on board. We are in position to render assistance. We have an RDF on your signal and believe to have you on radar. Navigator's been plotting our position against your estimated position. We are altering course to intercept. If you'll come twenty-eight degrees west, we'll be on reciprocal headings. Over."

"Roger, *Odyssey.* Altering course for intercept. We're making good at just over twelve knots. Over."

"Roger that, *Vintage.* We're pushing to maximum green...twenty-four knots. Stand by." After about a ten-second pause, "*Vintage*, given our combined speeds we should be on site in twenty-six minutes. Over."

"Roger, *Odyssey.* That's great. Thank you."

"Roger, *Vintage.* Your turn confirmed our radar contact. We have a lock on you. Visuals should be within fifteen minutes."

"Roger, *Odyssey.* Be advised, we also have a young lady with a severely smashed hand. It looks like some broken bones. Plus, we have two other ladies in shock. Over."

There was a prolonged pause. "*Vintage*, are you a documented U.S. vessel? Over."

"Affirmative, *Odyssey*. We're a U.S. documented vessel."

"Roger *Vintage*. Understand you are documented United States. What are your vessel's documentation numbers, names of the owner, captain, crew and all passengers on board, please. Over."

"Roger, *Odyssey*. MV *Vintage*. U.S. Documentation Number, 505-099. Owner/Operator, Corey Phillips. Crew, Travis Wolf, Jennifer Comstock and Jasmine..." *Shit. I don't know Jasmine's last name.* "Stand by, please, *Odyssey*." I ran out of the wheelhouse and into the salon. "We've got help coming!" I blurted out as I hit the door. "A cruise ship with a doctor is about twenty-five minutes away! We're going to meet them!"

"Thank God!" echoed throughout the salon as Jennifer and Jasmine started asking questions at the same time.

"Hold on," I pleaded. "They're on the horn right now and I've got to get back to them. Jasmine, what's your last name?"

"What? My last name—why?" she asked.

"They need the names of everyone on board."

"Mackenzie." Jasmine said. "My last name is Mackenzie."

"Thanks," I said, glancing toward the girls we'd rescued. "What about them?" I was avoiding eye contact with them or addressing them directly because they were still so freaked out.

Jennifer stood up, shot me a quick nod, and put herself between the girls and me. Leaning down, I could hear her asking them for their full names. "Peterson and Fields." Jennifer said, thanking them and turning back toward me. "Becky Peterson and Carol Fields."

"Thanks," I said. "How's he doing."

"He's ice cold," Jasmine said. "We've got him all wrapped up, but he's still ice cold."

He was wrapped in blankets, but when I reached over and felt his forehead, it was cold to the touch. *Shit.* "Hang on Trav...helps on its way."

"*Odyssey, Vintage.*"

"Go ahead, *Vintage.*"

"Roger, *Odyssey*. Final crewmember, Jasmine Mackenzie. Passengers, Becky Peterson and Carol Fields. Over."

"Roger, *Vintage*. Copy. What happened to you guys? Over."

"It's a long story…but I'd like to transfer all four victims when we meet, if that's possible. Over."

"*Vintage, Odyssey*." There was a new and very commanding voice on the other end. "This is Captain Paul Mitchell. I've been monitoring your transmissions. Say again please. How many victims are you requesting be transferred? Please state the nature of their injuries. Over."

"Roger, Captain. We have a total of four, repeat four, injured personnel on board—two crew and two passengers. One is in critical condition in need of immediate help from a deep gaff wound to his upper chest. He's lost a lot of blood and has been unconscious since the accident. The other three are women, and are not, I repeat, not in critical condition, but still in need of medical attention. I would like them to receive help as soon as possible. Over."

"Understand, *Vintage*," he said, "We're making arrangements to lower a shore boat, and will be standing by to receive all four of your injured personnel once on scene. Copy."

"Roger—all four personal. Thank you, Captain. Thank you so much. *Vintage*, standing by on channel one-six."

"Cruse ship *Odyssey* standing by on channel one-six."

The few minutes it took before I could spot their lights coming head on in the distance flew by. It's amazing how quickly a combined 36 knots closes the distance between two vessels. We were on site in no time as the radio speaker broke the wheelhouse silence.

"*Vintage, Odyssey.*"

331

"Odyssey, Vintage returning. How do you want to handle this?"

"One mile and closing. Engines are now all ahead slow. We will be pulling them out of gear for a reduced speed of less than five knots shortly. We'll come about into the wind, new heading two four degrees. Once abeam, please position your vessel about a hundred yards amid ship off our starboard leeward side, and await our launch. Over."

"Roger, *Odyssey.* Understand. Would you please send over a couple of men to help lift our injured crewman? He's still unconscious and we're shorthanded over here. Over."

"Roger that, *Vintage.* No problem. We've already assembled our boarding team. Over."

"Roger. Thank you again. I don't know if he could have held on much longer."

The cruise ship's blazing deck lights transformed the area surrounding us into daytime. I held us off a hundred yards and watched them through the binoculars as they lowered their skiff.

"Vintage, Odyssey. Please be advised that our launch is wet and away. Please hold your position. Over."

These guys are so formal, I thought before replying. "Roger, *Odyssey.* Holding position."

Sliding down the stairs and entering the salon, I panicked for a second until I saw Travis' chest rise and fall quickly. He was white and definitely having a hard time breathing. His lungs must have been filling with fluids. He would not make it another six hours without medical attention.

"What do we need to do?" Jasmine asked as soon as I entered. "Are they sending over a doctor?"

"I'm not sure, but I think so. Let's get Travis on board first, and then we'll transfer the girls. I've requested they look after you, as well, Jennifer."

"I'm not going anywhere!" Jennifer announced. "Not without you anyway." She put her good arm around mine.

I pleaded, "You need to get that hand looked at. Please, sweetheart, don't fight me on this."

"Are you going?" she asked.

"No."

"Then neither am I." And that was that.

"I'm worried about your hand."

"Let's just worry about Travis and the girls." I wasn't about to argue. With her mind made up, Jennifer wouldn't leave this boat without me. She squeezed my arm tighter. "We're going to make it," she said softly. "All of us."

It took only a couple of minutes for their launch to pull alongside us. "Permission to come aboard, Skipper?" one of the team requested.

"Absolutely. Thank God you're here." I extended my hand and helped the first member of the cruise ship team on board. The others followed effortlessly, leaving the driver and an additional crewmember in the skiff. As soon as their team was on board, the skiff slid away from us, holding position about fifteen yards off our quarter.

Transfers at sea can be dangerous, but we were blessed with calm seas. The winds were virtually non-existent—tucked in under the lee of a fifteen-storey, five-hundred-foot ship blocking what little wind and swell there was. The doctor gave Travis a preliminary examination and announced we needed to get him into surgery immediately. With the assistance of the additional crewmembers and a Stokes board, Travis's transfer went off flawlessly. Jasmine and Jennifer led the girls outside and helped them aboard, too.

The doctor pulled me aside. "That man doesn't have a gaff wound—he's been shot."

"I know, Doctor, I know," I said, trying to explain. "But I couldn't very well broadcast that fact over an open channel in Mexican waters." He didn't care about any of that. All he knew was that I had lied to his captain. He hesitated for a split second, so I pressed on. "Doctor, please. He's my best friend. If you don't help him, he's going to die." The doctor shook his head, deliberating about what to do next. "I'll ride over with you and explain everything to your captain in person. We're not hiding anything here…I just couldn't put that kind of information out on the radio."

"All right, you're coming with us."

"Absolutely—I can explain everything."

Jennifer was standing by, listening. "Heard your little conversation with the doctor there. Looks like we're going after all."

"I have to explain what happened."

"Good luck," she said reflectively. She was right. How the hell was I going to explain what we'd been through? Jasmine was already on board the skiff with Travis. The doctor jumped onto the launch. "What about the boat? If we all transfer over, there will be no one left on board."

"Doctor, who's in charge here?" I asked, looking at the remaining crew on board the skiff.

"First Officer Powell."

Powell was at the helm and talking on the radio with the cruise ship. I couldn't hear what was being said, but he had a serious look on his face and didn't look too happy. I also noticed he was holstering a sidearm. He replaced the microphone and looked at me. "Sir, Captain Mitchell has instructed us to escort you, your crew and passengers back to the ship with us."

"Great. Could you leave a couple of your men on board here to look after the boat?"

"I was instructed to do just that."

"Perfect," I said, shaking hands with the crewmen as they climbed on board. "Let me give you a quick rundown on the systems."

"That won't be necessary," Officer Powell said curtly. "Please, the two of you get in the launch. My men can handle your boat." It dawned on me that this wasn't an invitation to a party. Jennifer had figured it out the minute they realized Travis had been shot. One of the other crewmen helped her on board...I followed.

"Sierra, you stay, girl. We'll be right back." And we were off, leaving two strangers in control of the *Vintage*.

An army of personnel greeted us when we arrived at the cruise ship. Travis was rushed into surgery, with Jasmine by his side. Two nurses escorted Becky and Carol to the infirmary. They wanted to take Jennifer as well, so they could attend to her hand, but she refused. "I'm staying with him."

Four officers and crewmen—two in front and two behind us, they escorted Jen and me silently through the catacombs of the ship. All were carrying weapons. We must have been traveling through passageways that apparently were off limits to all but the crew because we didn't see a single passenger. They reminded me of the underground corridors that run throughout large resort hotels. The ship was huge. Some of the brightly lit, pure white passageways looked endless. We made a couple of right-hand turns and ended up in front of a small elevator. I wouldn't have been able to find my way back through that maze if our lives had depended on it.

"Where are we going?" Jennifer asked.

"Captain's quarters," the Officer in charge of the detail answered curtly. Glancing at the panel beside the elevator door, I saw we went up to the top of the tree. After a short walk down a private passageway, we were shown into a spacious suite and asked to wait. "The Captain will be in shortly."

Two of the men left the room, but stopped just outside the door; the other two remained inside, stationed on either side of the doorway.

Jennifer took a seat on the plush leather couch as I walked over for a closer look at the display of the photos strategically hung on the wall opposite our guards. Individual photographs showcased a man in dress whites shaking hands with the likes of JFK, Lyndon Johnson, Frank

Sinatra, even Elvis...an impressive array to say the least. The more recent photos revealed more decorations on the officer's uniform and a full head of silver-gray hair, but the face remained stately, firm and in control. I assumed the room, which was bigger than our entire boat, was the captain's outer chambers. The walls were all hand-finished Burmese teak; spotless stainless steel portals broke up the photo gallery; angled, recessed lighting spilled a soft light against the teak giving the room a feeling of warmth and texture. The dark, perfectly worn, leather couches and overstuffed chairs gave one the unmistakable feeling that this was a man's room. Understated elegance. A private, powerful room, where men could talk without reservation.

I guessed the captain's sleeping quarters were behind one of several closed doors located around the room. Just then, he entered from the opposite side of the room. Two additional officers were with him. They were all dressed in whites—a sharp contrast to our ragtag appearance...or at least to mine. I hadn't shaved in days, my t-shirt and shorts stained with dried blood. I was a mess and hadn't even thought about it until I saw the looks on their faces. They looked at me like I was from another planet.

In contrast, Jennifer had somehow managed to put on a clean blouse and brush out her hair. She'd rewrapped her hand with a clean, white bandage and sling. As usual, she wore no makeup, but looked beautiful as she stood to meet the men. I was beside her when the captain and officers entered. Standing together, the two of us made an interesting looking pair. I started to thank them for their help, but the captain immediately cut me off.

"You lied to me...to this ship...to all of us." He'd obviously had received a full briefing about the gunshot wound.

"There's no excuse, sir," I said humbly. "Absolutely no excuse. Please accept my apologies, not only to you, Captain, and to your officers, but also to your entire crew. I am sorry I had to lie to you." That helped take a little of the edge off, but he was still angry.

"Go on."

"Sir, being in Mexican waters, I felt it wasn't prudent to broadcast on an open channel the fact that we had a gunshot victim on board."

The officers looked at each other. "We're in international waters," the captain said, "but, please, do continue."

"Sir, all we're looking for is medical help." I held out my arms in a gesture of innocence. "I'm no doctor, but I don't think Travis would have made it if you hadn't stopped. You may have saved his life."

For all he knew, we could be drug runners. He'd responded to the Mayday call in accordance with maritime law, but upon finding out we had a gunshot victim on board, he'd ordered me here and had taken control of our vessel with armed guards. He wasn't about to jeopardize his crew or anyone else on board his ship until he could fully assess the situation.

"Very well...continue," he ordered. "We're listening." Old school, strictly by the book, but his word was law on this ship. We both knew damn well he could arrest us on the spot.

"Sir, with all due respect, I honestly don't know what's going on." This brought a combined trio of frowns. "Five days ago, my girlfriend here..." I said, looking over at Jennifer. "Gentlemen, this is Jennifer Comstock." She gracefully extended her left hand. The officers were all instantly a bit embarrassed for having ignored a lady in their presence. They were, after all, officers and gentlemen. Her smile helped crack the ice as they extended their hands and introduced themselves.

"Please excuse our rudeness, Ms. Comstock." The curt edge in the captain's voice was replaced by tones of smooth sophistication.

"Please call me Jennifer," she said, disarming them further.

"Your hand...," the captain said, looking at her wrapping. "May we attend to it?"

"I'd appreciate that, sir, very much. But only after you're satisfied we've done nothing wrong." Her grace, dignity and loyalty made an impression on the Officers. They were all still in the midst of trying to figure out exactly what they'd stumbled upon.

"As you wish," the Captain said to Jennifer. "Please continue," he commanded, turning his attention back to me.

"As I was saying, sir…five days ago, we were running a charter service out of San Diego. One of the other boats needed a relief cook, and since we weren't booked, Jennifer volunteered to help them out."

"Wait a minute!" Captain Mitchell interrupted, a light bulb suddenly going off inside his head. "You're the ones everyone has been looking for—on that missing charter boat. It's been all over the radio."

"Yes, sir," Jennifer said. "I was on board the *Dorsal*. We were hijacked."

"My God, what happened? Where are the others? The reports the Coast Guard was putting out advised us to be on the lookout for a missing charter boat with full crew and six passengers."

"That's right, captain. There were five of us in the crew, plus the four girls the two men brought with them." She paused. A dark cloud passed across her eyes. "They killed the crew and two of the girls."

Shock was evident on their faces. "Get on the horn and notify Coast Guard we've found them."

"Yes, sir," answered one of the officers, who immediately left the room.

Upon hearing from the doctor that we had a gunshot victim, especially after I lied to him, the captain had responded appropriately. But what Jennifer had just said hit a nerve. His entire personality was transformed. As a man who had spent his entire life at sea, he could only imagine the horrors Jennifer must have been through. He had no tolerance for piracy. His compassion was evident in his voice. "Are you sure you're okay?"

Jennifer nodded.

"Call the doctor," he commanded the remaining officer.

"I'm all right," Jennifer assured him. Touching my arm, she continued. "Corey saved my life. He saved all of our lives. If he felt he couldn't tell you about the fight on the radio, I respect his decision. We're both sorry he had to lie to you, and again, we offer our sincerest apologies."

"Are you sure you're all right?" Captain Mitchell asked again, gesturing for Jennifer to sit, obviously concerned about her condition.

"I'm all right," she said, "now." A soft smile crossed her face as she looked up at me. The exchange wasn't missed by the Captain.

"Looks as if I owe you an apology, sir," he said, extending his hand.

"No apologies necessary, Captain." I said as my hand disappeared in his grip. "We can't thank you enough for the help."

"You know as well as I do that a Mayday call commands response."

"You run an extremely tight schedule, Captain. You could've easily ignored the call, especially down here."

"Not on my ship," the Captain said, holding his head erect. "I don't care what the unwritten, unofficial company policies 'suggest' we do with a Mayday call. Maybe outside the breakwater in L.A., when some idiot runs out of gas or doesn't have a clue what he's doing and blasts a Mayday like he's calling triple A...but down here...in open waters...Mayday means Mayday." He was going to hear about this from the company, which would come later. But now he wanted more details. "Please," he said to Jennifer, "if you're up to it, I'd like to know as much as you can tell me."

Jennifer recounted the entire ordeal—from the time *Dorsal* left San Diego, the first signs of trouble...every detail up until the *Odyssey* pulled alongside us. As she was finishing, the first officer returned with the doctor.

"Doc," the Captain said, "this is Jennifer Comstock and Corey Phillips." We shook hands.

"Doctor Garcia," he said. "I'm the ship's GP. The surgical staff is still working on Travis."

"Any word?" I asked.

"Not yet. Do you mind if I take a look at your hand, Jennifer?"

She winced as he gently helped her take it out of the sling. With the bandage off, we were all shocked at how swollen and black her hand had become. A dark, reddish black, substance oozed from the torn skin. The pain on her face was obvious as he turned her wrist and examined the damage. "From the swelling and bruising, it looks like we may have some fractures. You say it got smashed in a hatch?"

"Yes, sir. A hatch fell on it during the storm."

"We need to get you below and shoot some pictures to see what's broken. We'll get this cleaned up. How long ago did this happen?" he asked, looking into her tired eyes.

"Oh…," she thought out loud, the exhaustion starting to takes its toll. "A couple of days ago."

"That's fine. Let's get you below. Are you able to walk?"

"It's my hand, Doc, not my foot," she teased.

"Fine," he said, smiling at her courage and helping her off the couch.

She hesitated, looked at me and then at the captain, who suggested I go with her.

"We can continue talking after you've been looked after and get some rest."

"Thank you, Captain."

"You're welcome. Ring me when you're finished with her, would you please, Doctor?"

Things in the operating room weren't going well. Travis had lost a lot of blood and was barely hanging on when they brought him in. The surgical team had a tough job. The bullet had splintered his shoulder bone before ricocheting off and becoming lodged partway into the lung. Had the bullet fully penetrated his lung, Travis would already be dead; because it was partially lodged in the surrounding muscle tissue, it was acting like a dam, preventing his lungs from filling with blood while still allowing him to breath.

Jasmine was beyond words. Once they'd taken him away from her and into surgery, she'd lost it. They asked me to wait while they worked on Jennifer, so I went looking for Travis and found Jasmine outside the surgery, sitting on the floor wedged into a corner. Her arms wrapped around her legs, rocking back and forth, sobbing.

Words would have been futile. Up until the moment they wheeled Travis into surgery, Jasmine had fought through her fears, focusing every ounce of her strength on helping him. Now that he was out of her care, she was deluged with pain and fear. I sat next to her on the cold linoleum floor and put my arm around her shoulder. She let her headrest on my chest, her tears soaking through my t-shirt. We sat together; terrified we were on the verge of losing Travis. When the craziness stops, the consequences of events start to take hold. Until you have time to stop reacting and think, it's all pretty much a blur. In the quiet seclusion of an empty hallway, the fear, the remorse, the losses were weaving themselves into our souls.

How did all this happen? I thought to myself. *The whole fucking mess is my fault. I should never have brought them along.*

"Why? Why Travis?" Jasmine sobbed through her tears.

We fell asleep, sitting together on the floor, leaning against the wall— two exhausted souls.

******

"Sir, wake up." A nurse was touching my shoulder. "Wake up."

I didn't know where I was. I snapped my head around, startling the nurse and waking Jasmine up at the same time. "What! What is it?" I blurted out, still half asleep.

"Sir," the nurse said, "your friend is out of surgery."

"Is he all right?" Jasmine demanded, instantly awake and springing to her feet.

"He's out of surgery and stable," the nurse replied.

"So he's alive?"

"Yes."

"Oh, thank God." Tears welled in her bloodshot eyes. "Thank you. Thank you. Thank you."

"Can we see him?" I asked, attempting to stand. My legs had fallen asleep and I couldn't feel them.

"He's sedated…most likely will be for awhile."

"Can I at least see him?" Jasmine begged. "Please." Springing up effortlessly.

"Come with me."

Oh, to be young again, I thought with a twinge, still struggling to stand. They both extended their hands, offering to help me up. "Thanks," I said. "Some parts just don't wake up as fast as others. How's Jennifer?"

"She's asleep in the room next to Travis. She'll be fine," the nurse assured us. "Doctor put her under to set her hand. She had several broken bones in her hand, plus three broken fingers. With all the lacerations, Doctor didn't want to cast it until there was no further threat of infection. He gave her a sedative to help her sleep. He has also set her up for intravenous painkillers when she comes to. She'll have to keep that hand immobilized for a while. It'll be a lot easier on her."

We looked in on Travis, who was sleeping. Jasmine commandeered a chair and planted herself next to his bed. No one would be able to drag her out of there. Down the hall, I found Jennifer. She was also fast asleep. I left her alone and asked the nurse how the girls were doing.

"Let me get the psychiatrist," the nurse said pleasantly. "She'll be able to tell you. Please wait here. I'll let her know you're waiting."

"Thank you. If you don't mind, I'd like to wait in Jennifer's room."

"That'll be fine." A few minutes later there was a soft knock. The door opened and the psychiatrist introduced herself. We stepped outside.

"Physically, there're both going to be all right. They were dehydrated and full of drugs. We don't have the facilities on board to determine what they'd been given, but we drew some blood samples. When we get into port, we'll turn them over to the authorities. The doctors have the girls on IV's. They did a full examination." She paused before telling me the obvious. "They were both raped and sodomized. We ran a complete rape kit, and recovered seminal fluids and multiple hairs from both girls. Like I said, we can't run tests on board, but barring exposure to any venereal diseases, physically they should recover." Pausing again, she shook her head. "Dealing with the emotional trauma is another story."

"Fucking animals," I said, shaking my head. "I'm sorry…I didn't mean to say that out loud."

"Anyone who would do that to a woman doesn't even deserve to be called an animal. Don't apologize. I feel the same way. What happened to them, anyway?" she asked, referring to the bad guys.

"I don't know for sure. When we arrived on scene, Jennifer had them trapped below deck. When we weren't paying attention, they managed to grab one of the girls, and that's when all the shooting started." Having already heard the girls' version, she nodded. "I'm not sure if I hit 'em or not. All I know is that it got awfully quiet down there and they stopped shooting. We dumped a thousand pounds of anchor and chain on top of the hatches and ran for help."

"So they're still out there somewhere…floating around?" she asked.

"I guess. As far as I'm concerned, they can rot in hell."

"My sentiments exactly."

We nodded in agreement. "Thanks for taking care of the girls."

She looked me over. "If you'd like to talk further, I'm available…anytime."

"Thanks, Doc, but I've got a boat that needs tending to."

I peeked in on Jennifer again. It looked like she was going to be out for awhile, so I took the elevator up to deck level and pushed open the heavy double doors leading from the crew's interior companionway out to a kind of Lanai deck. *Vintage* was running parallel—about two hundreds yards off— Sierra was still standing in the cockpit, her eyes glued to the cruise ship. It looked as if she hadn't taken her eyes off the ship since we'd abandoned her. A painful twinge of guilt shot through me.

Normally, I stamp any feelings of guilt 'Return to Sender,' but because Sierra and I been through so much together, seeing her standing there with her eyes glued to the cruise ship broke my heart. I didn't want to leave her alone any longer than absolutely necessary.

I jumped back on the elevator and took it to the top deck. Until now, we hadn't seen a single passenger, but when I got off the service elevator and walked into a large open salon area, I stepped directly into a crowd of curious tourists. Dressed in Hawaiian shirts, Bermuda shorts, loafers, sun dresses and hats, they were looking at me as if I was some sort of criminal. Shipboard rumors had been flying ever since the rescue, but other than the captain, first officers and medical teams, no one on board really knew what was going on.

"That's him! That's the guy!"

"Did you see all the blood on his shirt?"

"Why isn't he in the brig?"

"Maybe he escaped!"

I wheeled away from the crowd and headed toward the bridge, leaving them talking amongst themselves. *Fucking morons.* "May I speak with Captain Mitchell, please," I asked, entering the exception room adjacent to the massive bridge.

"Please take a seat. I'll check...and you are...?" asked the receptionist.

"Corey Phillips."

She picked up the intercom and spoke softly into it. A few seconds later, she said, "Mr. Phillips, someone will be right out."

"Thanks."

"Captain Phillips." It was one of the officers we'd met during the initial meeting in the captain's quarters. "Please come with me. Captain Mitchell will see you straight away." These guys even had their own language.

"Captain Phillips," the captain said as we shook hands. "How is everyone?"

"Please call me Corey." I didn't feel like any captain, and certainly wasn't in anywhere near the same league as this man. "They're all resting, sir. Thank you again for everything you and you crew are doing for us."

"We've got a good team on board," he said, nodding his head. "Rest assured, son, they're doing everything they can."

"No question, sir. Travis would have been dead by now if it weren't for you guys. We'll be eternally grateful for everything you've done."

"How about Jennifer?" he asked. "She seems like a fine young lady."

"She's asleep, too. Her hand was worse than we thought. A number of broken bones, along with her busted fingers. They gave her some painkillers and a sedative." Seeing the reaction in his eyes, I realized he knew all this and was just being polite, so I shut up.

"The Coast Guard has ordered us to stand down and wait here for their arrival."

"Are you kidding me?" I asked.

"The federal government doesn't kid, Captain. We have a very serious situation here, sir. A captain and crew missing, reportedly murdered and assumed dead, two additional girls reported dead and left abandoned on the hijacked vessel, two, possibly three, young ladies drugged and raped, and an additional crew member shot and in critical condition."

"Three?" I asked. "What are you talking about...three! Jennifer wasn't raped! She told me they hadn't touched her."

"Perhaps not," he said, backing off his statement a little. "We won't have her test results back until we return to port."

"You ordered a rape kit on Jennifer!" *So that's why the doctor put her under—it wasn't because of her hand.* "That's bullshit." I was disgusted.

"I had no options." He was holding his ground. "I had to give that order." We stared at one another. Seconds passed and neither of us said a word.

Slowly, I realized he had had no choice, though the thought disgusted me. "As I was saying, the situation we're dealing with is perhaps a bit more grave than you thought."

"What the hell do you think I've been doing the past four days…."

"You seem to be the only one not injured," he said matter-of-factly.

"This is bullshit! I'm out of here. I'm getting Jennifer and we're leaving. I want my boat back."

"Not so fast. We've been instructed to hold you on board with all your crew until the authorities arrive."

"Are you kidding me?" I asked, stunned and confused.

"As we speak, Coast Guard has a jet ranger in flight, carrying federal and state authorities. We're in international waters, so no Mexican officials. Evidently, they weren't too pleased about being left out of the party."

"Some party." I said, surrendering to the situation.

"Your vessel is safe and in competent hands."

"What about my dog? If you're going to hold us here, can she be brought aboard?"

Then I realized he didn't like the situation any more than I did. He'd been given his orders. "She'll need to be quarantined to one room below, but I don't think it'll be a problem." He paused. "It's still my ship." At that moment I saw how truly pissed off he was about being told what to do on his own command.

Realizing the burden our presence was causing him, I offered an apology. "I'm sorry for going off on you like that."

"I'd have felt the same way," he said. "Probably should have explained to you what I'd been ordered to do. I know you had nothing to do with the hijacking. You most likely saved not only Jennifer's life but the lives of the other girls as well. The Feds don't want me talking to you…told me they want to do their own interrogations." I nodded. "Fuck 'em," he said. "This is still my ship, and as far as I'm concerned, you're a damn hero.

Want a drink?" Though I don't drink, one doesn't refuse an offer like that from a captain of his status. "What'll you have?"

Bottled water was out of the question. "Ah…whatever you're having will be fine."

Pressing the intercom on his desk, he said, "Two Cutties and water, please."

"Coming right up, Captain," answered a clear voice through the speaker.

"Normally, I never have a drink until we're back in port," he said.

"Me neither."

The drinks were brought in and the steward left. The captain held out his glass. "To the quick recovery of loved ones." We touched our glasses. The first sip just about knocked my shorts off—it burned all the way down and left me flushed. "Don't drink much, huh?" he asked with a smile.

"Hardly ever," I said, trying to cover up.

"Hardly ever…or never?" He was no fool.

"Never."

"Then why now?"

I didn't even need to say it, but did so anyway. "Out of respect, sir."

We'd taken our first step towards building that invisible bridge of trust. Putting down his drink, he smiled. "Why don't you ride over with the launch to pick up your dog?" he said with a hint of fatherly affection. "I'm sure there are a few personal things the girls might like. And," he said and smiled again, "you might want to grab a change of clothes before the boys arrive."

"I'd appreciate that, sir. Thanks."

"Go get your dog," he said. "But let's keep this between us. No sense in giving the Feds anything to get pissy over. You'd better get a move on. The chopper will be here in a little over an hour. I'll call down and have them get the launch ready."

******

Sierra was ecstatic. Her tail was wagging so hard it was twisting her entire body. "Hey, girl!" I said jumping on board, and giving her a big hug. "Told ya we'd be right back." She was so relieved; she kept wagging and weaving herself between my legs. After a couple of minutes of receiving my undivided and completely deserved attention, she settled down but wasn't about to leave my side. I could almost hear her say, *You're not pulling that crap again—leaving me here alone with strangers.*

The Officer in Charge introduced himself and the crew assigned to my boat. "No one seems to know how long the Feds are going to take or how long you're going to be detained, so if you don't mind, would you give us a quick rundown of her systems?"

"Be glad to, but from the look of things, you've already got her pretty well wired."

It took only about fifteen minutes to go over everything. Compared to the ship they'd been running, *Vintage* was a windup toy. The boat was pretty self-explanatory since we'd reworked everything, but, like any lady, she needed paying attention to. As we went over everything, the Second made notes on a little spiral notepad—the kind that fits in your shirt pocket. After they had all the information they needed, I went below to grab a change of clothes. I opened some of Jennifer's drawers and picked out a couple of her favorite cotton blouses, some shorts and clean panties. Then I hit Travis and Jasmine's room and picked out a few things for them as well. Throwing everything into a big canvas bag, I grabbed a ten-pound sack of Sierra's food and stuffed it in on top of the clothes.

Getting back on the skiff—Sierra leading the way—I felt all right about leaving the boat. They were competent men and knew if they needed anything, I was just a radio call and a couple hundred yards away.

******

The authorities arrived in full force. A joint FBI/Interpol taskforce lead the way, with Coast Guard officials and a San Diego detective in tow. I was amazed they all fit on board the bird. One of the FBI agents was obviously in charge. They immediately separated us for interrogation. We didn't appreciate the forced isolation treatment, but we understood they were following protocol interviewing us alone. Jasmine flat out refused to leave Travis' bedside. Since he was still unconscious, they conducted her interviews in the ICU.

We cooperated fully, but after twelve hours Jennifer had had enough and demanded to see me. "He saved our lives and you're treating him—in fact, all of us—like we're the damned criminals. What's wrong with you people?"

She had a point, but apparently we'd been sucked into the largest organized slave sex syndicate in the world. This was the closest the task force had come to breaking the case in years. They were creaming all over themselves trying to garner every scrap of information they could from us.

San Diego Coast Guard had dispatched a cutter within an hour after receiving the initial call from the cruise ship and, at forty knots, would enter the area where we left *Dorsal* by first light. Satellite surveillance photos had the boat pinpointed the. Part of the task force had done a fly-over and detected no apparent activity on board. Against the wishes of the cruise line owners, the FBI ordered Captain Mitchell to proceed on site and, with *Vintage* still tagging along in her wake, to rendezvous with *Dorsal* and the Coast Guard cutter. Sunrise found all four vessels hovering together. The task force followed a heavily armed Coast Guard boarding party onto the abandoned vessel. Radioing back, they reported four dead—two females, two males.

"Are you all right?" Jennifer asked me from her bed in the infirmary when we heard the report.

"Yeah, I'm okay," I replied, avoiding her eyes.

"Listen," she said, reaching out and taking my hand. Her voice was surprisingly strong and clear. "Those animals were scum. They raped and murdered those girls. They killed the crew and were going to rape me and then sell us."

I nodded but still didn't meet her eyes.

"Do you understand me?" she continues. "They were scum. They shot Travis, for Christ's sake."

"I know," I said, squeezing her hand, meeting her gaze. "I'm all right. I was pretty sure I'd hit them all along. But being told...having it confirmed."

We lay there for a few moments. My head resting on her chest, absorbing the steady beat of her heart. "To be honest with you, I've been wondering how I'd feel when I found out for sure I'd killed them."

"And?"

"Relief. Relief that it's over, and you're safe."

If Jennifer hadn't trapped them and if we hadn't found the boat when we did, we both knew we would never have seen one another again. We'd slain the dragon before it could destroy our lives.

"But the feeling I can't shake is the fact that I'm the one who got Travis shot and that other girl killed. You knew. You warned me...but I didn't listen. I didn't watch those hatches. It's my fault, plain and simple."

"Oh," she said, gently stroking my head. "No way that's on you." After awhile she whispered," How's Travis?"

"He's still in a coma."

"How's Jasmine doing?"

"I'm starting to worry more about her than Travis. She hasn't left his side since we've been here. She's not eating or sleeping."

"Ask her to come see me."

When I walked into the room, Jasmine barely moved. "Jennifer asked for you." There was no response. "Would you mind going in to see her for a few minutes? She's right next door." Still nothing. "I'll stay here with Travis." She slowly got up, stood over Travis and looked at him with dark sunken eyes, blinked and made her way into Jennifer's room.

"You've got to eat something," Jennifer pleaded.

"I'm not hungry."

"Come on," Jennifer begged. "Please."

Jasmine shook her head. "I'm just not hungry. I'm not anything."

Jennifer pushed herself up and swung her legs over the side of the bed. "Come on, let's go see if we can find something together."

"What are you doing?" Jasmine asked, stunned.

"Going with you to the galley. And if I have to, I'll spoon feed you."

"Get back in that bed."

"Not until you eat."

"Okay, I will, but get back into bed."

Jennifer lay back down, but not before handing Jasmine the phone. "Call the nurse right now and order something."

******

The low, steady beeping from the heart monitor over Travis's bed was the only sound in the room. He didn't look good. All the color was gone from his face. His cheeks were sullen, his eyes deep dark orbs, his lips parched and chapped. The entire left side of his torso was heavily bandaged and wrapped. A thick, yellowish mucus oozed slowly down a drain tube.

I took hold of his hand. "Come on, Travis, you're not ready to go. Not now. If you were, you would already be gone. There's no way you're leaving now. Not after you finally found someone dumb enough to love you the way Jaz does. How she puts up with your shit is beyond me, but she does. You know she does. You know she loves you…so quit jerking us all around and get back here." I went on babbling like an idiot for a while. Finally I shut up and sat in silence, watching my friend fighting for his life.

"She fell right asleep," Jennifer said softly as I came back into the room. "Poor thing was dead tired. After she ate, I convinced her to stretch out on the bed next to me. How's Travis?"

"Sleeping."

She scooted over in the bed and I laid down next to her. There wasn't much else to say.

******

Every hour the *Odyssey* remained on site, the cruise line lost hundreds of thousands of dollars. Captain Mitchell was catching hell from the ship's owners as well as from the passengers, who lost interest in our little drama when they realized the delay was affecting their return home plans. The cruise scheduled to follow this one had already been canceled. In spite of his years of outstand service, Mitchell's career was obviously on the line. After transferring the bodies to the *Odyssey*'s morgue, the FBI decided to release the ship. *Dorsal* was to be driven back to San Diego by a Coast Guard crew, and from all appearances, they no longer seemed to give a shit about us or *Vintage*. They'd picked our brains for every shred of information we had.

"Do whatever you want," one of the agents told us. "You're free to leave."

Captain Mitchell informed us that he needed his men back immediately, so Jennifer and I decided to get back onboard *Vintage* and run her the rest of the way down to Cabo.

"Before you go," Dr, Garcia suggested to Jennifer "we get your hand in a cast. I would have preferred waiting awhile longer to give the skin a little more time to heal before casting it, but since you're no longer going to be our guests, I think it's the best way to proceed."

Jennifer didn't hesitate, "Whatever you say ,doctor."

Jennifer's plaster cast was still drying when we went in to talk things over with Jasmine. She was staying with Travis no matter what. There had been talk about airlifting him off, but the medial team's consensus was that everything possible had been done for him, and moving him could cause complications. The ship had an excellent surgical staff and he was in good hands, but he still hadn't regained consciousness. Jasmine promised to let us know the minute there was any change in his condition.

"You sure you're going to be all right?" Jennifer asked her.

Jasmine nodded. "I hate to see you guys leave."

"If there was any other way, Jaz..."

"I know," she said, gently dismissing my concern. "You have to take care of the boat." She took a deep breath and sighed as she focused on Travis. "He wouldn't want it any other way...and neither would I. You take care of the boat, and I'll take care of Travis. I promise to call you as soon as he wakes up." Tears were starting to form again in her eyes.

Jennifer started crying as well. They wrapped their arms around each other. "He's going to be all right, Jaz. The worst is over—he's only going to get better now."

"God, I hope so."

The girls hugged each other in silence. One of the ship's officers, who had been waiting in the hall outside the ICU, poked his head in and indicated that it was time to go. I whispered in Jen's ear that we had to go.

"He's going to make it," I promised Jaz, giving her a hug. "While you were sleeping, we had a little chat. He told me he just wanted to make you realize how much you loved him. That's why he's been hanging out there in space. He'll be back any minute now."

"You're full of shit," she said.

"Forget the boat," I said, turning to Jennifer. "We can't leave them like this."

Jasmine didn't miss a beat. "Get back to the boat right now—the both of you. He's going to be fine...we're going to be fine...and if either of you let anything happen to that boat, you know he's going kill you. So get her down to Cabo and wait for us there. We'll be along in awhile. You promised…remember?" She managed a half-smile through her tears.

Getting word that *Dorsal* was going to be returning to San Diego, and Jennifer and I were taking *Vintage* to Cabo, the crew tending to her had taken time to retrieve our ground tackle off *Dorsal's* deck before we arrived.

The same First Officer and crew that had initially picked us up shuttled us back to *Vintage*—minus the sidearms. First, they pulled up to the *Dorsal* to offload some supplies for the Coast Guard crew that was going to be running her back to San Diego. Both of *Dorsal's* mains were purring like kittens.

"What happened to her in the first place?" Jennifer asked one of them.

"Clogged fuel filters," he said, shaking his head.

You are a child of the universe, no less than the trees and the stars; you have a right to be here. Therefore, be at peace with God, whatever you conceive Him to be.

Chapter 13

Cabo San Lucas, Baja California Sur, Mexico

The ride south to the Cape was uneventful. Jennifer and I loved being back on board *Vintage*. On the cruise ship, we'd lost all sense of the ocean's rhythm, but back on the boat, feeling her hull riding up and over the gentle south swells, the healing process began. We didn't talk much. We were together again, and that was all that mattered. For the most part, we just sat together in the wheelhouse, allowing the soothing, steady hum of her diesels mixing with the spray coming off our bow to lull us into a world all our own. Sierra curled up next to us, asleep. The horrors of the past days beginning to dissolve from our memories like the wash of the wake disappearing behind our stern.

Rounding the arch and pulling into Cabo is one of the most beautiful sights on earth— Land's end. For us, a new beginning. We dropped the hook in front of the Hacienda, splashed the Achilles, fired up the Suzuki outboard and headed into town. We'd never met Minnie, but the second she saw us, she threw her arms around us like we were family and started talking a mile a minute, mixing her Spanish and English to point we could barely understand her.

"The whole town has been talking about the bandidos pirates. You're all over the TV." She went on and on, taking Jennifer's face in her hands. "Usted hermoso ángel. You are hero, no! Usted es el uno who captured pirates in fish hold!" Jennifer smiled shyly and started to speak, but was immediately cut off. " Ah, usted es héroe! You saved the other girls! El barco. Everything! Everyone wants to meet you. Come! Comer conmigo. I introduce you to husband, Roberto. We show him women are strong, no?" She flexed her arm, laughing out loud. You couldn't help falling in love with Minnie the minute you met her. She oozed warmth from every ounce of her being. She was one happy lady, that's for sure.

"Have you heard anything from our friends...from Travis and Jasmine...our friends we had to leave on the cruise ship?" Jennifer managed to ask.

"No. Nada. But I know your friend will be okay. I know it in my heart, okay?" Minnie said, looking into Jennifer's eyes. "You come now."

She closed the shop and hurried us to her home to meet Roberto and her family. She must have known everyone in town. There wasn't a person we passed who didn't hear that we were the ones who had captured and killed the pirates. By the time we reached her house, the town was abuzz.

Roberto was as warm as she was. Before we knew it, a party had begun. People arrived, bringing food and drink. Within an hour, it was a full-blown fiesta attended by the port captain, the mayor, the chief of police and so many 'officials' we couldn't even begin to keep track. We were heralded as heroes for killing the *pirates banditos*.

As evening turned into night, and the agave continued to flow freely, the party lost its focus on us and instead became a celebration of life. Jennifer and I tried to sneak back to the boat, but before we could make our getaway, Roberto pulled me aside and wanted to know all the details. He spoke English very well and I told him so.

"I'm an American," he said, waving his had in front of my face to see if I was blind. "Blue eyes, blond hair, six-four." He was a big man with an infectious laugh. "Been here going on twenty years. I'll tell you one thing—there isn't enough money in the world to get me to go back. I love it here. I love these people, my wife and family, my life." He stopped, held out his arms and closed his eyes. Looking up toward the heavens, he said a short prayer in Spanish. "Start at the top," he said seriously, coming back to earth. "I want to hear it all...every detail."

His sudden seriousness caught me by surprise. Only moments before he'd been so jovial. As his guest, I sat with him on a thick adobe wall under a little cluster of mango trees and felt obliged to tell him the whole story. I finished by saying, "We had an easy run down after leaving the cruise ship...and that's about it. We're just glad it's over."

"Don't be so sure it's over."

"What are you talking about? The motherfuckers are dead!"

"It's not them I'm worried about, amigo. One of the things that concerns me is the fact the Feds let you just mosey on down here like nothing ever happened."

"What do you mean?"

"The scumbags you wasted weren't operating on their own. Come on, think about it. They were just part of a crew and the Feds know it. After everything you guys have been through, it's pretty shitty of them to do this." He paused. "But I would have done the same thing."

"Done what?"

"Cut you loose as bait."

A chilling fear washed over me, as I grasped what he was saying. It had been too easy. Initially, the Feds had treated us like we were the criminals. They were all over us. But after the interrogations, it was like we didn't even exist. Thinking back on the way they acted, it was too abrupt, the reversal too fast. One minute the entire area was a crime scene, the next we're whisked back to *Vintage,* the cruise ship and Coast Guard cutter are booking it north.

"We've got to get back to the boat."

"I'll give you a ride back down to the wharf and ride out with you," Roberto said.

"Thanks. Let's find Jennifer. You really think we're in danger?"

"Don't know for sure, but twenty years with the LAPD taught me never to assume anything. We're dealing with some very bad people—people who are used to having things their way. Doubt if they appreciate you throwing a monkey wrench into their little party."

Inside the house, everyone was eating, drinking, dancing and singing. They knew how to have a good time. Jennifer was happy and laughing for the first time since this mess started. "Don't alarm her, okay? I'll just tell her that you and a couple of your friends want to see the boat."

"No problem," he said. "No reason to worry her."

Roberto's buddies just happened to be the Chief of Police, along with a couple other high-ranking *federales*. When word spread through the party that we were heading out to the boat, everyone wanted to come. After some yelling, a little arguing and a few more drinks, only those with the biggest badges were eventually selected to accompany us. We thanked Minnie, who promised to see us in the morning.

"Thank you for everything," we said, breaking away from her bear hugs.

Even after all the arguing and jockeying for position, the boarding party was still far to large for everyone to fit into our inflatable, so a couple pangas were commandeered from the beach. "Official police business," the chief told a couple of curious onlookers, as he flashed his badge.

Sierra greeted us with the usual tail wagging and whimpering, but a few of the boarding party were too frightened of the dog to get out of the skiffs. After some coaxing, the reluctant ones managed to get on the swim step but still wouldn't come through the transom door. They were content to keep their distance from Sierra and just look over the rail, while the rest of their *compadres* went through the boat.

Satisfied we weren't in any danger, Bob rounded up his posse and pointed them toward the beach. "You two have a good night's rest," he said as they shoved off.

"Will do," Jennifer said, waving as they left. "Thanks again for making us feel so welcome."

"Appreciate your hospitality," I added. "Tell Minnie thanks again for everything."

"No worries," he said, waving along with the others.

As the skiffs made their way toward the beach, Jennifer's arm found its way around my waist as she nestled her head up against my chest. The sweet scent of her shampoo blending with the salty evening air stirred my senses and pulled my mind away from the craziness that had dominated our lives since the abduction. We'd spent the ride down to the

Cape wrapped in the nurturing blanket of being back together. But as I held her, the embers stirred. A slow burning passion was building below the surface. I resisted for fear of not wanting her to have to deal with something she might not be ready for. But I was wrong—so wrong. She turned in my arms, raised herself up on her tiptoes and pressed her lips against mine. The softness of her kiss…the gentle probing of her tongue…the shortness of her breath growing heavy with passion...eliminated my initial fears. Her body needed to be touched, caressed, cared for, loved. She had stared death in the face and come out alive. Now nothing in the world was going to stop us from losing ourselves in each other. The sparks erupted into a raging wildfire. We couldn't get enough of each other. Our mouths parted just long enough for her to pull her white cotton blouse over her head. She wasn't wearing a bra. My mouth was instantly on her breasts. Her nipples tight and erect. Moaning, she pulled me to her. Her breath was coming fast and hard. Her heart pounding in my ears. I felt my shorts being yanked down. She wrapped her hand around my penis as her mouth engulfed it, her flowing hair cascading down the inside of my thighs. I frantically reached for her. She dropped to her knees, reached around with her one good hand and grabbed my bare cheek. My legs felt weak. I ran my fingers through her hair, holding onto her head.

"I want you inside me so bad it hurts," she pleaded in a harsh whisper. Pulling down her shorts and panties, she lowered herself onto the warm teak deck. She kicked off her panties the rest of the way and spread her legs. My tongue ached for her waiting vagina, but she grabbed my hair and pulled me up. "I have to have you now. Please."

Arching her back and lifting her pelvis to receive me, she moaned softly, closing her eyes and rolling her head as I entered her. She was swollen and moist, allowing me to glide effortlessly into her. Her love was flowing, her body quivering in anticipation. We surrendered, letting go of everything. The passion was all consuming. She began coming instantly, the very core of her being wrapping itself around my penis. I felt gripping waves of pulsating contractions. She screamed, demanding I come with her. Our orgasms echoed off the water.

We lay there in each other's arms, breathing heavily from the violent release we both had needed so badly. She was still holding me inside her, gently squeezing my penis and not letting it slip out. As I softened, she started contracting her vaginal muscles, massaging me back to another full erection. Effortlessly turning, she slid on top, her beautiful body glistening in the night. Looking me in the eye, she smiled as she lowered herself all the way down onto me. Our bodies moved together in perfect rhythm, slowly building. Then she began thrusting herself up and down faster and faster, abandoning all thoughts to passion. She came over and over again. Small quivering tremors turned into full-blown multiple orgasms. This time, I was able to hold on and stay with her, letting her take us wherever she wanted to go. Her wings spread wide and strong. We soared into heavenly bliss. Our bodies melted as we became one. Time stood still. There was no universe other than ours. Life flowed effortlessly through us. We were a cocoon. Our love isolated us in a womb of rebirth…of healing…of life renewed. Our souls were purging themselves of the horrors we'd been through by demanding that our bodies, our minds, our hearts surrender to one another, leaving nothing but love—pure, complete and absolute surrender. Knowing that death had been so close, every fiber of our souls rejoiced and celebrated…demanding to be touched, caressed, held, nurtured and loved. It was our bodies' dance of life.

Long after every ounce of our strength and passion had been drained, we lay entwined and naked on the deck. The warm night spread a blanket of stars over us. As I gazed at my sleeping princess, I became overwhelmed by her purity and beauty. She'd never looked more graceful. She was glowing and alive. Her sandy blond hair was strewn across her shoulder. Her breasts were still swollen from making love. Her heartbeat settled into a slow, steady rhythm, making her breathing relaxed and content—a stark contrast to the gasps and cries that had earlier sent us to a place beyond words

If ever there was love, this was it. I closed my eyes and gave thanks for her safety, for her love, for this moment, for the fact that she was alive and we were together. I thanked God for the gentle roll of *Vintage* beneath us, the sea and the sky. Our souls were at rest, at peace….together. The sea's breath of life matched our own in perfect harmony.

"What are you thinking?" she whispered without moving.

"That we're the luckiest people on earth."

Her murmur coupled with the gentle nestling of her head on my chest confirmed her sentiments were identical. "I never knew it could be like this," she said. "I've never felt so complete. So full…. Thank you. Thank love."

"For everything," I whispered.

The following week brought more of the same—our bodies moving effortlessly together through moments of unhurried tenderness. The love was soft, slow and gentle, with an occasional flurry. For the most part, the raging wildfires were spent. We savored every moment together. The smile in her eyes was coming back.

******

There was an easy pace about the town. For the most part, the people who called Cabo home were kind hearted, genuine people. Generation after generation here had scratched a living by working the sea and by managing to get a few fruits and vegetables to grow out of the rugged Baja terrain. We fell in love with the place—the quaint shops, the smell of freshly baked bread in the morning, rickety wooden fish taco carts and dirt streets. It was amazing watching these hardy souls carve out an existence in the middle of nowhere. The sun-drenched days melted into one another. We'd take Sierra into town and let her play with the kids or run along the endless sandy beaches. We walked hand in hand...in no hurry to do anything.

The day we heard Travis had come out of his coma and was going to make it was amazing. Neither of us had realized how worried about him we'd been, holding it in, not talking about it. Lloyd and Larry had been waiting for them when the cruise ship arrived, and along with Jasmine, they'd been by his side. Larry finally had to get back to San Diego, but Lloyd never left the hospital. Between Lloyd and Jasmine, Travis couldn't have been in better hands. When Jasmine told us he was pissed off we'd shipped him home, I knew he was going to be all right. He was out of danger, but had months of rehab ahead of him. The doctors on the cruise ship had saved his life and set his splintered collarbone superbly. No nerve damage was reported, and the prognosis was for a full recovery. We listened to the spark in Jasmine's voice over the telephone with Travis complaining in the background about wanting to get out of the place. We knew he was going to be alright. That day, the Baja sun never felt better.

Becky Peterson, one of the girls we'd rescued, was an eighteen-year-old from an extremely wealthy family, who had been very worried. As far as her family knew, Becky had been going out with friends on weekends and working at McDonald's after school. They just about shit a brick when they found out their little girl was working as a topless dancer. Had they found out before the kidnapping, she would have been grounded for life. Holding her hand in the hospital, they were just thankful she still had a life.

Clearing things with the Feds beforehand, they asked to be introduced to Jasmine at the hospital. Without any fanfare or publicity, they offered us a reward. Upon hearing the offer, Jasmine flat out refused. She thanked them, but said it wasn't necessary. Her gracious refusal only endeared her more to Becky's parents—especially the father. He was an extremely powerful individual accustomed to getting what he wanted. Nothing he'd done had helped locate his daughter.

"Young lady," he began, his smooth voice a unique combination of sophisticated charm, elegance and power, "our offer would have been pubic record, but the Feds told us any reward offer prior to Becky being found would have made the search more difficult. They asked us to remain silent. So you see, my dear, we're not singling you out—the offer was on the table long before you found her."

"It doesn't make any difference," Jasmine assured him. "We're just glad we were able to help and thankful your daughter's alright."

"Are you kidding me? Help? You and your friends saved my daughter's life!" The conversation was taking place in the hall outside Travis's hospital room. He gestured toward Travis's door. "I was informed your friend in there almost lost his life." Jasmine nodded, looking down at the linoleum floor. "Please, accept this," he pleaded, handing her a check.

Jasmine didn't even look at it. "We can't," she said. "We didn't do this for money. I don't feel right taking it."

"What about your friends?"

"They'd feel the same way."

"You don't understand. Ever since Becky disappeared, my wife and I have been a wreck. We were going out of our minds. We wanted to do something—anything—but the Feds told us not to—no rewards, no behind-the-scenes investigators, nothing. The waiting and not knowing…it was making us crazy. Especially not doing anything. Then you guys show up out of nowhere and save Becky's life…" His voice was trailing off. "I should have done more."

Jasmine could see the pain and regret in his eyes.

Unfortunately, sometimes it takes losing someone to realize how much they mean to you. It was obvious he felt as if he'd failed his daughter, and the reward was his way of doing something to make things better. She realized it wasn't about the money, or even about us for that matter. It was about allowing him to give in one of the only ways he knew how.

He tried once more. "You've given our family a second chance. You've given Becky a second chance. You know as well as I do that if you hadn't found my baby, she'd be dead right now…or, God forbid, from what the Feds have told us, she was going to be sold." His voice caught in his throat, and his words trailed off again as the image of his little girl being sold for sex overwhelmed him. "Please," he begged, "take this. Start a foundation…give it to charity…I don't care. Do whatever you want to do with it, but please take it."

Jasmine hesitated.

Sensing an opening with his sharp instincts, he pressed. "What about your friends? I know none of you are wealthy. Travis has months of rehabilitation in front of him. And what about all these hospital bills? You're hard working individuals, right?" She nodded and he continued. "Just trying to earn a living, right?" She nodded again. "Running a charter boat—it's not my field, but I'd venture to guess it's a pretty tough business. Lots of overhead and maintenance."

"You're right on all accounts," Jasmine said. "But we didn't do this for a reward. They took Corey's girlfriend and that was it. He knew something was wrong. No one would believe him, but after a couple of days, there was no stopping him. Where he went, Travis went. And I wasn't about to let Travis go running off alone. We had no idea what we were doing or where we were going."

"That's exactly why I'm begging you to take this. I didn't do anything and it's eating me alive inside. You helped Becky. Please, let me help you guys. You'll never know what you've given us. You brought my little girl back. She's alive, she's safe."

"I don't know—" Jasmine replied.

"This is between us. There's no press here, nobody...just you and me." He paused, waiting until Jasmine looked him in the eye again. "I know how you felt when Travis was in a coma and you thought he was going to die. I know...I thought Becky was already dead and it was killing me. We've both been given a second chance." When he saw the acceptance in her eyes, he smiled and his face lit up. Jasmine could see why he was so successful. "I never figured it would be so hard to give a little money away," he added, handing her the check.

Without looking at the check, Jasmine reached out and gave him a hug. At first he resisted, but then melted. The two of them held each other in the empty hallway. Stepping back, he looked her in eye again. "Thank you."

"Thank you," she said, smiling and looking at the check for the first time. She was stunned. "No...I can't..." she said, backing against the wall, "I can't take this."

"You already have," he said with a smile as he turned and walked away, leaving her alone in the hallway—a million dollars richer.

******

This time it only took about half an hour for the call to go through. Calls originating from our end were a nightmare. Calling southbound from the States wasn't as bad—you just never knew who was going to answer. We knew where Jasmine and Travis were whenever we tried to call Stateside, but Jaz had no idea who she'd end up talking to when she called us. So after a few complete cluster fucks, we worked out a plan— Jennifer and I would be at Minnie's tackle shop every morning at 10:00 a.m. If there was any news, Jaz would call; if not, we'd hang with Minnie and Robert for an hour or so. If no call came in, that was it—our only obligation for the day was fulfilled.

The phone was ringing as we walked in. Jaz asked for Jennifer over the poor connection. "Are you sitting down? You're not going to believe what happened last night."

"What?" Jen asked. "Did Travis get up and walk out?"

"No. He'd like to but knows I'd kill him if he tried. Listen to me…." Ten minutes later, Jennifer hung up the phone, looked at me with a huge grin on her face, but didn't say anything.

"Well?" I asked. She gave me the condensed version. "Unbelievable," I said, the reality of it just starting to sink in. "So you're telling me…we're going to be rich?"

"We already are," she said, wrapping her arms around my neck. "But now we're going to have a lot of money as well." She was right. We couldn't have been any richer than we already were, but finding out we'd just been handed a million bucks instantly took the edge off a lot of things I'd been quietly worrying about…like how were we going to eat. "I never had any doubts," she said, reading my mind.

"Doubts?" I looked at her, playing dumb. "Doubts about what?"

"About anything," she said all-knowingly deep from within her woman's intuition. "Even when I thought I was going to die… I knew in my heart that you were coming. So when it comes to the little things…"

"Like money?" I interrupted.

She smiled. "I don't let that stuff bother me. I know we'll always find a way."

Her faith in the ways of the world was way beyond mine. Just one more reason to love her. We decided to head back to the beach and go for a walk. Holding hands, we headed out of town on one of the dusty street leading toward the Pacific. The day was starting to get hot. "Thanks for letting me in on your little secret," I said.

"What secret?"

"That you know things are always going to work out."

She reached down, picked up a stick and threw it for Sierra. "Choices, baby. We make them every second of every day."

"We do. That's a fact."

"So I choose to believe in myself, in life, in us, in love.... in God. I don't care what you call it. It all comes from within and it's all still a choice." She squeezed my hand.

Nodding in agreement, "Like you so wisely said, we make 'em every day."

"It's a lot healthier than eating your guts out worrying about stuff you can't control. Don't you think?"

"Yeah, absolutely. But what about when you were on the boat? I know you were scared shitless."

"Fuckin' A," she said. "It's not like I walk around with my head up my ass. You know me better than that. When the shit's hitting the fan, you'd better damn well duck."

"Or swing a mean bat," I said.

She smiled. Tossing the stick again for Sierra. We hadn't really talked that much about what happened. We weren't avoiding the subject...it just didn't come up. Watching her eyes reflecting back at me—the memories still fresh, haunting her—I knew healing was going to take a long time. We both knew it and accepted it. We also knew there was no hurry and so long as we were together, we knew we would be alright.

Back at the boat, we packed up a little ice chest and ran the dingy over to an isolated stretch of sand called Lover's Beach and spent the rest of the day snorkeling, lying in the sand, soaking up the sun...doing nothing.

That night we had dinner at the mayor's house; we were his personal guests of honor. Minnie promised us this would be the end of all the notoriety. We'd been the center of attention since we arrived. It was flattering until it became obvious that we were just an excuse for these people to throw a party.

"I promise," Minnie said, "this will be the last time."

Rolling my eyes, I shook my head.

"I know, I know," she said, her hands in the air, shaking her head back like it was out of her control. "But you have to go. Él es el alcalde."

"El alcalde?" Jennifer asked.

"The mayor. El jefe," Minnie continued. "Es en la casa de los alcaldes. It would be an insult if you didn't come. You're the damn guests of honor, causa de Cristo," she said laughing, knowing full well the gig was up.

"You are so full of shit," I told her.

"I promise—no more parties…well, maybe we could have one more small one. You know, just us…to celebrate no more parties." You had to love her. "Anyway, the mayor's the highest ranking official in town. All the previous gatherings were just the lead-up to this one."

Jennifer and I looked dubiously at her. "You promise?" Jennifer asked. We wanted her word that this was going to be the last of these ordeals. We'd been to so many dinners and official functions the past few weeks we'd lost count. Not that we weren't grateful—we were. But enough is enough.

"Juro sobre la tumba de mi madre," she promised, crossing her heart and kissing her crucifix.

"All right, we'll be there. But this is the last one."

"How could one little village have so many damned officials?" I asked jokingly.

"God only knows. Give a Mexican a badge and an official rubber stamp, and you're in big trouble." Minnie said cracking herself up.

"No shit," I said.

"What time?" Jennifer asked.

"Same as always," Minnie said, turning to help an American tourist who was asking for the hottest marlin lure.

"You can't go wrong with this one," Minnie said, handing the gentleman the lure. "Zucker's black and purple."

******

Every official function we'd been invited to, as the guests of honor had basically been the same. In Cabo, dinner parties didn't start until around nine o'clock. The more time we spent in Baja, the more we began to think they really have life wired—they get up early, work until it gets hot, close up shop, take a few hours off for lunch and a siesta, sleep until after the midday heat passes and then go back to work for a few hours until it's time to eat again.

The networks had been sending down news crews to interview us. The story had broken big-time Stateside. An international sex slave organization specializing in the abduction and selling of teenage girls was just too sleazy for the media to ignore. They were milking the story for every ounce it was worth, ignoring the fact that families had lost loved ones and many, many young people were still missing.

The Feds thought they had their hands full before the story broke, but now the CID was in overload. Every family that had a missing daughter was convinced their little girl was being held hostage by some sheik selling her to the highest bidders across the globe. It turned into a full-blown circus. Even gays were protesting, wanting equal rights and demanding to know why the FBI wasn't also investigating every young male disappearance in connection with sex slavery.

The media was eating up the story—the cold blooded executions of *Dorsal's* crew, beautiful young girls held captive as sex slaves; rape and piracy; a daring high seas rescue; one of the heroes, a former USCG officer, recovering in a Long Beach Naval hospital with one shoulder wrapped in bandages, his strong pecks and sleek physique catching everyone's eye. Especially with his beautiful girlfriend never leaving his side. The story and photo ops were just too good to be true. We were headline news—lead story front page all the way.

Fortunately, being in Cabo, Jennifer and I had been spared, initially. Then the ENG crews started arriving—vultures offering us money for exclusive interviews. We refused, but they wouldn't leave us alone. They set up long lenses on the beach, out of the Hacienda rooms facing the boat, filmed our every move, and even hired skiffs to circle us while we were at anchor, holding out microphone booms, shouting questions at us. When we realized after several days that they weren't gong away, we agreed to do a press conference. Roberto set the whole thing up on the patio of the Hacienda at sunset. Surprisingly, as the hour grew near, the butterflies started fluttering around inside us.

"I'm a little nervous about this. Are you?" Jennifer asked, as we showered and dressed.

"Yeah, I am," I admitted. "It's funny…after everything that's happened, you'd think this would be no big deal."

"You ever do anything like this before?" she asked.

"No. Have you?"

"Never, but I'm getting nervous," she said, pulling a simple peasant blouse over her head and tanned shoulders.

"You need any help with that?" I asked.

"No," she said. "Thanks for asking, though. My shoulder's getting back to normal. I almost have full range of motion." She demonstrated by rotating her arm like an old-fashioned pitcher warming up before a big game. "I can't wait to get this cast off. It's driving me nuts."

"But you look so cute and helpless in it," I said, teasing her, "with just your fingertips sticking out the end."

"I'll show you helpless," she threatened, raising her cast like a club to mimic an overhead attack.

I picked her up around the waist and dove with her onto the master queen-sized bed, tickling her as we landed. Laughing in each other's arms…just like that, the butterflies were gone.

******

To say the cameras loved Jennifer was an understatement. She was radiant. The fact she still had a cast on, a black eye and lacerations on her face, was icing on the cake. The questions were endless. The reporters wanted to know every detail and the TV cameras didn't miss a frame. At first the interviewers were polite.

"How did you end up on the boat?

"Were you scared?"

"Have you seen your parents since this happened?"

"Have you been back to the States?"

But after the preliminary questions, things started heating up. The reporters acted like a pack of hyenas, circling in for a kill, hungry for those juicy sound bites they knew would make air.

"Were you raped?" one reporter shouted.

"No," Jennifer said, shaking her head, as she tried to field the onslaught of questions.

"How did you kill them?"

"How many times were the other girls raped?"

"Did they make you watch?"

"Weren't you a stripper at the same club the girls were abducted from?"

The volley of questions came from all directions like shots from a semi-automatic. The segment producers smelled an Emmy. They wanted nothing to do with me. Jennifer was the money shot. Squeezing my hand during the questions about the rapes, she held her own. She was amazing. Whenever she felt things were about to spin out of control, she simply stepped back from the podium and stopped speaking. The questions flew for another couple minutes, but then stopped. Looking directly at the reporter who'd fired the last question, she stepped back to the mic. "Would you please repeat your question so everyone can hear it?" They loved her.

"What do you think would have happened to you if your boyfriend hadn't found you?"

"I'd be dead," she said matter-of-factly.

"How does that make you feel?"

"How do you think it makes me feel?" she asked back. "I was scared to death. After seeing what they'd done to the other girls and the crew, I was ready to die fighting for my life rather than let them drug me."

They ate it up. Another barrage of questions.

Holding up her hand, waiting patiently until they all shut up. "If it hadn't been for Corey, Travis and Jasmine, all of us on board *Dorsal* would have either been killed or gone forever. As it is, two of the girls are dead. So is the crew. Executed in cold blood," she paused, letting her words sink in.

"Our prayers go out to their families and loved ones. And to all the other families, who, as we speak, have no idea where their missing children are. The people behind this are horrible, despicable individuals. They do unspeakable things…things you can't even imagine. I was there. They treated us like scum. They rape, they kill, and they sell flesh to the highest bidders without even blinking. There are thousands of young girls still missing. They're the ones who need help now. You're interested in our story…and that's fine…but there are missing people out there who still desperately need your help. So please, use your resources. You want a story? Be the one to find these girls."

Like that, she'd taken control of the circus and ended it. Squeezing my hand again, pushing it toward the stairs, she had enough presence to let me lead her off the podium.

"Vultures," she said, stepping back into the manager's office out of sight. "I realize they're doing their jobs, but the only thing they wanted to hear about were the rapes. It makes me sick."

"I know, but you did a great job. You really did—answering all their questions, and then talking about the people that really matter."

"Yeah, maybe, but they'll never use it."

"There's nothing you can do about that."

"I just can't help thinking about the other girls," she said, sitting down, the adrenaline still pumping through her. Her emotions lay exposed, on the surface. "I could've been one of them."

"But you're not—you're here. You fought for your life and won. I'm so proud of you."

"How long has this been going on?" she asked, not hearing a word I was saying.

"It blows my mind no one figured it out until now. It just doesn't make any sense."

"If it hadn't been for you, they still wouldn't have a clue. You fucked up their whole operation." I gave her a hug, which she returned half-heartedly, because she was still thinking about the other girls. "You did good, real good." She saw I meant more than just dealing with the press. She'd saved her own life, the lives of the two other girls, and perhaps hundreds more now that the Feds were onto the gig.

"Let's hope so," was all she said, shaking her head as the adrenaline's adverse effects began kicking in.

"Let's get back to the boat, okay?"

******

Federal Bureau of Investigation
Washington, D.C.

"This better work, Beak," the Director of the FBI's Criminal Investigative Division said without taking his eyes away from the window. A sweltering heat wave had descended on Washington, adding to the heat he was feeling from the press. He watched the ripples of hot air rising off the distant asphalt between the endless streams of traffic along Pennsylvania Avenue, and his corner office six stories up in the J. Edgar Hoover Building.

"It's the best shot we've got," answered Beak, Special Agent in charge of the case.

Director Winslow hated using civilians, but with all the media attention this case had generated, the pigeons were just too ripe not to bring into play. Too much was at stake, including his job. Before the story broke, they'd been able to keep a low profile. There hadn't been a big celebrity-type case in years. The bad guys had figured out it was a lot easier keeping low profiles. But now this sex slave story was dominating the media and focusing the spotlight on his department, or to be more precise, on his head. "The whole Goddamned country's watching," Winslow complained. Turning away from the window, he finally looked across the room at Agent Beak, who sat cross-legged in one of the overstuffed leather chairs in front of the director's desk. "This better fucking work," he repeated, sitting down behind his desk. Beak nodded. He'd been around the old man long enough to know it wasn't time to answer. "You'd better make damn sure it works, you understand me? I don't want any screw-ups. These kids are becoming fucking celebrities, for Christ's sake." He pointed to the four TVs built into the centre of the floor-to-ceiling bookcase. Each monitor was tuned into one of the major networks. With the audio on mute, one was running clips of our recent interview from Baja.

"I know, sir," responded Agent Beak. "We've got teams covering both pairs…24/7."

"They suspect anything?"

"Not that we can tell, sir. The girl Stateside, Ms. Mackenzie, is completely immersed in looking after her boyfriend."

"The one who got shot?"

"Correct, sir."

"She's only left the hospital once since they brought them in."

"And?

"She went shopping, sir. They arrived with nothing. They didn't even have a change of clothes. He hasn't needed any yet…still in hospital garb. But the girl—she'd been in scrubs for a week before she went out and bought a few things from Sears." The director always wanted details, in quick simple fashion and without having to ask.

"What about the couple in Mexico?" His eyes were still on the clips from our interview.

"They're staying on board their boat, the *Vintage* anchored off the beach in Cabo San Lucas. It's located at the tip of Baja, sir."

"I know where the fuck Cabo is," he snapped. He'd never even heard of the place until the story broke, but he'd been well briefed and was anything but stupid. One of the best field agents the bureau had ever seen.

"What else?"

"Not much, sir." Agent Beak paused. "They've become local folk heroes in Cabo. Been attending dinner parties hosted by various city officials down there. Anyway, sir, they spend most of their time together—walking the beach, swimming, lounging around the boat. They seem content to just sit and wait."

"For what?

"They talk with the couple Stateside every day or so. We've got the hospital switchboard wired. All their conversations are taped." The director gave a slight nod of approval, indicating that Beak should continue. "The gist of it, sir, is they've decided once Jordaine is well enough to travel, he and the girl will fly down to Cabo. From there, it's anyone's guess."

The director grunted. "She's pretty—the one with the cast," he said, turning away from the monitor.

"Yes, sir.

"So they're just going to sit and wait for their friends?"

Beak waited just long enough to get a nasty look from the director. "It appears so, sir."

He loved baiting his boss like this. He knew it was risky, but couldn't help himself. It was a little game he played whenever he had to deal with the old man. The director was known for going off at the drop of a hat. His tirades were legendary within the agency.

"Don't fuck with me, Beak!" he snapped.

"No, sir.

"How long?"

"Before they release Mr. Jordaine, sir?" Receiving another dirty look, Beak knew he was really pushing his luck. "They're telling him at least another two weeks, sir, but the chief surgeon will do whatever we ask. They're at the Naval Hospital in Long Beach."

"Beak, I swear to God—"

"The longer the couple is there, the more press the hospital receives. They're not in any hurry to get rid of him. And we all know he can pay his bills now…this isn't on the tax payers."

"A million bucks…can you believe that shit?"

"No, sir."

"Knock it off."

"Yes, sir.

"I mean it, Goddamn it!" The director was getting pissed. It was all Beak could do to keep a straight face. "So it's a done deal?" he asked. "Even after we told Peterson not to do it?"

"That was before they found his daughter, sir. Once he had her back, we couldn't very well tell him what to do."

"I asked you if it was a done deal?"

"Yes, sir. But she hasn't done anything with the check."

"What do you mean?"

"It's just sitting there on the tray table beside his bed. The two girls joke about being millionaires on the phone."

"Appears they're a pretty tightly knit little group," the director commented. "Anything kinky?" The Director's obsession with freaky sex was even more legendary than his temper tantrums.

"No, sir," Beak answered instantly. Best to play it straight and move on whenever the Director got around to sex…which he always did. Fucking around with him during a case interview was one thing, but messing with him about sex was committing suicide. "From what we can tell, sir, just two couples…both straight. One of the girls was a stripper, but no evidence of anything sordid, sir."

The Director just couldn't let it go. He figured every crime was about either sex or money. He was right. This one was about both. "Let me know if there's anything strange going on with them between the sheets."

"Absolutely, sir.

"Anything more on the dead guys?"

"Background traces on both are still on going. We don't have much, sir. Neither of them had a sheet. No known ties, no hits off their prints or phone lugs, no credit cards, no paper trail. No vehicle registration and nothing from their last known address. The landlord was useless—said they always paid on time, in cash.

"Hmm…what about the landlord?"

"Straight up, sir. Was worried he'd done something wrong taking the cash. He'd deposited and reported every dime. Korean vet…Marine…like I said, sir, All-American. We went way back…traced through both sets of his and his wife's grandparents. Nothing, sir. He's clean. They knew exactly the type to rent from. They're pros."

"They *were*," the Director corrected, becoming bored. Nothing juicy—no sex, no leads—now he really was getting pissed. "Then what the fuck do you have?"

"The couples, sir," Beak answered immediately. "The couples."

"Don't fuck it up," the Director commanded in a dismissive tone. "Now get out of here. I've got work to do."

"Thank you, sir," Beak said, getting up to leave the room, cursing the old bastard under his breath.

"I'm holding you responsible for this whole fucking mess, Beak. It's your ass if anything happens to those kids. You understand me. It's your ass— not mine. This is your op."

Stopping in mid stride, Beak swallowed his pride. He turned to face his boss once again. "I understand completely, sir. Thank you."

"Fuck you! Get out of here!" the Director snapped.

"Yes, sir."

Agent Beak could hear the Director snarling as he left the room. The worst was over. He'd been told in no uncertain terms his career was on the line, which he knew before going into the meeting. Taking a deep breath, now he could quit playing politics and get back to his investigation. At this point, that meant babysitting two unsuspecting couples that were being offered up to the bad guys as live bait. Hopefully, that was an offer too tempting to resist. The press had done their job, just as Beak knew they would, playing up the foursome as the heroes who broke the sex slave ring. They hadn't broken anything, but Beak was counting on the fact that they'd been a big enough pain in the ass to get the maggots behind the operation to crawl out from under their rocks for a little revenge. All he needed was one shot at the bastards. Odds were that the brains behind this whole thing were way too smart to expose themselves, but who the fuck knows? Maybe, just maybe, they'll get a shot at the bastards. Now it was a game of cat and mouse.

******

"I'm fine," Travis said, complaining over the phone. "I don't know why they're keeping me here. I feel like a damn prisoner."

"If it weren't for Jasmine," I said, "they would have thrown your sorry ass out of there weeks ago. You should be counting your blessings instead of whining like a little girl."

"You get your fat ass up here and sit around this stinking room for a month and say that. I'm going stir crazy. I swear to God, man, I'm going nuts."

"Glad to hear you're feeling better, amigo."

"You're a dick," Travis said, chuckling. "Saw you guys on TV. Jennifer looked good."

"She's going to be all right."

"How's the boat?"

"Fine—we got a coat of varnish on her the other day. Any idea of when you're getting a hall pass?"

"No," Travis snapped back. "They don't tell me a fucking thing."

"What about rehab?"

"I can handle it on my own…if they'd let me out of here."

He was feeling better—a lot better. "Hey, Jen wants to talk to Jasmine for a minute. Take care. We're waiting for you guys."

"Yeah, right. I'm going to be an old man before they let me out of here."

He kept complaining because I was the only one who'd listen. He was still bitching when I handed the phone to Jennifer. The girls talked for a while, just like they did every time. Jennifer couldn't wait to tell Jaz her cast was removed that morning. Her fingers had healed perfectly. "They're stiff and weak, but other than being ghost white and pealing, my hand's fine."

Their conversation then turned into some kind of code. Neither Travis nor I could keep up listening from our respective ends of the conversation, but when they hung up, they both seemed happy and content at having discussed and solved at least some of the world's problems. What shoes had to do with it all, I had no idea, but new shoes seemed to play an important part in their conversations.

"How much longer does she think?" I asked Jennifer when she hung up.

"A week…maybe a little longer, but not much. Says they're going to have to chain him down if they want to keep him any longer than that. He's feeling stronger every day—no infections, no complications. Looks like he's going to be fine. They've got the shoulder isolated and his left arm is in a sling strapped around his chest. Still too early to tell, but they think he'll regain full use of his arm and have full range of motion. He's been moving it around a lot the past week, and I think he's driving them all crazy with his bitching."

"That's my man," I said, smiling. "Told me he was climbing the walls. Couldn't for the life of him figure out why they're keeping him."

"Jasmine said after the first few days, the hospital administrators started asking her about insurance and how Travis was planning on paying for his visit…they called it a 'visit,' for God's sake. Jasmine told them not to worry, but they kept hounding her. Then, mysteriously, the day after accepting the reward money, there were no more visits from the administration office. Instead, the head of surgery himself started looking in on Travis. She figures word's out about the money we got— thinks the hospital is milking this whole publicity thing for all it's worth…now that they know the bill's covered."

"Hate to think of hospitals like that," I said, "but she's probably right."

*****

We left Minerva's. You could feel the entire area was posed for major changes. It was just too beautiful a place to remain a sleepy little fishing village. Located at the end of one of the most remote, rugged and breathtakingly beautiful peninsulas in the world, you could feel it was only going to be a matter of time before developers discovered it. Acapulco, Mazatlan, Zewatt, Cancun had been the resort destinations of choice for decades, but times…they are a changin'. *Sometimes you don't know what you got 'til it's gone. Pave paradise and put up a parking lot.* (Joni Mitchell had it right.)

But on this particular day, Cabo was as it had been for a hundred years— a little fishing village, where no one was in any hurry to do anything or go anywhere. Walking down the main street, we admired the hand-stitched embroidery that decorated much of the native garb—intricate floral designs with bright colors, peasant blouses with lace, beautiful scarves and shawls. There were hand-carved iron wood marlin, hammerheads, dorado and roosterfish, and sun-bleached shell necklaces strung with monofilament. There were silver bracelets, St. Christopher's medallions and crosses, dried puffer fish, as well as shark jaws, big individual shark tooth necklaces, paper machete piñatas and faded post cards—inexpensive trinkets for all the tourists that swarmed off the cruise ships once a week, taking over the town and transforming its way of life. It was sad seeing the changes and knowing the place would never be the same again.

Today, Cabo felt perfect. We walked along one of the dirt paths that led to the north out of town. Kids were swinging from an old tire tied to a branch of an even older tree, chickens scratched at the dirt, picking off unwary prey. A spotted mama goat and her skinny kid looked up out of curiosity for a second before continuing to munch at a tiny patch of wild grass that had somehow made its way up through the dry soil. None of the houses had any locks. Many of them didn't even have doors—just dusty horse blankets tied off to one side with a short hunk of rope. No fences, no boundaries. No crime, no punishment. Simple people, living simple lives.

"I could stay here forever," Jennifer said, looking at nothing in particular. "I love it here—it feels right." With Jennifer beside me, any place felt right. I'd never felt so complete, so whole, in my life. It didn't matter what we did or where we went, as long as we were together.

We continued our walk between a two small ancient adobe houses. Cutting west toward the Pacific, we crossed a low, flat area, and then climbed a hillside that took us three or four hundred feet above sea level and left us breathless as we reached the top. The view was spectacular. Sierra didn't hesitate—she raced down the front side of the giant dune to the water. We sat and watched her for a long time. Finally making our way down, we stripped off our clothes and dove into the crystal-clear blue water. It was the first time Jennifer had been able to really enjoy the water because of her cast. But getting it cut off earlier, she was soaking up every minute of being back in the water. A small shore break provided just enough push to have fun. Every time we'd ride a wave in, Sierra would come bounding through the foam to greet us. Without another soul in sight, we spent the day in bliss.

"We'd better be getting back," Jennifer said as the afternoon wore on. "I'm starving. We haven't eaten since this morning. Feed me before I wilt."

Pulling our clothes back on, we reached the crest of the dune in time to catch the sun kissing the horizon—a huge, glowing ball of orange, melting into the rich, blue Pacific. The day relinquished itself to night. Bright streaks of radiant yellow pieced the sky, turning the entire canvas into a golden hue, its highlights silhouetting the few wispy clouds hanging above the distant horizon. Pure white sand stretched endlessly in both directions. Less than a twenty yards off the beach, a few birds were working a bait ball, picking off their last meal of the day. A couple of big roosterfish had the bait balled up—we could see their combs flashing under the birds. Turning around to head home, we stopped in our tracks at the sight of the full moon making is way over the eastern horizon. We stood motionless…hand in hand…absorbing nature's gift of beauty and harmony. Peace stretched from horizon to horizon.

We made our way down the hillside at dusk. Back in town, we stopped at the first street vendor we saw. His rickety wooden cart tilted slightly. A smile radiated from his weathered, tanned face, even though he had few teeth. The aromas emanating from his covered pans were tantalizing. "Dor'rra'do," he said, still smiling. Reaching over, he lifted off one of the covers, and showed us the pure white filets grilling on some sort of homemade BBQ he'd built into the top of the cart. The fish was definitely fresh.

"Está delicioso? He asked expectantly as we took our first bites of the fresh homemade tortillas he'd carefully wrapped around the fish, adding a pinch of cilantro, some salsa and a hearty squeeze of fresh lemon. Dorado didn't need any other condiments and he knew it. His smile got even bigger as we both nodded, our mouths too full to answer him right away. "Ellos son deliciosos," Jennifer managed to get out between bites.

"Bueno bueno muy fresco," he said.

"Estos son los mejores tacos de pez que yo jamás he tenido," I told him, "Gracias. Le cuánto debemos nosotros?

"Cuarenta pesos," he asked politely.

"Four dollars," I mumbled through my food as I handed him a U.S. five dollar bill. As he started to make change, I held up my hand and shook my head. "Los demás son para usted.

"Gracias. Gracias," he said, bowing his head slightly.

"Mucho gracias. Estos son el mejor," Jennifer said, as he contentedly began pushing his old cart down the dirt road.

We walked down to the beach, devouring our first taco along the way, and sat together in the warm sand to finish the rest of our feast. Sierra got little bites from both of us, but knowing she was hungry, we jumped into the inflatable and headed towards *Vintage*.

******

As we pulled up I about shit. Karyn was sitting in the cockpit like she owned the place. Her legs casually crossed over the combing. Wearing only a bikini, her stunningly body, impossible to ignore, causing Jennifer to look at me expectantly, but before I could say a word, Karyn spoke.

"Glad you're O.K." Karyn said, getting up, looking directly at me, totally ignoring Jennifer.

"What the hell are you doing here," I said as we secured the dingy. Sierra jumped off, greeting our unwelcome guest.

She ignored Sierra as well. "Saw what happened to you on the news. I had to come down to make sure you were alright."

"Bullshit." I snapped back at her. Reaching out, giving Jennifer a hand onboard. Never in a thousand years would I have expected her to just show up like this. Not here. Not in the middle of nowhere. And especially not now.

Jennifer politely extended her hand, "I'm Jennifer."

Karyn glared back at Jennifer, not taking her hand, but announcing, "I'm Karyn, Corey's wife."

******

"Whose the new babe," one of the new team of agents that had us under surveillance, asked from behind the tented windows of the Hacienda, watching through the high power glasses. "She's hot."

"We're checking now. She showed up an hour ago. A panga dropped her off and left. She's just been sitting there. Looks like she was waiting for them to get back."

"They're back now. Wish we'd been able to mic the boat. I'd love to hear that conversation."

******

"You're married?" Jennifer said, collapsing into Karyn's vacated chair. "Married."

"Jennifer, I can explain everything," I pleaded to her. But it was too late. Karyn had planned it perfectly. From not wearing any cloths, to dropping a bomb I couldn't do anything to stop.

"God damn it, Karyn!" I shouted. "What are you doing here! I never wanted to see you again."

"Cheer up," she said laughingly, "things could be worse. You're little *kitten* here could still be with the bad guys. I'm not the enemy."

"Fuck you!"

"Come now, *dear*, don't be so rude. We have a lot of catching up to do."

"We don't have a thing to talk about. Get off this boat."

"Temper, temper."

"God damn it. I mean it."

Standing up, Jennifer looked Karyn right in the eyes, and in a very calm and polite voice, asked, "May I get you something to drink?"

Shocked, I could only stand there... watching.

The women never took their eyes off one another. Assessing... probing...evaluating. The intensity growing by the split second.

After what seemed like an eternity, Karyn finally said, "Thank you, I'd love a Tab."

Nodding, Jennifer turned towards me, "Corey?"

"What?" I mumbled.

"Would you like something to drink?"

"Ah, no. No, thank you."

With that she slipped into the galley.

My turn to collapse into the vacated deck chair.

Karyn settling on the cockpit combing directly in front of me, with clear eyeshot of the salon door, she slowly crossed her legs.

"Why are you here?" I finally asked quietly, the anger... and any logical explanation beyond me.

"I've missed you."

I almost puked. I couldn't even look at her.

She continued, "I'm so sorry for what happened. I never meant to hurt you. I still love you, and you are, still, my husband."

"We were over the minute I saw you and Shane together."

"I know you've been hurt, but that's all over now."

"Bullshit. You don't know what you're talking about. I feel sick just hearing your voice."

She reached over, trying to brush some locks of hair out of my eyes.

I pushed her arm away. "Don't ever touch me again."

"After all this time, you're still mad."

"I'm not mad. I just can't stand you. You're poison."

"I made a mistake. A big one. I know that now. It's over with Shane me. Like I said, I'm sorry. I really am. I want you to come home."

Again, her timing couldn't have been better. She must have rehearsed this little scene to a tee. All Jennifer heard was "... I want you to come home."

"Jennifer," I said standing up, looking her in the eyes. "This was my train wreck." Praying that she'd understand. "I'm sorry I never told you any of the details, but it just didn't seem to matter."

"You didn't think it mattered that you never told me you were married?" Jennifer asked flatly.

Karyn, feeling as if she were gaining the upper hand, started to say something, but Jennifer instantly cut her off, steel in her voice. "I'm talking to Corey. Don't interrupt me. You two had your little chat, now it's my turn." She refocused her attention on me, "Well?"

"I love you."

"Don't." she said, holding up her palm.

"O.K. yes, I was married. But it was over a long time ago. Over long before I met you."

"Then why is she saying she's your wife?"

"I don't know," I said shaking my head. "I talked to my grandfather, and he told me she wanted a divorce. I told him I did, too. It was over. I asked him to have the papers drawn up, and I'd sign whatever she wanted me to."

"But you never did?"

I bowed my head. "No."

Jennifer waited.

I shook my head in disgust at myself for being so lame. "With everything that was happening with us, I didn't think about it... Didn't want to think about it. Never wanted to think about her again.... I just assumed it was getting taken care of."

"By whom?" Jennifer asked, "The divorce fairy." But she'd made her decision. I could hear it in her voice... I just didn't know what her decision was.

"Corey," she said, gently putting her hand under my cheek, tilting my head up to meet her eyes. "I love you. But don't you think it's time we ask our guest to get off *our* boat."

Relief flooded over me as she wrapped her arms around me.

Karyn was pissed. She'd given it her best shot, flaunting her raw sex appeal and perfectly time daggers, but Jennifer wasn't buying it.

"Look," she said glaring at Karyn, "I don't know who you are, or what you did to this man, and to tell you the truth, I don't want to know. What I do know is that he's a good man. A kind man with a caring heart. Whatever you did, you're going to have to live with that. You can't change history. But what I'm not going allow, is for you come into our lives and try and ruin our future."

Jennifer was glaring at Karyn, challenging her with her eyes and elegantly selected words.

"Somehow he managed to get through whatever happened between you two, and now, he loves me. And as far as I'm concerned, that's all that matters. So if you don't mind, please step into the dingy and we'll escort you back to the beach. You are no longer welcome on our boat."

******

"Shit," one of the agents said. "I thought we were in for a cat fight with those two."

******

Karyn could only scowl in contempt and hatred at Jennifer. Without so much as saying another word, she picked her small backpack up off the teak deck, and stepped into the dingy. Sierra bounding in after her, oblivious to most of what had just transpired. Wagging her tail she took her spot in the bow, front paws hanging over the edge. Her entire life just one adventure after another. *Living in the present* was all I could think of as I started the motor. Helping Jennifer in, we stood together behind the center console. Her arm locked inside mine. As we got to the beach, Karyn jumped out.

"Stay, Sierra." I said. Disappointed she slouched back down without jumping into the water. *Adventure aborted.*

Karyn looked back over her shoulder at us. "Nice dog," was all she said as we backed away leaving her alone on the beach.

"That wasn't too strange," Jennifer said as we headed back to the *Vintage*.

"I'm sorry," I said. "I should have told you everything."

"I don't know," she said, shaking her head. "I really don't. On the surface, yea, I wish I'd known because of the way things came down. But I don't feel like you were keeping anything from me... hiding anything from me."

"I wasn't. I swear to God. It just never felt like we needed to talk about my past like that. Shit, we've hardly talked about anything like, you know...romantically, that either of us have been through."

"That's what I mean," she said. "I don't feel betrayed. Ambushed, yes. But not by you. She had this whole thing planed. It wasn't your fault."

"But you're the one who.... I was so lost. I didn't think I'd ever be able to feel anything for anyone again." I paused. "Not the way I feel for you."

"Sometimes, it's better to leave the past in the past. God knows we've both been hurt before... made mistakes... but why drag all that crap into a new relationship."

"I agree."

"You are what you are. Simple as that. You either learn how to live with your past...your mistakes... learn... and move on, or you just keep replaying them over and over again with new partners."

"I don't know many women that would have handled the situation the way you did."

She smiled as we pulled up to the swim step.

"When you asked her if she wanted something to drink, I about fainted."

"I knew you guys needed some time alone to talk... and I needed a few minutes to think."

"Thank you for finding a way to stand by me. It would have been so easy for you just to get pissed off. You had every right to be."

"I was, but not at you," she paused again before saying. "Finding love is hard enough. Keeping it alive is... well I don't know," she said. "...almost impossible. But I wasn't about to let her destroy what we have. So I decided to do the only thing I know how to do with you, and that was to just keep on loving you."

"If there's anything you ever want to know about my past, just ask."

"Likewise," she offered, "...but for now, I think we've had enough for one afternoon."

Helping her out of the dingy she added, "Oh, there is one thing," she said, "I do want to be the first to know when you're divorce papers are final."

******

It was starting to get late, so I climbed into the engine room to fire up the generator. Jennifer poured Sierra a bowl of crunches.

"We're out of stuff for breakfast," Jennifer said when I came out of the hatch. "Why don't I run back into town and grab a few things so we don't have to do it in the morning."

"I'll go with you."

"You don't have to," she said.

"I want to. Sierra's eating, so let's leave her. It'll only take a few minutes." Sierra barely glanced up at us from her food, as we got back into the inflatable. Completely content with her meal, she'd had a big day. We knew she was going to crash as soon as she finished eating. "We'll be right back, girl," I told her, casting off the bowline. We got a little wag as we left.

Jennifer wanted to drive. The water was glass—with no wind, there wasn't a ripple. The lights reflected off the smooth surface like a mirror image, and with the full moon, you could see all the way across the bay to the arch. "Let's run over there before heading into town," I suggested. "It looks cool like this, all silhouetted."

Turning, we ran across the entrance of the harbor. The tide was up, so Jennifer ran us right up to the arch. Idling, we slipped under it and through. It was the first time we'd done it, which made it all the more exciting. Watching the moon disappear through a hole carved out of stone by hundreds of years of pounding waves, I thought about the amazing forces it took to create something like this. We idled on the outside for a while before running up the beach. Then, turning back again, we shot through the arch at full speed. Jennifer—still at the wheel and loving the rush—screamed with delight as we passed under it. I loved seeing her so happy.

"It feels so good having my hand out of that cast," she said, waving it over her head.

The streets were almost empty by the time we got to the little market. They'd closed up for the night. They didn't have any fixed hours, so we didn't feel bad. There was always mañana.

"We'll just come back and get things in the morning," Jennifer said, without a worry. She took my hand and we headed back to beach where we'd left the inflatable. Once on the sand, Jennifer issued a sudden challenge. "Race ya!" She kicked off her shorts and thongs, pulled off her blouse and dived into the warm water stark naked. She was an excellent swimmer and glided through the water effortlessly. If I were going to have any chance of catching her, it wouldn't be wearing a pair of shorts with big pockets acting as sea anchors. Pulling them off, I went in after her—the race was on.

Vintage was anchored about a hundred yards off the beach. She had a good head start, but I was able to catch her just before we got to the boat. I slid up on her back, pushed her head underwater, then reached up for the swim step, pulling myself out of the water in one easy motion.

She came up hollering, spitting out a mouthful of salt water. "You cheater! Disqualified. Illegal lane change!" Catching her breath and laughing, she spluttered, "You are hereby officially D-Qued and banned from any further Olympic competition for the rest of your unsportsmanlike, cheating life. You're a disgrace to the sport. Banned for conduct unbecoming an officer, whom I had mistakenly thought to be a gentleman."

"Sore loser," I said, reaching down to help her up. During her little speech, she'd subtly braced her feet against one of the stainless steel brackets supporting the swim step. As soon as our hands locked, she jerked down hard and pulled me back into the water. She was already on the swim step when I came to the surface. "Talk about a poor loser," I complained, watching her strut her stuff, her body glistening in the moonlight. Laughing and tossing her golden hair in defiance, she left me in the water and turned to step though the transom door.

Her gut-wrenching scream stopped my heart. Pulling myself out of the water towards her, I started to ask what was wrong. Suddenly my heart jammed in my throat, keeping any sound from coming out. Sierra lay motionless on the deck. Her head was twisted sideways... the dark pool around her was blood. There was no doubt she was dead—her throat had been slit wide open. Dropping to my knees, I took Sierra in my arms, only to see her limp head snap backwards in a grotesquely horrifying motion.

I didn't even feel the blow that struck the back of my head.

******

"Holy shit!" screamed the FBI agent. He'd been watching us through one of the government's high-powered night vision scopes. "There's someone on board. They just clobbered the guy and grabbed the girl. Call for backup now. Let's move!"

Agent Beak had assigned a six-unit team to keep an eye on us—just as he had done for Travis and Jasmine in Long Beach. Until now, the assignment had been a dream vacation for the Cabo team. In pairs, one male, one female, the agents worked eight-hour shifts. If it hadn't been for the females assigned the detail, the men would have been in bliss—watching us making love on the deck, seeing Jennifer lying out topless in the sunshine wearing nothing more than a string. But the female agents had put an end to voyeurism once it was obvious we were alone and just making love. At first the male agents fought them, claiming it was part of the detail and they couldn't afford to take any chances. The female agents threatened to file formal reports if the men continued shooting rolls of 35 mm close-ups with high powered lenses for their personal viewing.

Since we'd left the boat all day, the surveillance team on duty trailed us. No one had given a second thought to watching the boat. The bad guys had gotten on board unnoticed just before dark. They had taken the bait, but no one was watching. They forced Jennifer to the deck, face down, jammed a knee into her back, duct-taped her mouth shut and covered her head with a hood. Then they zip-tied her hands tightly behind her back. They did the same to me before dragging me to the swim step. A stealth black inflatable slid up on cue. Within seconds, they had us both off *Vintage* and on board the inflatable...leaving only Sierra lying dead in her own blood. The agents couldn't believe what they were seeing. The entire operation took less than twenty seconds.

"We're fucked," said the agent, before screaming into her handheld radio. "Move! Move! Move! Suspects are on the move with both items." They never expected anything like this, especially after weeks of nothing but sunshine and love. The Baja had lulled them into a false sense of security—as if evil would never find this place.

The second and third units reacted immediately, but were screwed from the get go. They raced down to the skiff they had chartered when they first arrived. Even though they hadn't used it yet, they paid for it in advance, a week at a time. *Not a good idea.* With nothing to do but just sit there, the captain had started drinking—he'd been looped for going on two weeks now. When the agents got to the boat, their captain was passed out in the sand, and the boat's battery was dead from constantly running a bilge pump wired directly to it.

"Fuck this!" screamed the field agent in charge. "Get another boat! Grab that one!" he yelled in desperation, pointing to another panga with a newer-looking outboard tied to the rocks near them. One of the agents leaped off the boat, sprinted the few paces to the panga, jumped in and started the 25 hp Suzuki on the first pull.

"Come on!" he shouted, hearing the motor fire up. The other agents were already halfway to the boat. Within seconds, they were racing towards the *Vintage.*

The two agents in the hotel surveillance room heard the radio crackle "We're en route." Both of them were watching the cluster fuck with the drunken captain. The one on the night scope took his eyes off the bad guys for just a few seconds, but it was a costly mistake. In the time it had taken to commandeer the panga, the bad guys were gone.

"Shit," said the agent with the night scope, frantically swinging it back and forth.

"What's wrong?"

"They're gone. I don't see them anywhere."

"Let me see!" she said, jamming her eye into the scope. "You shouldn't have taken your eyes off them!"

"I know…it was only for a second."

"Hold on…I've got something!" she shouted excitedly. "Can't make it out…low profile…looks like an inflatable. They're hauling ass…with no running lights. It's got to be them." Grabbing the hand-held radio, she yelled into it. "Be advised. Suspects are northbound, running full speed. Repeat. Appears suspects are northbound in a black inflatable."

"Goddamn it!" yelled one of the agents. "Is this as fast as this piece of shit will go?"

There was no way they could catch the inflatable with a 25 hp motor.

The agents in the hotel room heard their boss yell into the radio. "Get another boat—a fast one! We'll check out *Vintage*. Wait for you there."

"Yes, sir. We're on our way."

Approaching the *Vintage* with weapons drawn, they swooped onto the boat in perfect precision. Stepping over Sierra, through the blood, they swept the boat. "Clear!" yelled the agents from below, emerging from their search of the interior.

"Clear up here," came the shouts from the wheelhouse.

"You guys got anything?" demanded the officer in charge, yelling into his hand-held unit.

"Negative. There are no other boats along the breakwater." The voice sounded out of breath.

"What are you doing?"

"We're running towards the harbor. We'll be there as soon as we can," was the crackling response back through the radio.

"This is bullshit!" screamed the agent to no one in particular. Releasing the transmit button he continued barking orders. "Let's go!" he yelled. "There's nothing. We're wasting time here." The agents jumped back into the panga and headed up the coast into the darkness. "We're going after them."

"Roger," came the response from those looking for another boat. "We've got our night vision gear. As soon as we get a boat, we'll find you."

The officer in charge didn't even bother responding. He'd been with the bureau long enough to know they were screwed. Winding that 25 to the limit, they were barely making twenty knots—in the dark, with no compass no lights...nothing. Everything had happened too fast. They were highly trained professionals—some of the best America has—but they were all land-based. None of them had any experience on the ocean. It only took a few minutes out there in the middle of nowhere for them to realize they were way out of their element.

"Where do I head?" yelled the agent on the tiller over the high-pitched scream of the outboard. No one answered him. They were too busy holding on. Even in a light chop, running at 20 knots in the dark was nuts. They couldn't see the next wave and had no way of bracing themselves before flying over it. It was like riding a mechanical bull blindfolded. They were being pitched and banged against the sides of the boat. "I can't see a thing," yelled the agent again.

The lights on the beach in front of the Hacienda were disappearing in their wake. More lights could be seen further up the beach. "Keep those lights off to the left," the agent in charge yelled into the hand-held unit, pointing at the lights. "Anything? You got anything? We're running blind."

"We got you guys. We're right behind you, hauling ass." They'd gotten lucky. A big yacht had pulled into Cabo that afternoon, loaded with toys that included the 23-foot center console that was now doing close to 50 knots.

"Roger," cracked the radio in response. "Did you grab all the gear?"

"Roger. We got it. Slow down—we're right behind you." The agents scrambled onto the center console, leaving the panga adrift.

"Let's go get them."

******

Like most successful plans, the hijackers' scheme had been simple—use the element of surprise, incapacitate the victims, remove them immediately from the point of contact and get to a secure location. In our case, the secure location was the 190-foot mega yacht *Allah's Desire*, owned by Prince Kareem Remesh Paymon, the eldest son of one of the wealthiest oil sheiks in Saudi Arabia.

The prince and his ship were on an extended goodwill tour of the world. Sanctioned by his government, the ship and her entire crew enjoyed diplomatic immunity wherever they went. They were treated like royalty, which, of course, the prince was. He was also acting as a representative for the oil cartel that supplies the world with over thirty percent of its crude. *Allah's Desire* had been cruising the Mexican Riviera for months. Only the highest-ranking Mexican officials were invited on board as guests. Mexico, just like the U.S; is dependent upon a continuing flow of raw petroleum from the Saudis, so the prince and his crew were being treated with the highest respect.

After leaving the mainland and heading into the Sea of Cortez, the charade of entertaining an endless parade of officials stopped. There wasn't a Mexican official residing in Baja worthy of an invitation. Besides…they had work to do. They'd been awaiting delivery of their next shipment for over a week. Everything had been planned in meticulous detail months in advance and was being executed to perfection—until we got involved.

The prince was not accustomed to anything going wrong. In his kingdom, if a subordinate screwed up, he was killed and replaced. This wasn't the first glitch they'd had in their illicit sex trade, but it was the first in a long, long time…and it was the first since the prince had taken charge. He ran the operation with an unmerciful iron fist. He enjoyed administering gruesome punishments and spent hours thinking up horrible tortures. The poor souls serving him lived in fear of being his next victim.

Unhappy with his meal, the prince ordered the chef to be brought to his table with a meat cleaver. After spitting the food in the man's face, he commanded his guards to hold the man's hand on the table so he could hack off his fingers and send them to the kitchen to be deep-fried. He then began feeding them to the poor man—one digit at a time. After gulping down the first finger, the chef threw up.

"Just like your hyena's food," smirked his tormentor as he forced another fried finger into the man's throat. The chef threw up again. "Goddamn it!" the prince shouted and grabbed an industrial stapler from a side table. (Evidently, he'd planned his evening's entertainment in advance— the meal had nothing to do with it.) After forcing another finger into the man's mouth, he began stapling his lips shut.

"Now try and puke," the prince laughed, as the man choked on his own vomit. "Toss him overboard. I'll have my *crème brûle* in my room."

When he learned we had fucked up his latest delivery, he went into a rage and ordered the execution of the head of his U.S. operations. In a press release, the FBI reported the death of one of their own as a tragic traffic accident. The prince ordered the same for his Mexican liaison. He had him flown into La Paz and invited him for an afternoon cruise on board *Allah's Desire,* complete with lunch and some skeet shooting. Once on board, the prince personally blew the man's balls off and had him tossed overboard into a chum slick that was attracting a number of large hammerheads. The man didn't last fifteen seconds.

Now the prince wanted nothing more than revenge on the heathen 'American heroes' he'd been watching on satellite television for the past month. Outraged by the endless news stories about us, he was particularly furious that the girls had played such important roles. Women fucking up his operation drove him crazy. The prince hated women—all women—especially those who had places of respect and power. "Women are whores. That's all they're good for, giving me sons, cowards!" he screamed at the television. "Letting women do your work for you...cowards! I will kill you with my own hands!"

He wanted nothing more than to fuck to death the bitches that had messed up his plans. He couldn't wait to jam his cock up their asses before shoving his gun up there and blowing them apart. He planned every detail in his twisted mind, getting hard just thinking about it. After beating Travis and me, he would make us watch while our whores begged for mercy. He'd have some of his men fuck them as well. Then, when he could almost taste the blood, he was going to cut off our balls and jam them down the girls' throats before killing them. He was hoping that the shotgun blast in their pussies would force our balls out of their mouths to land at our feet, where he'd stomp on them before executing Travis and me as well. The sharks were going to feast!

"Fucking Americans—I hate them all," he'd scream, jerking off. He hated everyone—except himself...and, of course, his father. He hated his brothers. His sisters weren't even worth thinking about. The rest of the world could suck his dick. "Where the fuck are they?" he demanded.

"My Prince," snapped his first lieutenant. "They are on their way here now. They will arrive in only a few minutes. You will have to wait no longer. Everything went according to your plan. Your father will be most pleased."

The hell he will. Not after all the problems these cowards caused us, he thought to himself. "Are you that stupid?" he barked back at his cowering subordinate. "They have jeopardized our entire operation." *Father will never forgive me.*

Your punishment will be nothing more than a stern look before being embraced by your father—no torture, no pain, nothing, the lieutenant thought to himself. Out loud, he said, "My Prince, you are cleaning up the mess now. You are...how they say...taking care of business." He was proud of the term he learned from watching American movies.
"True," said the prince, inwardly acknowledging what he knew to be the truth. *If I weren't the Sultan's eldest, I'd die for this incompetence.* "Inform me the moment the cowards are on board." When he reported to his father the infidels were dead, he knew he'd be completely forgiven.

******

Coming to, bouncing on the aluminum floor of the inflatable tender, it took awhile to figure out where I was. It felt like we were doing a hundred knots over the short chop. I had a hood over my head, so I couldn't see a thing. I tried to focus on what I could feel—tight string cutting into my wrists. I couldn't move. I mistook the blood dripping down the back of my neck for water. My head was pounding, but that was nothing compared to the dread that descended on me as I put the pieces together. Wriggling my wrist, I succeeded only in digging the restraints deeper into my skin. I felt a warm body lying body next to mine…I hoped it was Jennifer. I grunted and received a swift kick to the ribs.

We're fucked, I thought to myself. I felt the boat slow down. Someone from behind and above me was barking out orders in a foreign language. A minute later, the boat bumped against something solid. More commands. I felt several pairs of strong hands jerking me up off the floor, pushing me toward the side of the boat. My knees banged into something hard. I stumbled blindly under the black hood. More short, quick, foreign commands. I felt my feet plant themselves on a solid platform. *This doesn't feel like a boat…it's too steady. But there aren't any marinas or docks between Cabo and La Paz.* There was no sound of any shore break or waves. They had to be putting us on board another boat—a big one.

Our hoods were yanked off. We stood side by side, blinking while our eyes adjusted to the bright aft deck lights. Seeing Jennifer brought a momentary wave of relief. They hadn't removed the tape from our mouths and our eyes met for only the briefest of moments. I saw the sheer panic in her eyes before a sharp slap snapped my head forward. "Finally we meet," the prince hissed in disgust. "The big, brave Amerr'ican heroes." His words dripped of sarcasm, and he rolled the 'r' in American.

As my eyes continued adjusting to the light, his dark features came into focus. Shiny black hair…distinct jaw line and jet black eyes…medium height, lean and athletic. His clothes were casual, but expensive…tailor-made. A crisp white shirt, open at the neck, tan slacks, loafers. His well-manicured fingernails caught the light. His English was smooth and polished—obviously that of a well-educated man. He was standing on the lanai deck above us, which was backlit. I caught glimpses of the opulent decor of the salon behind him. We were led up the stairs into the huge, open salon.

He maintained his sarcastic tone, an undercurrent of rage within each word. "You must be so proud of yourselves," he hissed, "my famous Amerr'ican heroes." It pissed me off the way he rolled the r to intentionally mispronounce our country's name. He walked slowly around us while he spoke...made full circle stopping inches in front of my face. Without so much as a flinch of his eyes, his knee flew up into my groin, crushing my balls. My legs collapsed, sending me tumbling to the floor in pain.

My scream was forced back down my throat by the tape. I felt a wave nausea. I thought I was going to pass out again. My vision burred as his loafers came in and out of focus. I forced myself to focus on a spot of carpet just past my nose, but I never saw the next blow coming. The kick exploded into the side of my face. I felt Jennifer crouch down, trying to protect me. She took his next kick in the ribs for her efforts. It lifted her clean off me, knocking the wind out of her lungs. With nowhere to go, it also blew her eardrums out. I tried to force my eyes open...to fight through the blackness. I couldn't see. I thought maybe he'd kicked my eyeball out. I spat out blood and little chips of broken teeth, trying to catch my breath.

"Get him the fuck out of here. He's bleeding all over my carpet." Instantly, sets of strong hands jerked me off the carpet, dragged me out the door and tossed me down the steps. I landed hard on the aft deck. They left Jennifer where she lay. Curling herself into a ball, she knew she was going to die.

Fighting to stay conscious, I shook my head and got another kick in the face. I saw this one coming out of the corner of my eye, and was able to turn just before it landed, taking the blunt of the blow in my ear. My eardrum ruptured—blood flowed down the side of my neck. Half conscious, I wondered what we had done to make them so mad. It didn't seem to matter any longer. Nothing did. Nothing hurt any more, either. *That's weird...a minute ago everything hurt like hell.*

A blanket of serenity descended over me as another shoe caved in my ribcage. I didn't feel a thing. *Never figured it would be like this.* Distant thoughts. *This isn't so bad. I wish I could see where we're going.* The next blow never came. Instead, I heard the angels above me speaking in some strange tongue. *Bummer. I'm going to heaven and can't even understand what they're saying. Hey, excuse me, you guys. What do you want? I can't understand you.*

"That's enough!" The prince bellowed from above.

Thank God you speak English, my brain told the Lord in our first encounter. *I was starting to worry.*

"I don't want him dead yet. He's got a show to watch first."

Oh good, a show...I love the movies. The angels were moving around above me, but then they started talking again in that weird language. *Must be angel speak,* I thought. *Heaven is going to take some getting used to. Why don't you just speak English? Doesn't seem fair. I'm here, but I can't understand a word you're saying. Always assumed you'd speak English.* More funny angel speak. They acted as if they hadn't heard me. *Hey, guys, can I talk to God again?* No answer...only more angel mumbo-jumbo.

The first thunderous cracks of lightning that exploded over my head scared the shit out of me and shattered my already dubious concepts of heaven. The angels started screaming, as bolts of thunder and lightning spewed forth from under their wings. *Now I know I'm fucked. This isn't heaven. There's no thunder and lightening in heaven. It doesn't even rain in heaven. That's it—I'm in hell. That's why I can't understand what they're saying.*

The thunder was deafening and there was lightning flashes everywhere...exploding all over the place...coming from every direction. *I've never seen it rain so hard. This really sucks... But where are the raindrops?* Blinding bright flashes of white light exploded right in front of my face. I could feel the heat of hell descending upon me.

I must have done something really bad to piss Him off, I thought deliriously. *Maybe it's because I cuss too much. My mom always told me not to. That's got 'a be it.* The thunder and lightning continued exploding all around me. One of the angels fell from the sky and landed right next to me. *Holy shit! It must have been hit by lightning. Yeah, while he was trying to deliver me. I'm sorry* was the last thing I remember thinking.

******

The FBI team had located the boat. With the crew's attention on us, they'd managed to get close enough to open fire. A firestorm was raging above me. The first volley was returned by one of the thugs who had been kicking me. They didn't see the taskforce until they were already on the swim step. The automatic fire sent a cascade of red hot shells spraying all over my limp body, but the gunman pulled high and to the left, missing all the agents. The other goon set his gun down inside the salon to lift me. The moment the first shooter let off the trigger long enough to regain control of the gun, the agents leveled them both, returning controlled fire.

Something else big and heavy fell from the sky, landing directly on me. I couldn't get any air. My mouth was still taped shut. My nose was clogged with blood. Writhing in panic and shaking my head violently, my instincts took over. *"I'm sorry,"* I cried out, pleading. *"Please, God, I'll do whatever you want. I just didn't understand you. Please, let me breathe again—just once more!"*

Enough air managed to get past the blood to keep me alive, but I still couldn't breathe. Panic raced through my body, supercharging my system with adrenaline. Any feelings of mercy were gone. I was done begging...my body was fighting for another breath...needing air desperately. Another volley of thunder cracked directly over my head. Lightning exploded all around me. Hot rain dropped on me from above. My flesh was burning.

"No!" I screamed in terror. *"No, Goddamn it! I'm not going!"*

With the two gunmen in the cockpit down, the agents leaped over the transom and spread out. They dived towards the forward starboard steps, finding shelter behind the bulkhead to port. Two more of the prince's elite guards rushed in to take up positions inside the salon. Fire from their AK 47's shattered the sliding glass doors. Going up against automatic weapons in confined quarters is a nightmare, but nothing can take the place of professional training. No one trained agents better than the FBI. While the portside agents drew fire, another FBI man crept up the stairs on the starboard side and dropped both the bad guys dead in their tracks.

The terror was all consuming. My lungs were on fire at they fought for air. My mind raced, screaming for a way out. My body fought, knowing if it didn't get air, it was over. I was shaking violently. Rocking back and forth, I tore the skin off my wrists. I was lying at the feet of one of the agents. Feeling me thrashing against his leg, he reached down, grabbed my hair and pinned me down long enough for one of the other agents to yank the tape off my mouth. Air instantly filling my lungs. I swallowed hard and gasped for more precious oxygen. I heard more thunder and lightning. *At least I can breathe again*, I thought before an all-consuming blackness fell.

The agents made their way forward, encountering heavy but poorly aimed panic fire from the remaining armed guards. At the end of each wild volley, they were able to pick off the guards without a single casualty. Securing the main salon, they split up. They worked in teams of two, moving methodically through the boat—one team headed below, another forward, a third toward the bridge. After blasting the crap out of the captain's quarters from behind the bed, one more armed guard was taken out with shots through the mattress he'd hidden behind for protection. Four direct shots blew his head apart.

"Clear," shouted the agents after sweeping the wheelhouse. With the top deck, wheelhouse and main floor secured, they retraced their steps to see if they were needed below.

At the sound of the first shots, the prince grabbed Jennifer by her hair and dragged her into his master stateroom. He was standing there calmly—his back to the far side of the wall—when the first team of agents made its way to his room. He wedged a 9 mm Glock into Jennifer's side, just below her armpit. "She dies if you don't place your weapons on the floor immediately and step back," he said calmly, in perfect English.

Jennifer's mouth was still taped shut. Her arms were zip-tied behind her and blood trickled out of her ears. The prince was holding her hair, forcing her body against the gun. "Now, please...or she dies." Jennifer tried shaking her head, pleading with her eyes, but they had no choice. The initial team lowered their weapons. "Thank you. Now, place them on the floor and turn around...slowly." The agents hesitated.

"Now!" commanded the Prince.

The second team had stopped in the hallway just outside the master stateroom—unseen and unheard—and was listening to the prince's orders. The agents who had swept topside joined them. "Stay here. Do whatever he asks," the agent in charge whispered. Turning, he quietly made this way back into the salon.

The prince smiled to himself, watching the two agents lowering their weapons. "Now step back and turn around." They did as instructed.

"Now," he said, "we're all going to move slowly out of here. If one of you so much as flinches, she's dead. Understand?" The agents nodded. "After you," the prince instructed.

Starting out of the master stateroom, they suddenly stopped, seeing their fellow agents, still armed in the hallway. The prince pushed Jennifer ahead of him, looking over the shoulders of the unarmed agents and into the hallway. "I suggest you do the same as your friends here." His voice left no doubt he'd kill Jennifer if they didn't do as he instructed. The agents hesitated for an instant—none wanted to give up their weapon.

"I'm not asking again." They lowered their weapons to the floor. "Wise decision. Now turn around and lead the way up to the salon. Keep your hands away from your bodies."

The procession made its way along the companionway up a wide, curving stairway and into the main salon. The smell of gunpowder filled the room. The automatic weapons had torn the place apart. Windows were shattered and remnants of the once fine wooden levelers hung in disarray. Stuffing from the expensive furniture was strewn all over the floor. Four of the prince's elite guards were dead, sprawled out in a disfigured death. The first body was at the top of the stairs. After stepping over it to make their way into the open area of the salon, they found another body under the dining room table and chairs. A third was facedown over the back of a leather couch, his blood pooling around him...and around the motionless body of the agent in charge.

One of the other agents gasped when she saw her boss lying at the base of the couch covered in blood. His neck, face and head were crimson red. His eyes, rolled back in his head, were open and staring blankly into oblivion.

A grin curved the corners of the prince's mouth when he saw the dead agent. "So, my men weren't total incompetents," he announced to his captives with some satisfaction. "Overall, though...a miserable performance." Glancing back down with satisfaction at the bloodied face, he added, "But not a total waste."

The agent had let all his breath out and hadn't moved an inch since the procession entered the room. Listening as the procession moved by him, he knew he had less than a minute. The prince walked by just inches from his head, his gun was still jammed into Jennifer's ribs. Without flinching, the agent followed him with his eyes. Withdrawing his strategically placed hand from underneath the couch, he leveled his gun and squeezed the trigger, blowing the front of the prince's head open. The bullet entered the base of this skull, severing his spine and exiting where his mouth had once been. Fragments of gray matter, teeth and hot blood splattered all over Jennifer. She screamed through the tape as the hand that had been holding her hair involuntary clamped down, pulling her to the floor. The prince was dead before he hit the carpet. One agent spun around immediately at the sound of the single shot to kick the gun away, but it was locked in the grip of the dead man. They had to pry open his fingers to remove it. Spinning wildly, Jennifer left him holding a clump of her

Whatever your labors and aspirations in the noisy confusion of life, keep peace with your soul. With all its sham, drudgery and broken dreams, it's still a beautiful world. Be careful. Strive to be happy.

Chapter 15

The Washington Post
Monday, October 1, 1973
WASHINGTON, DC

International Sex Slave Scandal Escalates

Following the death of Prince Kareem Remesh Paymon, killed by FBI agents during a fierce gun battle off the Mexican coast, an FBI spokesman today announced agents have uncovered an additional twenty-three American female hostages. All are reported between the ages of twelve and twenty-five. Identifications are being withheld, pending notification of the families. Some of the young women were reported missing as long as four years ago. Evidence points to all these women having been abducted by an international syndicate headed by the deceased prince. The number of Americans found and freed to date by the FBI, working in conjunction with international agencies around the world, totals three hundred thirty-three.

Several teenage boys have also been rescued. Spearheaded by the FBI, the joint investigation by law enforcement agencies involving six countries continues to grow. More cells of the syndicate are expected to be uncovered in the weeks to come.

CID, Director Winslow stated, "This is one of the most disturbing investigations in FBI history. Our children being abducted and sold into sex slavery is beyond civilized reason."

Governments from around the world are requesting access to the investigation, a source inside the Pentagon reported. The White House is threatening military action against the royal family if it doesn't fully cooperate. A spokesman for the royal family denies any knowledge of the alleged sex slave operations and claims it was all the act of the deceased Prince Paymon.

In an exclusive interview with the Post, a spokesman said, "The royal family does not have, nor has it ever had, any knowledge of Prince Paymon's alleged illegal activities. Furthermore, the family wishes to cooperate fully with the United States government in finding those responsible and bringing them to justice."

Despite the denials, federal investigators continue combing through massive international banking records reportedly linking many high-ranking Saudi government officials to the investigation.

"The scope of the case is stunning," said Special Agent Beak, head of the CID field task force that broke the case. "The deeper we dig, the broader the investigation grows. We believe that we've just uncovered the tip of the iceberg."

Families of the rescued captives have nothing but praise for the investigation, while relatives of the thousands of missing children still unaccounted for are frustrated. The mother of fourteen-year-old Berkley Brown, missing for two years from Draper, Virginia, told this reporter, "We're terrified that our little girl was kidnapped by those sickos. She's still missing. Her daddy and I can't even imagine what she must be going through. We're praying they find her."

To date, none of the rescued victims and their families has been allowed to speak to the media for fear of hindering the investigation. However, reports of connections linking a number of still missing persons to what investigators have already uncovered creates hope for many the families.

Director Winslow added the FBI "…is doing everything we can to find these missing persons. I have three children of my own. I promise you, every resource we have at our disposal is focused on this investigation. With the excellent cooperation we're receiving from international agencies around the world, we're not going to stop until every missing child is accounted for."

******

Sea of Cortez
Isla del Camen
Baja California Sur, México

"Seen this?" Travis asked, handing me the a copy of the worn out, week-old newspaper the girls picked up when they'd run into Loreto for supplies.

"I read it already."

"They'll be lucky if a dozen of those kids are still alive. I'm amazed they found as many as they have."

"They're doing everything they can."

"I know, but the assholes buying those kids are sick motherfuckers. I'd be surprised if they haven't already killed 'em and burned their bodies out there in the fucking desert somewhere. When the heat's off, they'll just buy fresh meat."

"It makes me sick."

"No shit," Travis said, tossing the paper on the deck. "It's amazing we made it out alive."

Thinking about what might have been...still made me light-headed. After being taken off *Allah's Desire*, Jennifer and I had been airlifted from Cabo to the Naval base in San Diego. Hearing the news, Travis demanded to be released and drove to San Diego with Jasmine. They got a hotel room near the hospital and spent the first week sitting with us every day.

Jennifer and I both sustained broken ribs and head trauma. It hurt to breathe, and we avoided sneezing at all costs. They put us in adjacent rooms initially, but the night duty nurse would find us curled up together in one of the beds every shift.

"Against hospital policy," one of the Naval surgeons informed us when we asked to have our beds moved into the same room. After a couple days of us doing nothing but complaining, the hospital decided to bend the rules a little. Given in no small part to the extensive media the hospital was receiving and the demands of Naval Officer Lloyd W. Wolf, Ret. The bedside interviews and front-page newspaper shots of us lying together made whoever approved the rule change look like a PR genius.

Because my shattered jaw was wired shut, Jennifer was doing all the talking, which was fine with me. We were both healing, and to be honest, the attention helped to pass the time.

"Just like rock stars," Jennifer would say when we were alone.

A couple of days after we arrived in San Diego, Lloyd and Larry flew down to Cabo to look after the boat while we were laid up. They were having the time of their lives. I think they would have been happy spending the rest of their days down there. We decided to put the reward money into a joint account under all our names, and paid off all our fuel and bait bills. We were debt-free and earning interest on the substantial balance left over. The moment Jennifer and I were released, the four of us flew back to Cabo on one-way tickets.

The night before we were scheduled to leave, Minnie and Roberto threw a huge farewell party for us on board the boat. There were so many people; I honestly thought we were going to sink. The swim step was six inches below water. The party lasted well into the wee hours of the morning. We practically had to kick Lloyd and Larry off the boat—they didn't want to go home.

As Roberto returned in their skiff to pick up Minnie after dropping off the last guests on the beach, he had a funny look on his face. "Why are you smiling like that?" Jennifer asked him. Before he could answer she saw it—they'd brought us a new puppy. The thing couldn't have been more than six weeks old. Where they'd found a golden retriever in Baja was beyond us.

"Don't even ask," Roberto said, holding up both hands like he was innocent. We knew full well there wasn't a purebred dog within a thousand miles. The girls cried as they hugged the sleepy bundle.

We pulled anchor before dawn the following morning, slipping out of town unnoticed to head up into the Sea of Cortez. The sun and the sea were working their magic on our tattered souls. The days began melting into one another. Our bodies were healing and turning a dark brown. We lost track of time as *Vintage* slowly worked her way through uncharted islands. We ran without any schedule or agenda, staying as long as we liked in a place before moving on. We fished or dived whenever we felt like fresh food. We bought from or traded with the locals. No sooner would we set the hook than out of nowhere they'd show up in old pangas. Where they got fuel or how they kept their outboards running was beyond us. They were always friendly, preferring fishing line and hooks to money. They'd leave us happy and well stocked with local fruit, vegetables and, on occasion, a slab of beef or fresh chicken.

Eventually, we pulled into a secluded and totally deserted cove on the northwest corner of a little island south of Loreto. Time had lost all meaning. The only thing that mattered was that we were together and safe. *Vintage* had become our home, our universe.

Late that afternoon, Jasmine and Travis slipped off the swim step, snorkeling over the shallow crystal clear turquoise cove. The pup following right behind them.

"She loves the water," Jennifer said. "I love watching her swim."

"Me, too. She's so cute out there."

After awhile, Travis and Jasmine climbed back on board. We'd rigged a little ramp for the pup so she could get back on board by herself. She scrambled up the ramp and bounced into the cockpit to shake herself off.

******

As the sun dropped behind the distant hills, Jennifer and I headed topside, stretched out behind the wheelhouse with the pup in our lap and settled in to watch the show. We quietly drank it all in...our new pup falling asleep...Jennifer slipping her hand into mine, resting her head on my chest...*Vintage* gently rocking beneath us.

Closing her eyes, Jen murmured softly, "We're cradled in the wings of an angel."

Tonight, no doubt, the universe was unfolding as it should.